TEEN TITANS GO!™ TO CAMP!

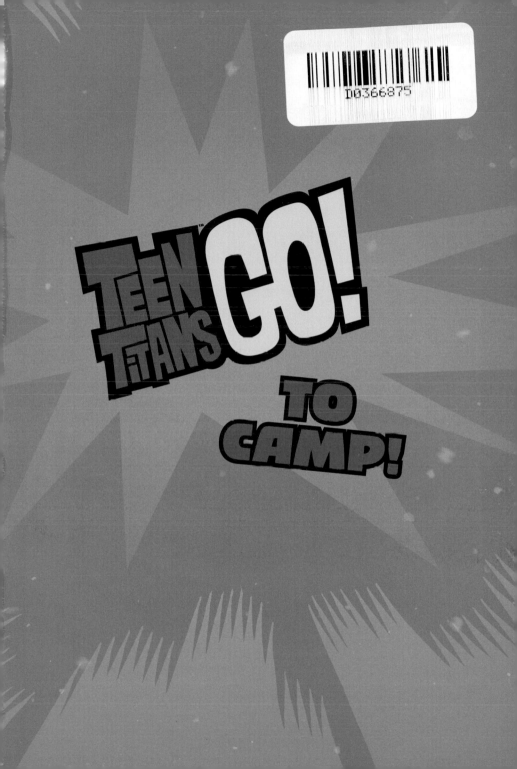

Written by

Sholly Fisch

Illustrated by

Marcelo DiChiara

with Agnes Garbowska, Dario Brizuela, Abigail Larson, Emma Kubert, Leila del Duca, Erich Owen, Jamal Igle, and Franco

Colored by

Franco Riesco

with Silvana Brys, Dario Brizuela, Abigail Larson, Emma Kubert, Marissa Louise, Erich Owen, Jamal Igle, and Franco

Lettered by

Wes Abbott

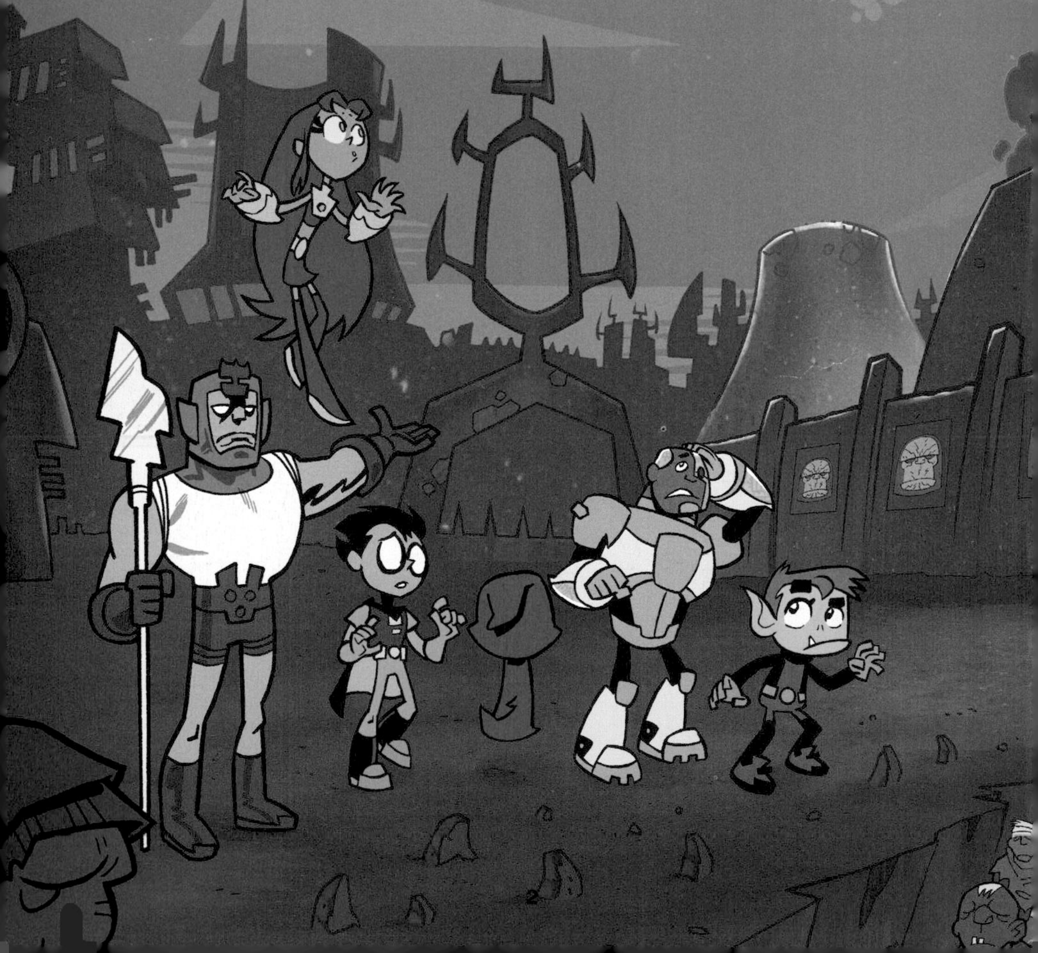

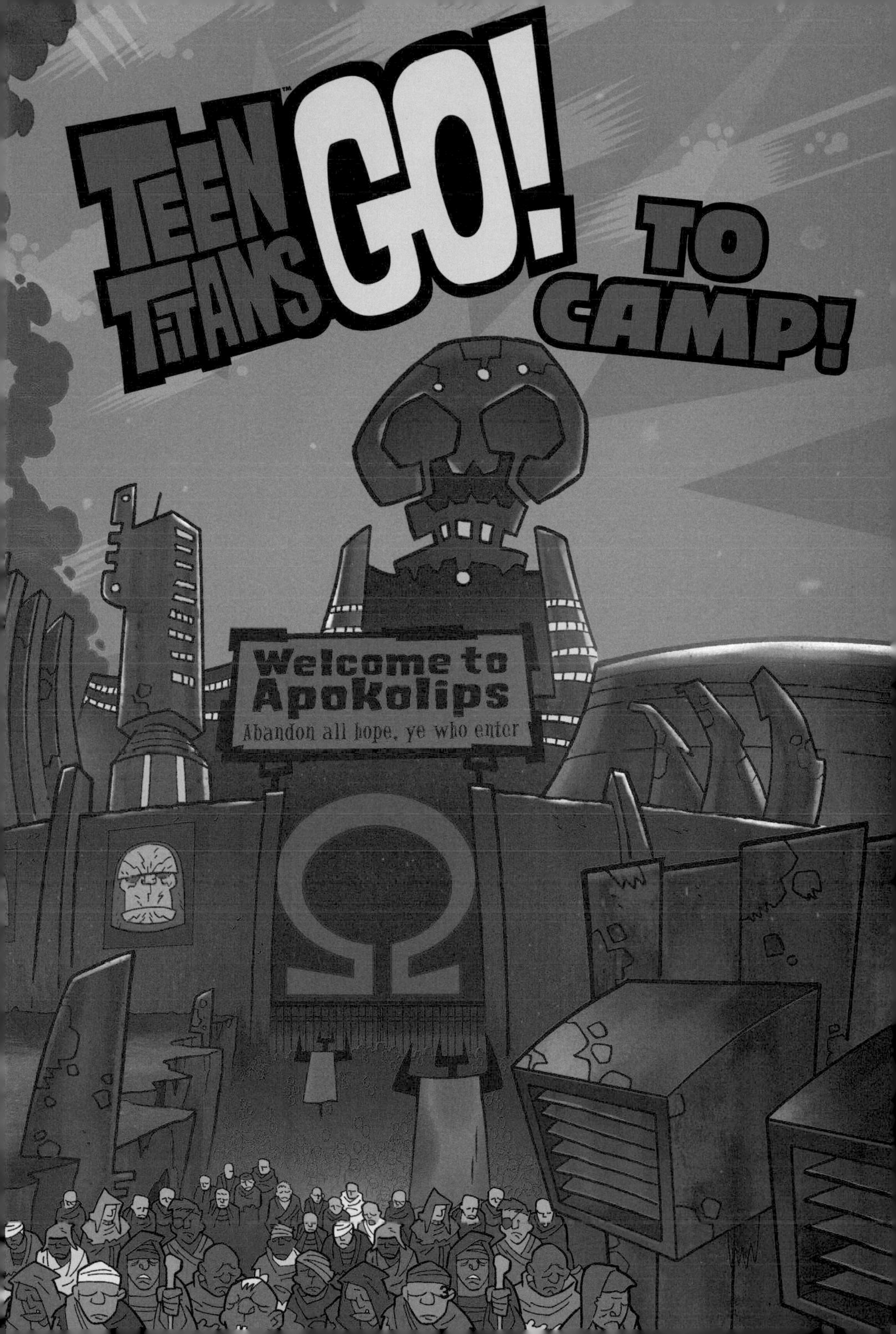
TEEN TITANS GO! TO CAMP!
Welcome to Apokolips
Abandon all hope, ye who enter

KRISTY QUINN Editor
STEVE COOK Design Director - Books
AMIE BROCKWAY-METCALF Publication Design

BOB HARRAS Senior VP - Editor-in-Chief, DC Comics
MICHELE R. WELLS VP & Executive Editor, Young Reader

DAN DiDIO Publisher
JIM LEE Publisher & Chief Creative Officer
BOBBIE CHASE VP - New Publishing Initiatives
DON FALLETTI VP - Manufacturing Operations & Workflow Management
LAWRENCE GANEM VP - Talent Services
ALISON GILL Senior VP - Manufacturing & Operations
HANK KANALZ Senior VP - Publishing Strategy & Support Services
DAN MIRON VP - Publishing Operations
NICK J. NAPOLITANO VP - Manufacturing Administration & Design
NANCY SPEARS VP - Sales
JONAH WEILAND VP - Marketing & Creative Services

DC - a WarnerMedia Company

Printed at LSC Communications,
Crawfordsville, IN, USA.

6/26/20. First Printing.

DC Comics, 2900 West Alameda
Ave., Burbank, CA 91505

ISBN: 978-1-77950-317-6

Library of Congress Cataloging-in-Publication Data

Names: Fisch, Sholly, writer. | Dichiara, Marcelo, illustrator. | Riesco,
    Franco, colourist. | Abbott, Wes, letterer.
Title: Teen titans go! to camp! / written by Sholly Fisch ; illustrated by
    Marcelo DiChiara [and eight others] ; colored by Franco Riesco [and
    eight others] ; lettered by Wes Abbott.
Other titles: Teen Titans go! (Television program)
Description: Burbank, CA : DC Comics, [2020] | Audience: Ages 8-12. |
    Audience: Grades 4-6. | Summary: "Summer's in the air, and the Teen
    Titans are leaving Jump City behind for six fun-filled weeks of
    mosquitoes, sunstroke, and poison ivy at summer camp! What the Titans
    don't realize until they arrive is that this is Camp Apokolips, where
    the "bug juice" is made with real bugs, the swimming pool is a fire pit,
    and the camp director is heartless Granny Goodness. Things only get
    worse when they encounter the bunks they'll be competing against in the
    camp's games: the Titans East and the H.I.V.E. Five! Given all of that,
    there's only one thing on Robin's mind. No, not escape. It's how to beat
    the other bunks to become the camp champions. This is Robin,
    remember?"-- Provided by publisher.
Identifiers: LCCN 2020010483 (print) | LCCN 2020010484 (ebook) | ISBN
    9781779503176 (paperback) | ISBN 9781779503183 (ebook)
Subjects: LCSH: Graphic novels.
Classification: LCC PZ7.7.F57 Tc 2020 (print) | LCC PZ7.7.F57 (ebook) |
    DDC 741.5/973--dc23
LC record available at https://lccn.loc.gov/2020010483
LC ebook record available at https://lccn.loc.gov/2020010484

Chapter One

Starfire's letter drawn by Agnes Garbowska,
colored by Silvana Brys

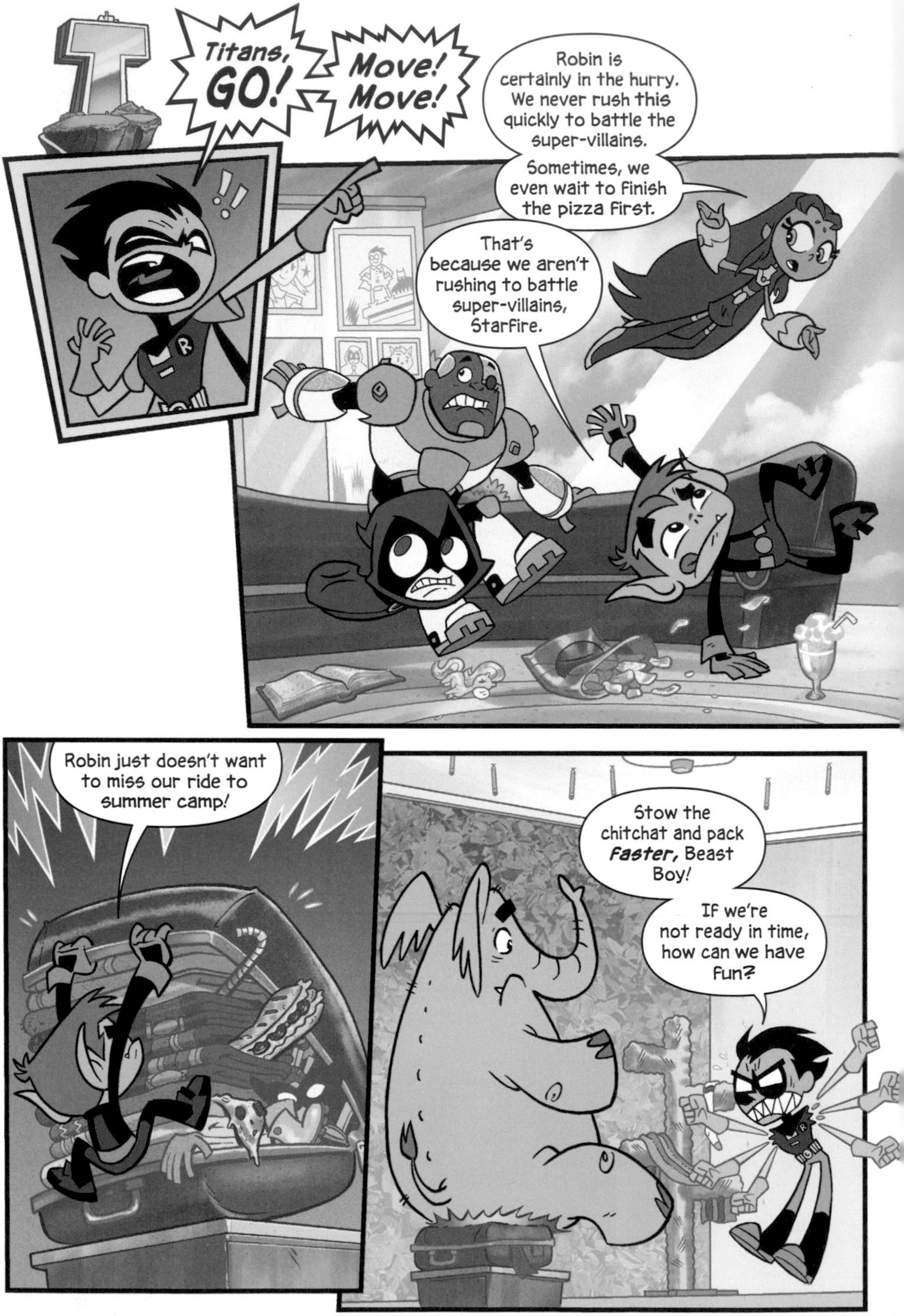
Titans, GO!
Move! Move!
Robin is certainly in the hurry. We never rush this quickly to battle the super-villains.
Sometimes, we even wait to finish the pizza first.
That's because we aren't rushing to battle super-villains, Starfire.
Robin just doesn't want to miss our ride to summer camp!
Stow the chitchat and pack *Faster,* Beast Boy!
If we're not ready in time, how can we have fun?

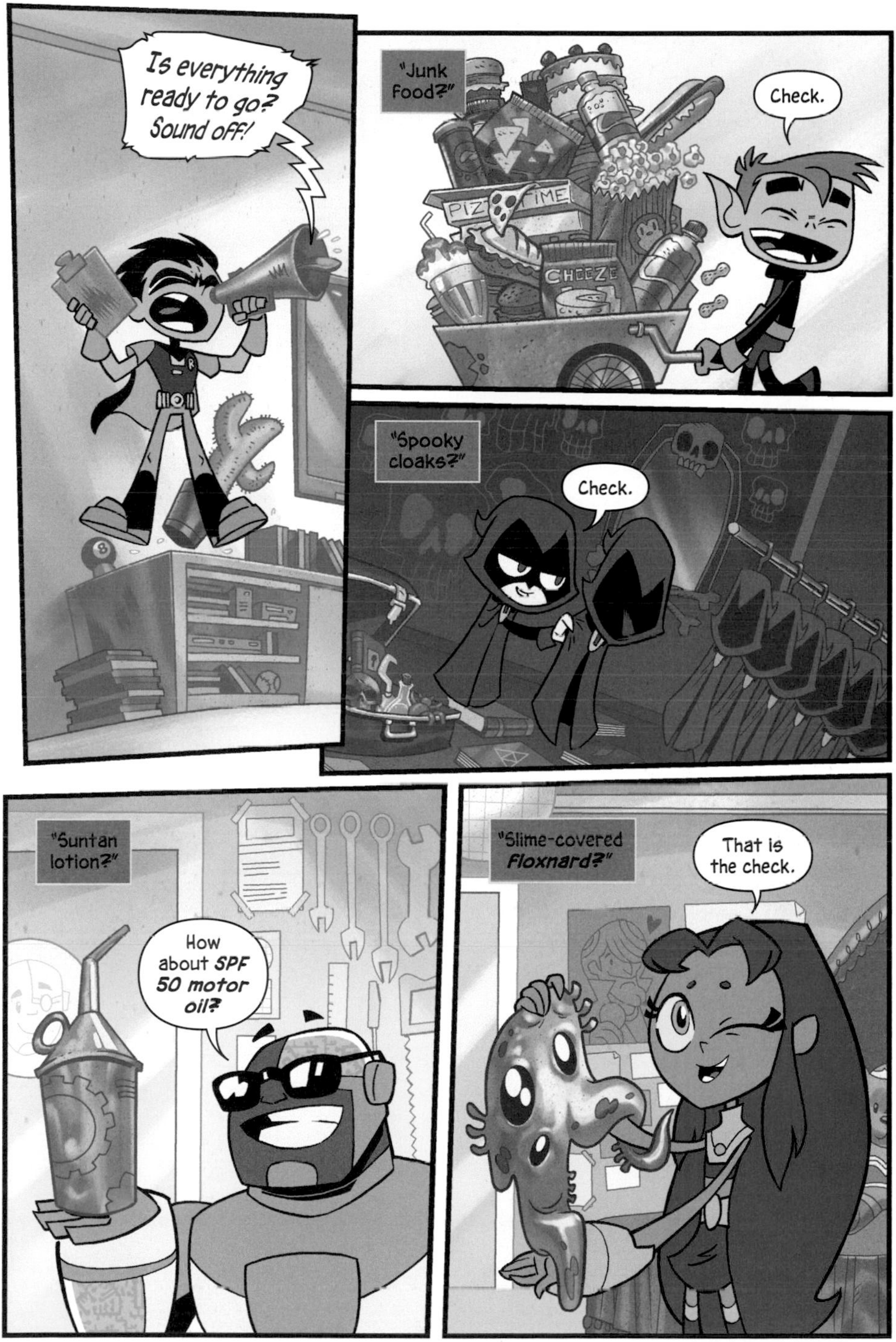

Is everything ready to go? Sound off!
"Junk food?"
Check.
"Spooky cloaks?"
Check.
"Suntan lotion?"
How about *SPF 50 motor oil?*
"Slime-covered *Floxnard?*"
That is the check.

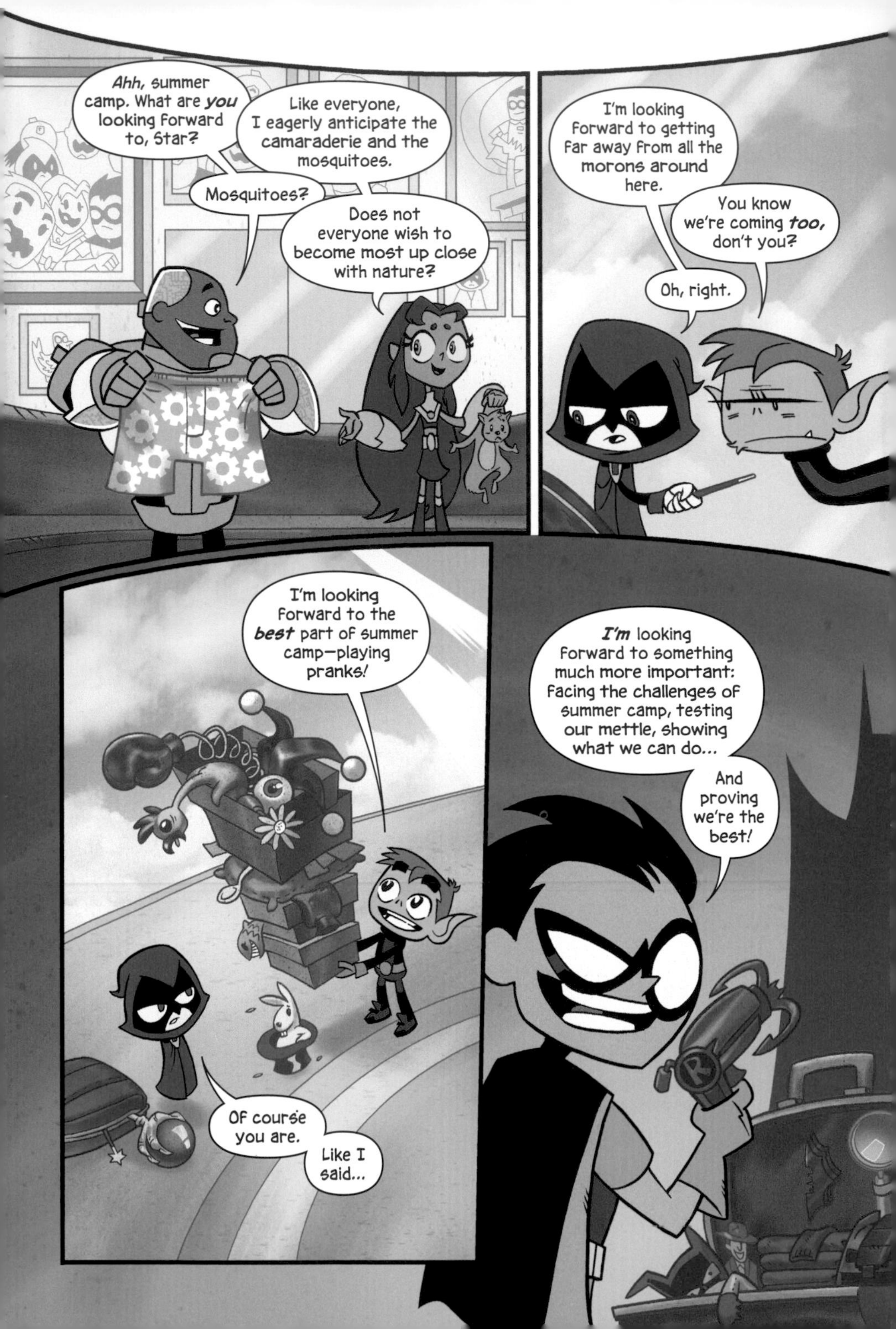

Ahh, summer camp. What are ***you*** looking forward to, Star?
Like everyone, I eagerly anticipate the camaraderie and the mosquitoes.
Mosquitoes?
Does not everyone wish to become most up close with nature?
I'm looking forward to getting far away from all the morons around here.
You know we're coming ***too***, don't you?
Oh, right.
I'm looking forward to the ***best*** part of summer camp—playing pranks!
Of course you are.
Like I said...
I'm looking forward to something much more important: facing the challenges of summer camp, testing our mettle, showing what we can do...
And proving we're the best!

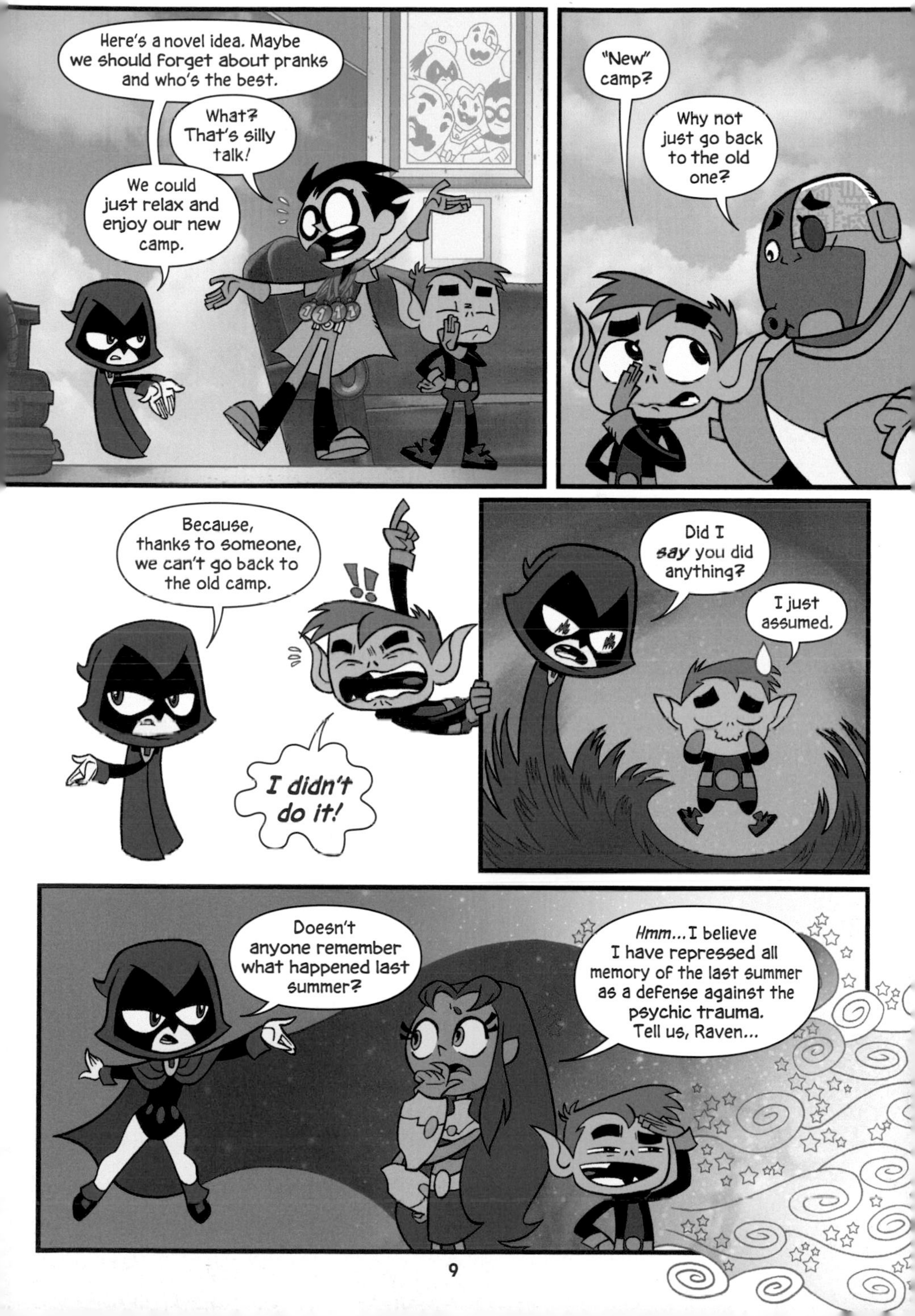
Here's a novel idea. Maybe we should forget about pranks and who's the best.
What? That's silly talk!
We could just relax and enjoy our new camp.
"New" camp?
Why not just go back to the old one?
Because, thanks to someone, we can't go back to the old camp.
!!
I didn't do it!
Did I *say* you did anything?
I just assumed.
Doesn't anyone remember what happened last summer?
Hmm... I believe I have repressed all memory of the last summer as a defense against the psychic trauma. Tell us, Raven...

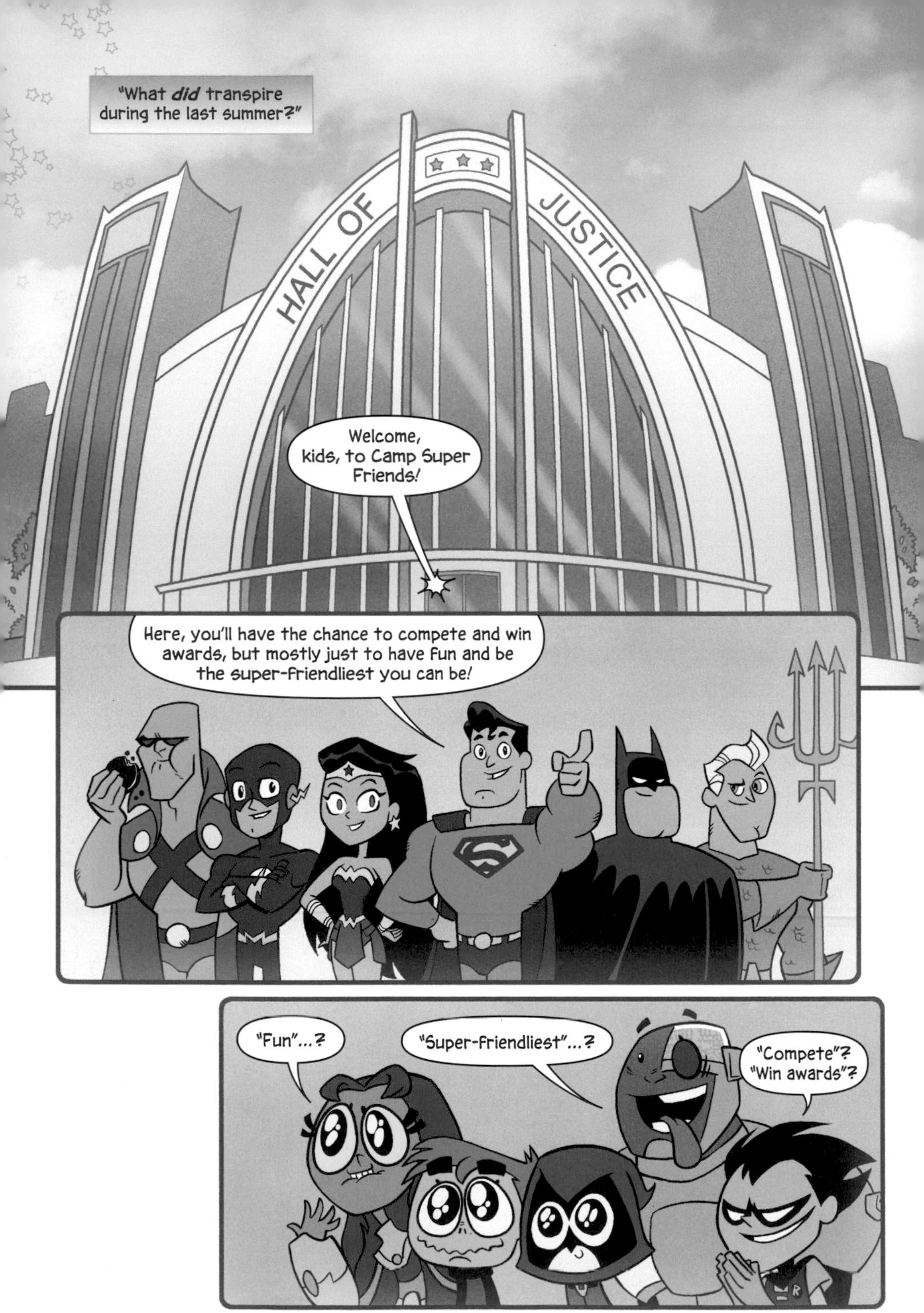
"What *did* transpire during the last summer?"
HALL OF JUSTICE
Welcome, kids, to Camp Super Friends!
Here, you'll have the chance to compete and win awards, but mostly just to have fun and be the super-friendliest you can be!
"Fun"...?
"Super-friendliest"...?
"Compete"? "Win awards"?

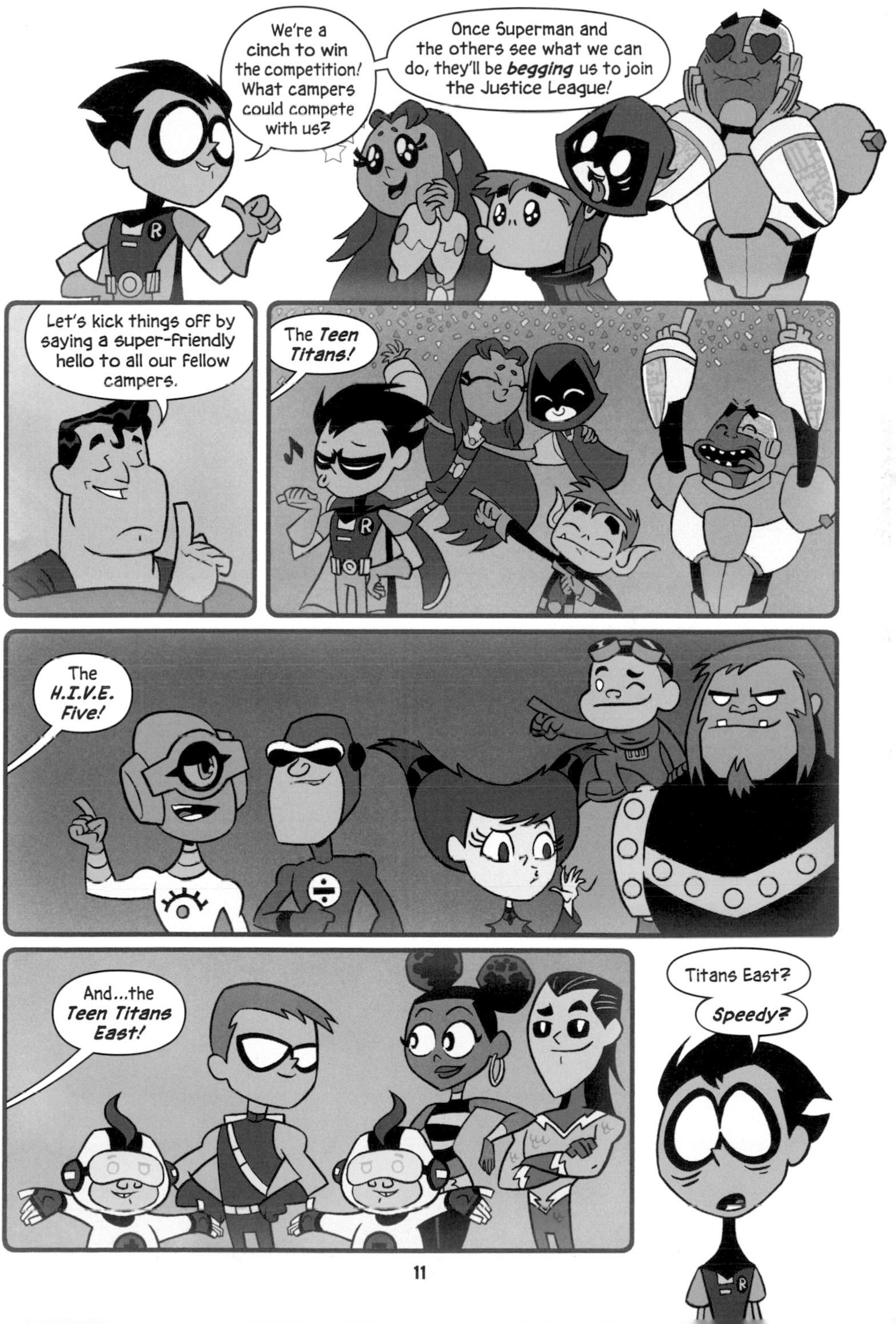
We're a cinch to win the competition! What campers could compete with us?
Once Superman and the others see what we can do, they'll be *begging* us to join the Justice League!
Let's kick things off by saying a super-friendly hello to all our fellow campers.
The *Teen Titans!*
The *H.I.V.E. Five!*
And...the *Teen Titans East!*
Titans East?
Speedy?

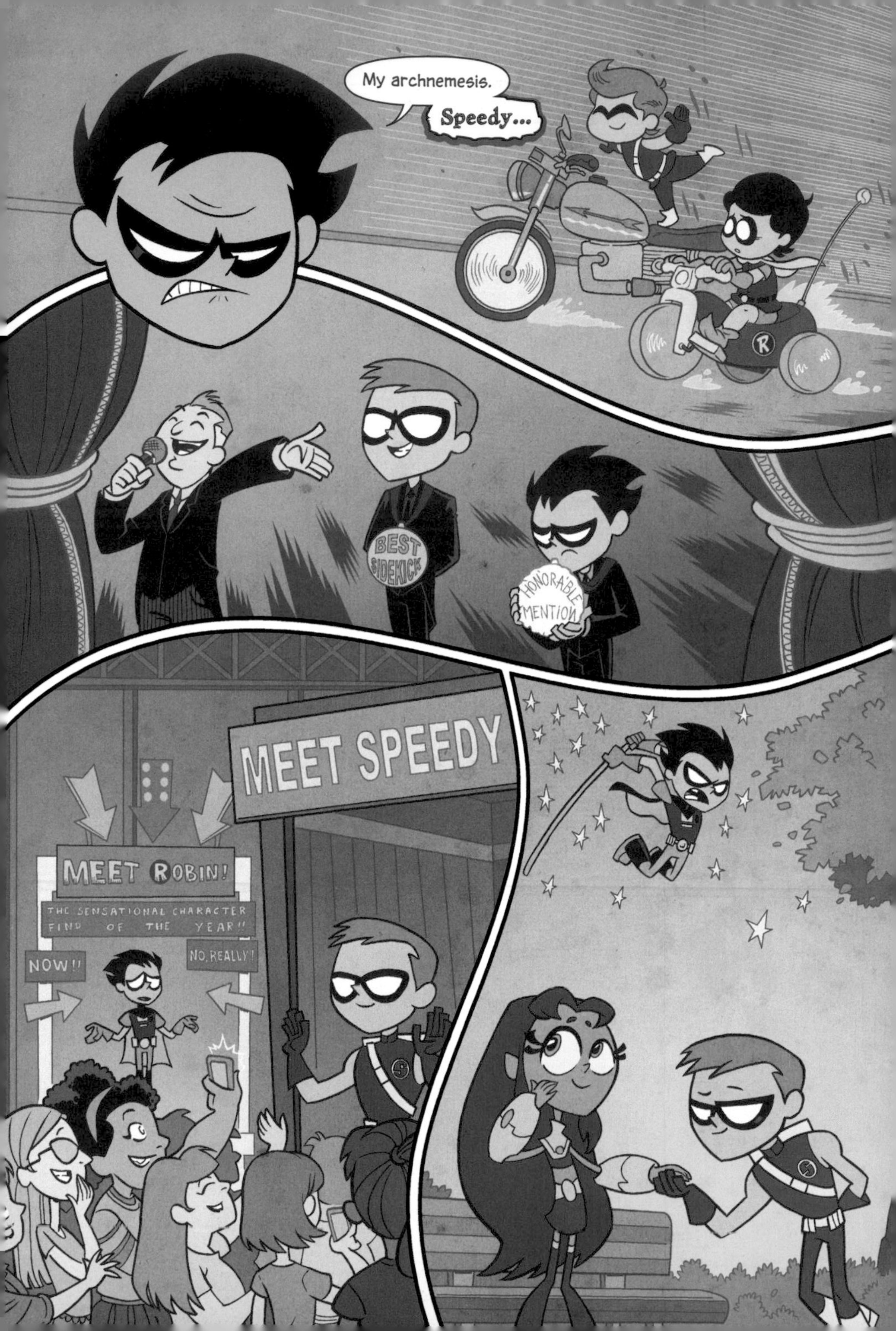
My archnemesis.
Speedy...
BEST SIDEKICK
HONORABLE MENTION
MEET SPEEDY
MEET ROBIN!
THE SENSATIONAL CHARACTER FIND OF THE YEAR!!
NOW!!
NO, REALLY!

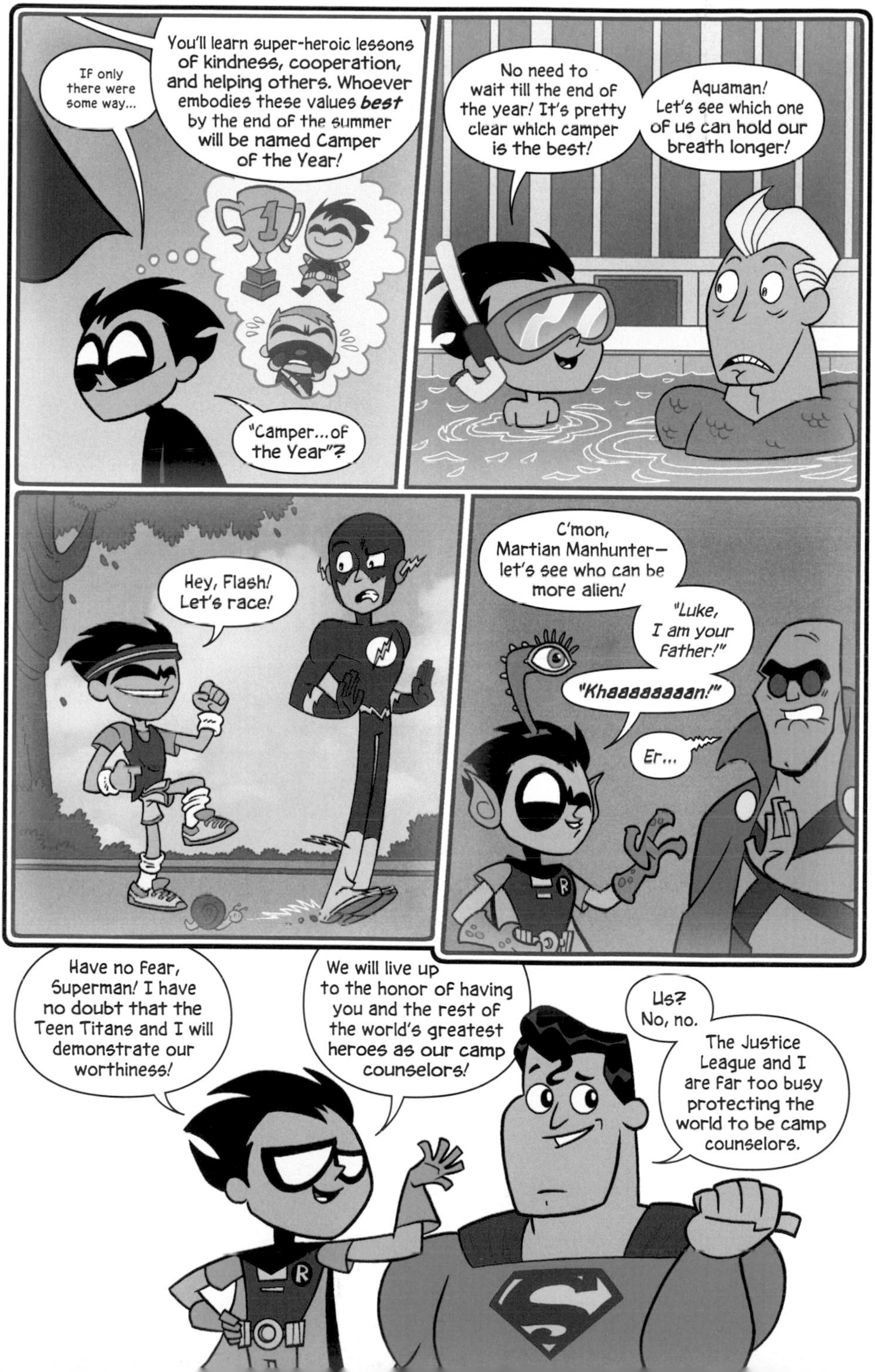
If only there were some way...
You'll learn super-heroic lessons of kindness, cooperation, and helping others. Whoever embodies these values *best* by the end of the summer will be named Camper of the Year!
"Camper...of the Year"?
No need to wait till the end of the year! It's pretty clear which camper is the best!
Aquaman! Let's see which one of us can hold our breath longer!
Hey, Flash! Let's race!
C'mon, Martian Manhunter— let's see who can be more alien!
"Luke, I am your Father!"
"Khaaaaaaaan!"
Er...
Have no fear, Superman! I have no doubt that the Teen Titans and I will demonstrate our worthiness!
We will live up to the honor of having you and the rest of the world's greatest heroes as our camp counselors!
Us? No, no.
The Justice League and I are far too busy protecting the world to be camp counselors.

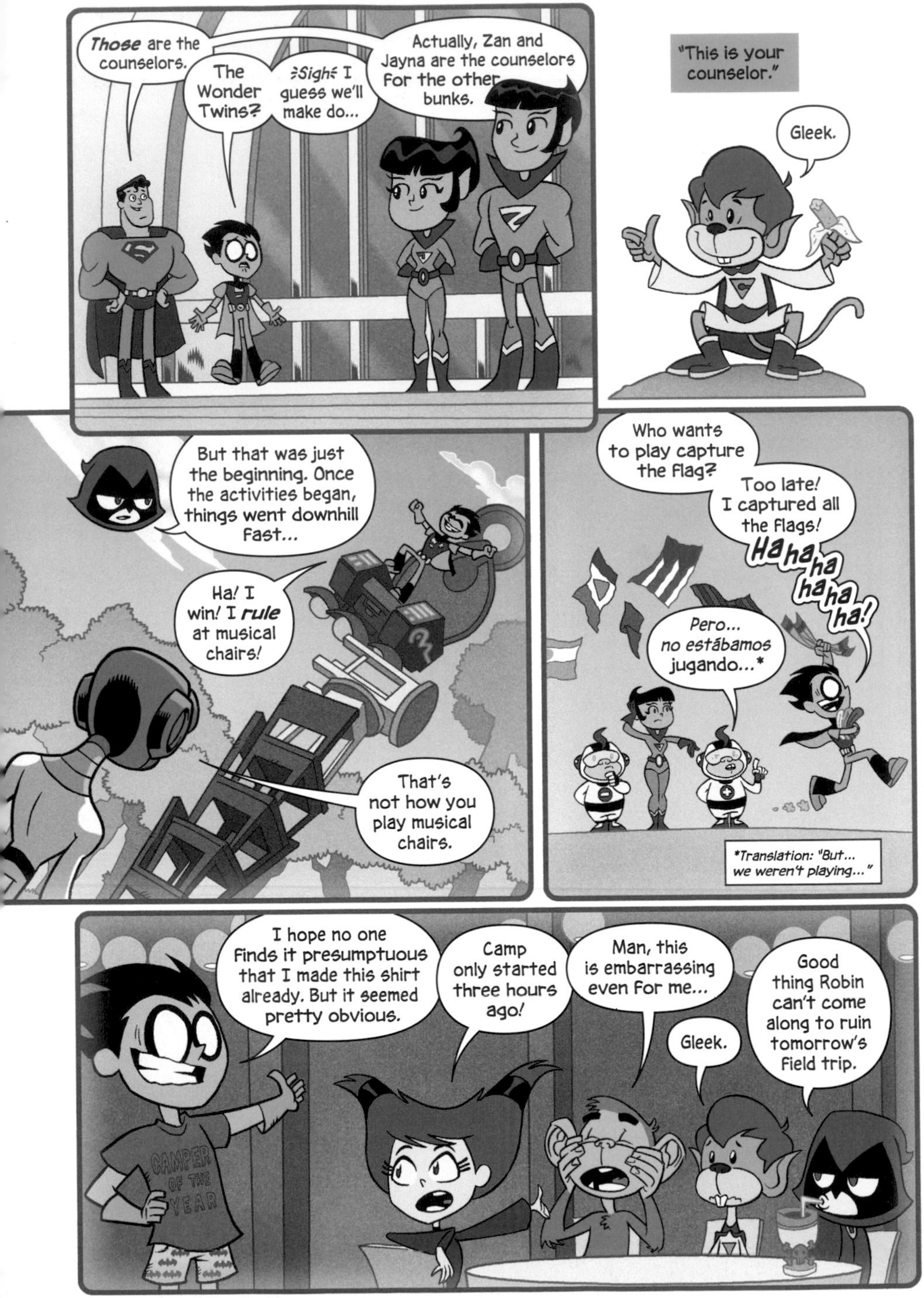
Those are the counselors.
The Wonder Twins?
Sigh I guess we'll make do...
Actually, Zan and Jayna are the counselors for the other bunks.
"This is your counselor."
Gleek.
But that was just the beginning. Once the activities began, things went downhill fast...
Ha! I win! I rule at musical chairs!
That's not how you play musical chairs.
Who wants to play capture the flag?
Too late! I captured all the flags!
Hahahahahahaha!
Pero... no estábamos jugando...*
*Translation: "But... we weren't playing..."
I hope no one finds it presumptuous that I made this shirt already. But it seemed pretty obvious.
CAMPER OF THE YEAR
Camp only started three hours ago!
Man, this is embarrassing even for me...
Gleek.
Good thing Robin can't come along to ruin tomorrow's field trip.

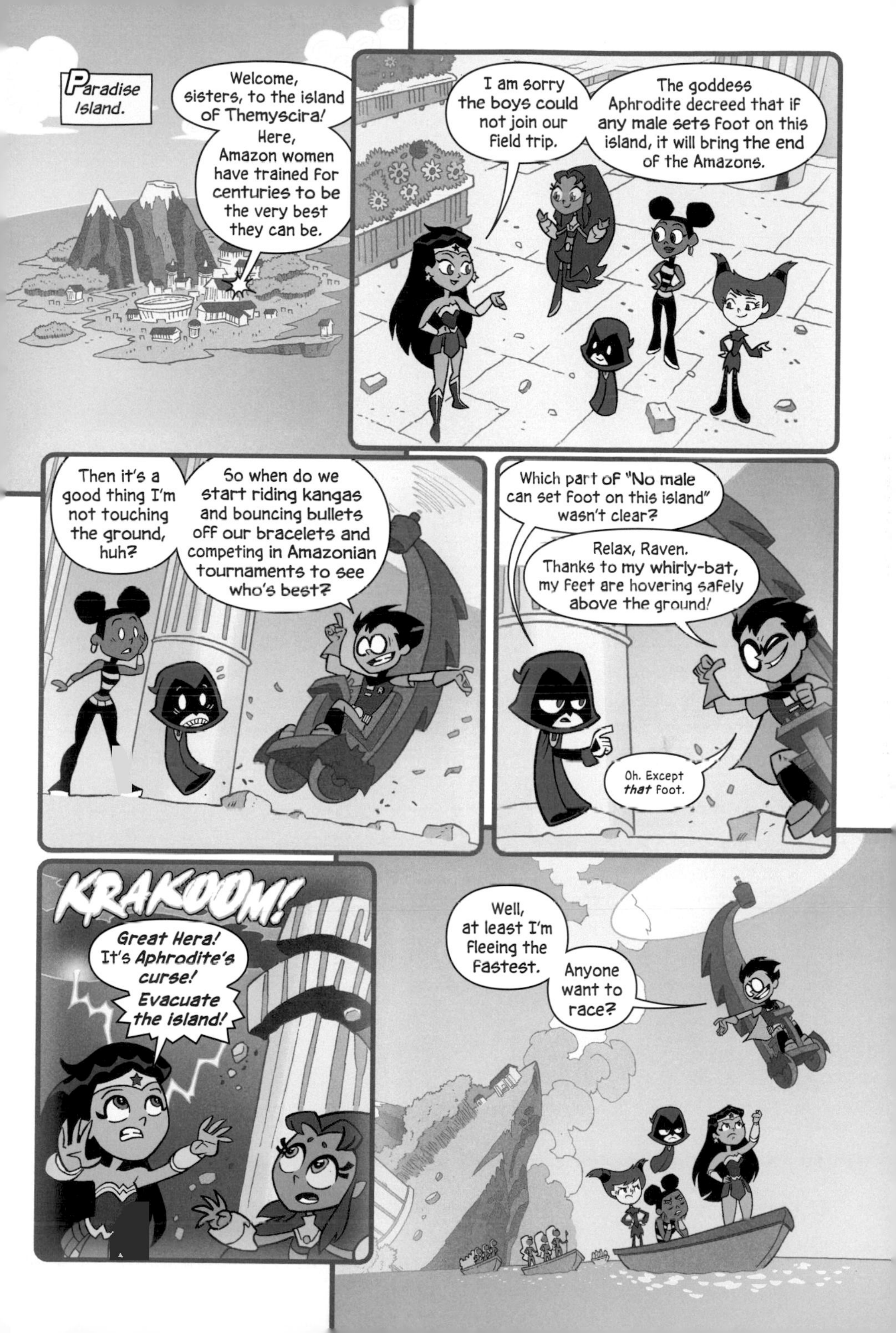

Paradise Island.
Welcome, sisters, to the island of Themyscira!
Here, Amazon women have trained for centuries to be the very best they can be.
I am sorry the boys could not join our field trip.
The goddess Aphrodite decreed that if any male sets foot on this island, it will bring the end of the Amazons.
Then it's a good thing I'm not touching the ground, huh?
So when do we start riding kangas and bouncing bullets off our bracelets and competing in Amazonian tournaments to see who's best?
Which part of "No male can set foot on this island" wasn't clear?
Relax, Raven. Thanks to my whirly-bat, my feet are hovering safely above the ground!
Oh. Except *that* foot.
KRAKOOM!
Great Hera! It's Aphrodite's curse! Evacuate the island!
Well, at least I'm fleeing the fastest.
Anyone want to race?

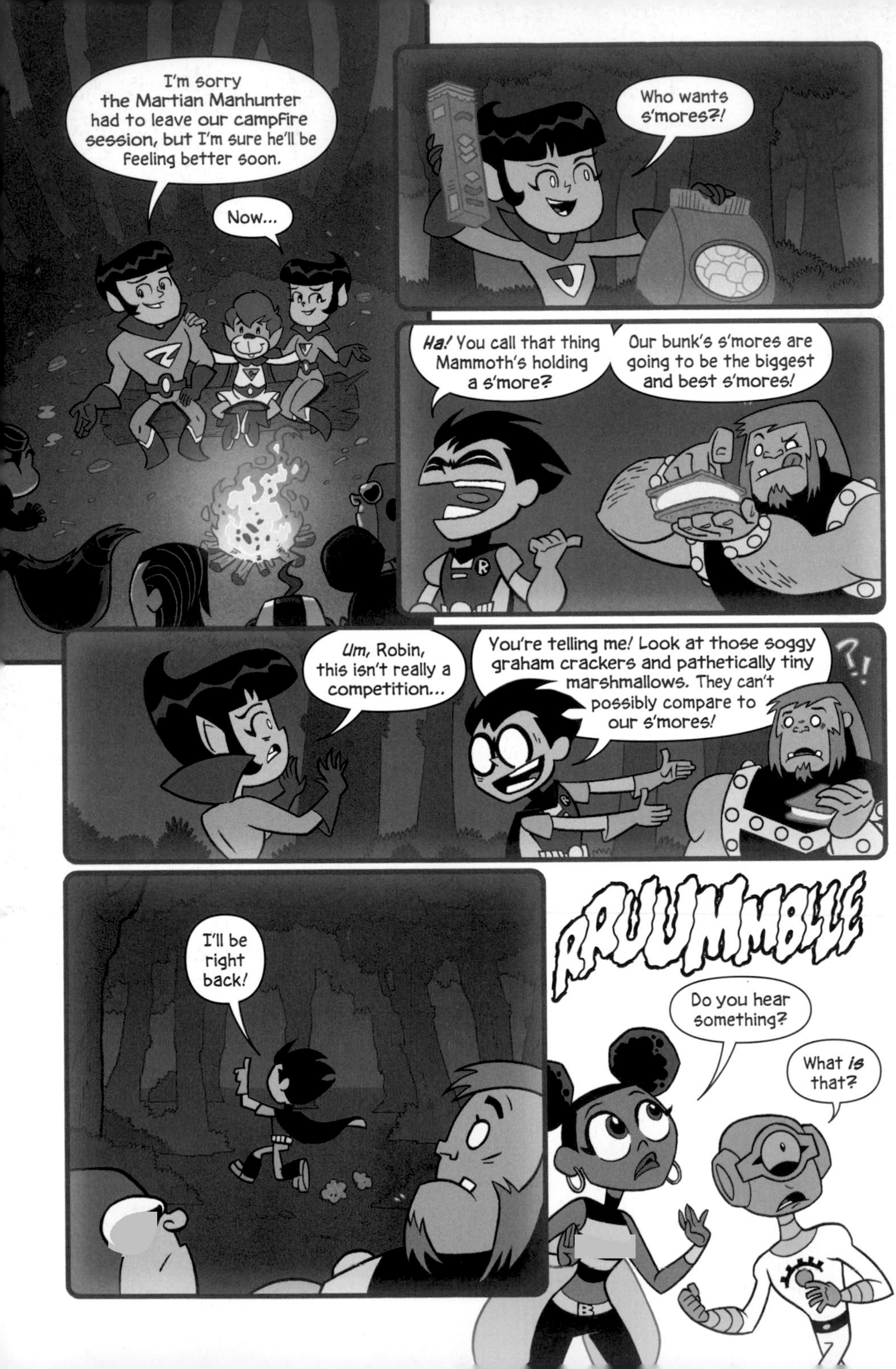
I'm sorry the Martian Manhunter had to leave our campfire session, but I'm sure he'll be feeling better soon.
Now...
Who wants s'mores?!
Ha! You call that thing Mammoth's holding a s'more?
Our bunk's s'mores are going to be the biggest and best s'mores!
Um, Robin, this isn't really a competition...
You're telling me! Look at those soggy graham crackers and pathetically tiny marshmallows. They can't possibly compare to our s'mores!
?!
I'll be right back!
RRUUMMBLLE
Do you hear something?
What is that?

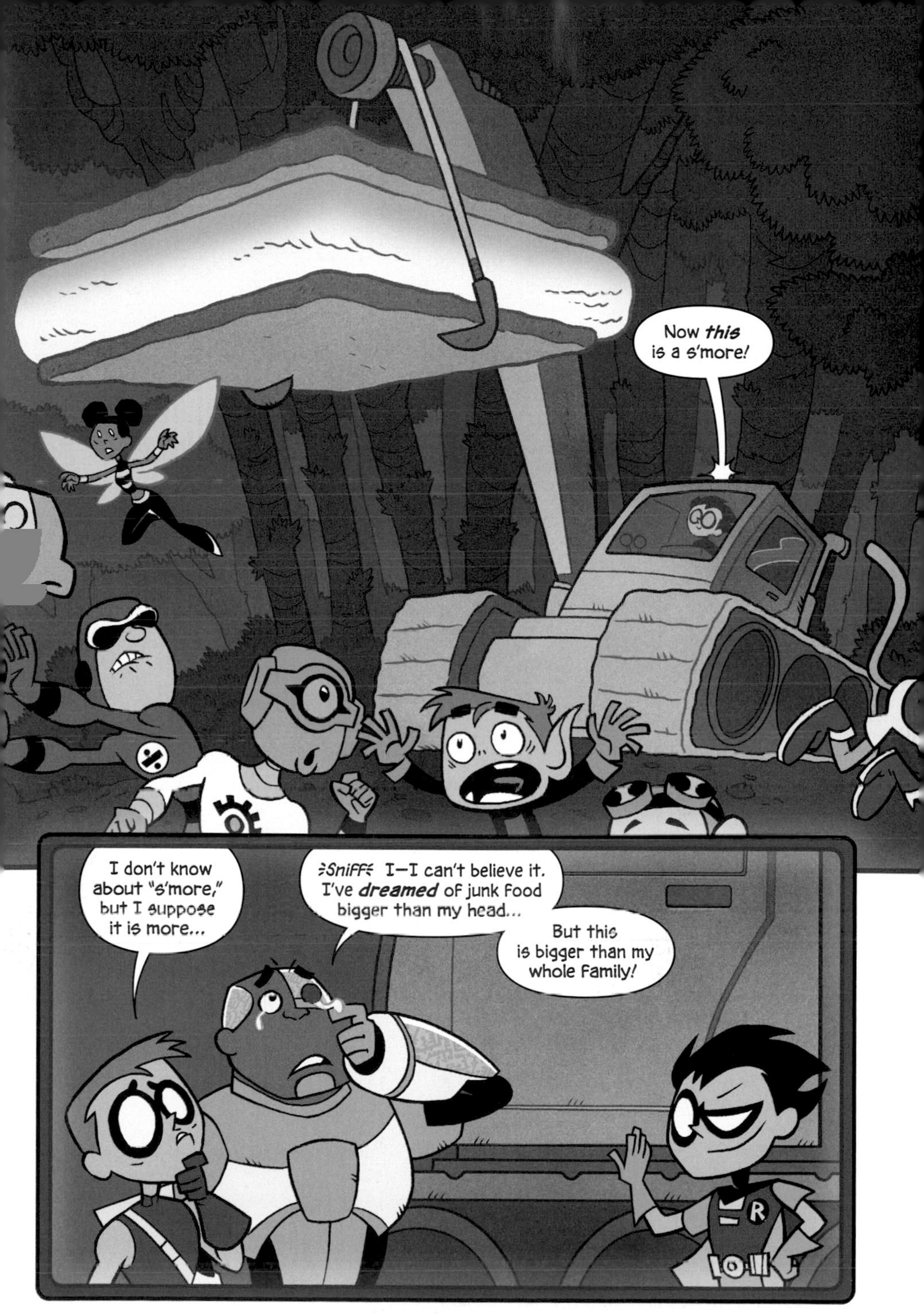
Now *this* is a s'more!
I don't know about "s'more," but I suppose it is more...
≑Sniff≑ I—I can't believe it. I've *dreamed* of junk food bigger than my head...
But this is bigger than my whole family!

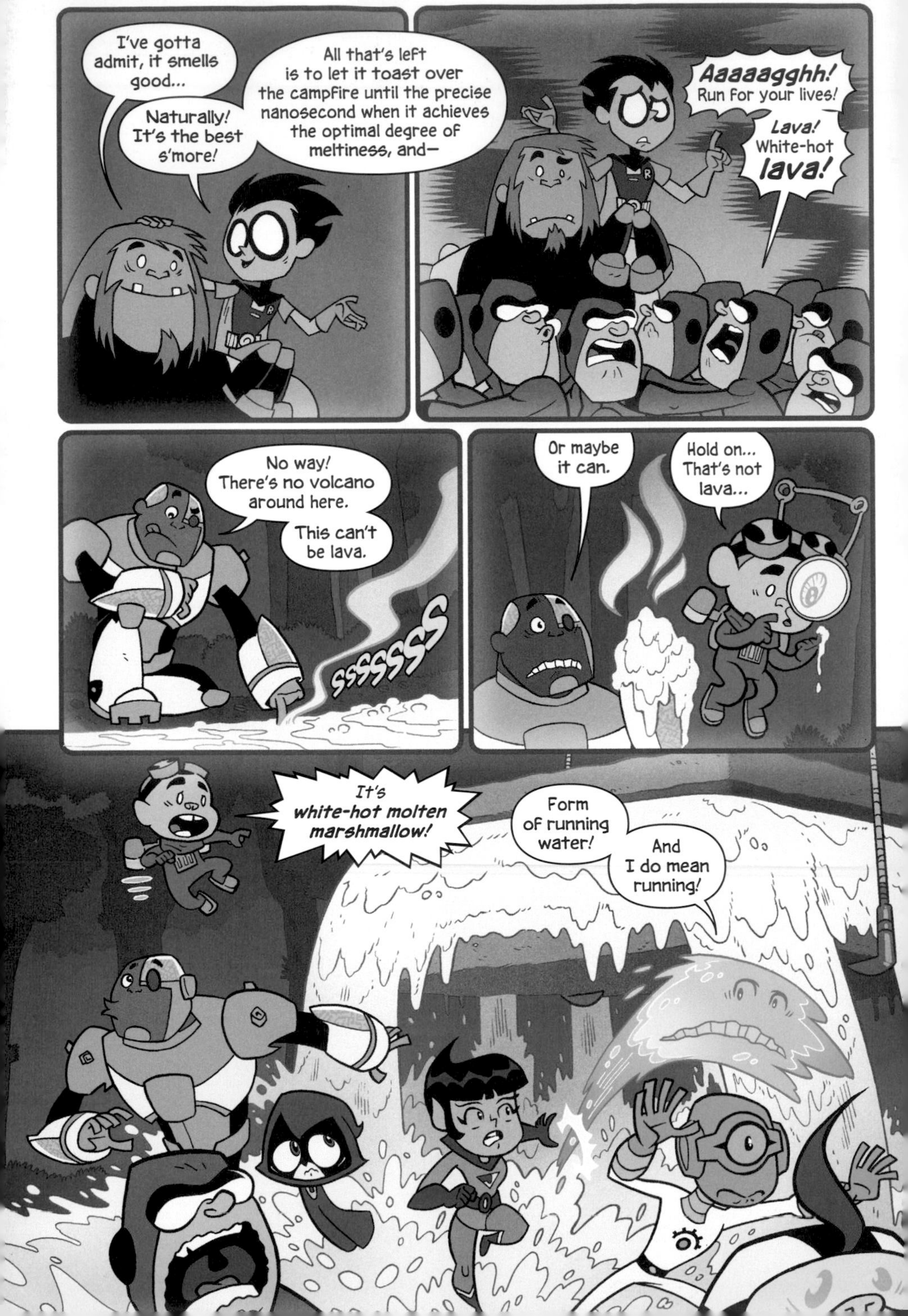
I've gotta admit, it smells good...
Naturally! It's the best s'more!
All that's left is to let it toast over the campfire until the precise nanosecond when it achieves the optimal degree of meltiness, and—
Aaaaagghh! Run for your lives!
Lava! White-hot lava!
No way! There's no volcano around here.
This can't be lava.
SSSSSSS
Or maybe it can.
Hold on... That's not lava...
It's white-hot molten marshmallow!
Form of running water!
And I do mean running!

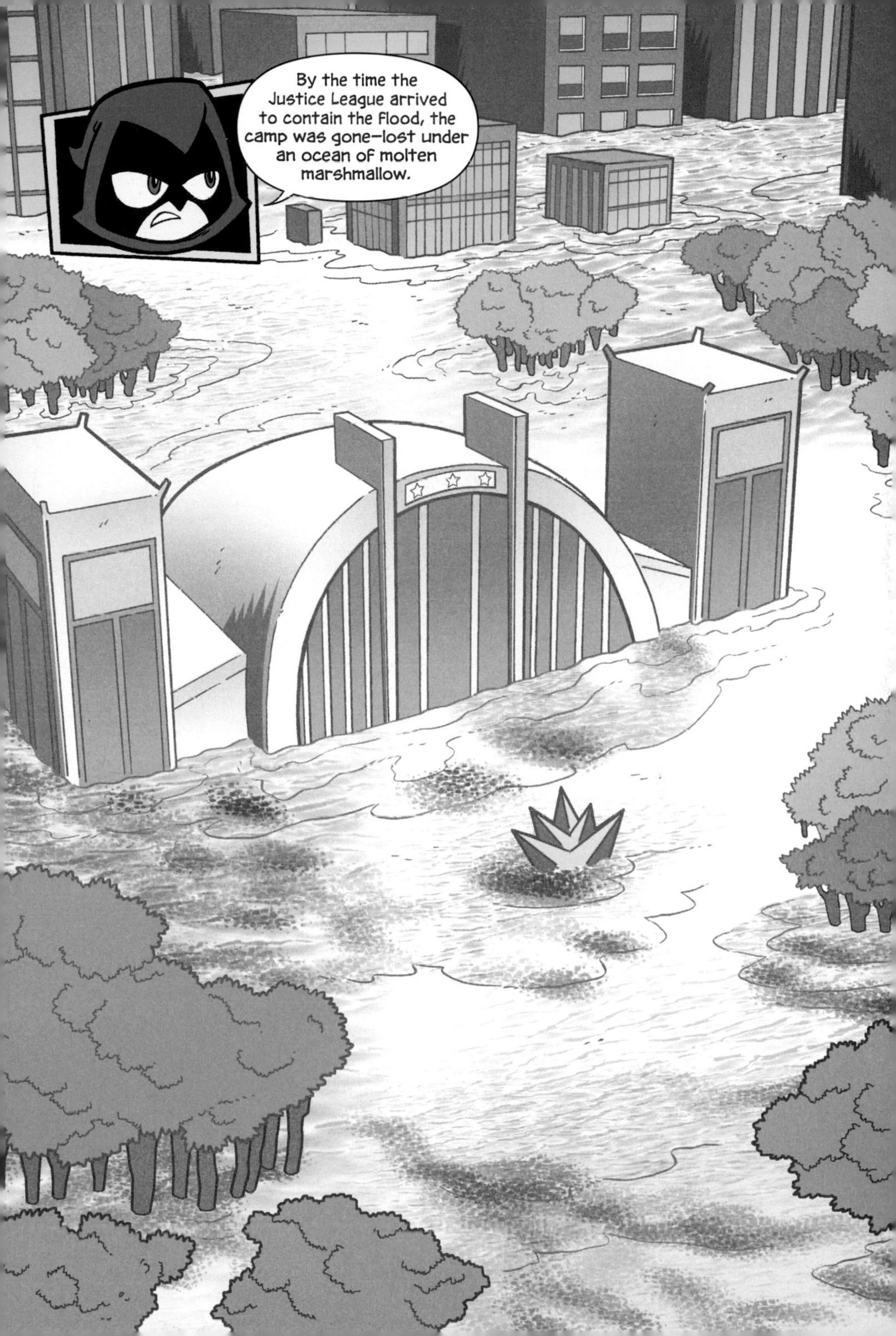
By the time the Justice League arrived to contain the flood, the camp was gone—lost under an ocean of molten marshmallow.

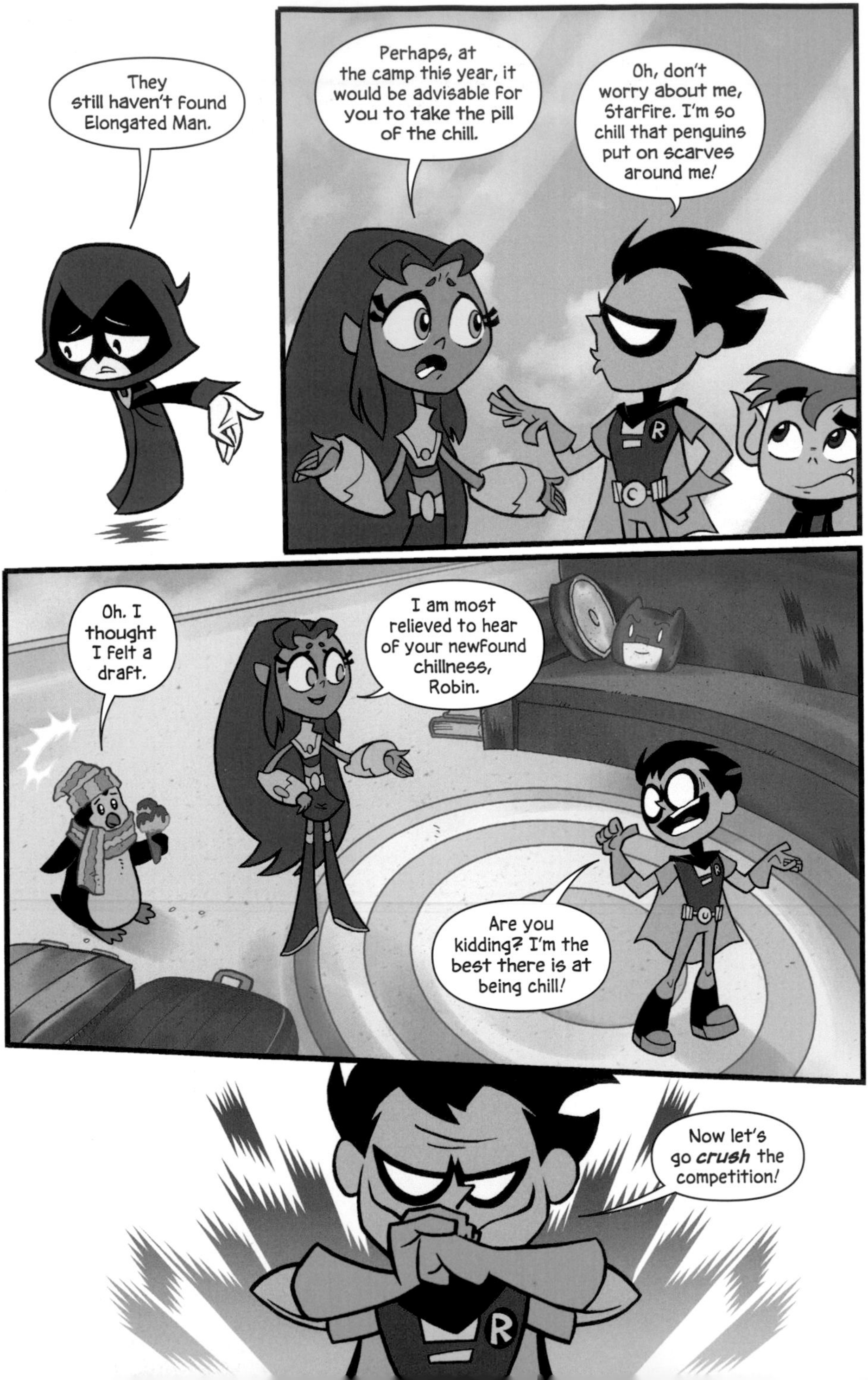
They still haven't found Elongated Man.
Perhaps, at the camp this year, it would be advisable for you to take the pill of the chill.
Oh, don't worry about me, Starfire. I'm so chill that penguins put on scarves around me!
Oh. I thought I felt a draft.
I am most relieved to hear of your newfound chillness, Robin.
Are you kidding? I'm the best there is at being chill!
Now let's go *crush* the competition!

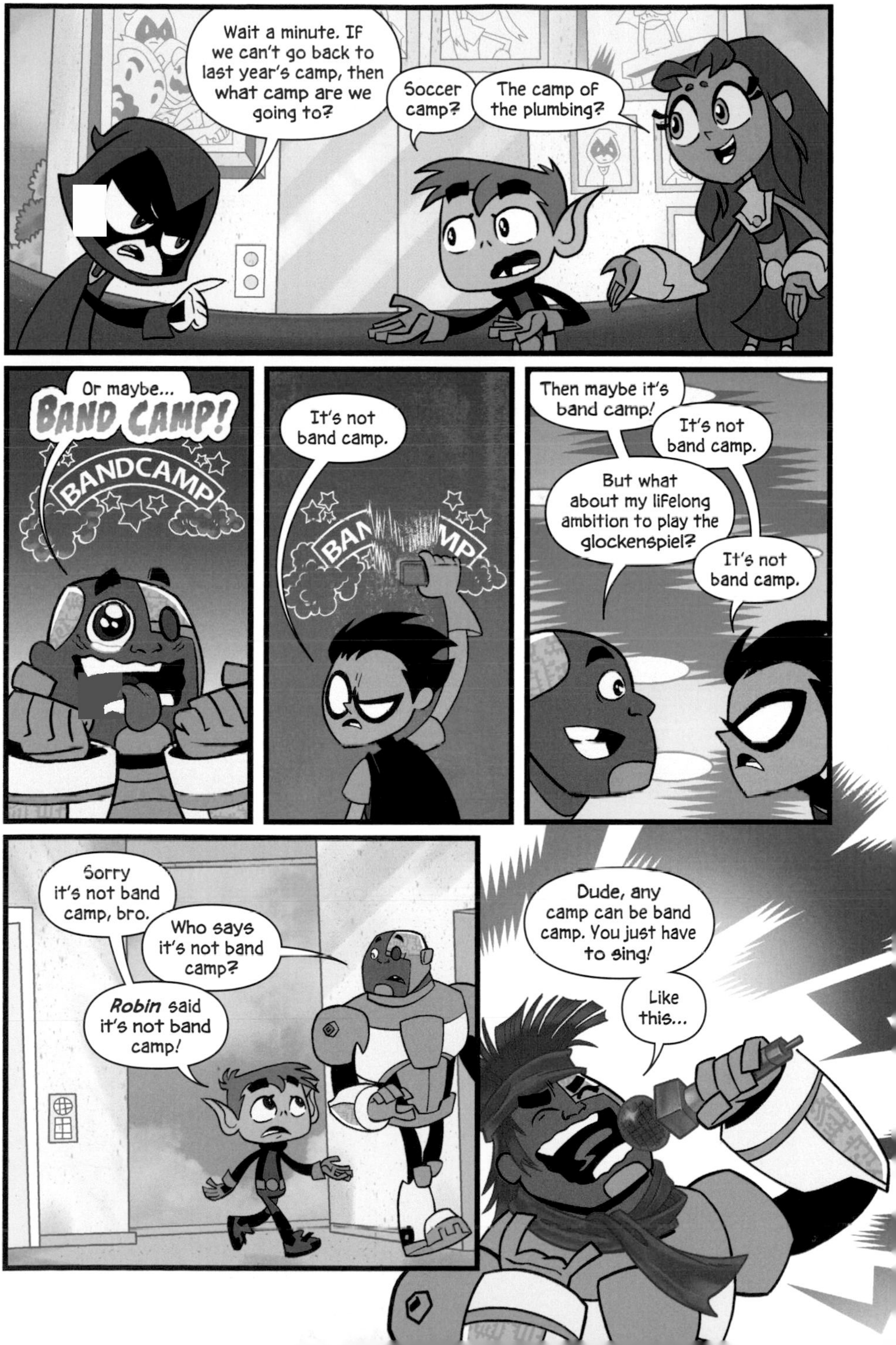
Wait a minute. If we can't go back to last year's camp, then what camp are we going to?
Soccer camp?
The camp of the plumbing?
Or maybe... BAND CAMP!
BANDCAMP
It's not band camp.
Then maybe it's band camp!
It's not band camp.
But what about my lifelong ambition to play the glockenspiel?
It's not band camp.
Sorry it's not band camp, bro.
Who says it's not band camp?
Robin said it's not band camp!
Dude, any camp can be band camp. You just have to sing!
Like this...

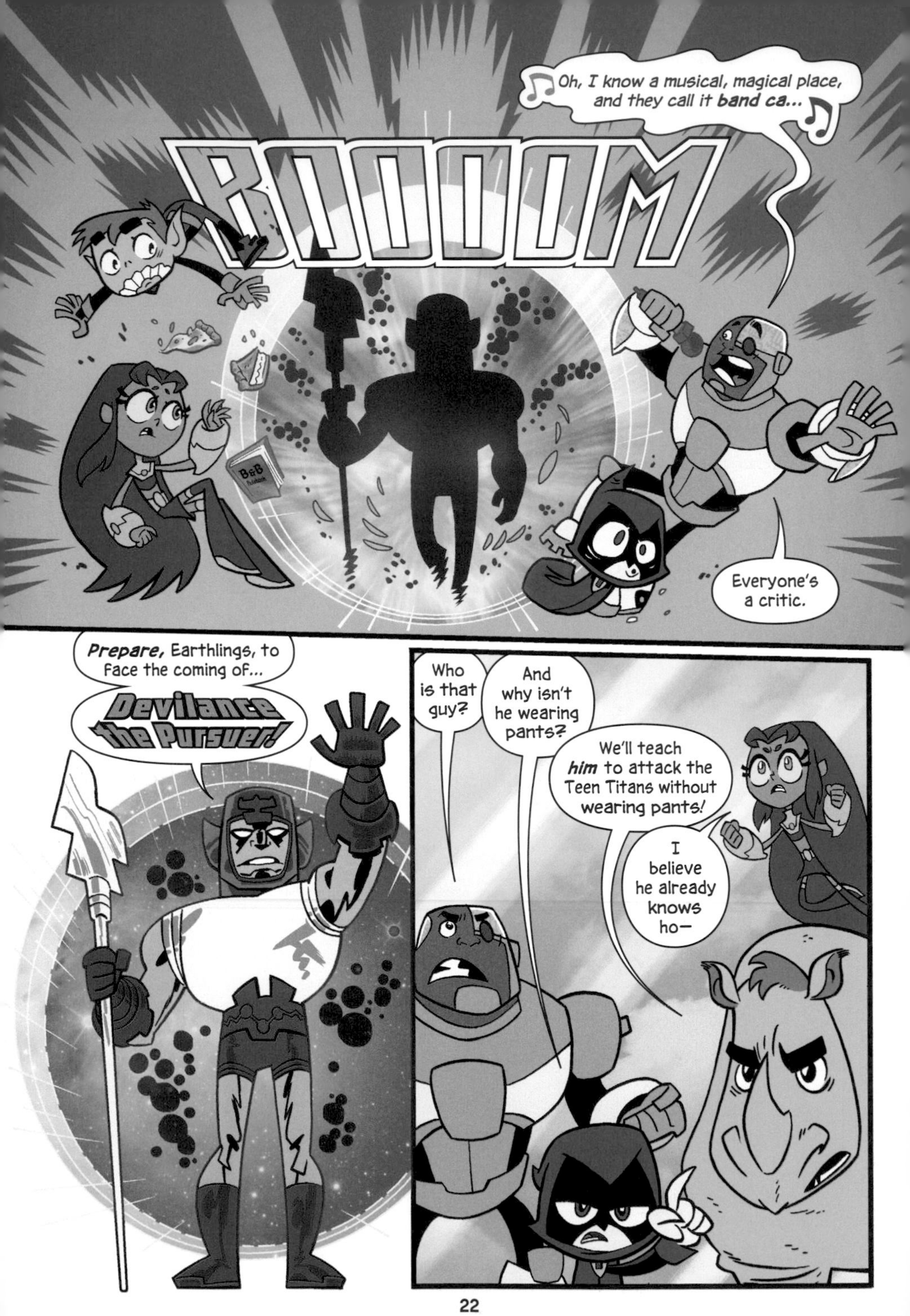
Oh, I know a musical, magical place, and they call it **band ca...**
BOOOOM
B&B
Everyone's a critic.
Prepare, Earthlings, to face the coming of...
Devilance the Pursuer!
Who is that guy?
And why isn't he wearing pants?
We'll teach ***him*** to attack the Teen Titans without wearing pants!
I believe he already knows ho—

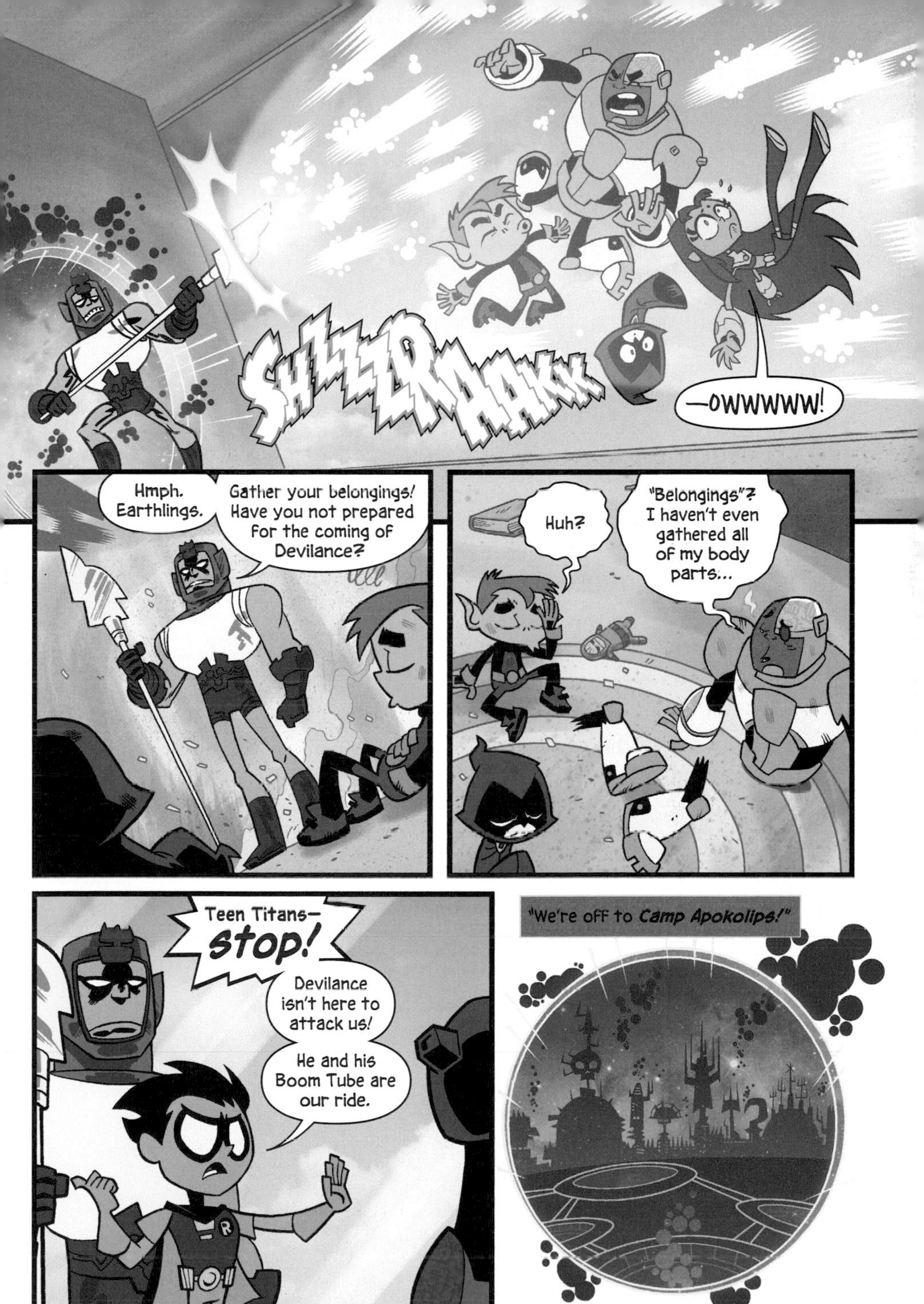

SHZZZRAAAKK
—OWWWWW!
Hmph. Earthlings.
Gather your belongings! Have you not prepared for the coming of Devilance?
Huh?
"Belongings"? I haven't even gathered all of my body parts...
Teen Titans— Stop!
Devilance isn't here to attack us!
He and his Boom Tube are our ride.
"We're off to Camp Apokolips!"

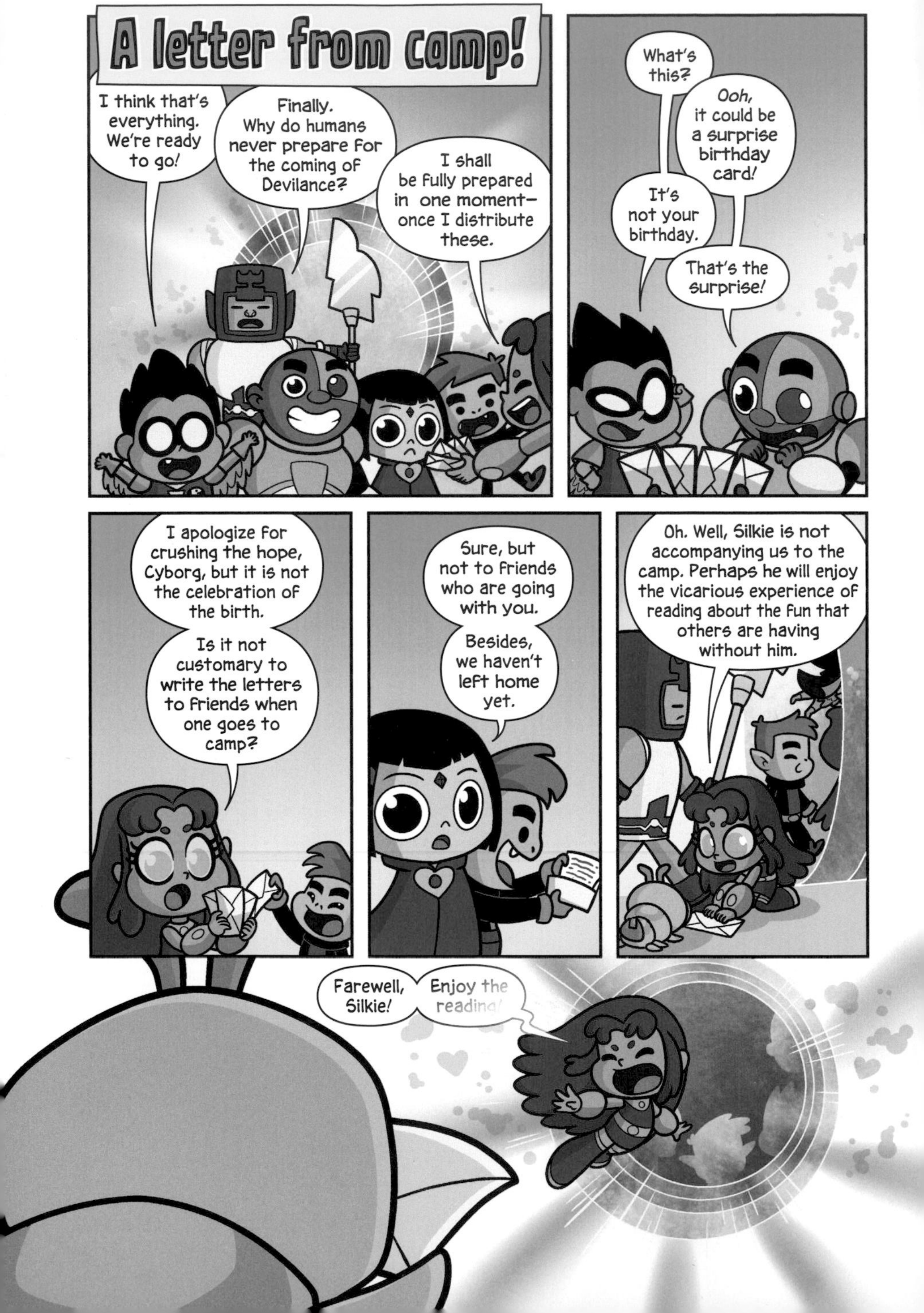
A letter from camp!
I think that's everything. We're ready to go!
Finally. Why do humans never prepare for the coming of Devilance?
I shall be fully prepared in one moment— once I distribute these.
What's this?
Ooh, it could be a surprise birthday card!
It's not your birthday.
That's the surprise!
I apologize for crushing the hope, Cyborg, but it is not the celebration of the birth.
Is it not customary to write the letters to friends when one goes to camp?
Sure, but not to friends who are going with you.
Besides, we haven't left home yet.
Oh. Well, Silkie is not accompanying us to the camp. Perhaps he will enjoy the vicarious experience of reading about the fun that others are having without him.
Farewell, Silkie!
Enjoy the reading!

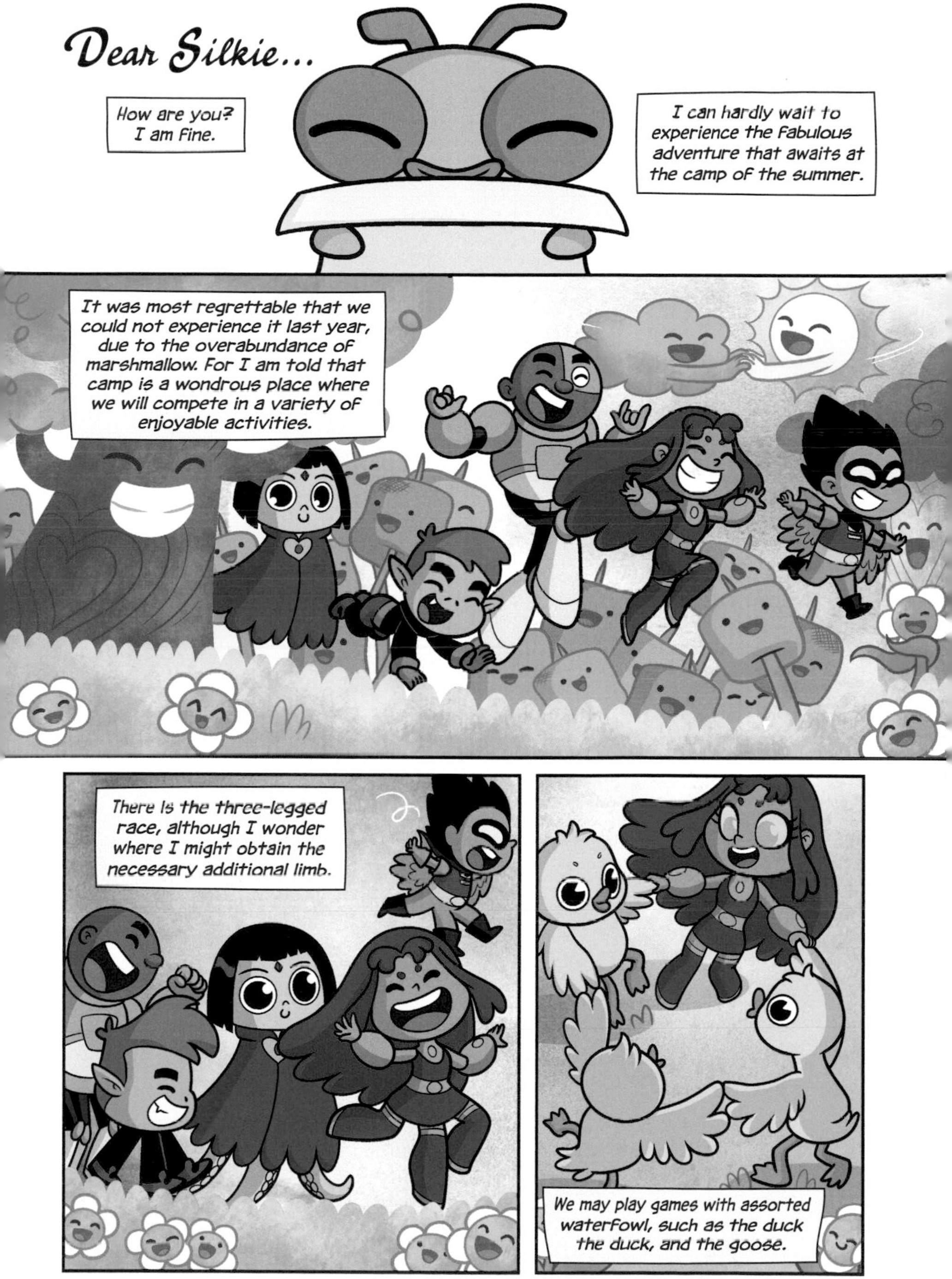
Dear Silkie...
How are you? I am fine.
I can hardly wait to experience the fabulous adventure that awaits at the camp of the summer.
It was most regrettable that we could not experience it last year, due to the overabundance of marshmallow. For I am told that camp is a wondrous place where we will compete in a variety of enjoyable activities.
There is the three-legged race, although I wonder where I might obtain the necessary additional limb.
We may play games with assorted waterfowl, such as the duck the duck, and the goose.

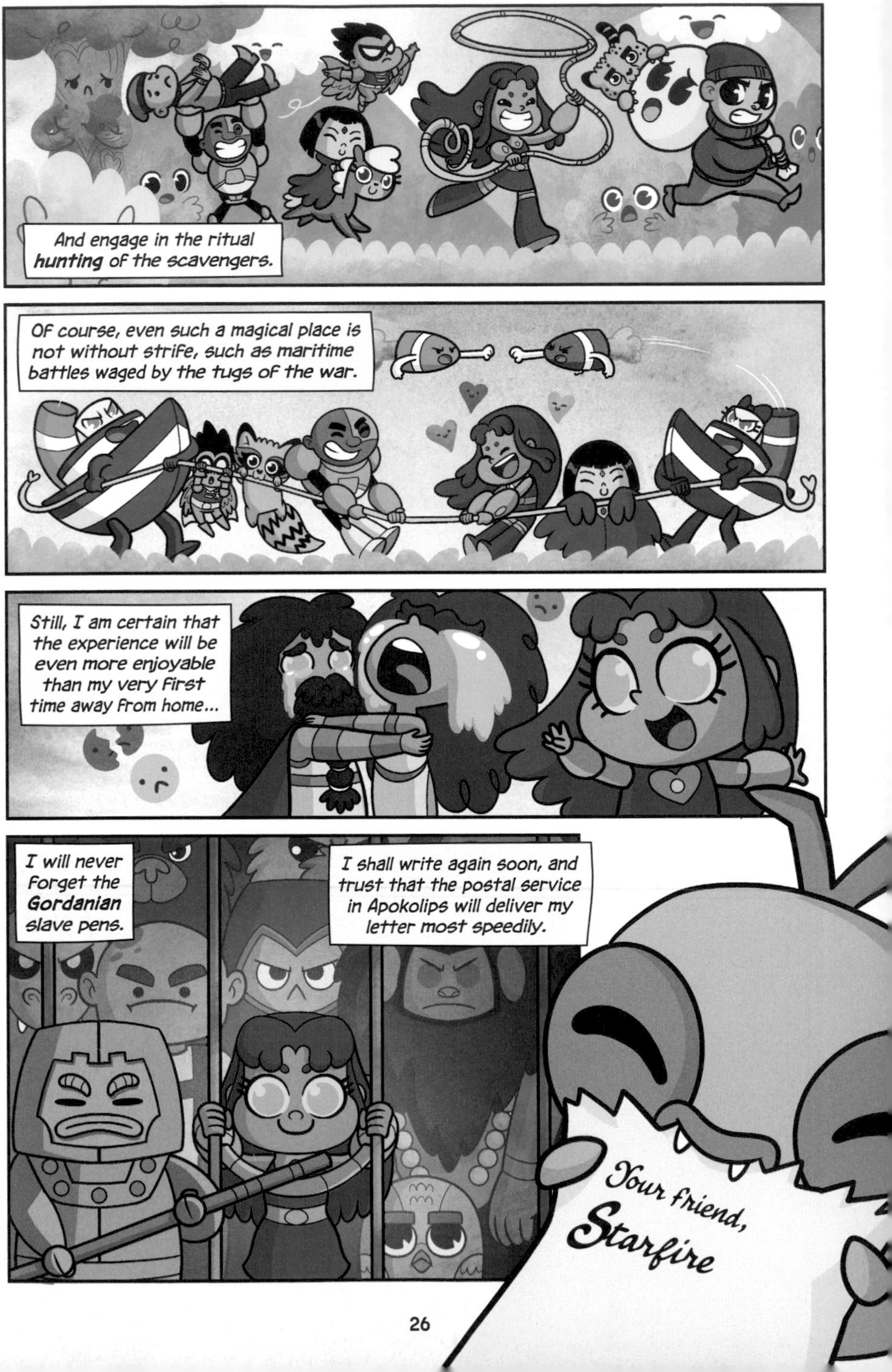

And engage in the ritual **hunting** of the scavengers.
Of course, even such a magical place is not without strife, such as maritime battles waged by the tugs of the war.
Still, I am certain that the experience will be even more enjoyable than my very first time away from home...
I will never forget the **Gordanian** slave pens.
I shall write again soon, and trust that the postal service in Apokolips will deliver my letter most speedily.
Your friend,
Starfire

Chapter Two

Beast Boy's letter drawn and
colored by Dario Brizuela

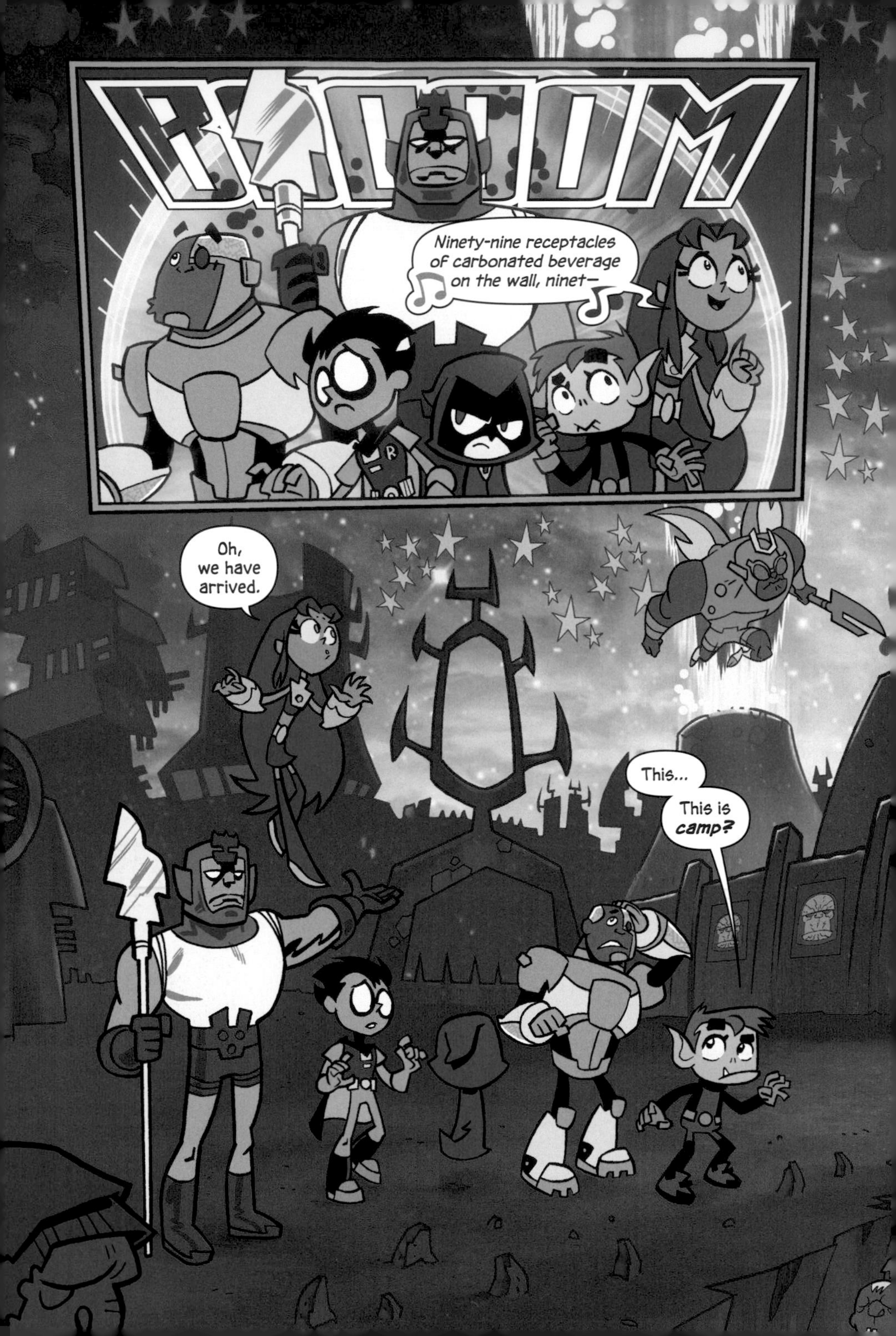
Ninety-nine receptacles of carbonated beverage on the wall, ninet—
Oh, we have arrived.
This...
This is *camp?*

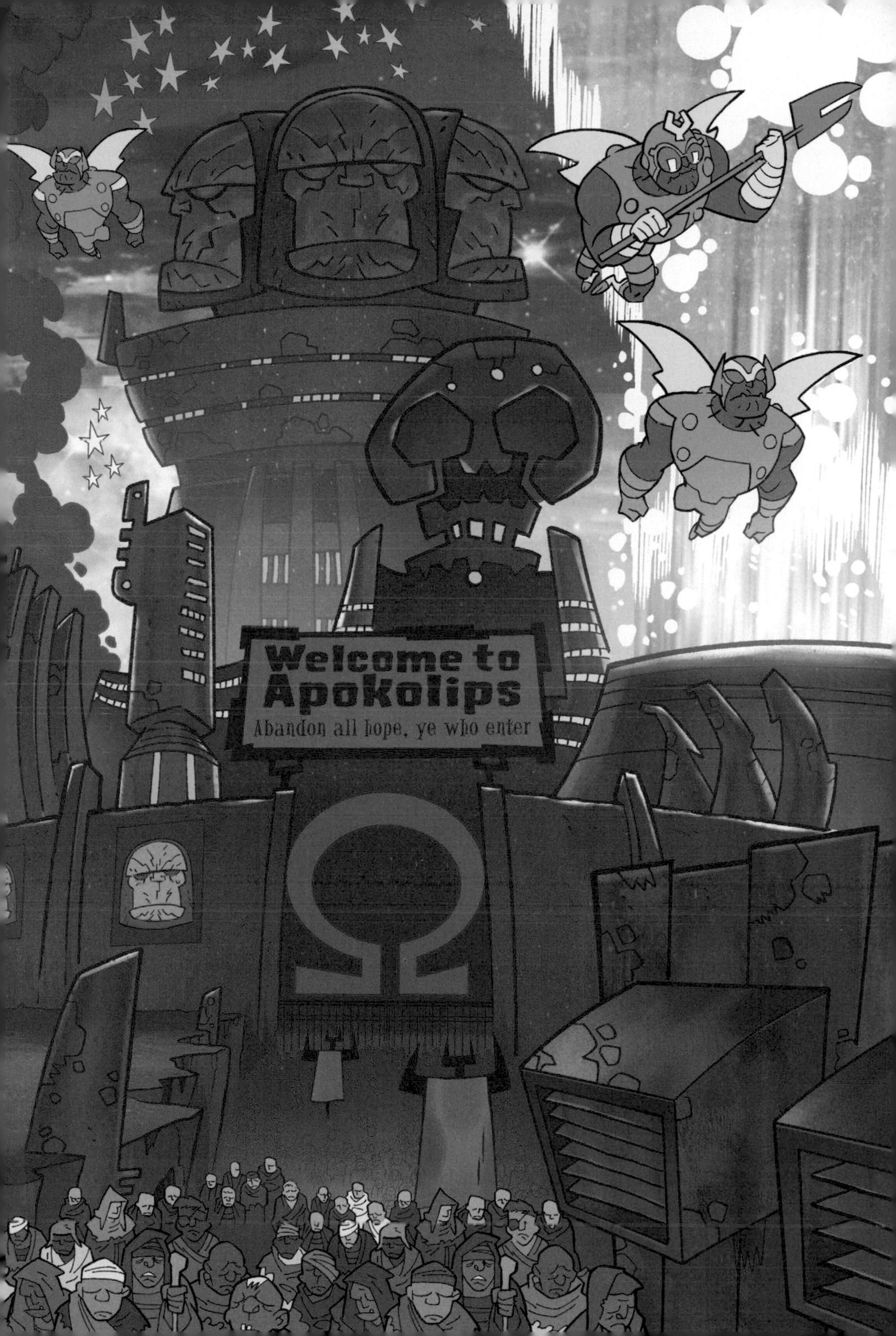
Welcome to Apokolips
Abandon all hope, ye who enter

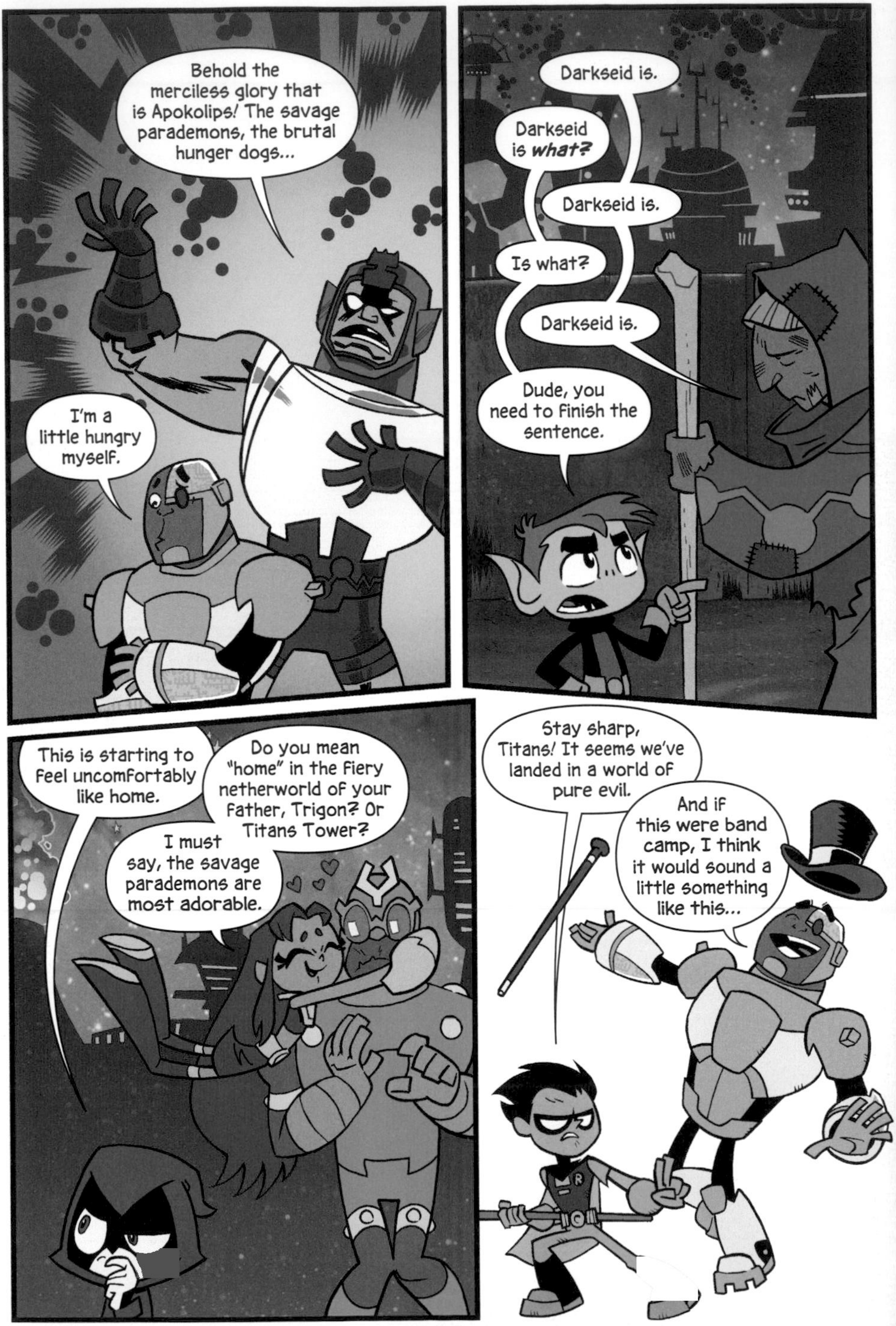
Behold the merciless glory that is Apokolips! The savage parademons, the brutal hunger dogs...
I'm a little hungry myself.
Darkseid is.
Darkseid is *what?*
Darkseid is.
Is what?
Darkseid is.
Dude, you need to finish the sentence.
This is starting to feel uncomfortably like home.
Do you mean "home" in the fiery netherworld of your father, Trigon? Or Titans Tower?
I must say, the savage parademons are most adorable.
Stay sharp, Titans! It seems we've landed in a world of pure evil.
And if this were band camp, I think it would sound a little something like this...

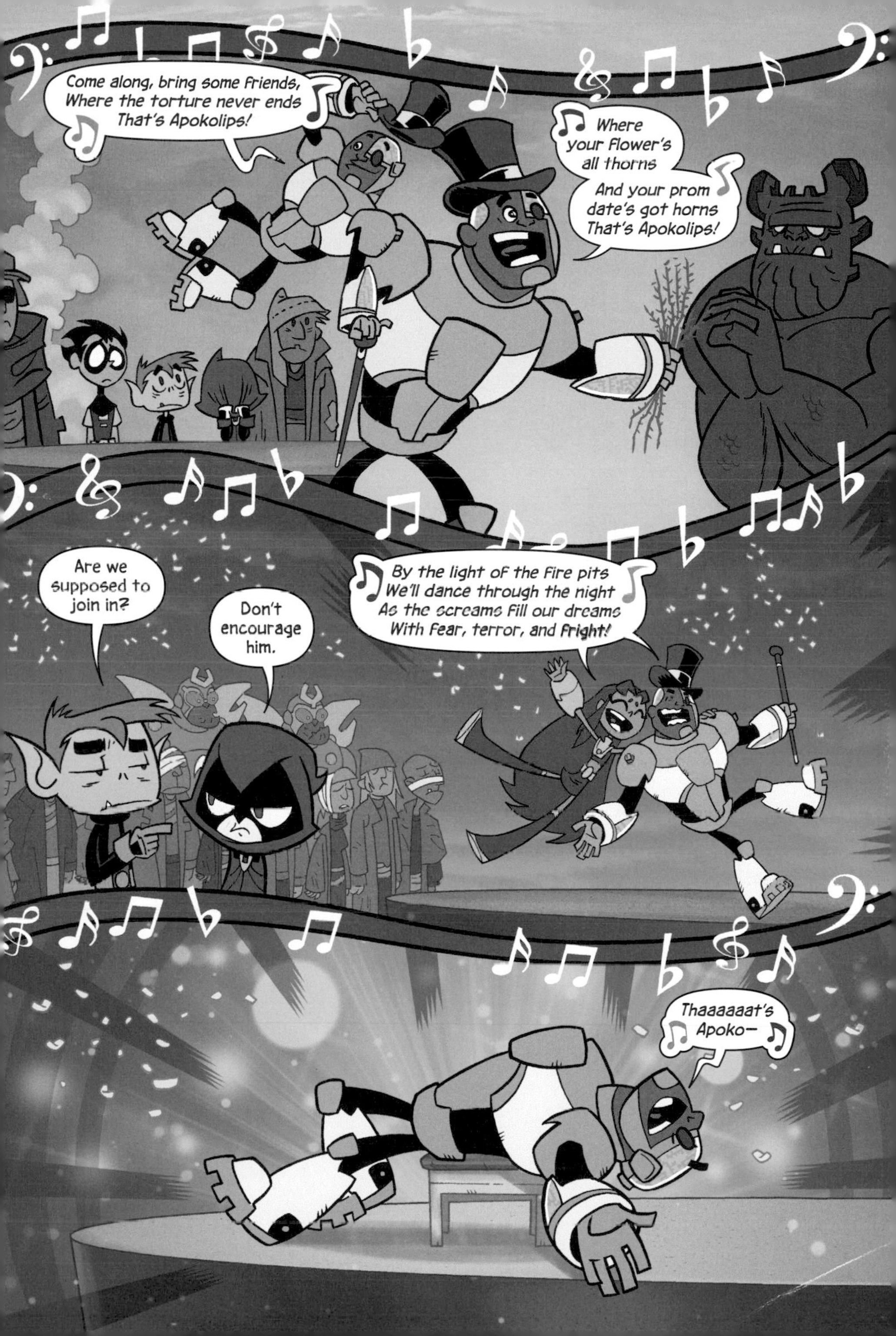

Come along, bring some friends,
Where the torture never ends
That's Apokolips!
Where your flower's all thorns
And your prom date's got horns
That's Apokolips!
Are we supposed to join in?
Don't encourage him.
By the light of the fire pits
We'll dance through the night
As the screams fill our dreams
With fear, terror, and fright!
Thaaaaaat's Apoko—

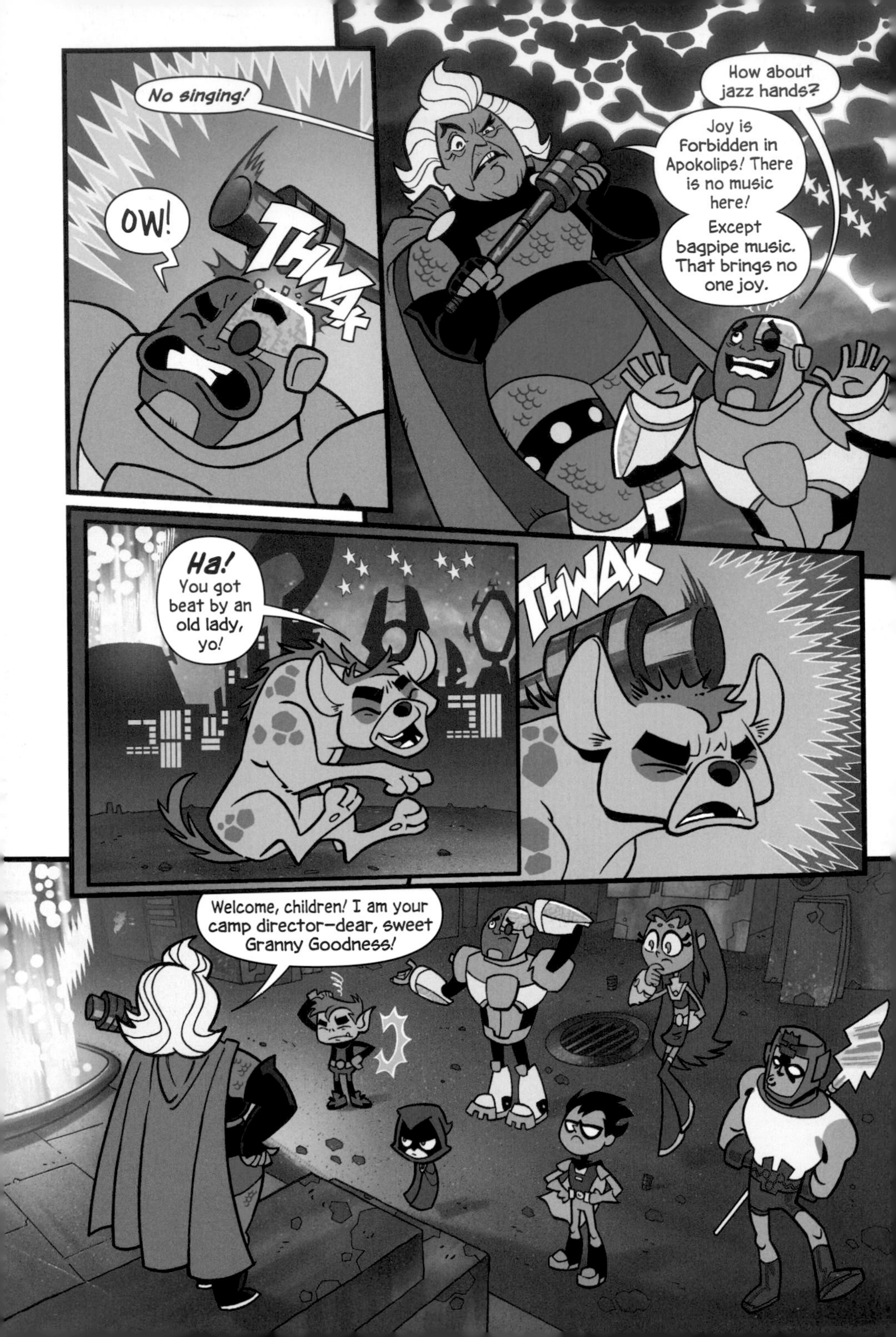
No singing!
OW!
THWAK
How about jazz hands?
Joy is Forbidden in Apokolips! There is no music here!
Except bagpipe music. That brings no one joy.
Ha! You got beat by an old lady, yo!
THWAK
Welcome, children! I am your camp director—dear, sweet Granny Goodness!

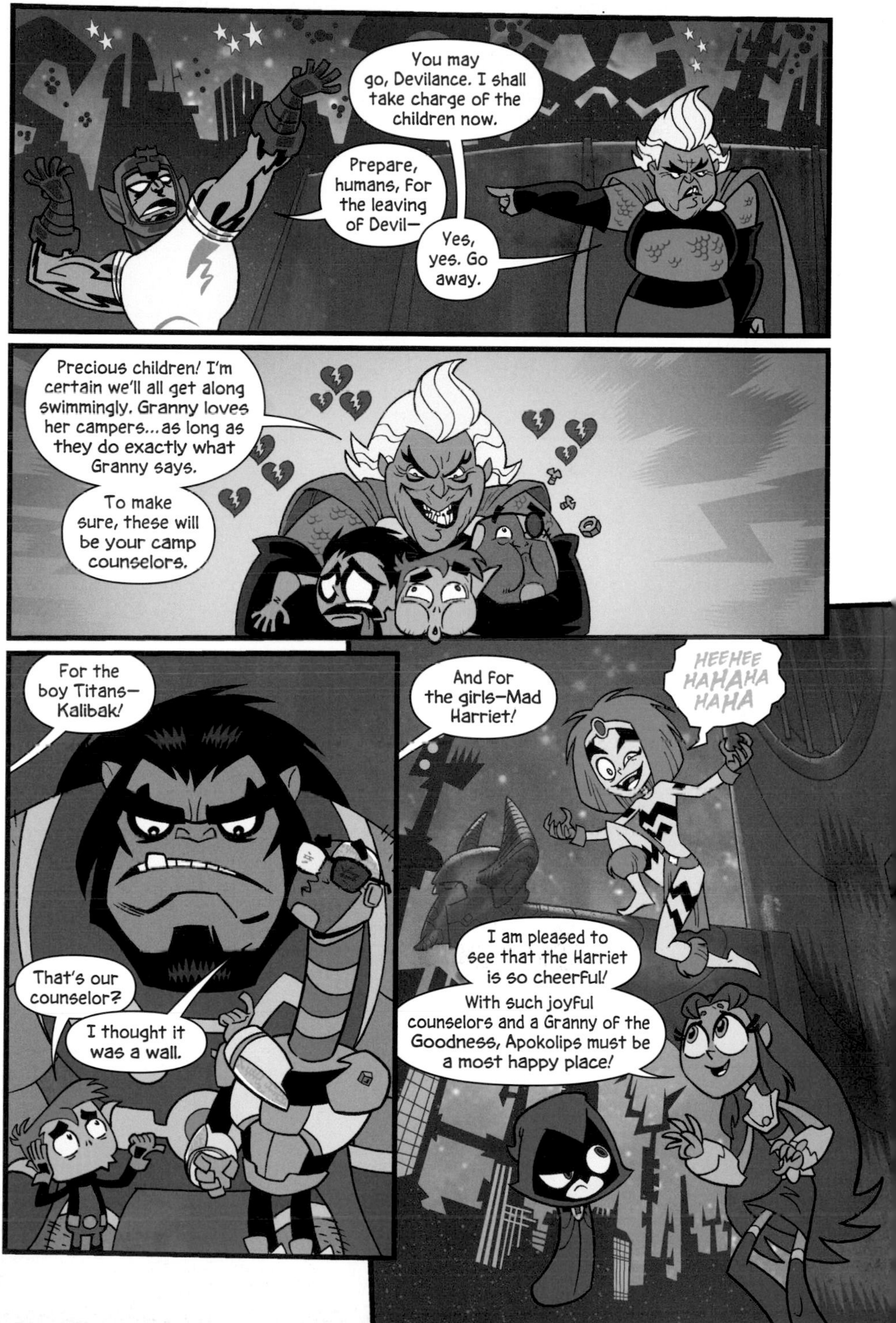
You may go, Devilance. I shall take charge of the children now.
Prepare, humans, for the leaving of Devil—
Yes, yes. Go away.
Precious children! I'm certain we'll all get along swimmingly. Granny loves her campers...as long as they do exactly what Granny says.
To make sure, these will be your camp counselors.
For the boy Titans—Kalibak!
That's our counselor?
I thought it was a wall.
And for the girls—Mad Harriet!
HEEHEE HAHAHA HAHA
I am pleased to see that the Harriet is so cheerful!
With such joyful counselors and a Granny of the Goodness, Apokolips must be a most happy place!

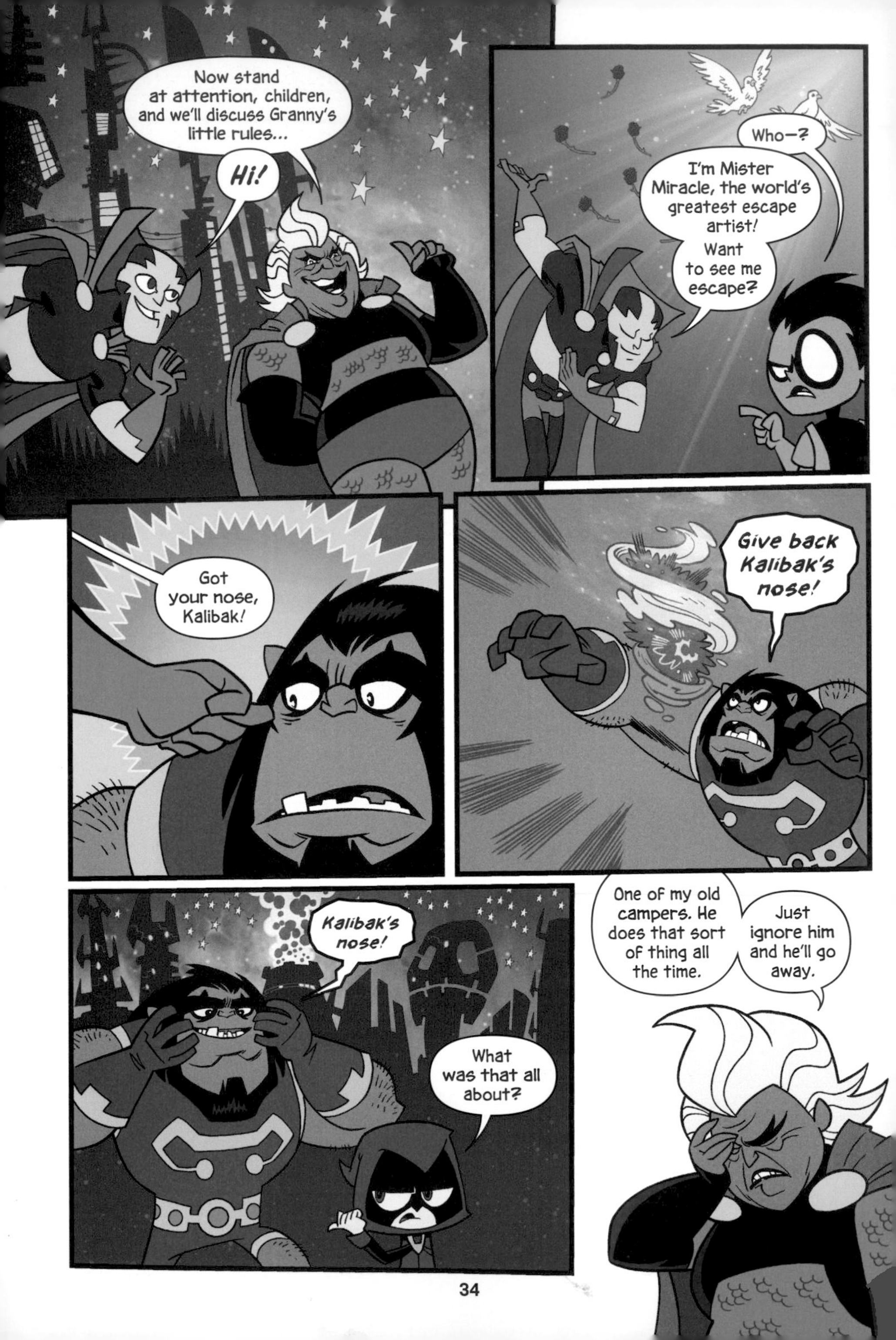
Now stand at attention, children, and we'll discuss Granny's little rules...
Hi!
Who—?
I'm Mister Miracle, the world's greatest escape artist!
Want to see me escape?
Got your nose, Kalibak!
Give back Kalibak's nose!
Kalibak's nose!
What was that all about?
One of my old campers. He does that sort of thing all the time.
Just ignore him and he'll go away.

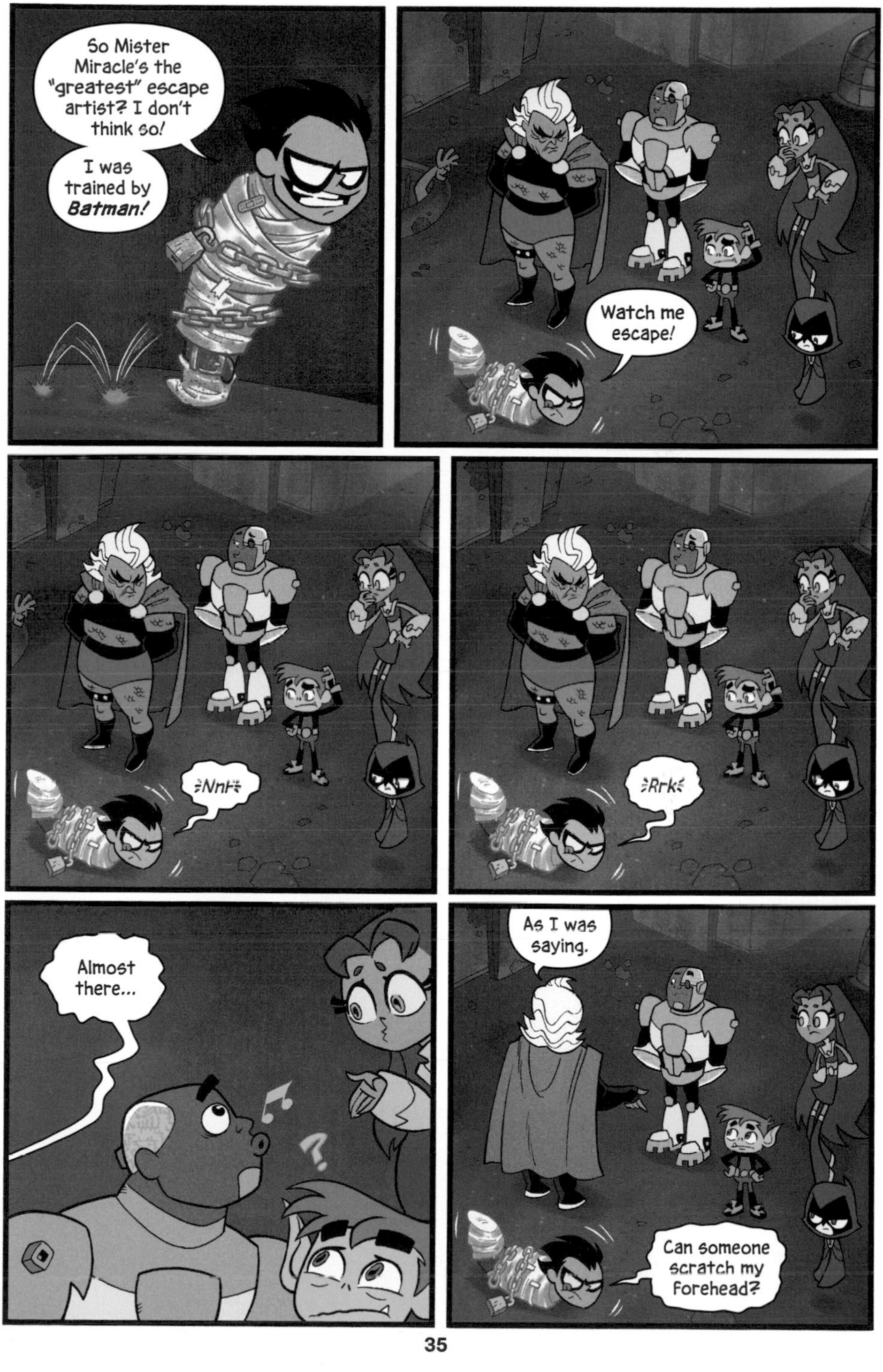
So Mister Miracle's the "greatest" escape artist? I don't think so!
I was trained by Batman!
Watch me escape!
Nnf
Rrk
Almost there...
As I was saying.
Can someone scratch my forehead?

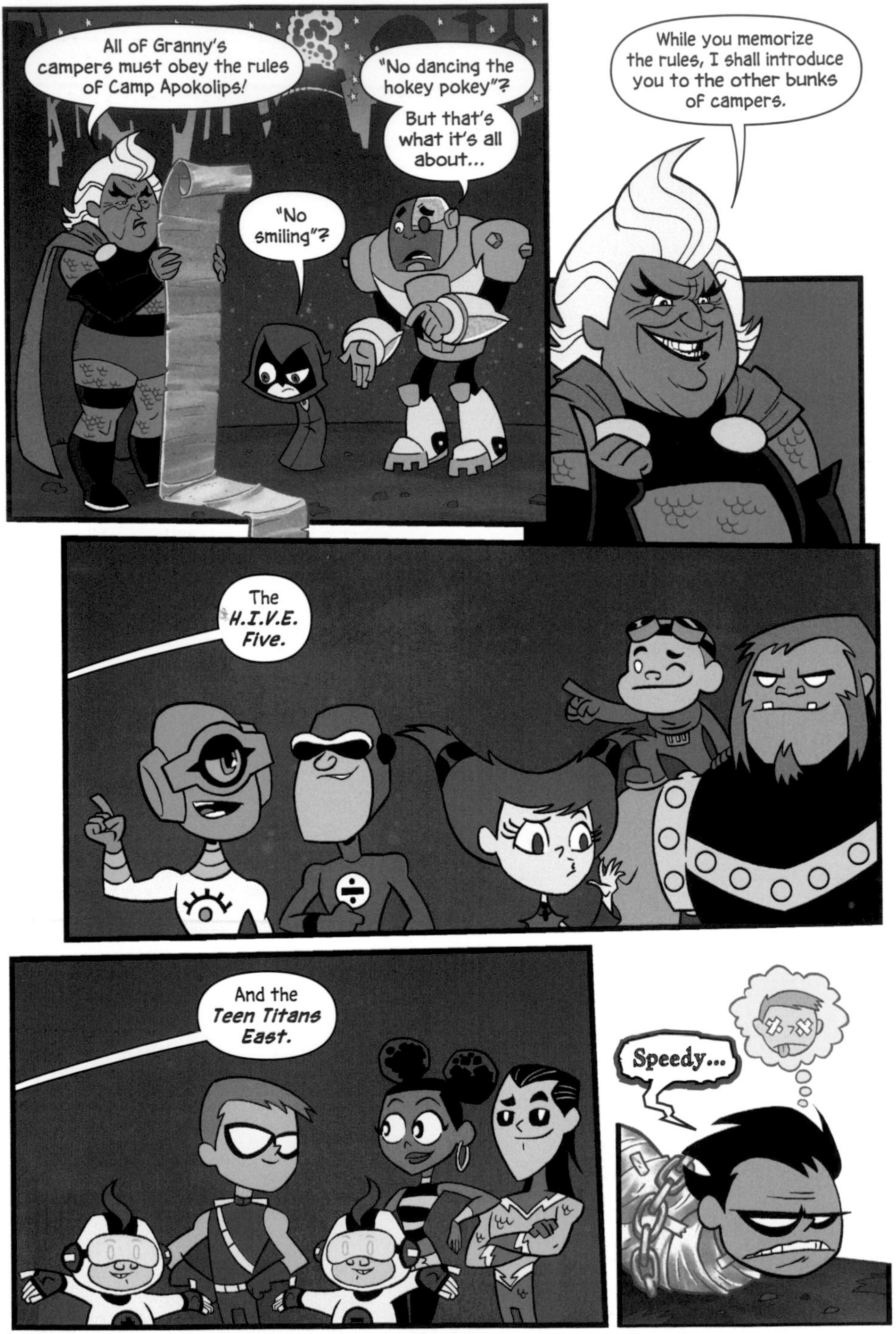
All of Granny's campers must obey the rules of Camp Apokolips!
"No dancing the hokey pokey"?
But that's what it's all about...
"No smiling"?
While you memorize the rules, I shall introduce you to the other bunks of campers.
The H.I.V.E. Five.
And the Teen Titans East.
Speedy...

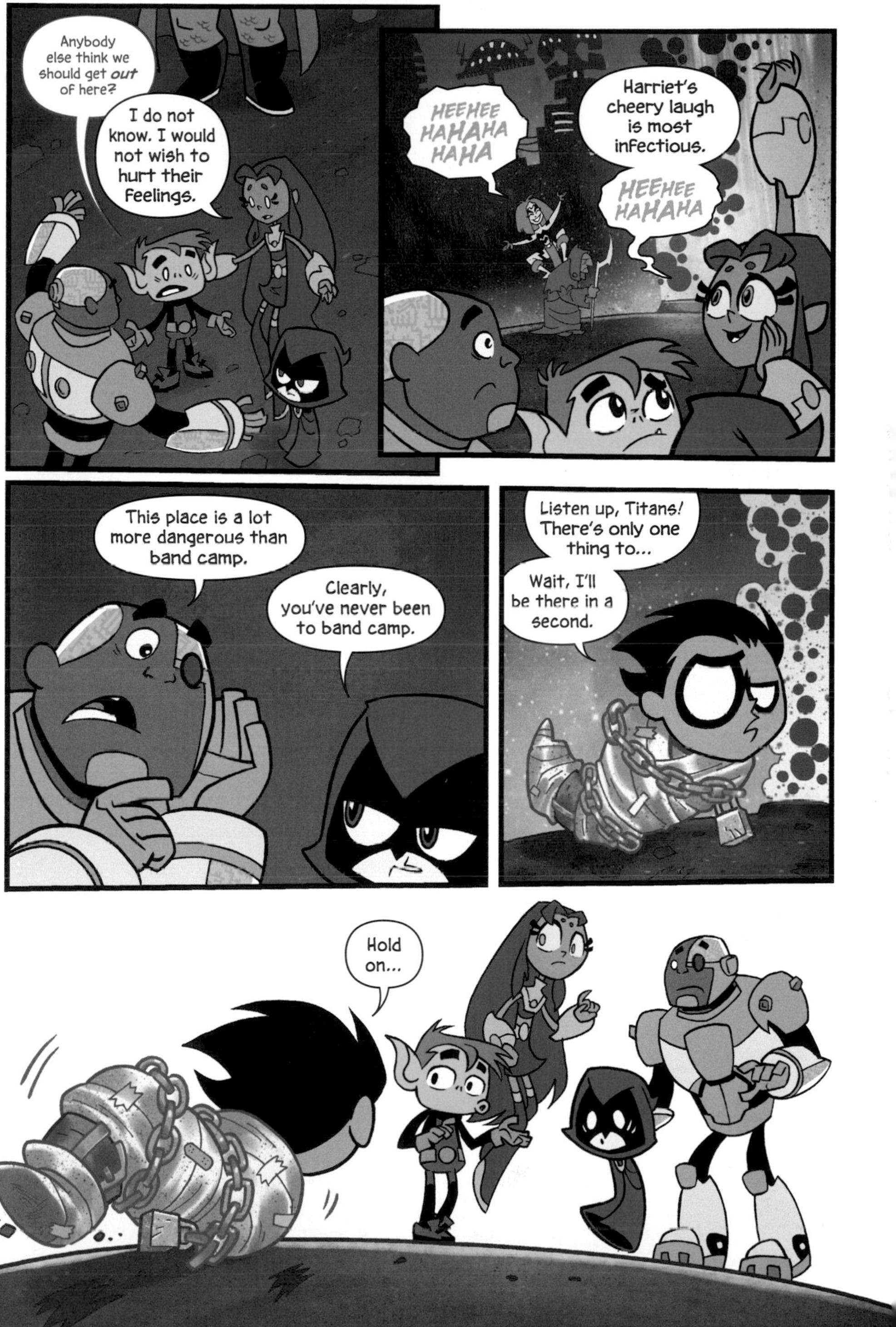
Anybody else think we should get *out* of here?
I do not know. I would not wish to hurt their Feelings.
HEEHEE HAHAHA HAHA
Harriet's cheery laugh is most infectious.
HEEHEE HAHAHA
This place is a lot more dangerous than band camp.
Clearly, you've never been to band camp.
Listen up, Titans! There's only one thing to...
Wait, I'll be there in a second.
Hold on...

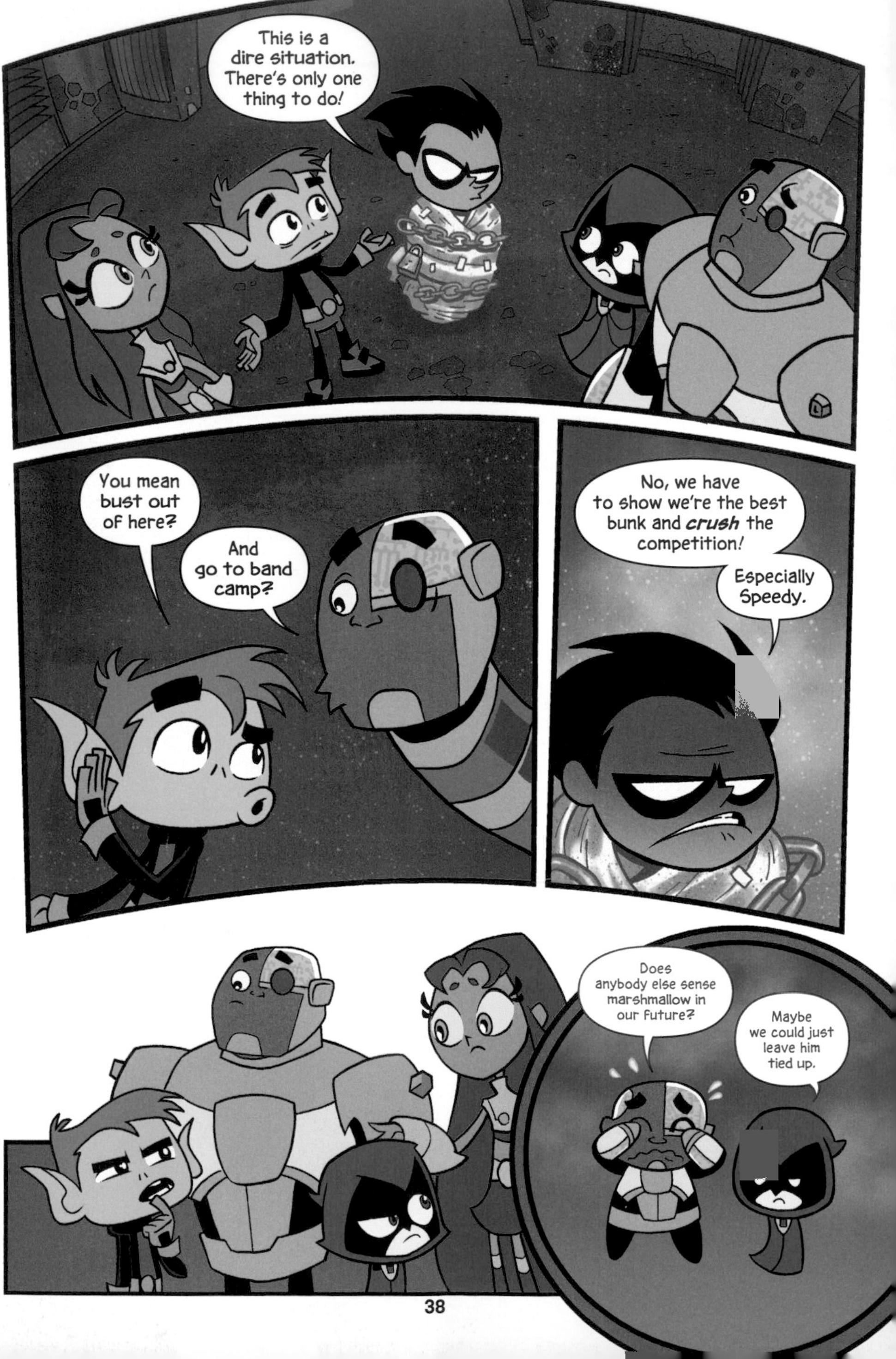
This is a dire situation. There's only one thing to do!
You mean bust out of here?
And go to band camp?
No, we have to show we're the best bunk and *crush* the competition!
Especially Speedy.
Does anybody else sense marshmallow in our future?
Maybe we could just leave him tied up.

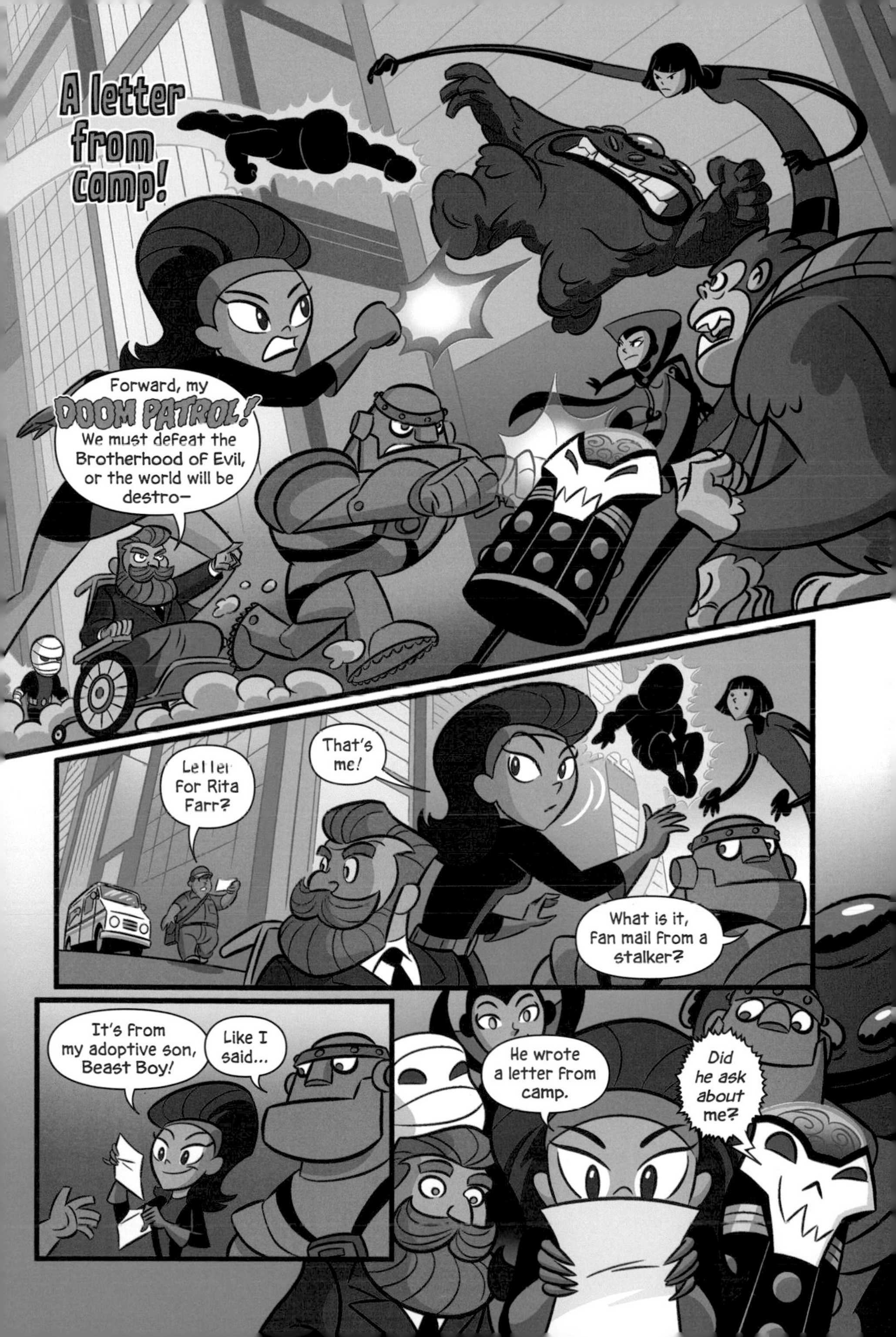
A letter from camp!
Forward, my DOOM PATROL! We must defeat the Brotherhood of Evil, or the world will be destro—
Letter for Rita Farr?
That's me!
What is it, fan mail from a stalker?
It's from my adoptive son, Beast Boy!
Like I said...
He wrote a letter from camp.
Did he ask about me?

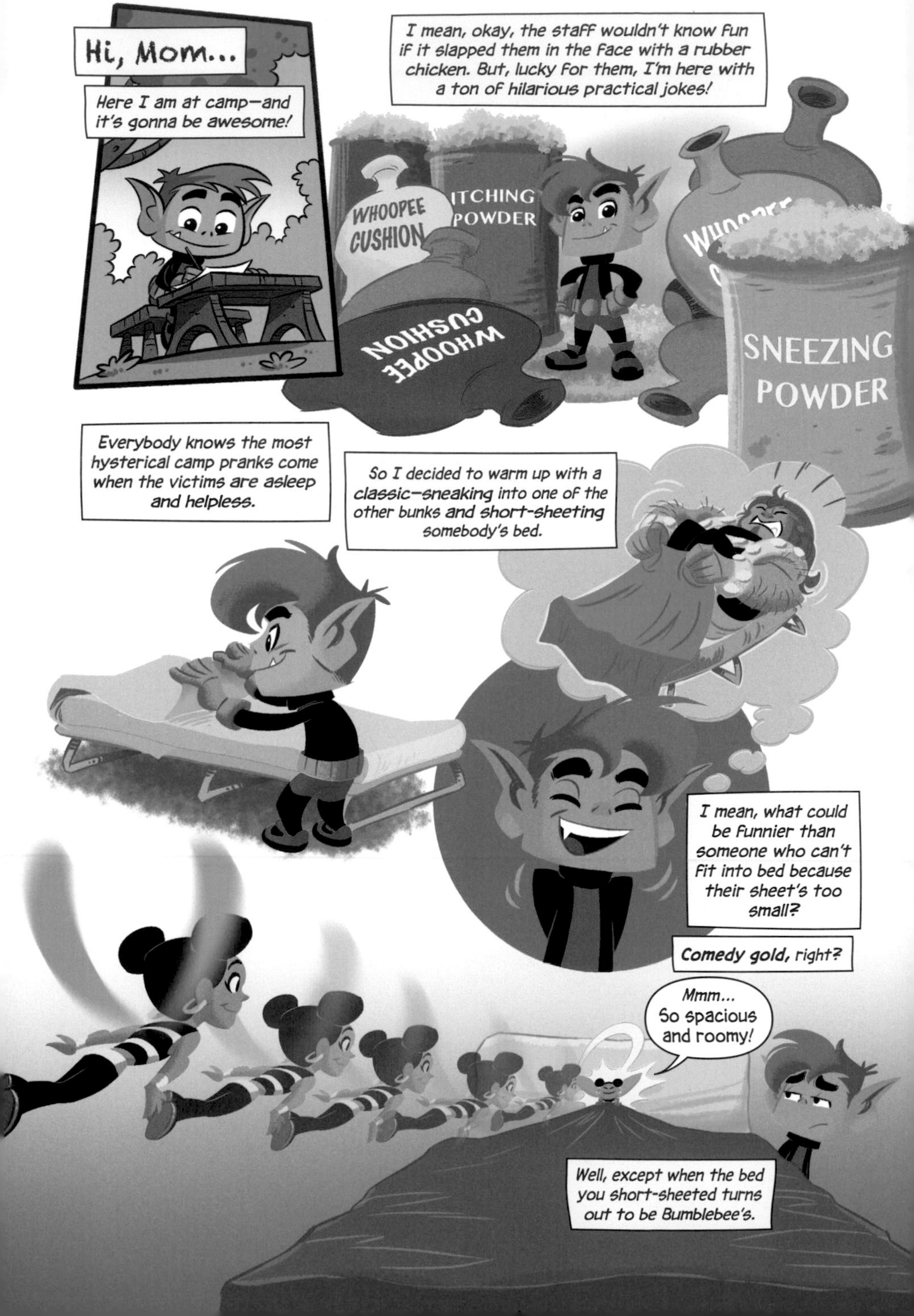
Hi, Mom...
Here I am at camp—and it's gonna be awesome!
I mean, okay, the staff wouldn't know fun if it slapped them in the face with a rubber chicken. But, lucky for them, I'm here with a ton of hilarious practical jokes!
WHOOPEE CUSHION
ITCHING POWDER
WHOOPEE CUSHION
SNEEZING POWDER
Everybody knows the most hysterical camp pranks come when the victims are asleep and helpless.
So I decided to warm up with a classic—sneaking into one of the other bunks and short-sheeting somebody's bed.
I mean, what could be funnier than someone who can't fit into bed because their sheet's too small?
Comedy gold, right?
Mmm... So spacious and roomy!
Well, except when the bed you short-sheeted turns out to be Bumblebee's.

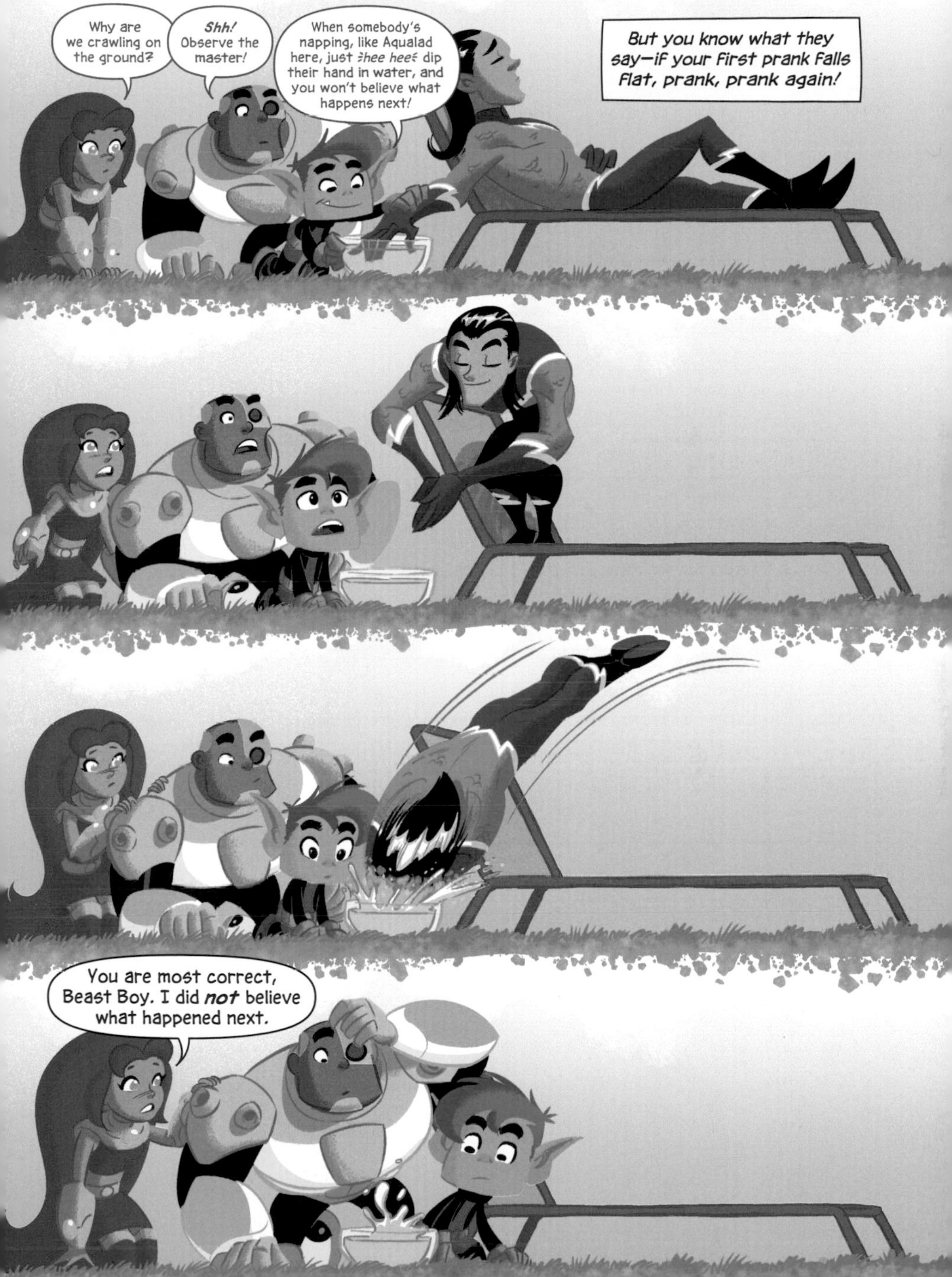
Why are we crawling on the ground?
Shh! Observe the master!
When somebody's napping, like Aqualad here, just ≷hee hee≶ dip their hand in water, and you won't believe what happens next!
But you know what they say—if your first prank falls flat, prank, prank again!
You are most correct, Beast Boy. I did *not* believe what happened next.

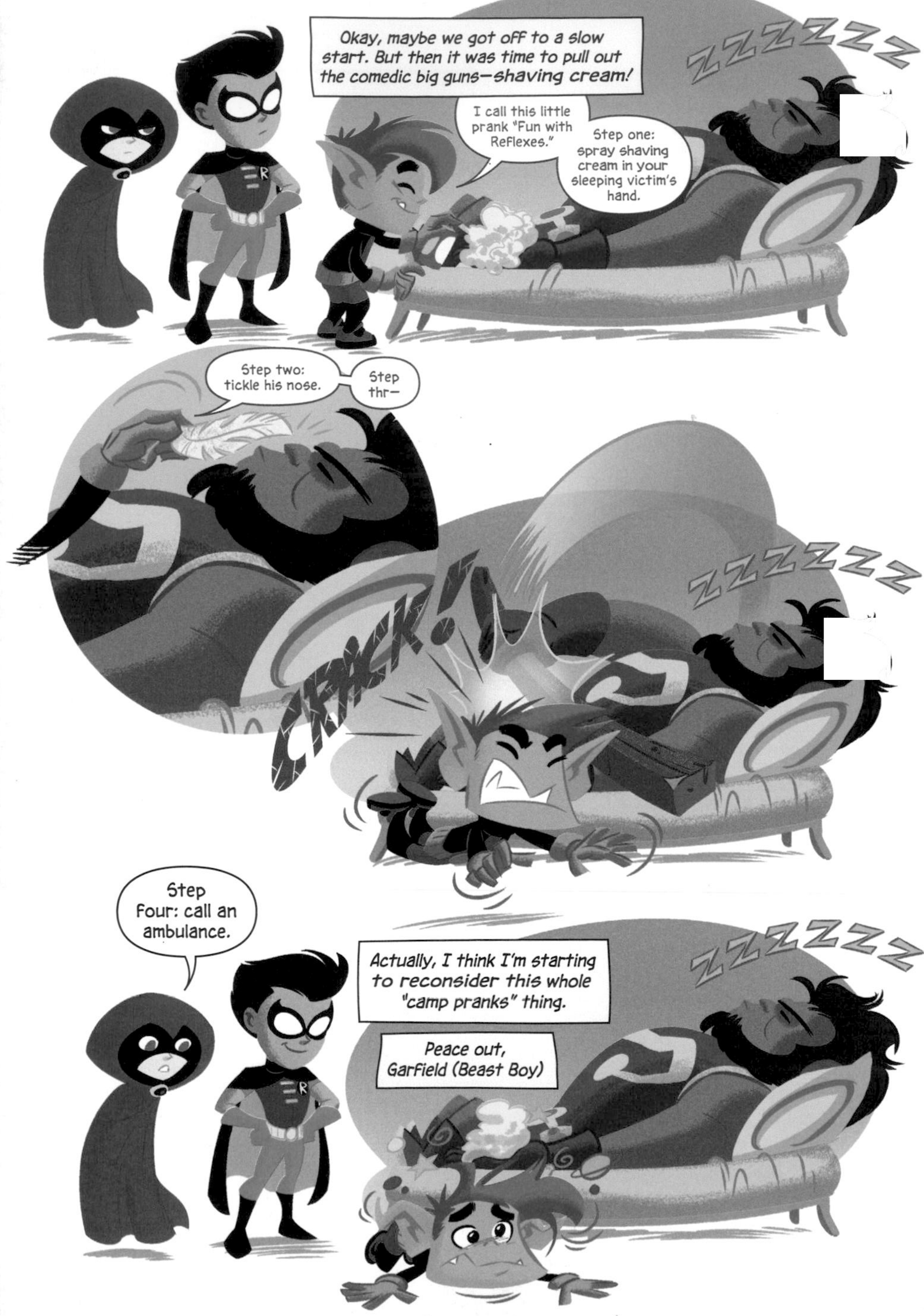
Okay, maybe we got off to a slow start. But then it was time to pull out the comedic big guns—shaving cream!
ZZZZZZZ
I call this little prank "Fun with Reflexes."
Step one: spray shaving cream in your sleeping victim's hand.
Step two: tickle his nose.
Step thr—
ZZZZZZZ
CRACK!!
Step four: call an ambulance.
ZZZZZZZ
Actually, I think I'm starting to reconsider this whole "camp pranks" thing.
Peace out, Garfield (Beast Boy)

Chapter Three

Raven's letter drawn and colored by Abigail Larson

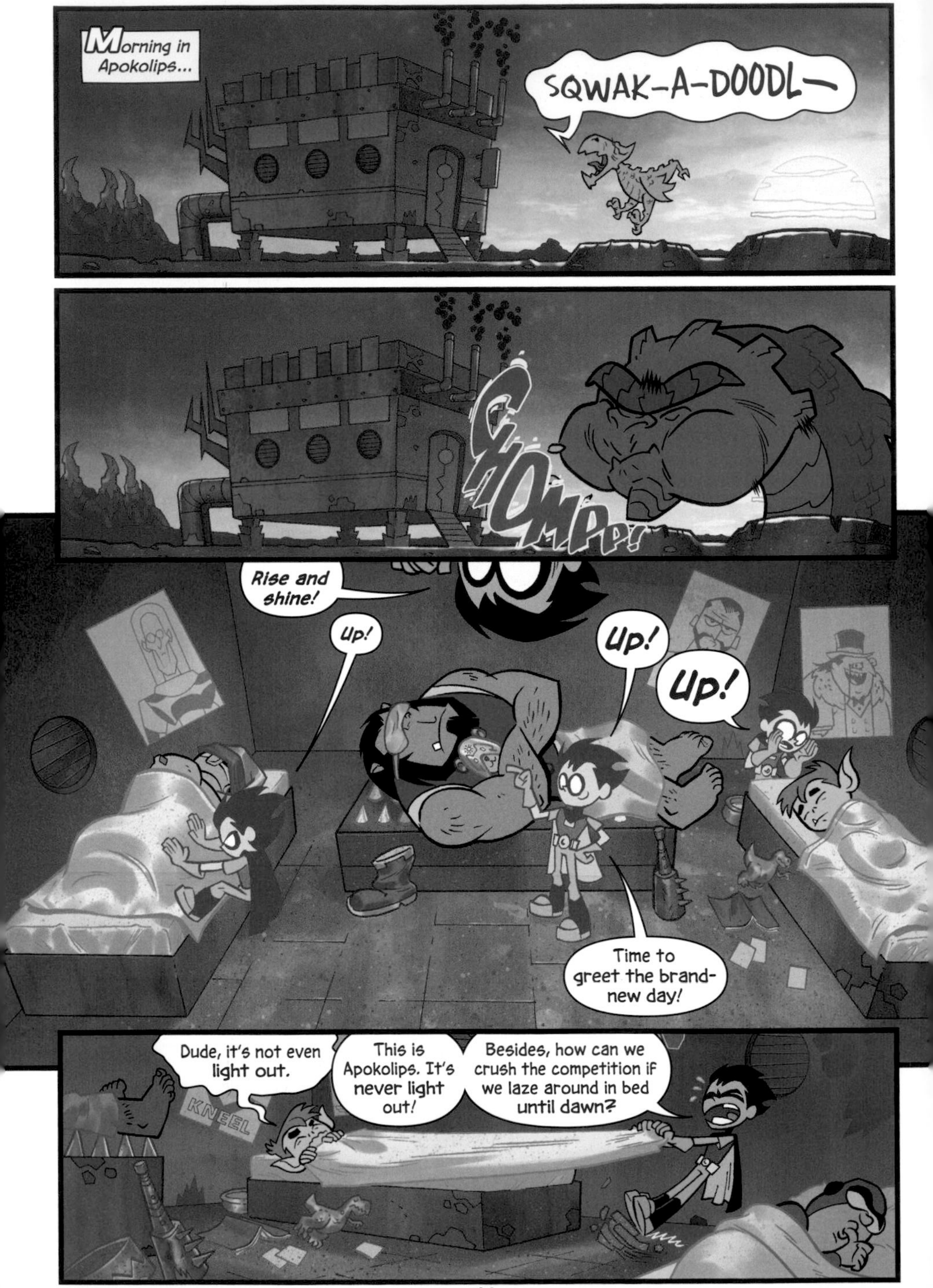
Morning in Apokolips...
SQWAK-A-DOODL—
CHOMPP!
Rise and shine!
Up!
Up!
Up!
Time to greet the brand-new day!
Dude, it's not even light out.
KNEEL
This is Apokolips. It's never light out!
Besides, how can we crush the competition if we laze around in bed until dawn?

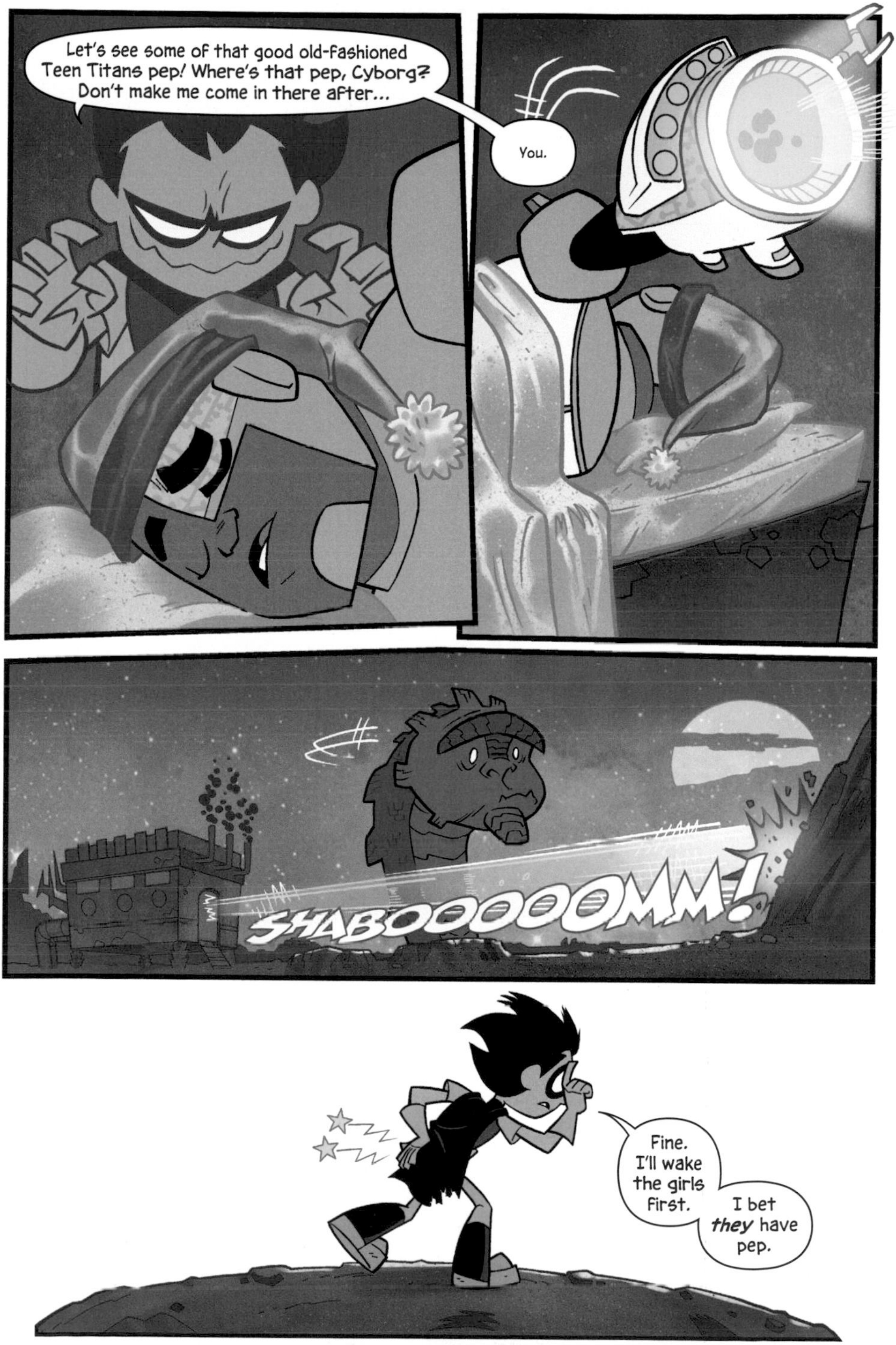

Let's see some of that good old-fashioned Teen Titans pep! Where's that pep, Cyborg? Don't make me come in there after...
You.
SHABOOOOOOMM!
Fine. I'll wake the girls first.
I bet *they* have pep.

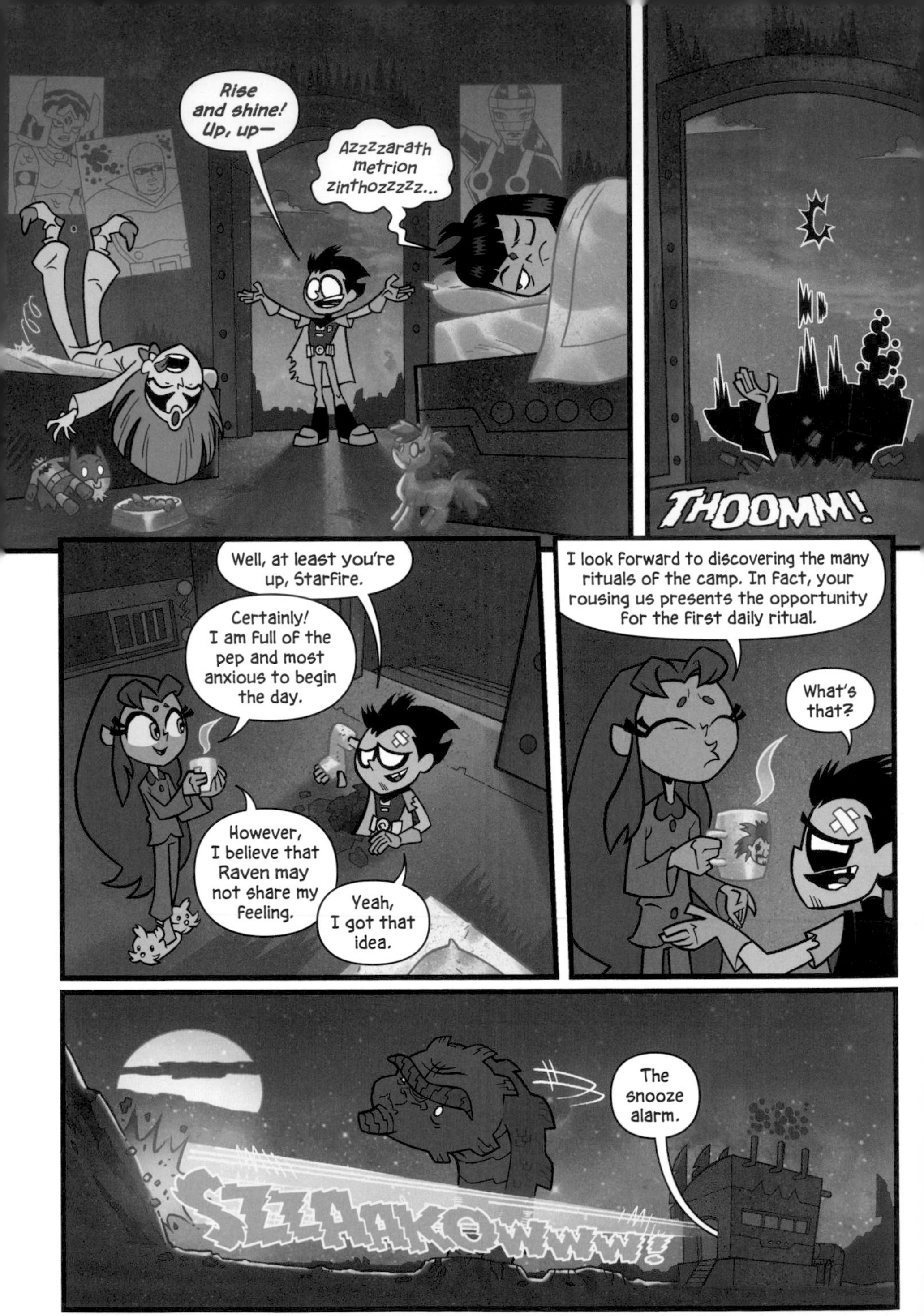
Rise and shine! Up, up—
Azzzzarath metrion zinthozzzzz...
THOOMM!
Well, at least you're up, Starfire.
Certainly! I am full of the pep and most anxious to begin the day.
However, I believe that Raven may not share my feeling.
Yeah, I got that idea.
I look forward to discovering the many rituals of the camp. In fact, your rousing us presents the opportunity for the first daily ritual.
What's that?
The snooze alarm.
SZZAAKOWWW!

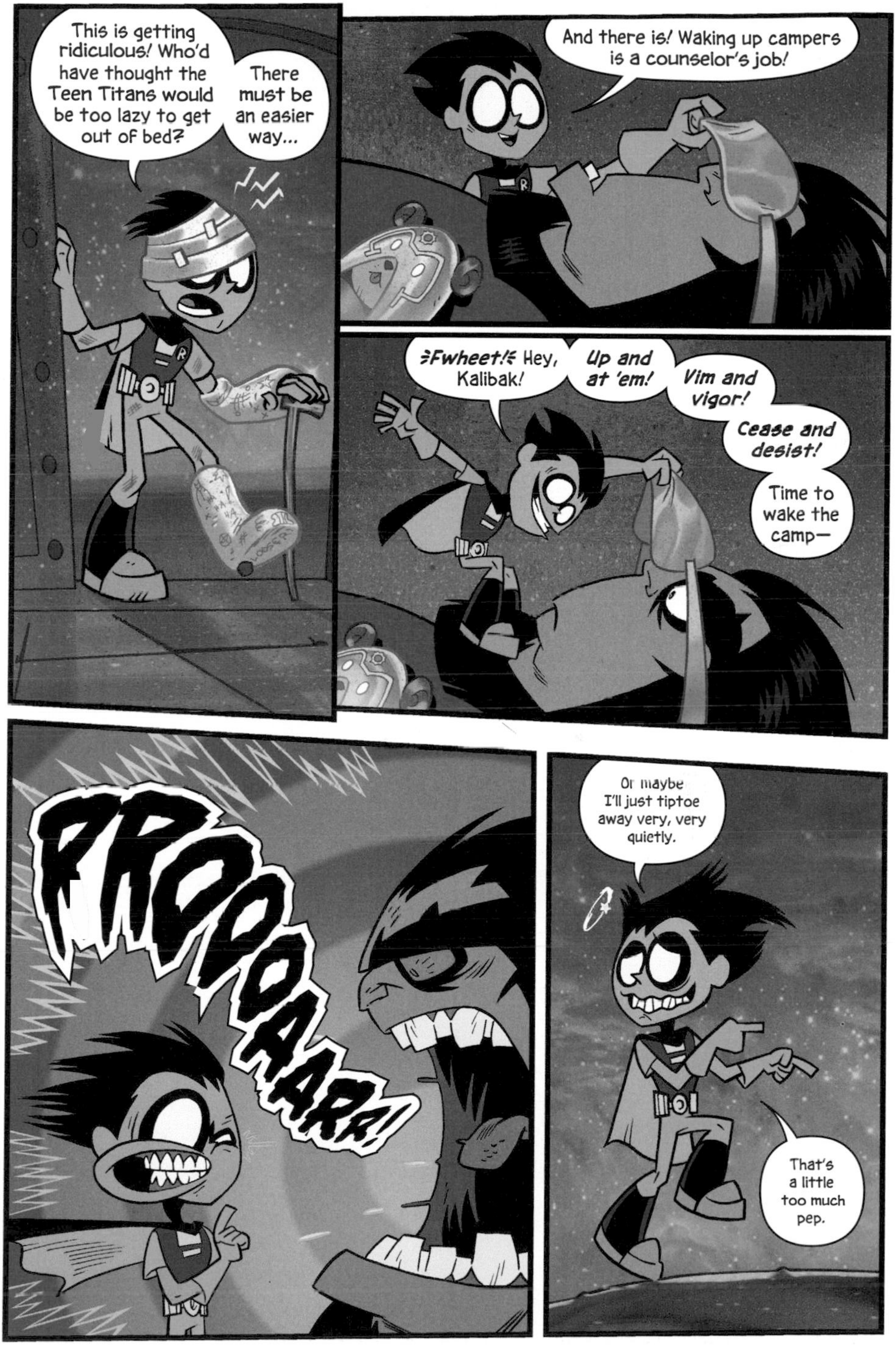
This is getting ridiculous! Who'd have thought the Teen Titans would be too lazy to get out of bed?
There must be an easier way...
And there is! Waking up campers is a counselor's job!
Fwheet! Hey, Kalibak!
Up and at 'em!
Vim and vigor!
Cease and desist!
Time to wake the camp—
RROOOAARR!
Or maybe I'll just tiptoe away very, very quietly.
That's a little too much pep.

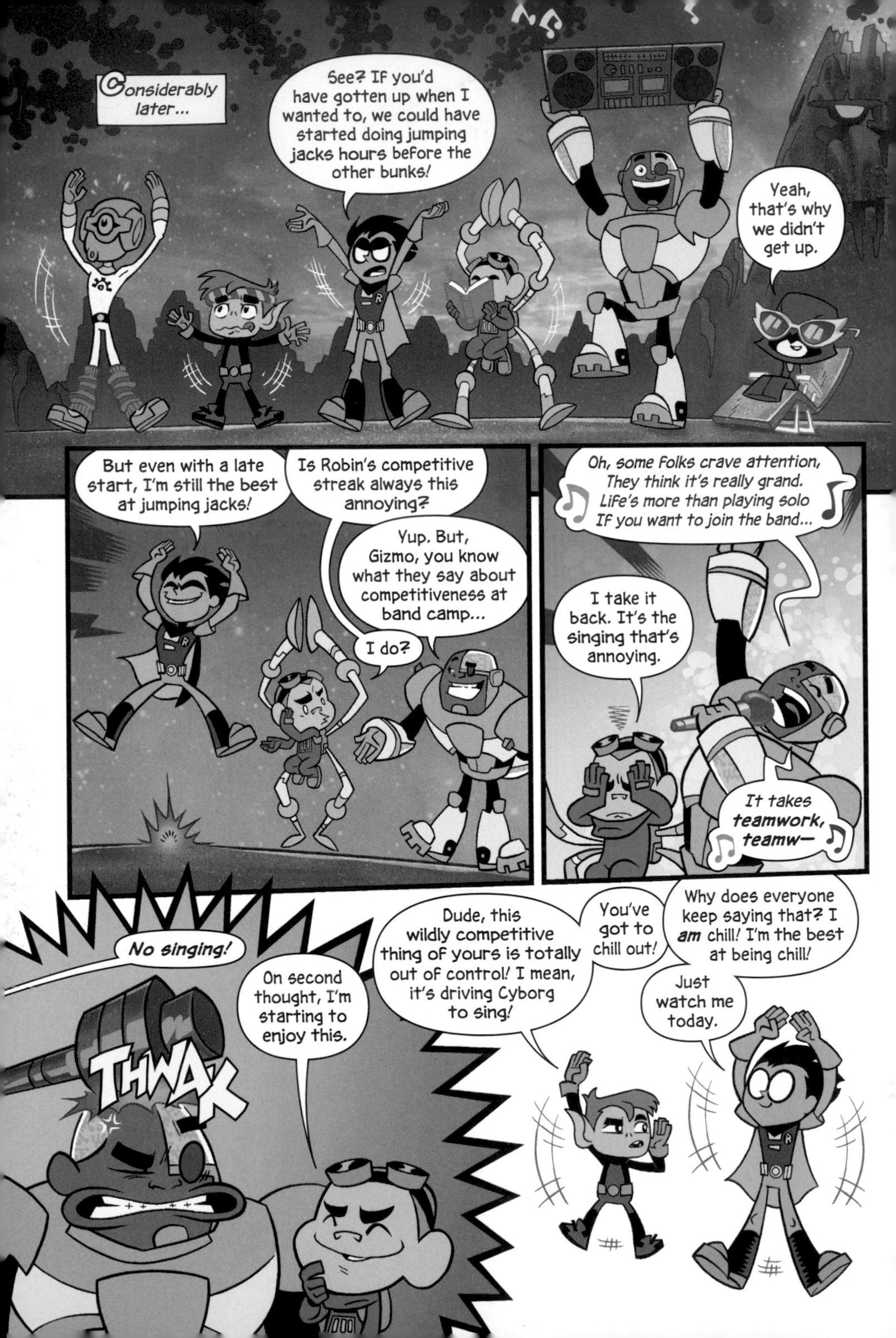
Considerably later...
See? If you'd have gotten up when I wanted to, we could have started doing jumping jacks hours before the other bunks!
Yeah, that's why we didn't get up.
But even with a late start, I'm still the best at jumping jacks!
Is Robin's competitive streak always this annoying?
Yup. But, Gizmo, you know what they say about competitiveness at band camp...
I do?
Oh, some folks crave attention,
They think it's really grand.
Life's more than playing solo
If you want to join the band...
I take it back. It's the singing that's annoying.
It takes teamwork, teamw—
No singing!
THWAK
On second thought, I'm starting to enjoy this.
Dude, this wildly competitive thing of yours is totally out of control! I mean, it's driving Cyborg to sing!
You've got to chill out!
Why does everyone keep saying that? I am chill! I'm the best at being chill!
Just watch me today.

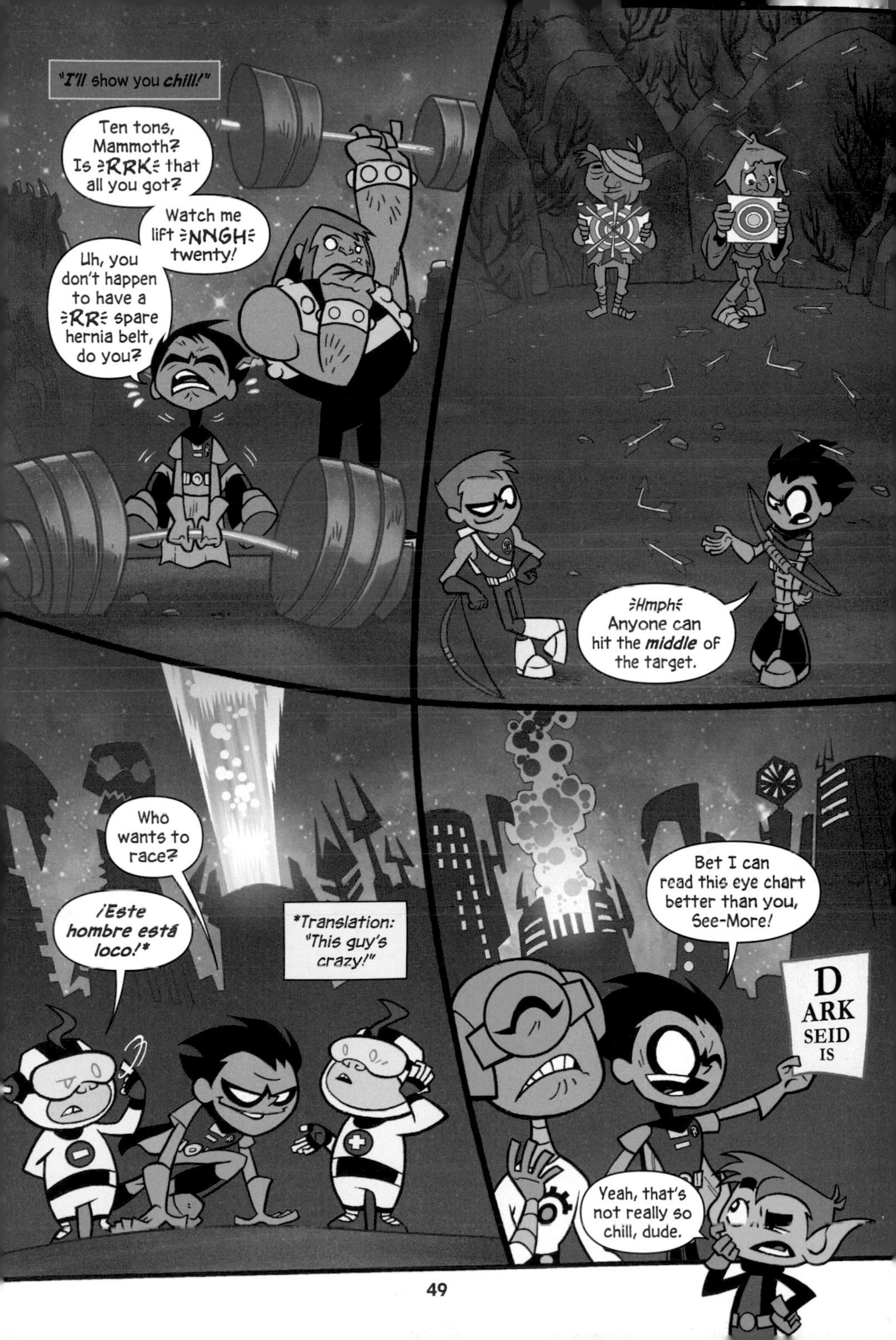
"I'll show you chill!"
Ten tons, Mammoth? Is ⩶RRK⩶ that all you got?
Watch me lift ⩶NNGH⩶ twenty!
Uh, you don't happen to have a ⩶RR⩶ spare hernia belt, do you?
⩶Hmph⩶ Anyone can hit the middle of the target.
Who wants to race?
¡Este hombre está loco!*
*Translation: "This guy's crazy!"
Bet I can read this eye chart better than you, See-More!
D
ARK
SEID
IS
Yeah, that's not really so chill, dude.

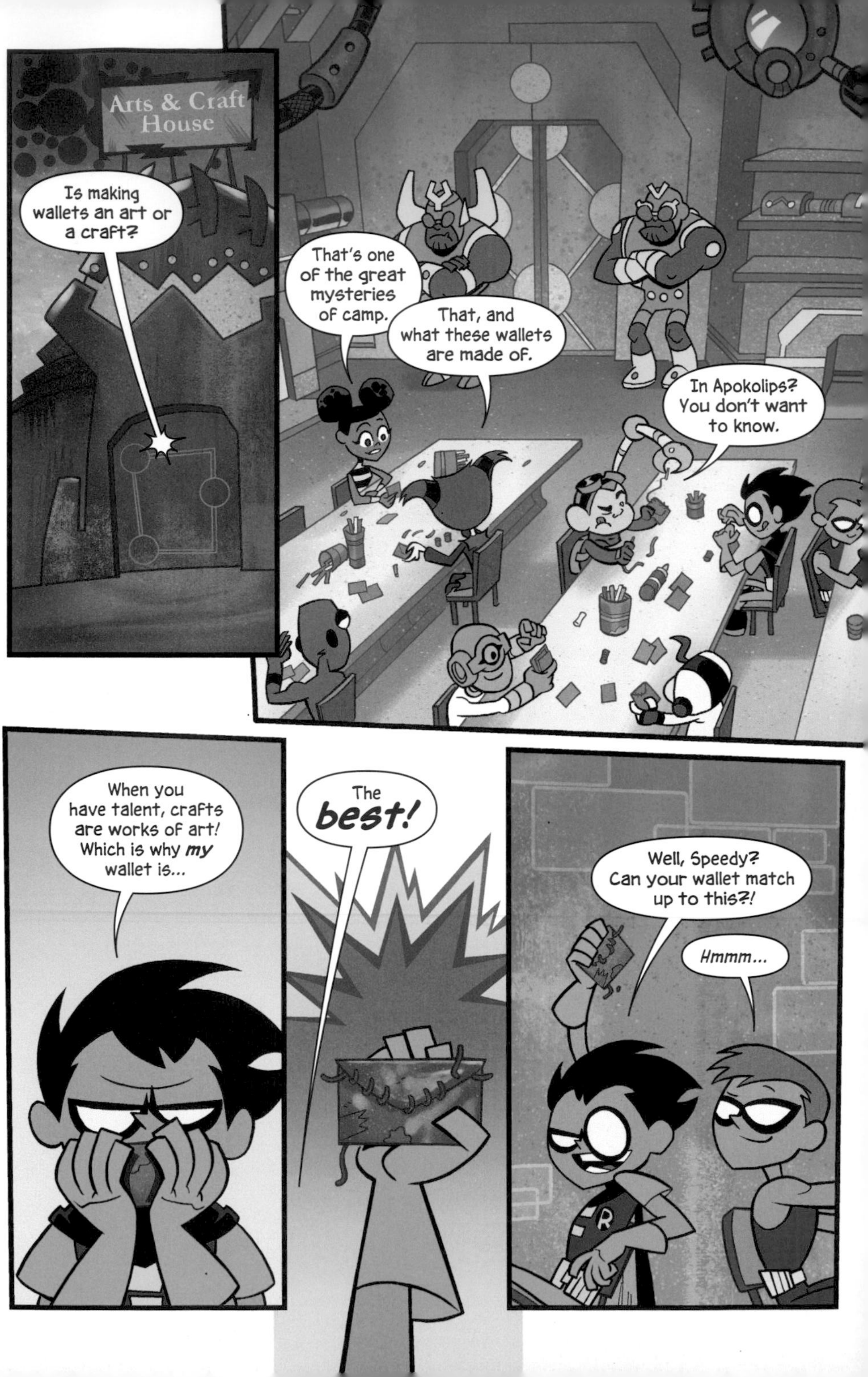
Arts & Craft House
Is making wallets an art or a craft?
That's one of the great mysteries of camp.
That, and what these wallets are made of.
In Apokolips? You don't want to know.
When you have talent, crafts are works of art! Which is why *my* wallet is...
The **best!**
Well, Speedy? Can your wallet match up to this?!
Hmmm...

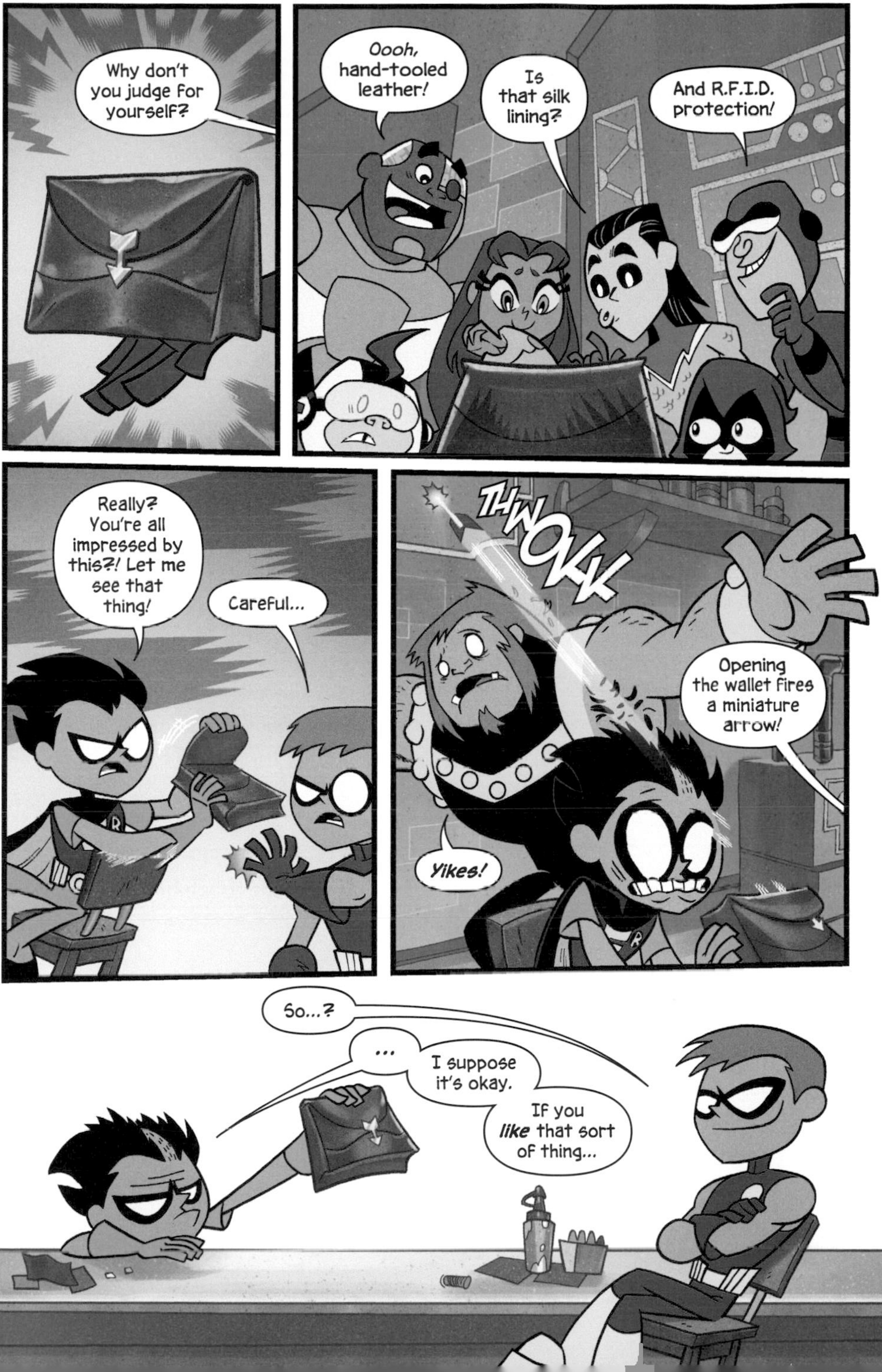
Why don't you judge for yourself?
Oooh, hand-tooled leather!
Is that silk lining?
And R.F.I.D. protection!
Really? You're all impressed by this?! Let me see that thing!
Careful...
THWOKK
Opening the wallet fires a miniature arrow!
Yikes!
So...?
...
I suppose it's okay.
If you *like* that sort of thing...

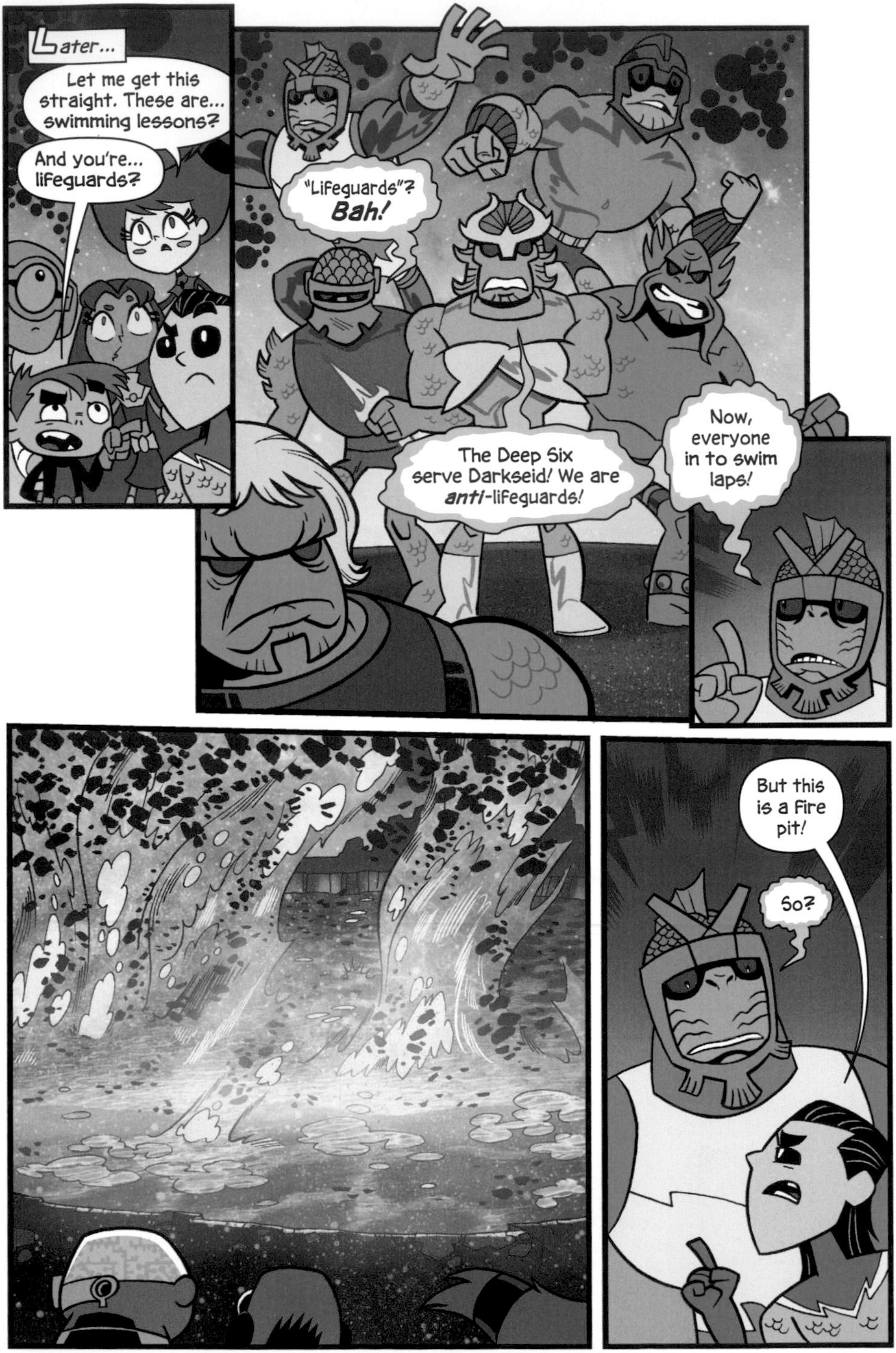
Later...
Let me get this straight. These are... swimming lessons?
And you're... lifeguards?
"Lifeguards"? Bah!
The Deep Six serve Darkseid! We are anti-lifeguards!
Now, everyone in to swim laps!
But this is a fire pit!
So?

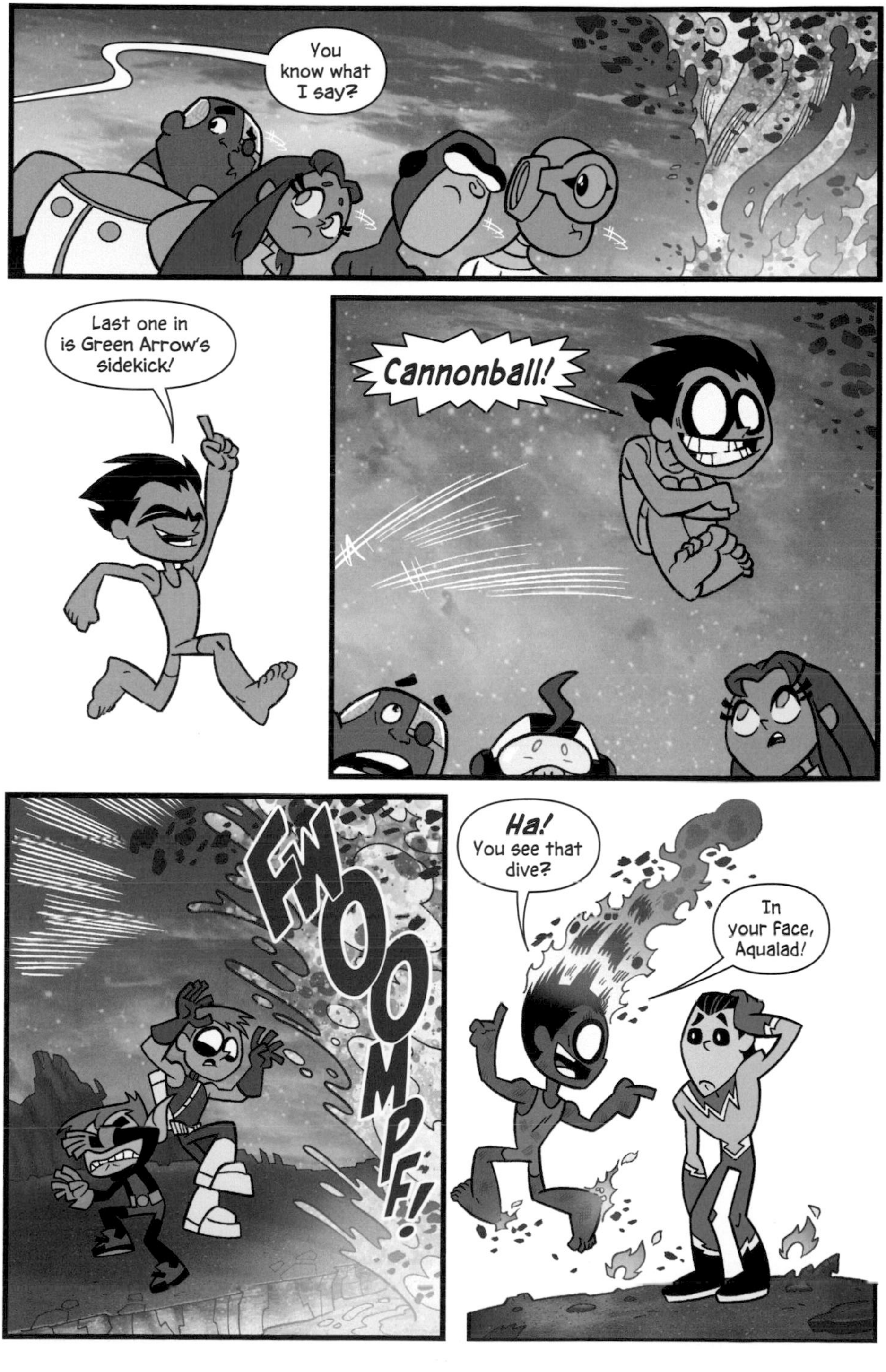
You know what I say?
Last one in is Green Arrow's sidekick!
Cannonball!
FWOOOMPF!
Ha! You see that dive?
In your face, Aqualad!

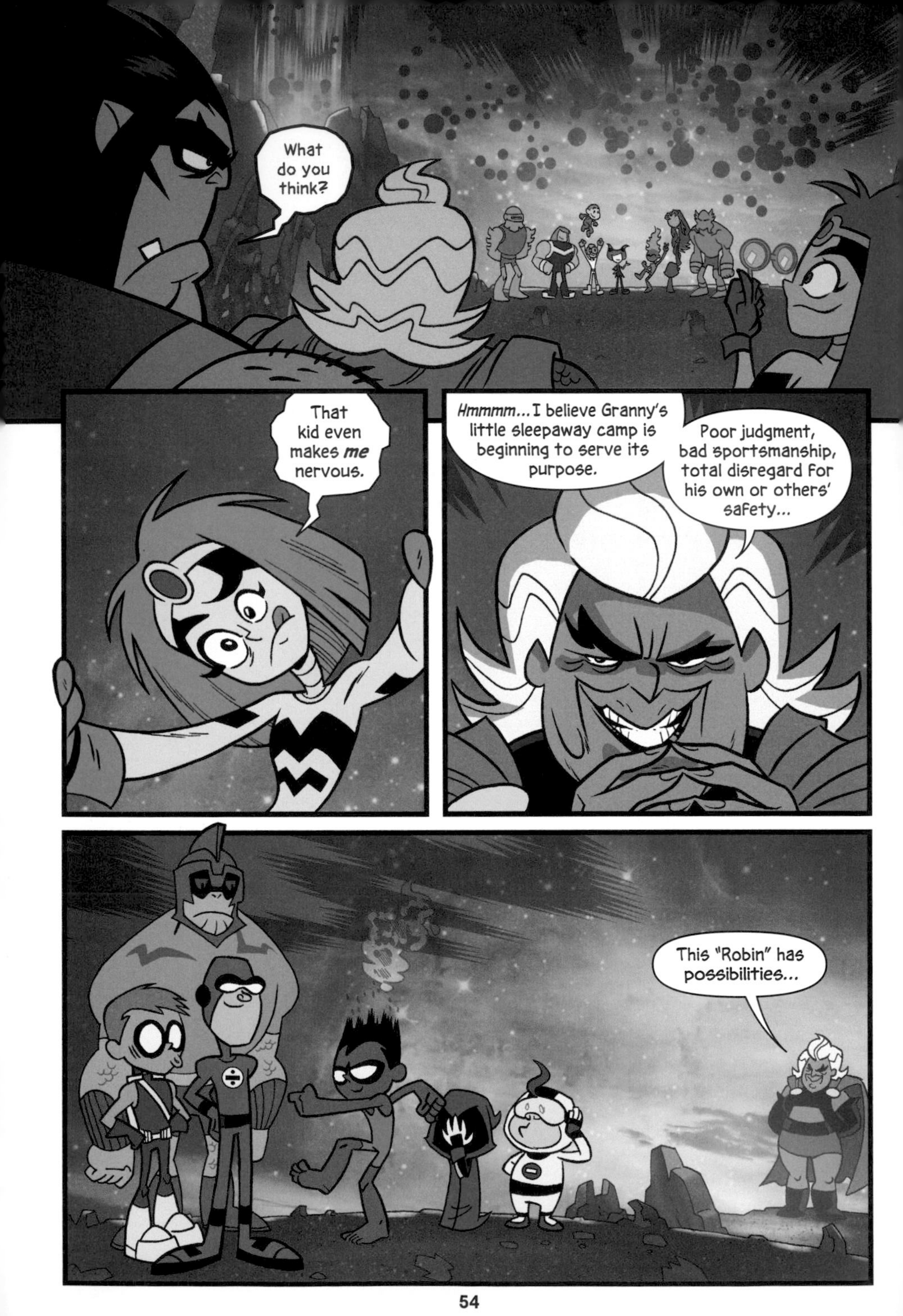
What do you think?
That kid even makes *me* nervous.
Hmmmm...I believe Granny's little sleepaway camp is beginning to serve its purpose.
Poor judgment, bad sportsmanship, total disregard for his own or others' safety...
This "Robin" has possibilities...

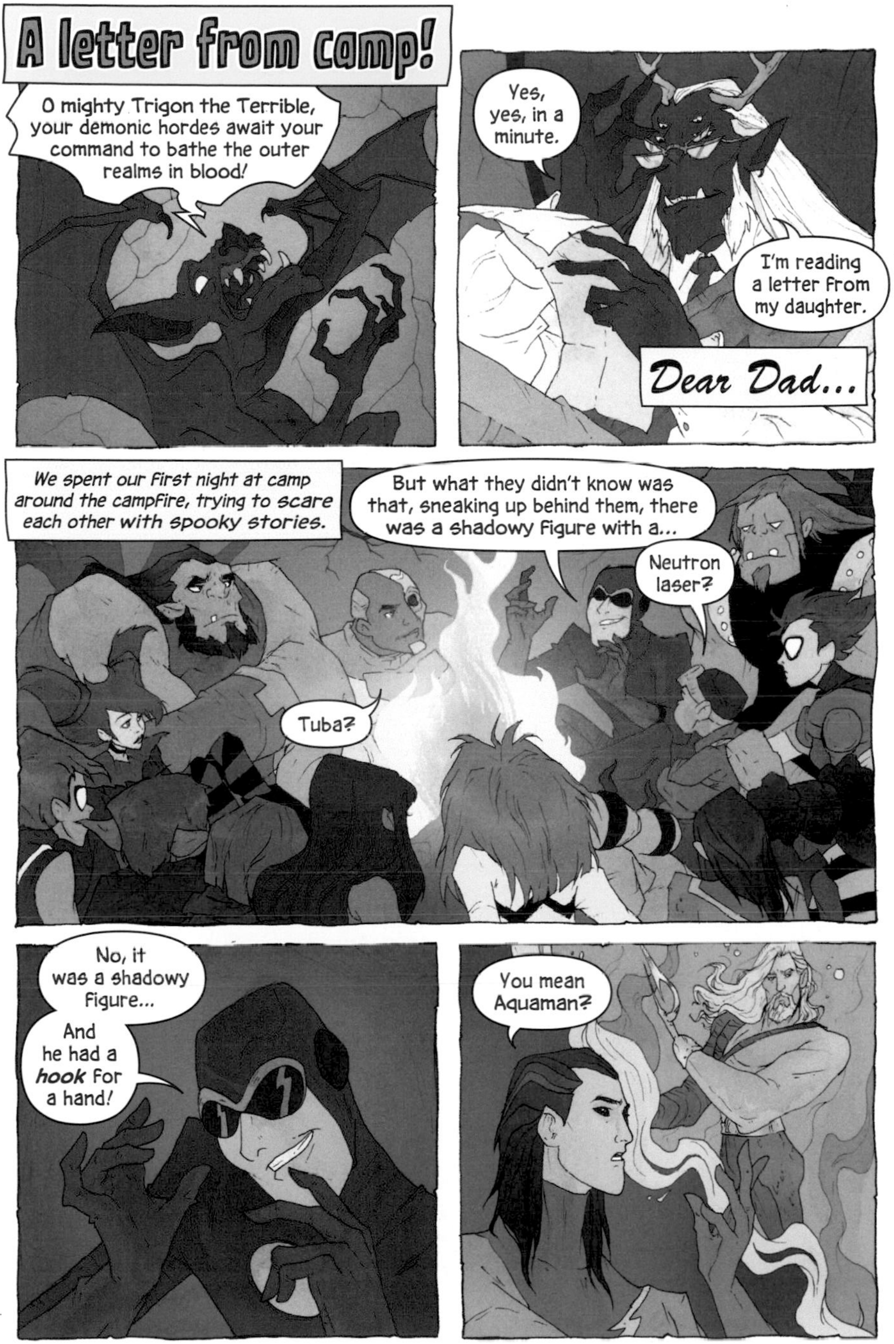
A letter from camp!
O mighty Trigon the Terrible, your demonic hordes await your command to bathe the outer realms in blood!
Yes, yes, in a minute.
I'm reading a letter from my daughter.
Dear Dad...
We spent our first night at camp around the campfire, trying to scare each other with spooky stories.
But what they didn't know was that, sneaking up behind them, there was a shadowy figure with a...
Neutron laser?
Tuba?
No, it was a shadowy figure...
And he had a *hook* for a hand!
You mean Aquaman?

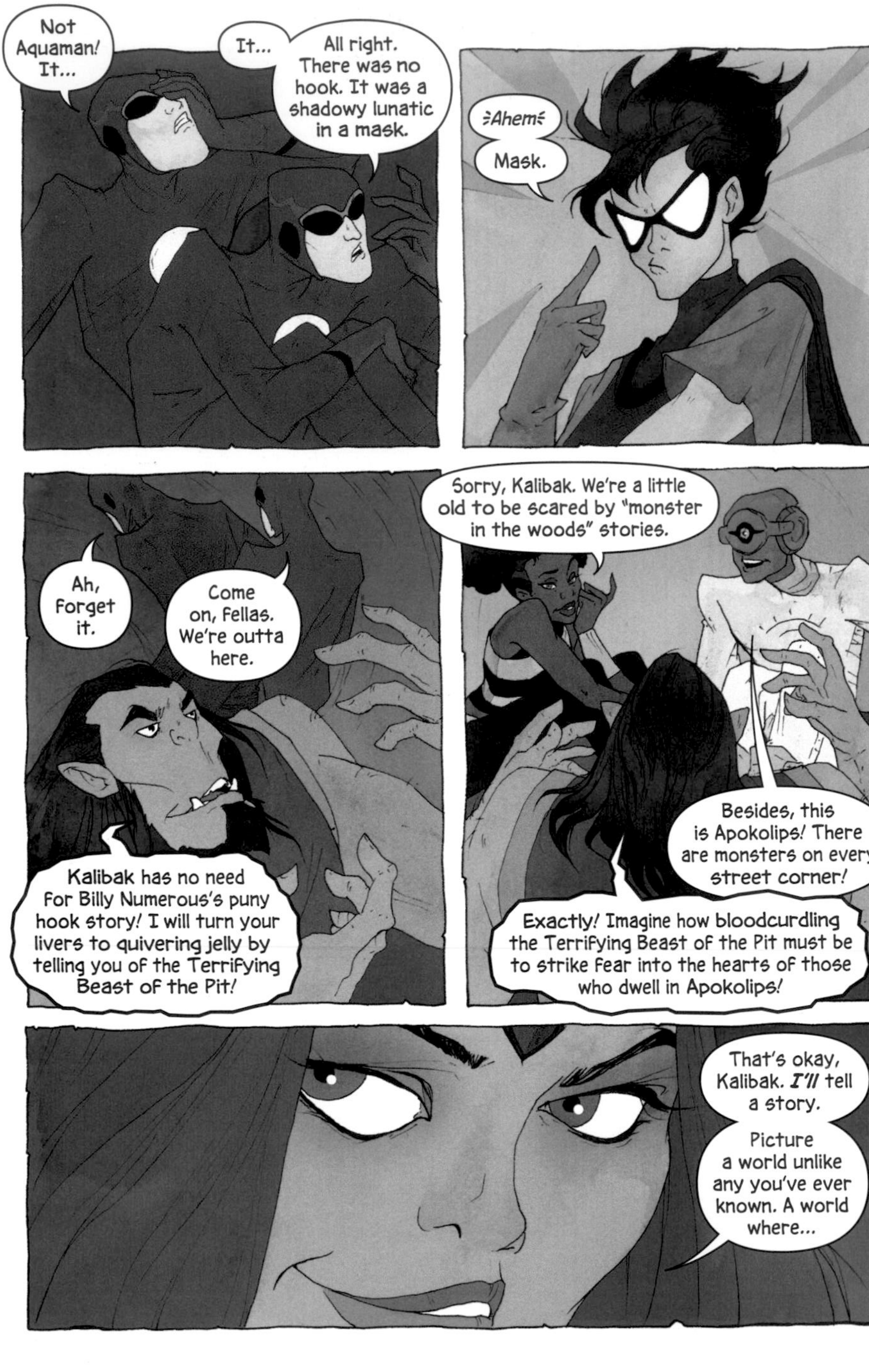

Not Aquaman! It...
It...
All right. There was no hook. It was a shadowy lunatic in a mask.
Ahem
Mask.
Ah, forget it.
Come on, fellas. We're outta here.
Kalibak has no need for Billy Numerous's puny hook story! I will turn your livers to quivering jelly by telling you of the Terrifying Beast of the Pit!
Sorry, Kalibak. We're a little old to be scared by "monster in the woods" stories.
Besides, this is Apokolips! There are monsters on every street corner!
Exactly! Imagine how bloodcurdling the Terrifying Beast of the Pit must be to strike fear into the hearts of those who dwell in Apokolips!
That's okay, Kalibak. *I'll* tell a story.
Picture a world unlike any you've ever known. A world where...

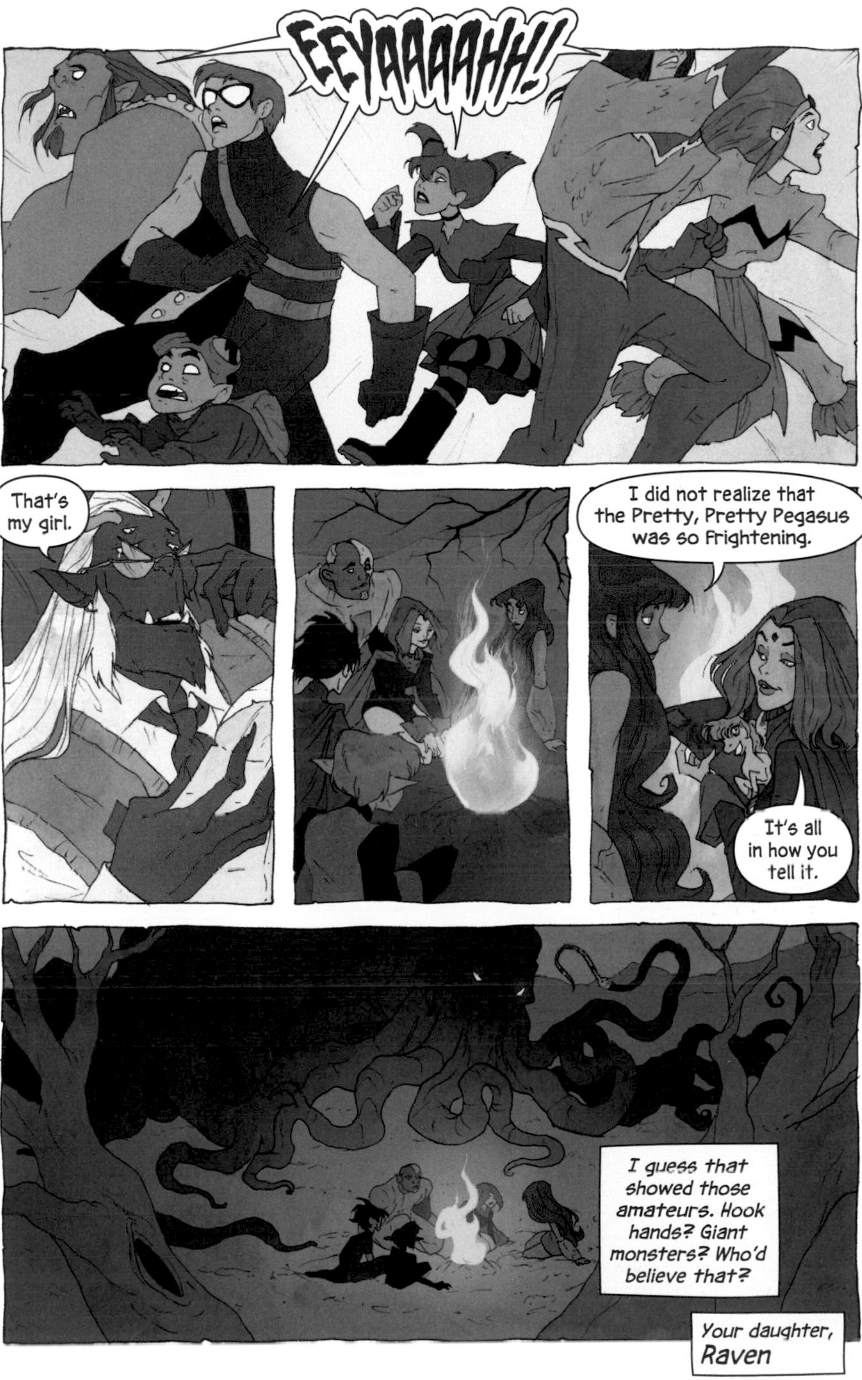
EEYAAAAHH!
That's my girl.
I did not realize that the Pretty, Pretty Pegasus was so frightening.
It's all in how you tell it.
I guess that showed those amateurs. Hook hands? Giant monsters? Who'd believe that?
Your daughter, Raven

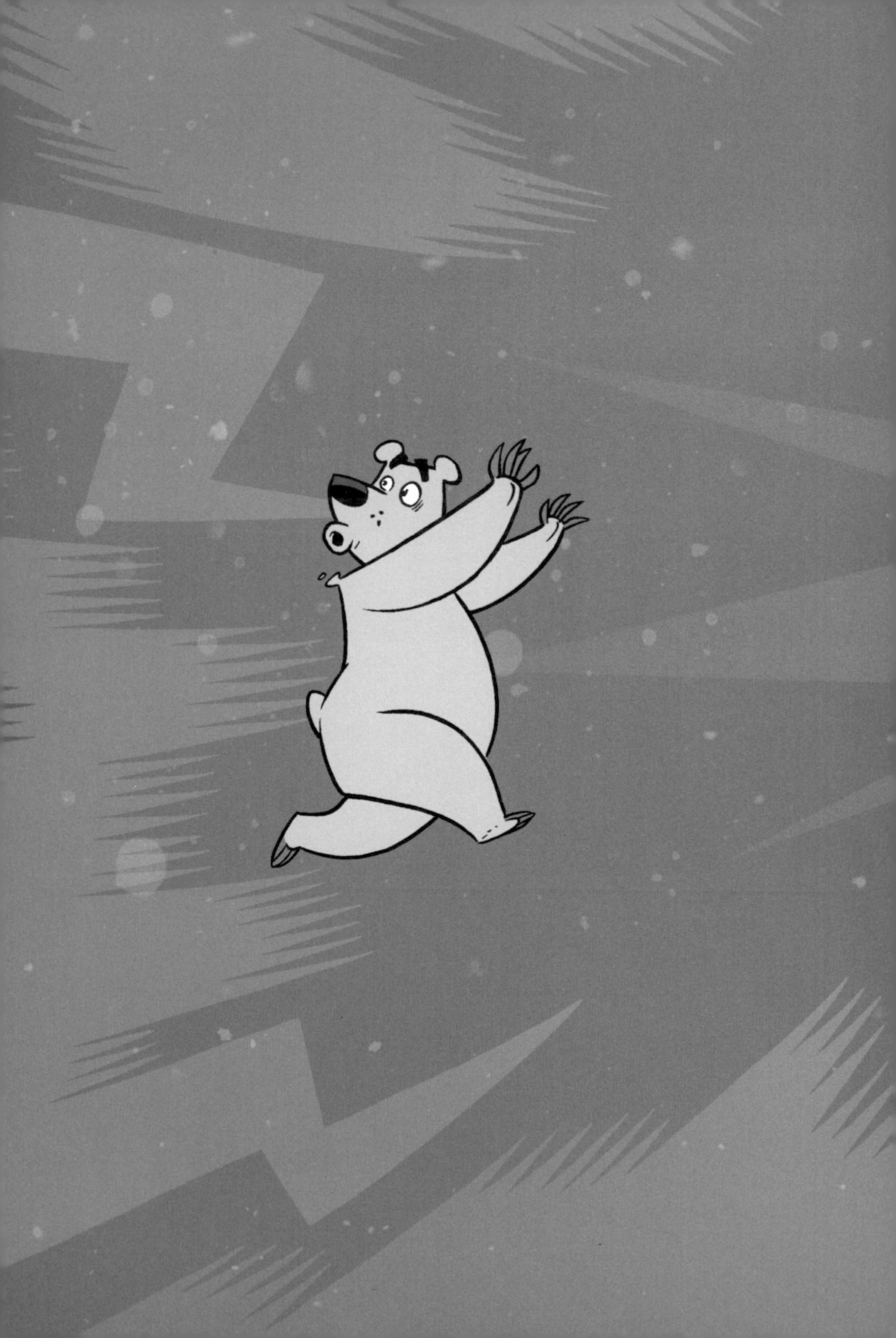

Chapter Four

Robin's letter drawn and colored by Emma Kubert

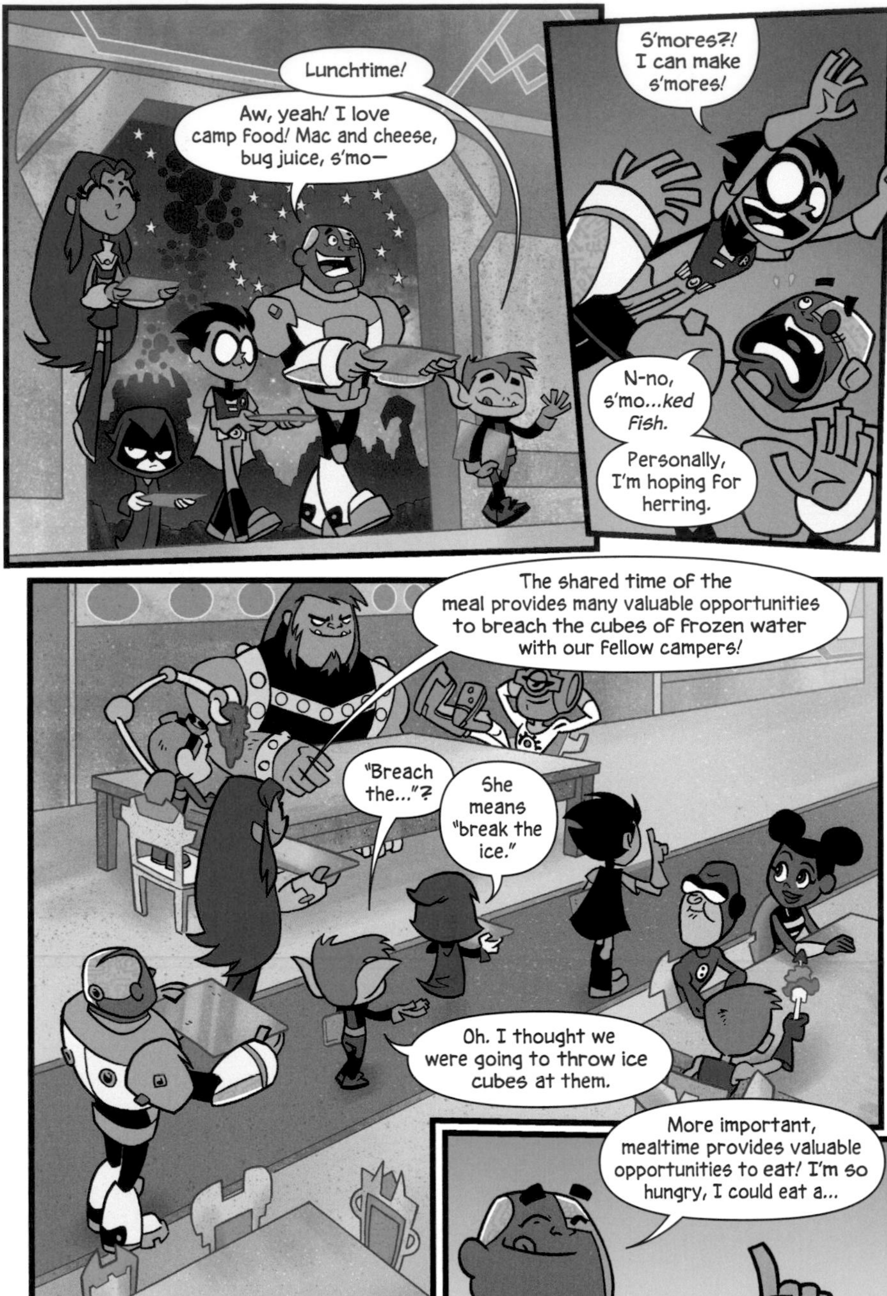
Lunchtime!
Aw, yeah! I love camp food! Mac and cheese, bug juice, s'mo—
S'mores?! I can make s'mores!
N-no, s'mo...*ked Fish.*
Personally, I'm hoping for herring.
The shared time of the meal provides many valuable opportunities to breach the cubes of frozen water with our fellow campers!
"Breach the..."?
She means "break the ice."
Oh. I thought we were going to throw ice cubes at them.
More important, mealtime provides valuable opportunities to eat! I'm so hungry, I could eat a...

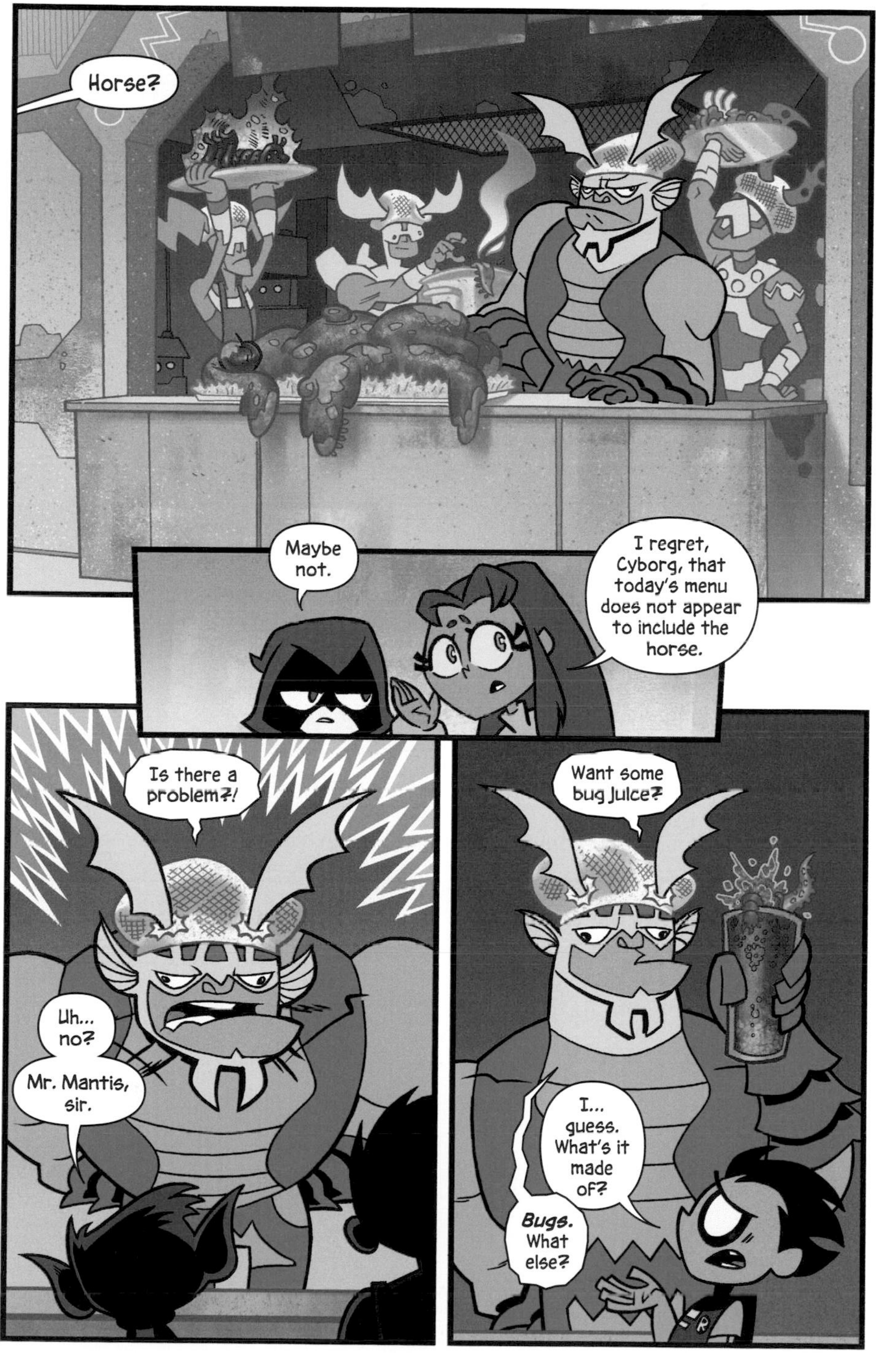
Horse?
Maybe not.
I regret, Cyborg, that today's menu does not appear to include the horse.
Is there a problem?!
Uh... no?
Mr. Mantis, sir.
Want some bug juice?
I... guess. What's it made of?
Bugs. What else?

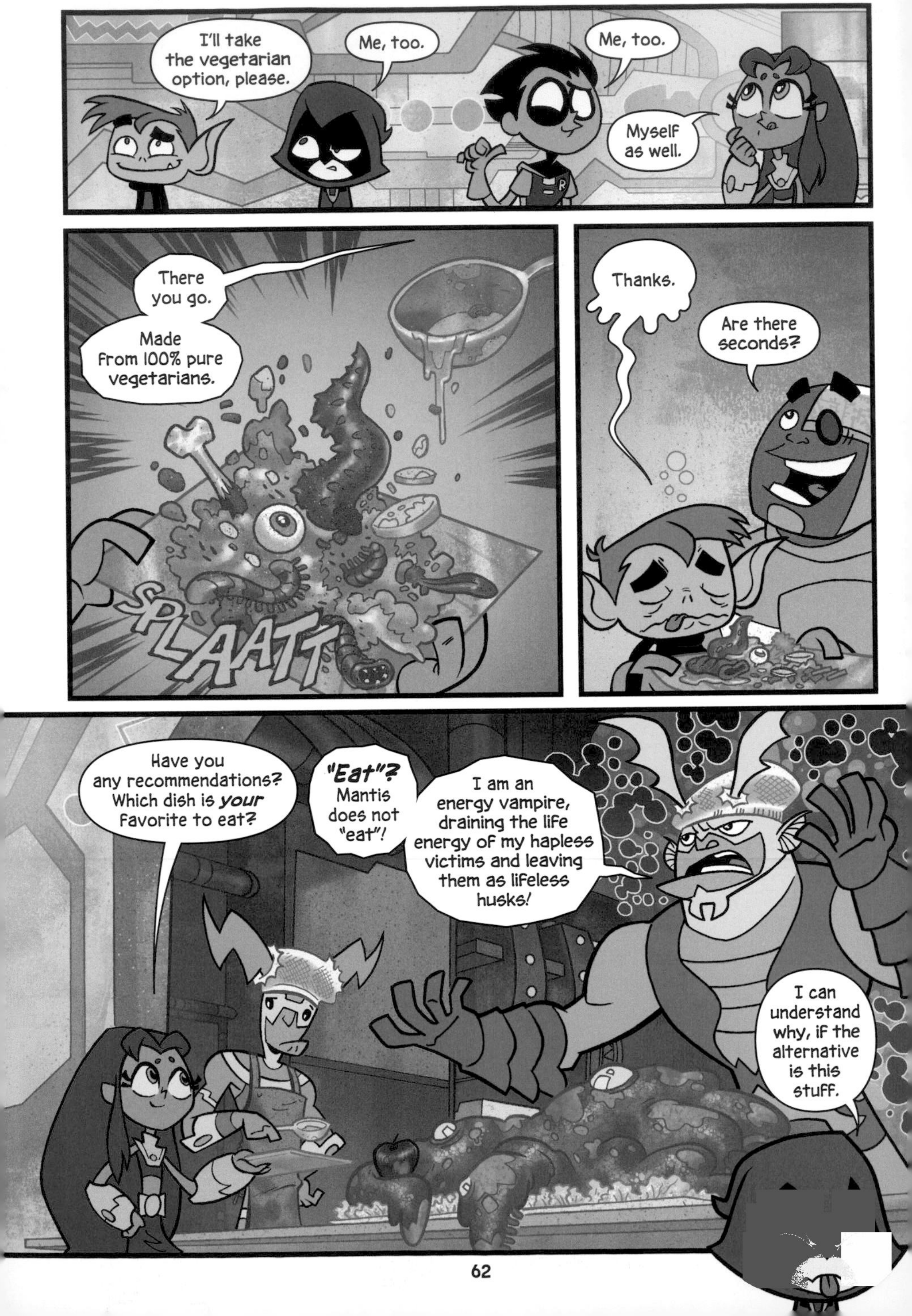
I'll take the vegetarian option, please.
Me, too.
Me, too.
Myself as well.
There you go.
Made from 100% pure vegetarians.
SPLAATT
Thanks.
Are there seconds?
Have you any recommendations? Which dish is *your* favorite to eat?
"Eat"? Mantis does not "eat"!
I am an energy vampire, draining the life energy of my hapless victims and leaving them as lifeless husks!
I can understand why, if the alternative is this stuff.

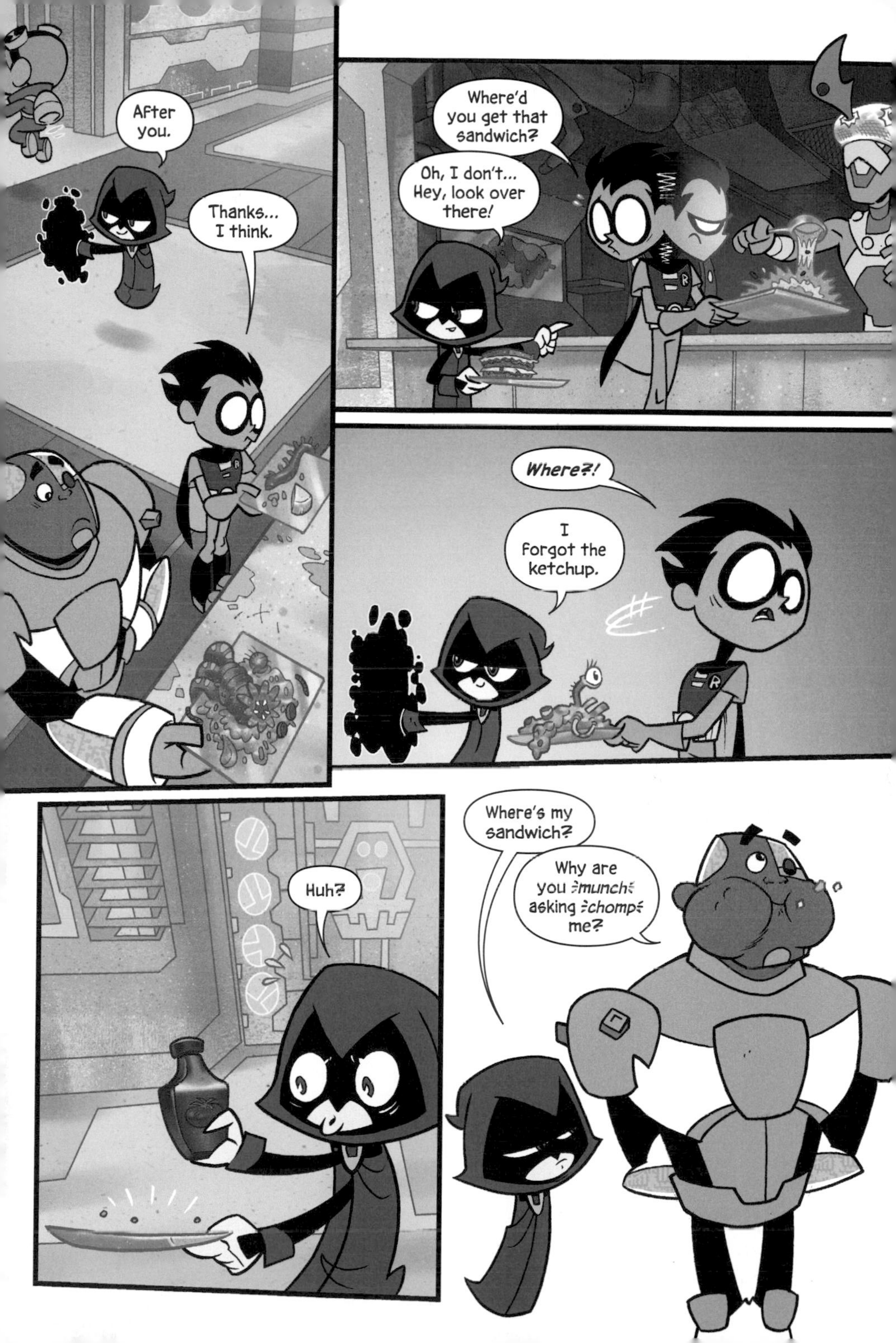
After you.
Thanks... I think.
Where'd you get that sandwich?
Oh, I don't... Hey, look over there!
Where?!
I forgot the ketchup.
Huh?
Where's my sandwich?
Why are you *munch* asking *chomp* me?

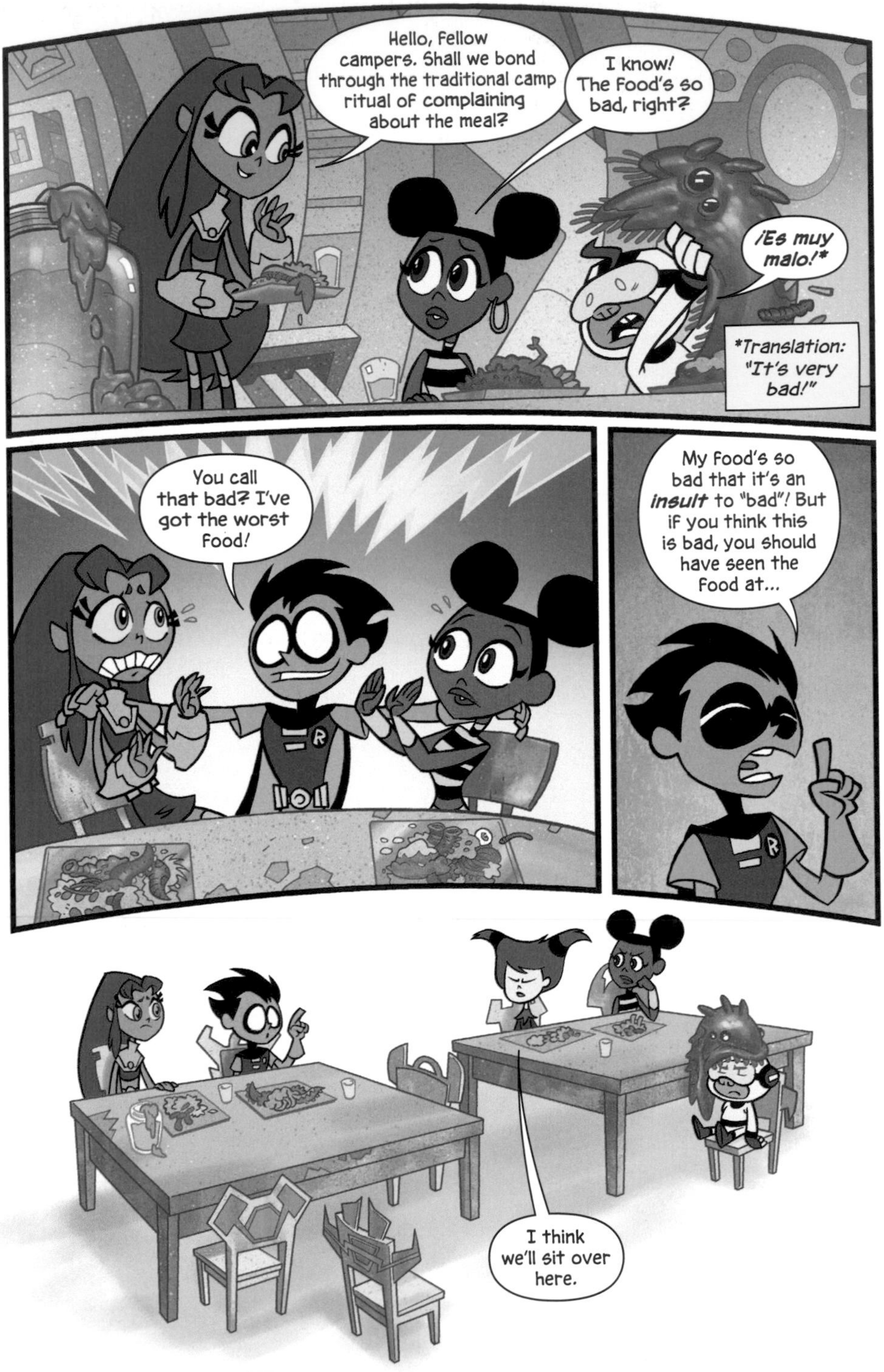
Hello, fellow campers. Shall we bond through the traditional camp ritual of complaining about the meal?
I know! The food's so bad, right?
¡Es muy malo!*
*Translation: "It's very bad!"
You call that bad? I've got the worst food!
My food's so bad that it's an *insult* to "bad"! But if you think this is bad, you should have seen the food at...
I think we'll sit over here.

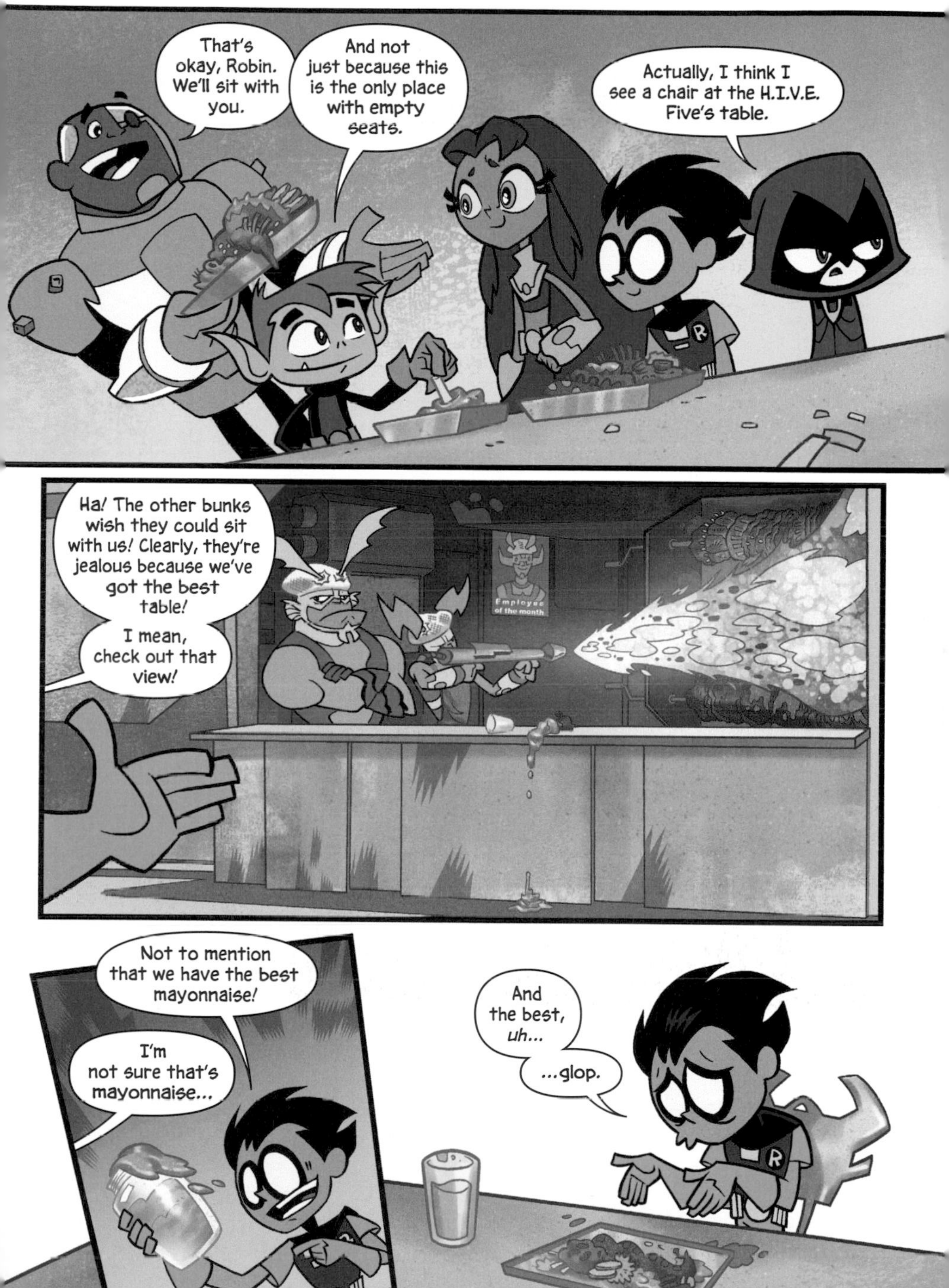
That's okay, Robin. We'll sit with you.
And not just because this is the only place with empty seats.
Actually, I think I see a chair at the H.I.V.E. Five's table.
Ha! The other bunks wish they could sit with us! Clearly, they're jealous because we've got the best table!
I mean, check out that view!
Employee of the month
Not to mention that we have the best mayonnaise!
I'm not sure that's mayonnaise...
And the best, uh...
...glop.

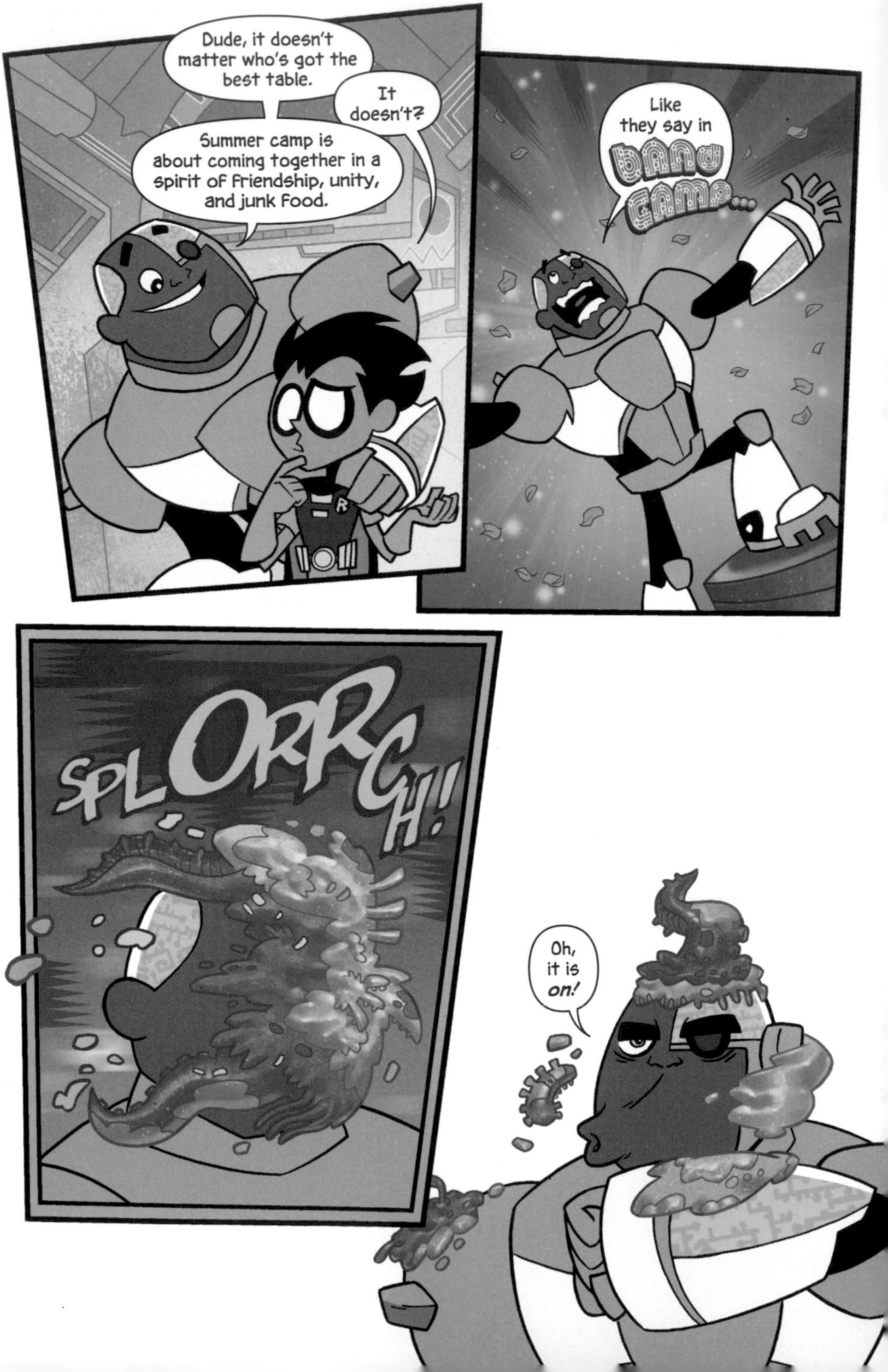

Dude, it doesn't matter who's got the best table.
It doesn't?
Summer camp is about coming together in a spirit of friendship, unity, and junk food.
Like they say in BAND CAMP...
SPLORRCH!
Oh, it is *on!*

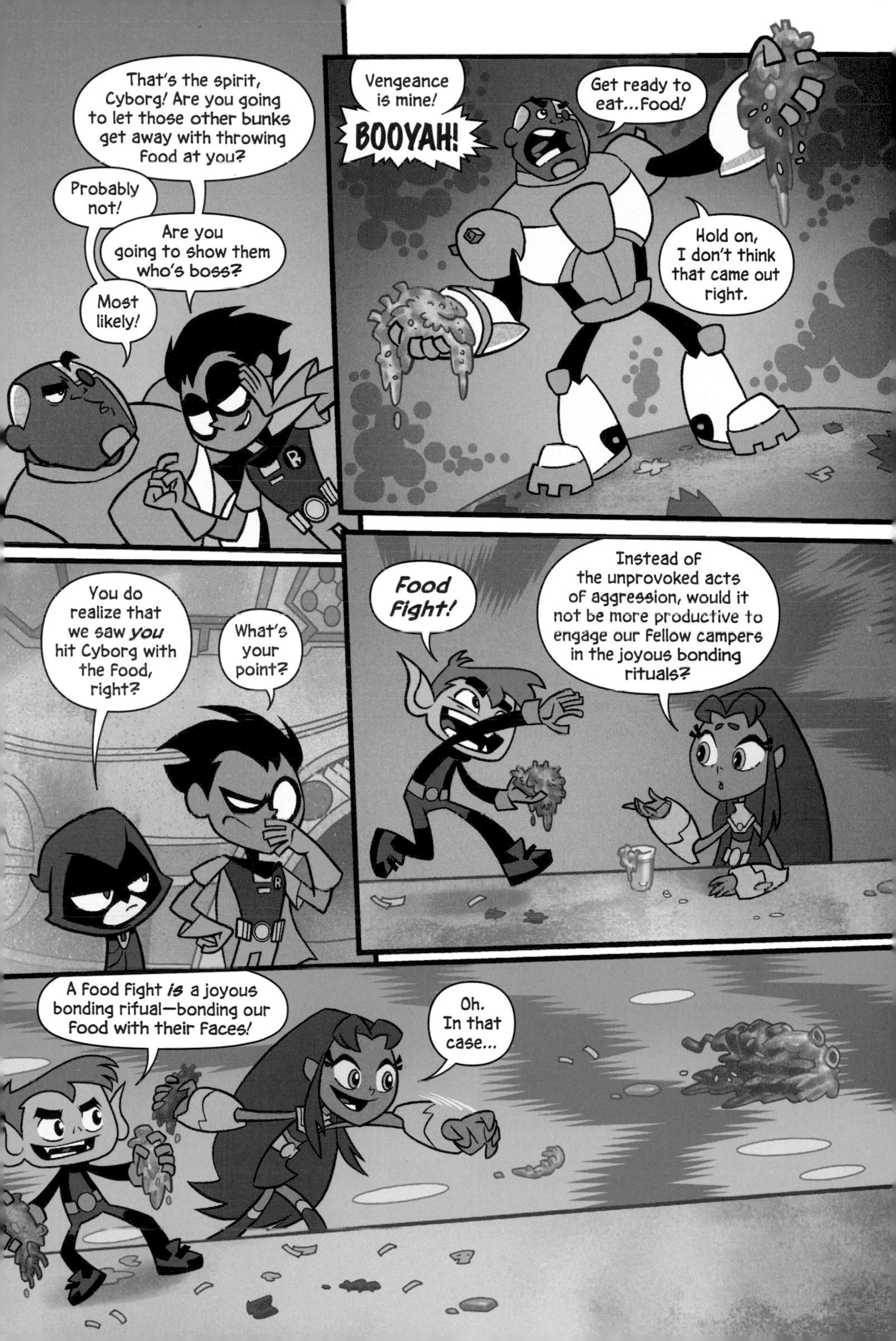
That's the spirit, Cyborg! Are you going to let those other bunks get away with throwing food at you?
Probably not!
Are you going to show them who's boss?
Most likely!
Vengeance is mine!
BOOYAH!
Get ready to eat...food!
Hold on, I don't think that came out right.
You do realize that we saw *you* hit Cyborg with the food, right?
What's your point?
Food fight!
Instead of the unprovoked acts of aggression, would it not be more productive to engage our fellow campers in the joyous bonding rituals?
A food fight *is* a joyous bonding ritual—bonding our food with their faces!
Oh. In that case...

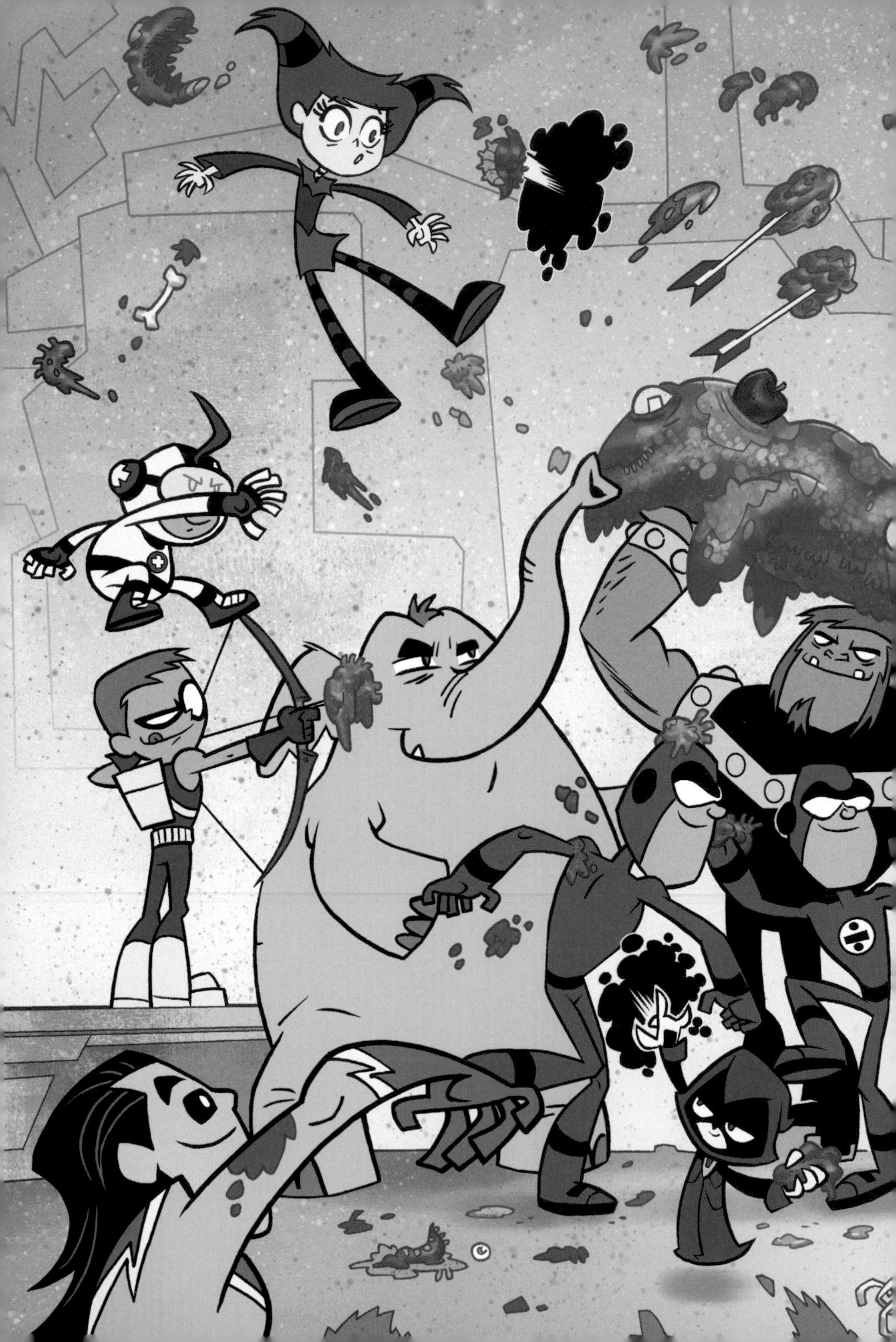

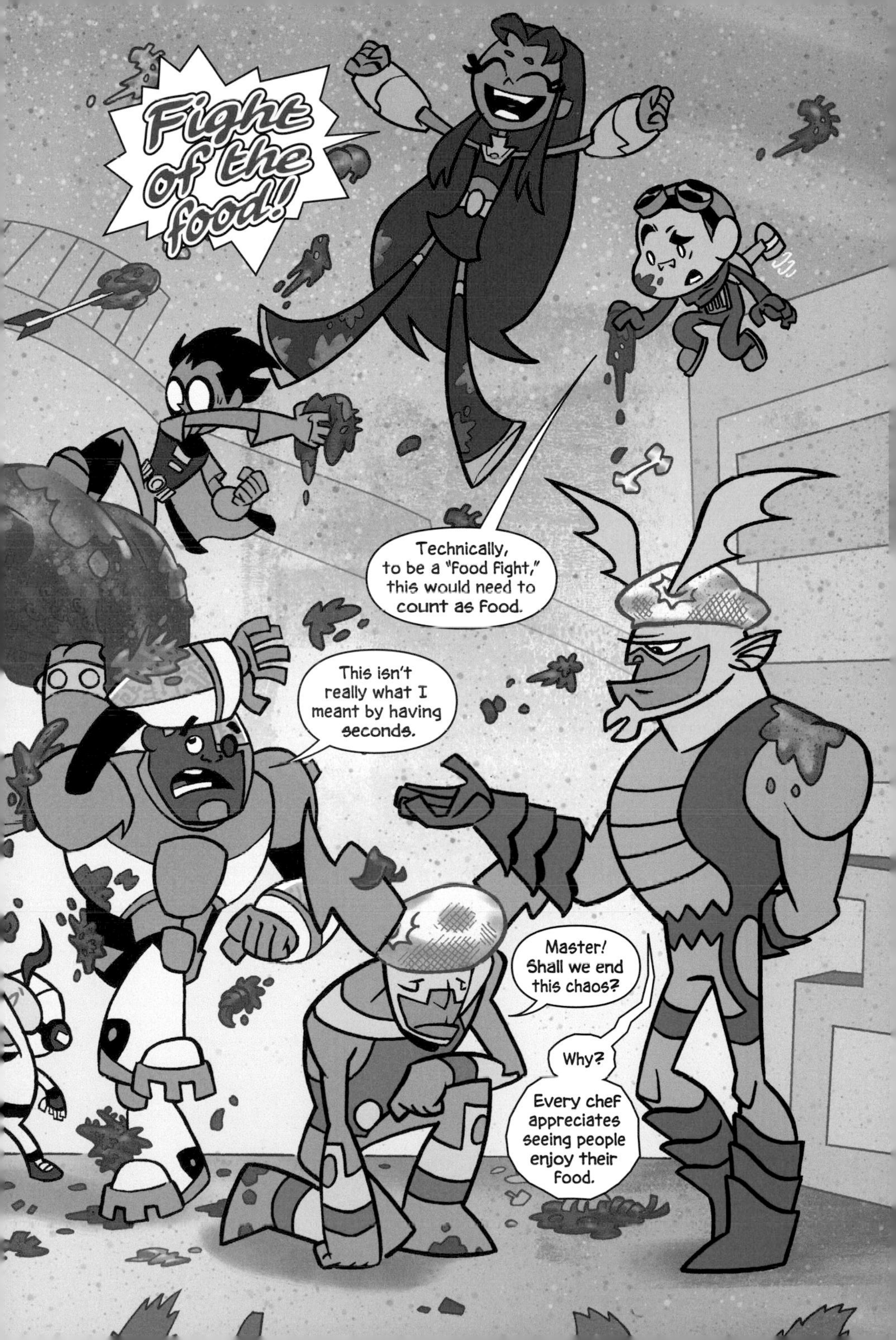

Fight of the food!
Technically, to be a "food fight," this would need to count as food.
This isn't really what I meant by having seconds.
Master! Shall we end this chaos?
Why?
Every chef appreciates seeing people enjoy their food.

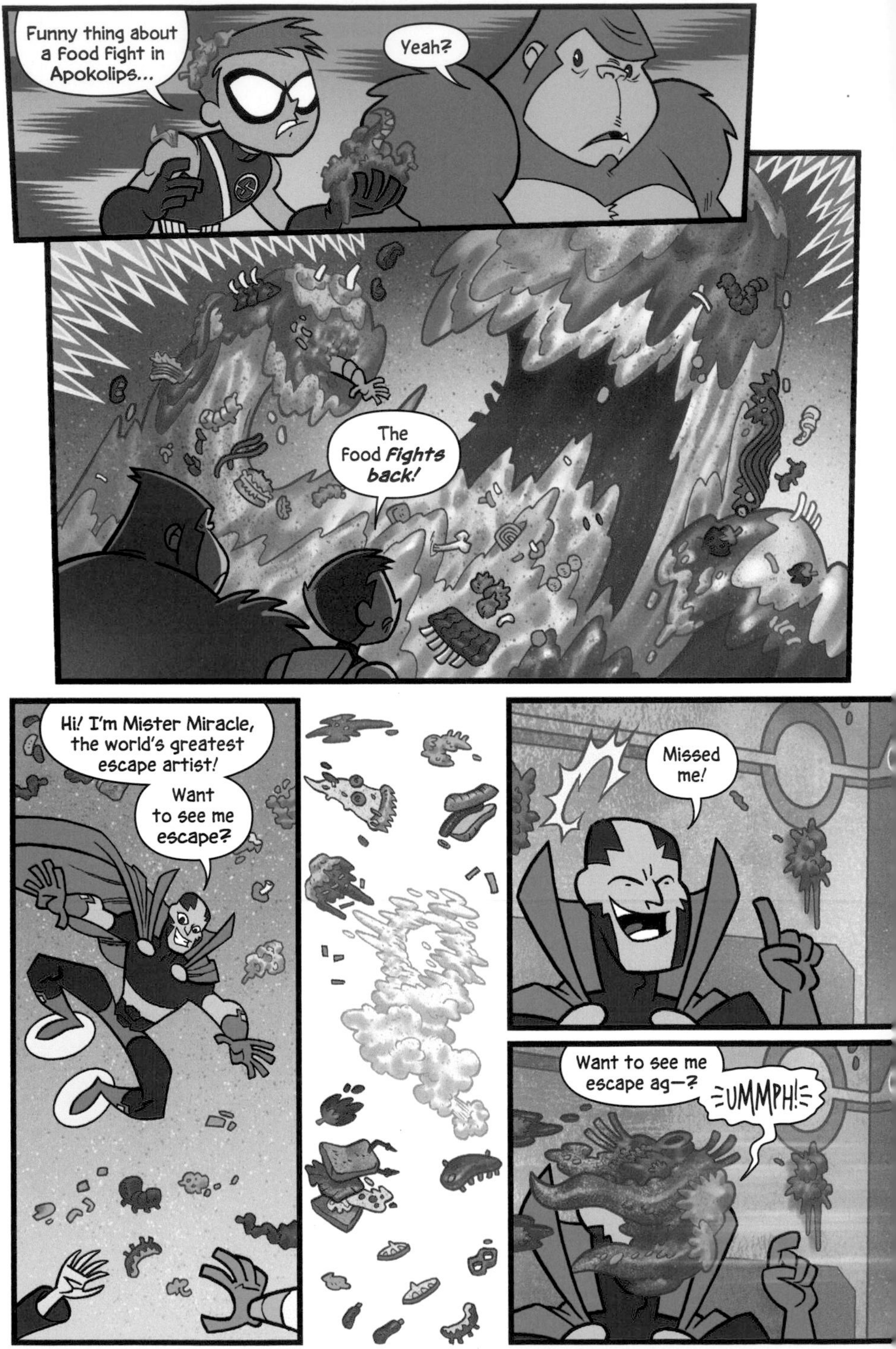
Funny thing about a food fight in Apokolips...
Yeah?
The food *fights* *back!*
Hi! I'm Mister Miracle, the world's greatest escape artist!
Want to see me escape?
Missed me!
Want to see me escape ag—?
UMMPH!

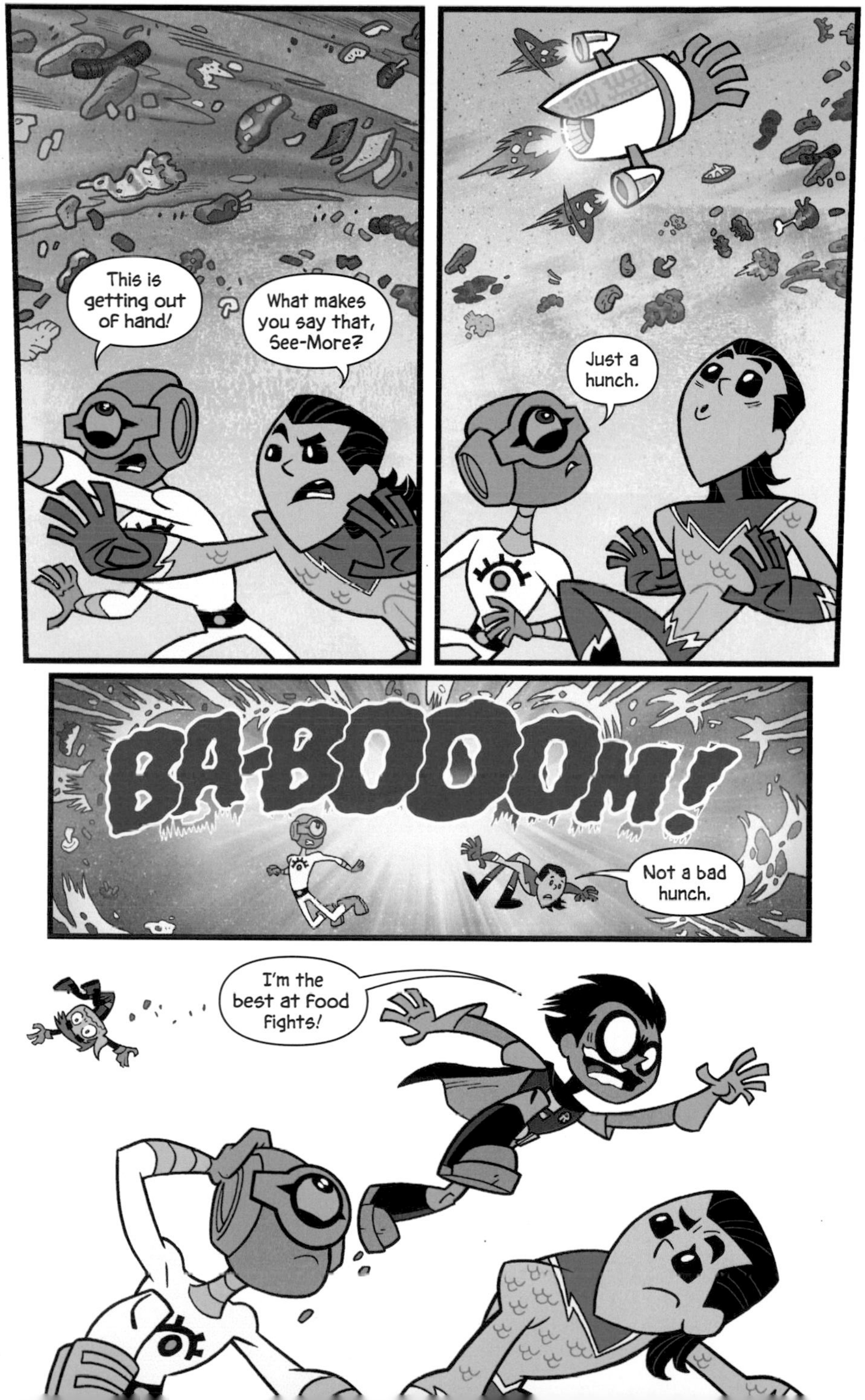
This is getting out of hand!
What makes you say that, See-More?
Just a hunch.
BA-BOOOM!
Not a bad hunch.
I'm the best at food fights!

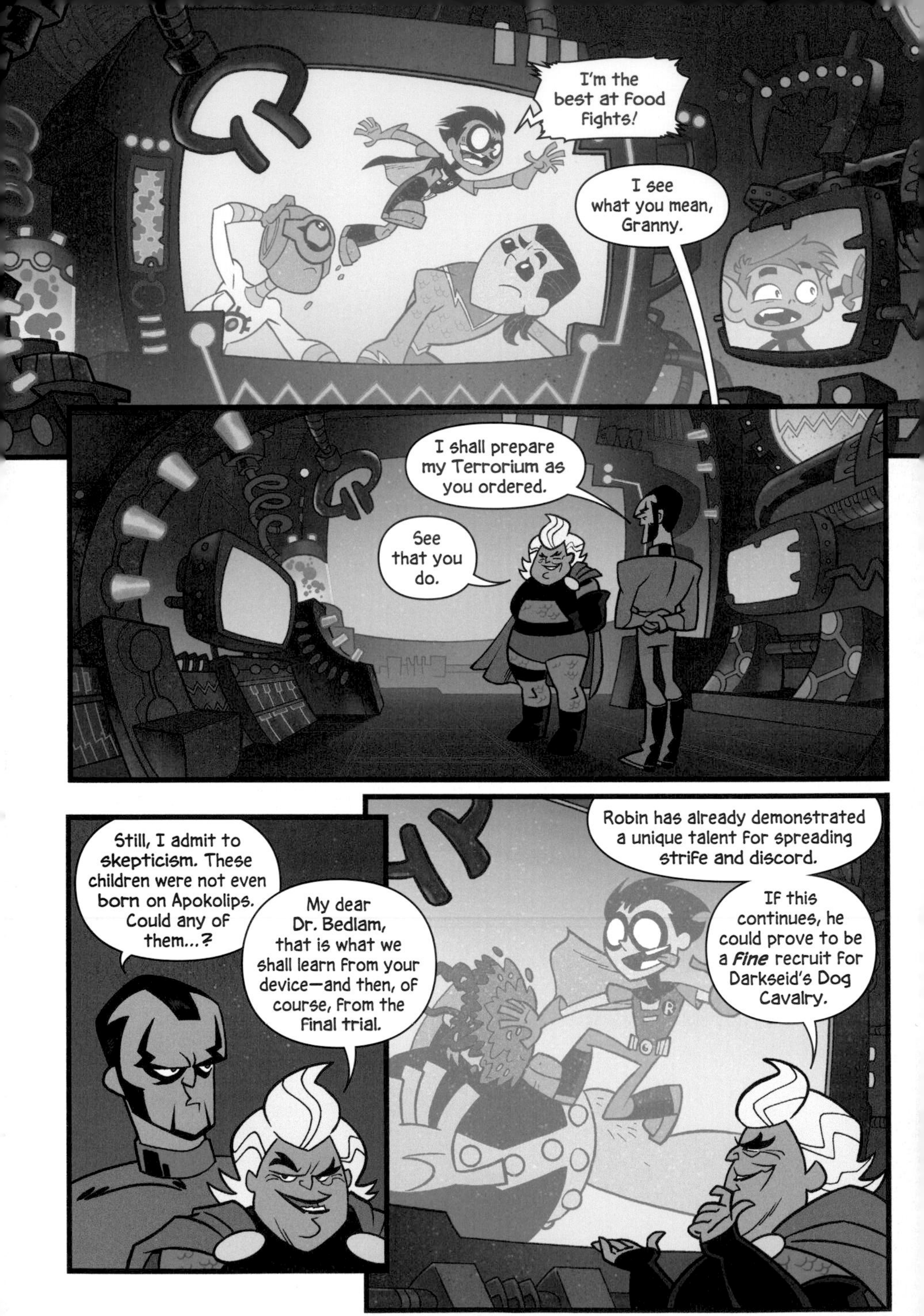

I'm the best at food fights!
I see what you mean, Granny.
I shall prepare my Terrorium as you ordered.
See that you do.
Still, I admit to skepticism. These children were not even born on Apokolips. Could any of them...?
My dear Dr. Bedlam, that is what we shall learn from your device—and then, of course, from the final trial.
Robin has already demonstrated a unique talent for spreading strife and discord.
If this continues, he could prove to be a *fine* recruit for Darkseid's Dog Cavalry.

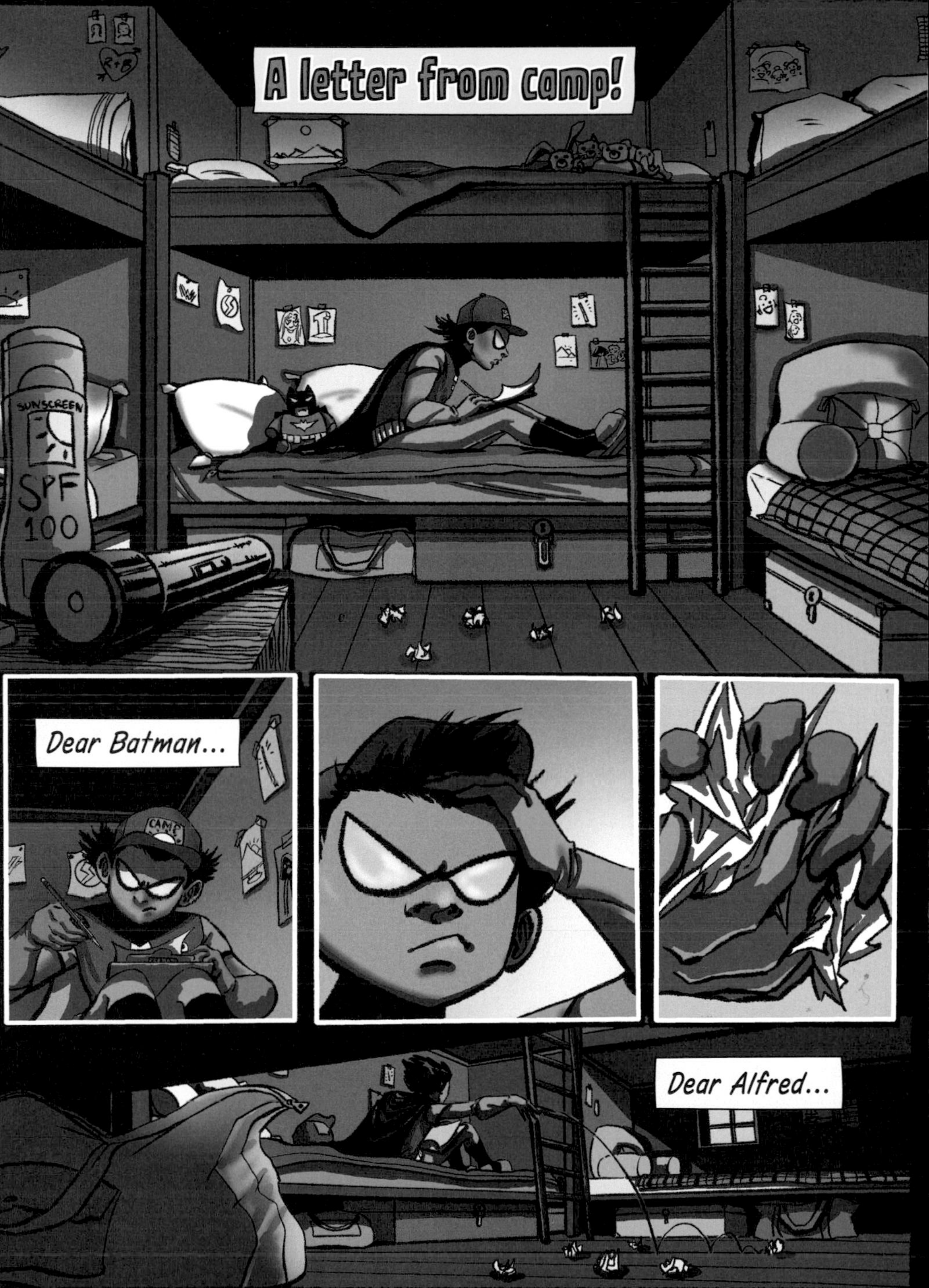
A letter from camp!
SUNSCREEN
SPF 100
Dear Batman...
CAMP
Dear Alfred...

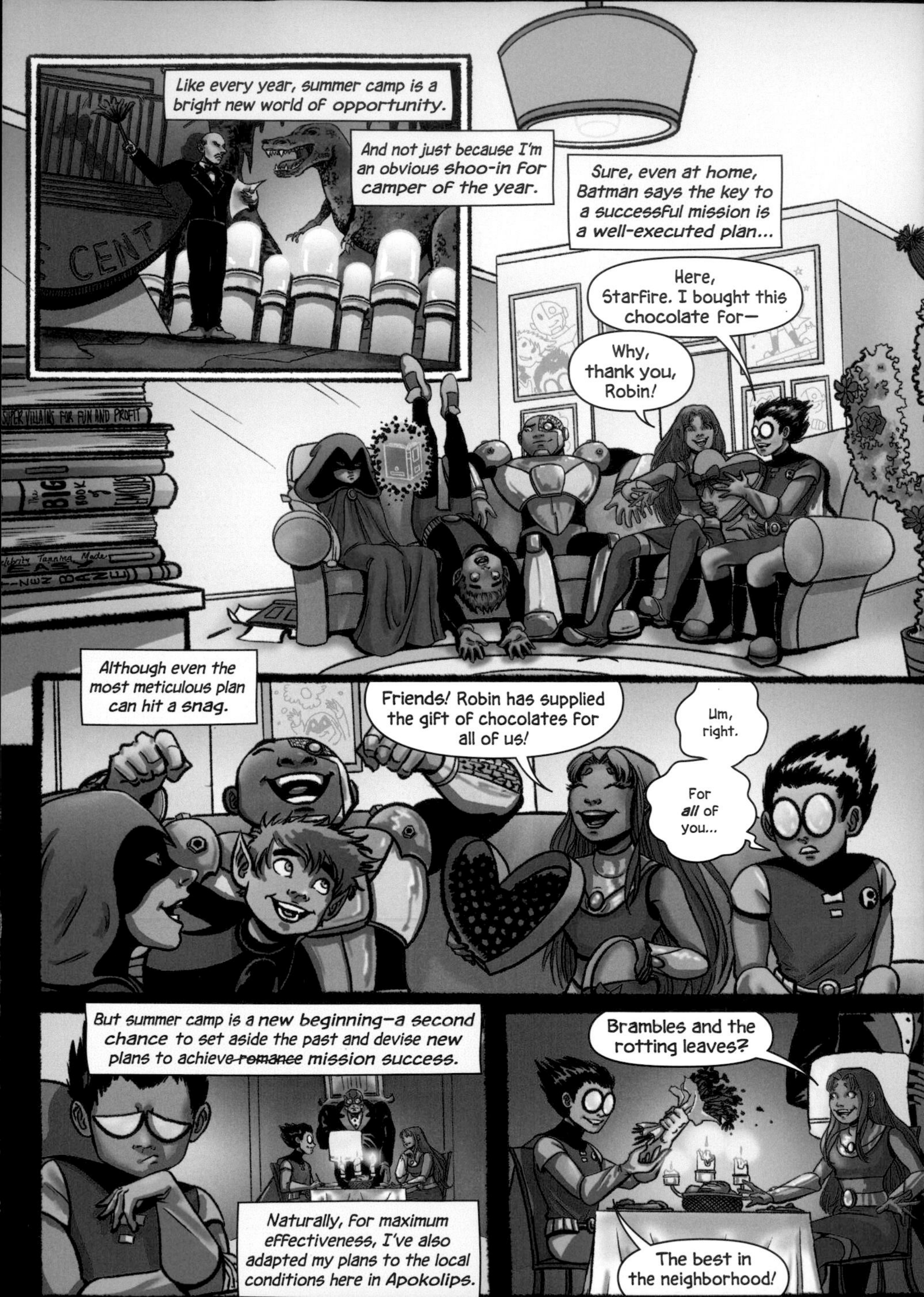
Like every year, summer camp is a bright new world of opportunity.
And not just because I'm an obvious shoo-in for camper of the year.
Sure, even at home, Batman says the key to a successful mission is a well-executed plan...
Here, Starfire. I bought this chocolate for—
Why, thank you, Robin!
SUPER VILLAINS FOR FUN AND PROFIT
THE BIG BOOK of
Although even the most meticulous plan can hit a snag.
Friends! Robin has supplied the gift of chocolates for all of us!
Um, right.
For all of you...
But summer camp is a new beginning—a second chance to set aside the past and devise new plans to achieve romance mission success.
Naturally, for maximum effectiveness, I've also adapted my plans to the local conditions here in Apokolips.
Brambles and the rotting leaves?
The best in the neighborhood!

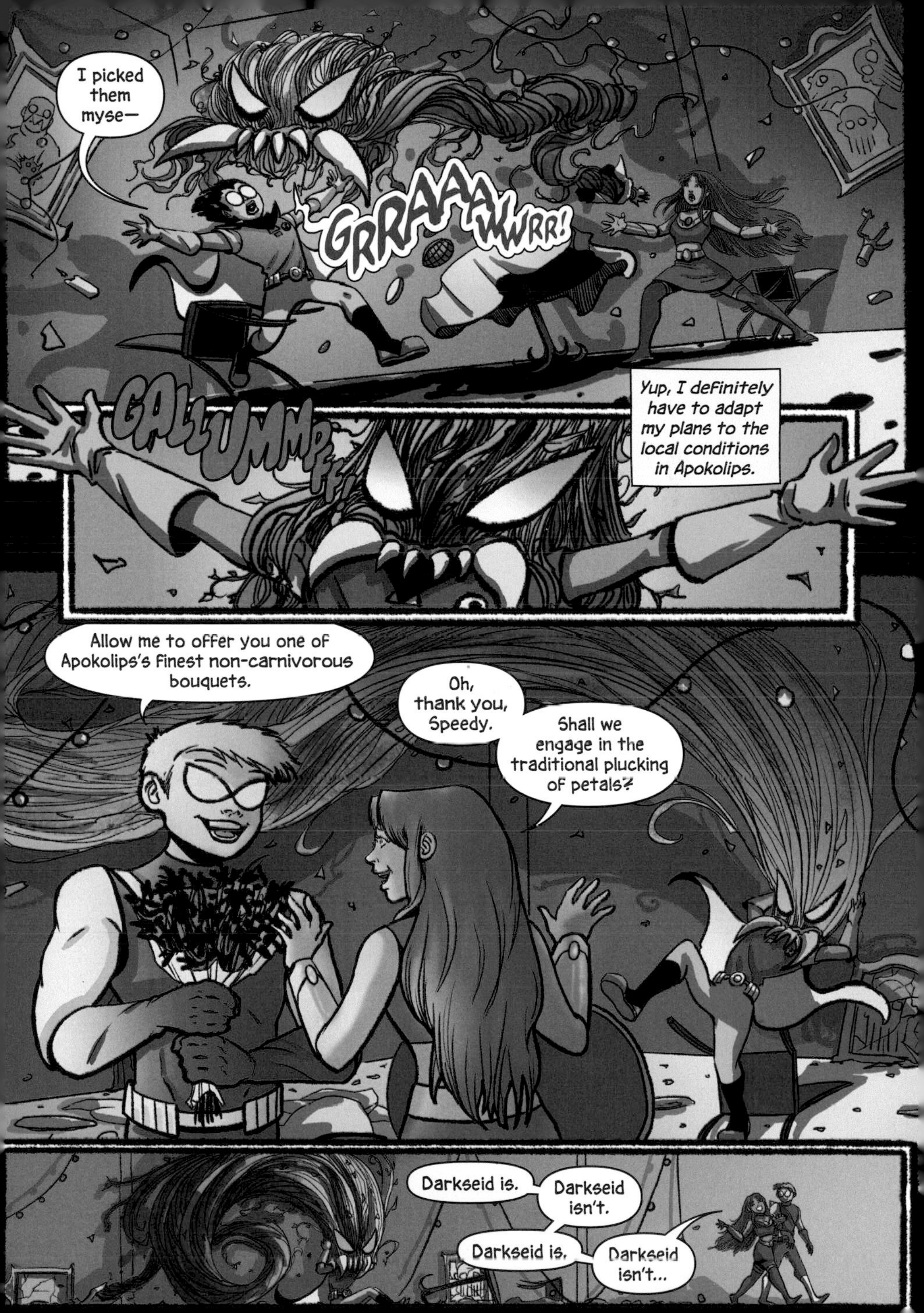
I picked them myse—
GRRAAAWWRR!
GALLUMMPFF!
Yup, I definitely have to adapt my plans to the local conditions in Apokolips.
Allow me to offer you one of Apokolips's finest non-carnivorous bouquets.
Oh, thank you, Speedy.
Shall we engage in the traditional plucking of petals?
Darkseid is.
Darkseid isn't.
Darkseid is.
Darkseid isn't...

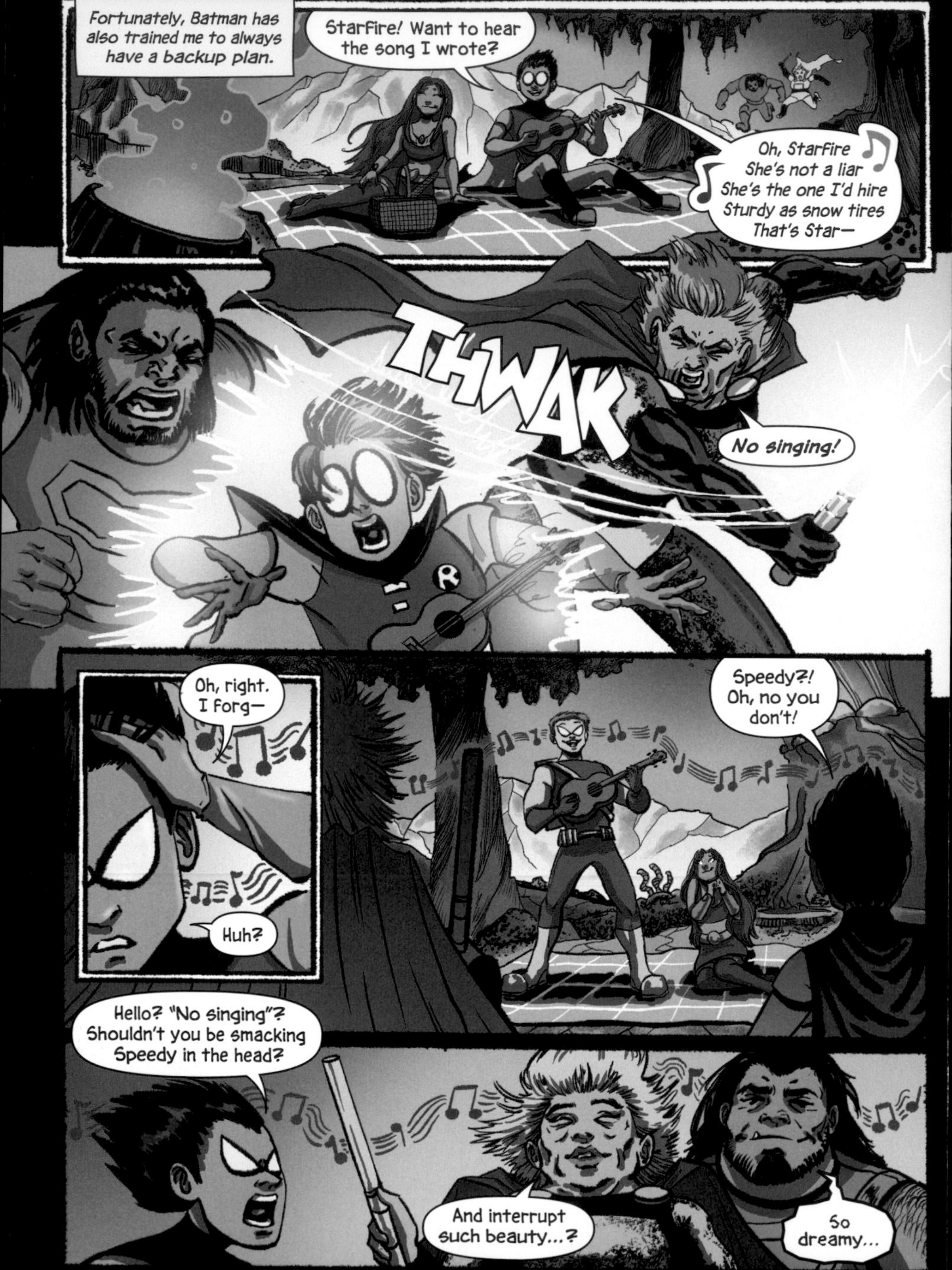
Fortunately, Batman has also trained me to always have a backup plan.
Starfire! Want to hear the song I wrote?
Oh, Starfire
She's not a liar
She's the one I'd hire
Sturdy as snow tires
That's Star—
THWAK
No singing!
Oh, right. I forg—
Huh?
Speedy?! Oh, no you don't!
Hello? "No singing"? Shouldn't you be smacking Speedy in the head?
And interrupt such beauty...?
So dreamy...

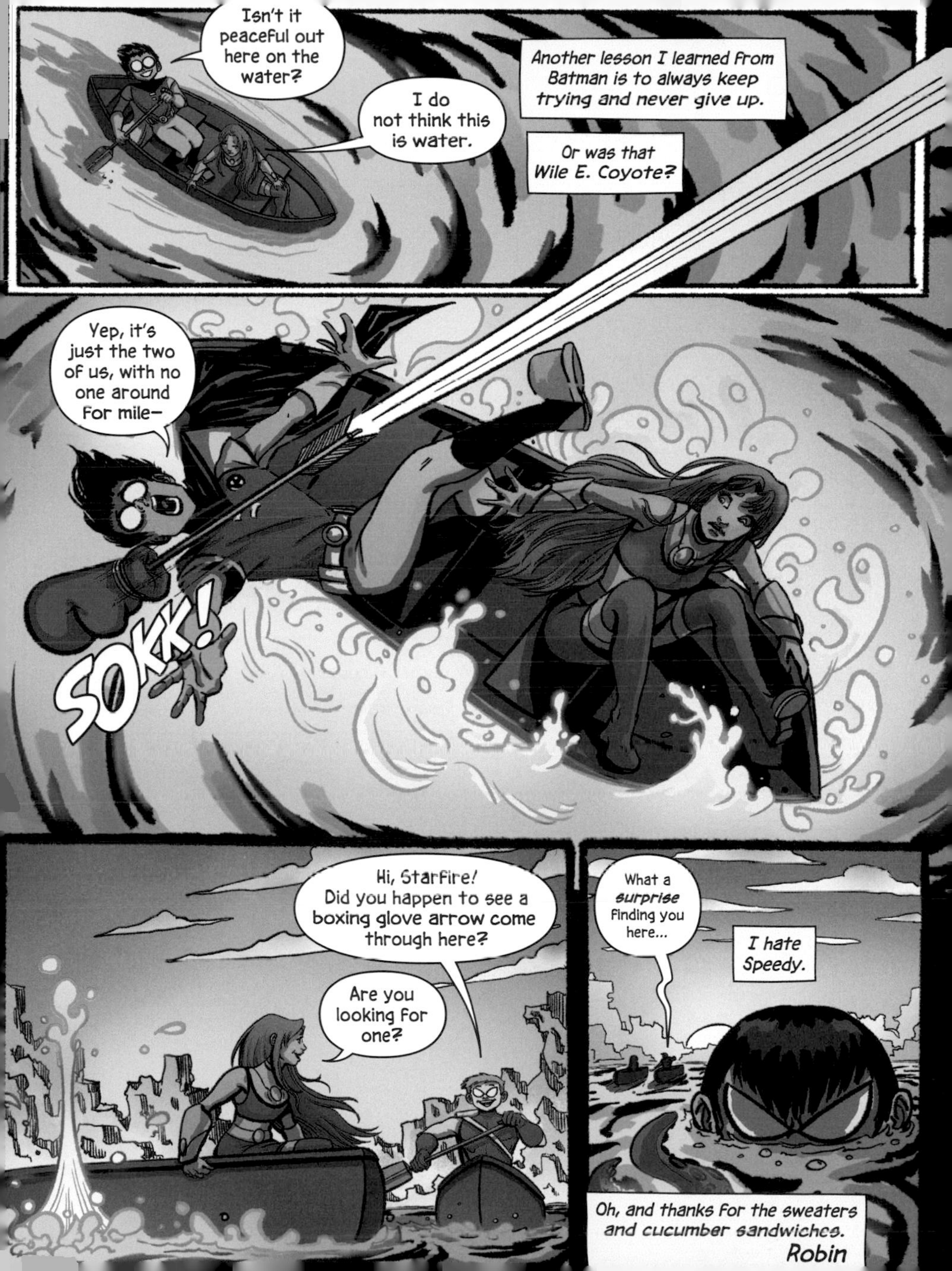
Isn't it peaceful out here on the water?
I do not think this is water.
Another lesson I learned from Batman is to always keep trying and never give up.
Or was that Wile E. Coyote?
Yep, it's just the two of us, with no one around for mile–
SOKK!
Hi, Starfire! Did you happen to see a boxing glove arrow come through here?
Are you looking for one?
What a *surprise* finding you here...
I hate Speedy.
Oh, and thanks for the sweaters and cucumber sandwiches.
Robin

Chapter Five

Speedy's letter drawn by Leila del Duca,
colored by Marissa Louise

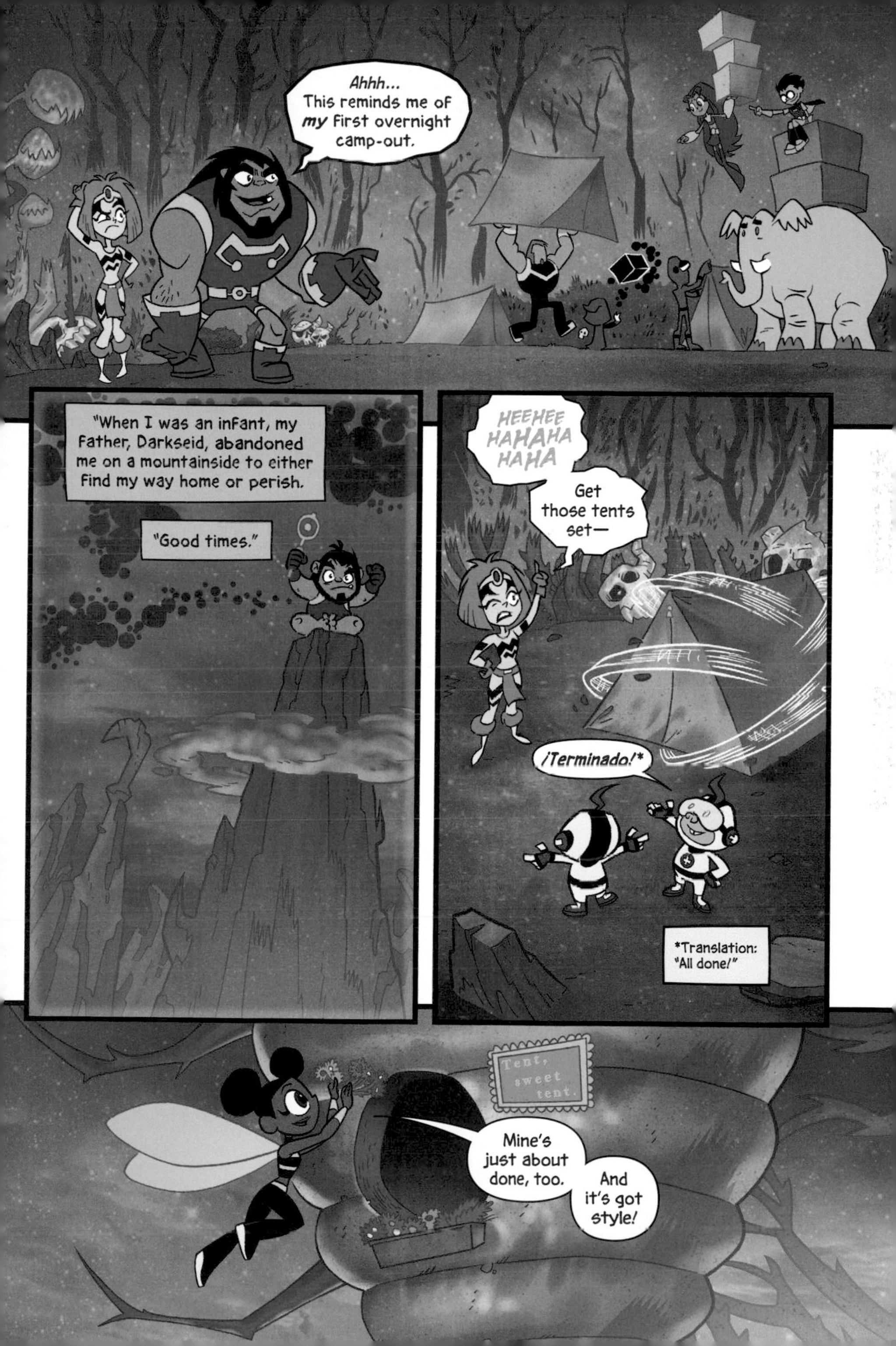

Ahhh...
This reminds me of *my* first overnight camp-out.
"When I was an infant, my father, Darkseid, abandoned me on a mountainside to either find my way home or perish.
"Good times."
HEEHEE HAHAHA HAHA
Get those tents set—
¡Terminado!*
*Translation: "All done!"
Tent, sweet tent.
Mine's just about done, too.
And it's got style!

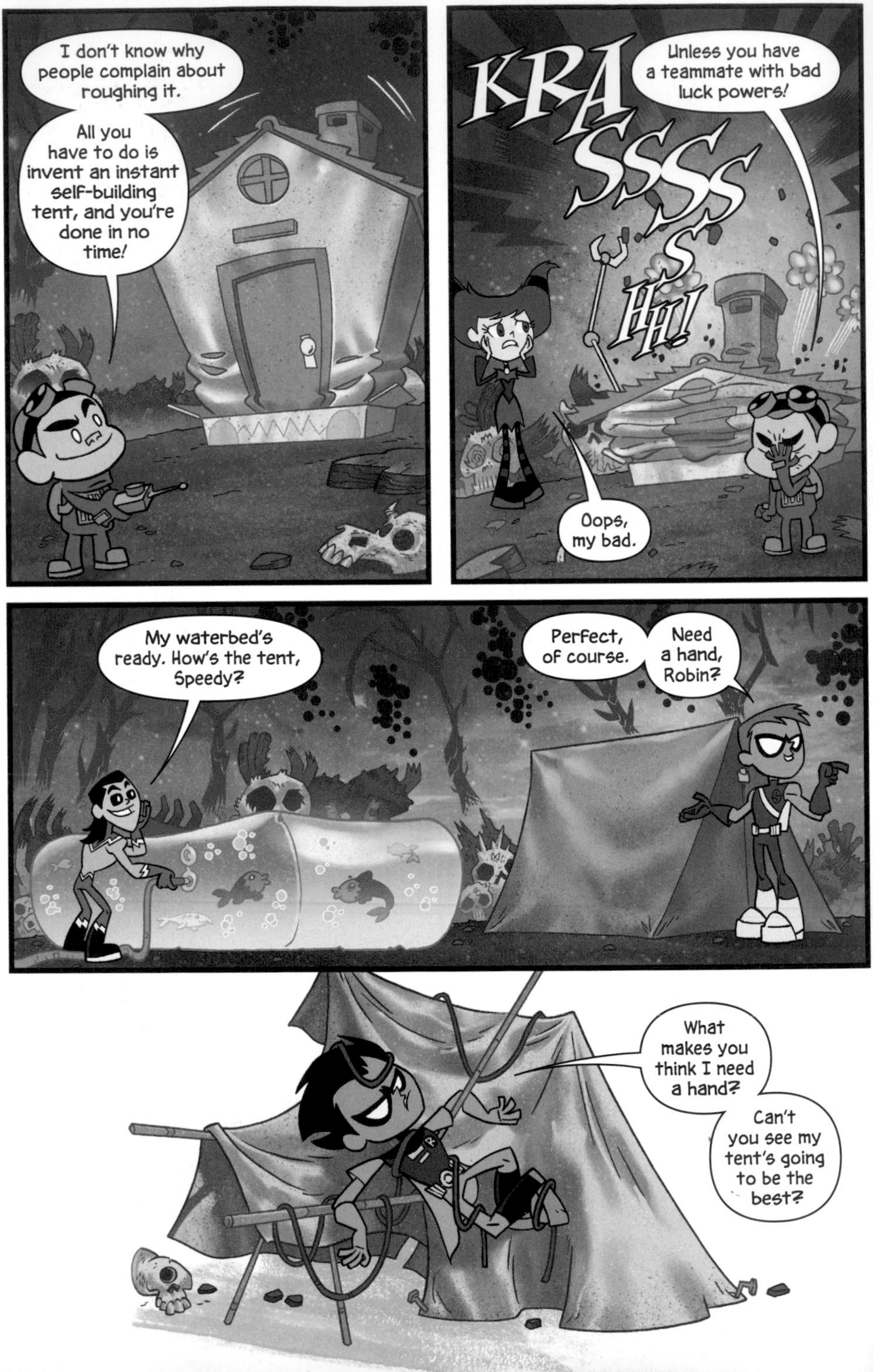
I don't know why people complain about roughing it.
All you have to do is invent an instant self-building tent, and you're done in no time!
KRASSSSSHH!
Unless you have a teammate with bad luck powers!
Oops, my bad.
My waterbed's ready. How's the tent, Speedy?
Perfect, of course.
Need a hand, Robin?
What makes you think I need a hand?
Can't you see my tent's going to be the best?

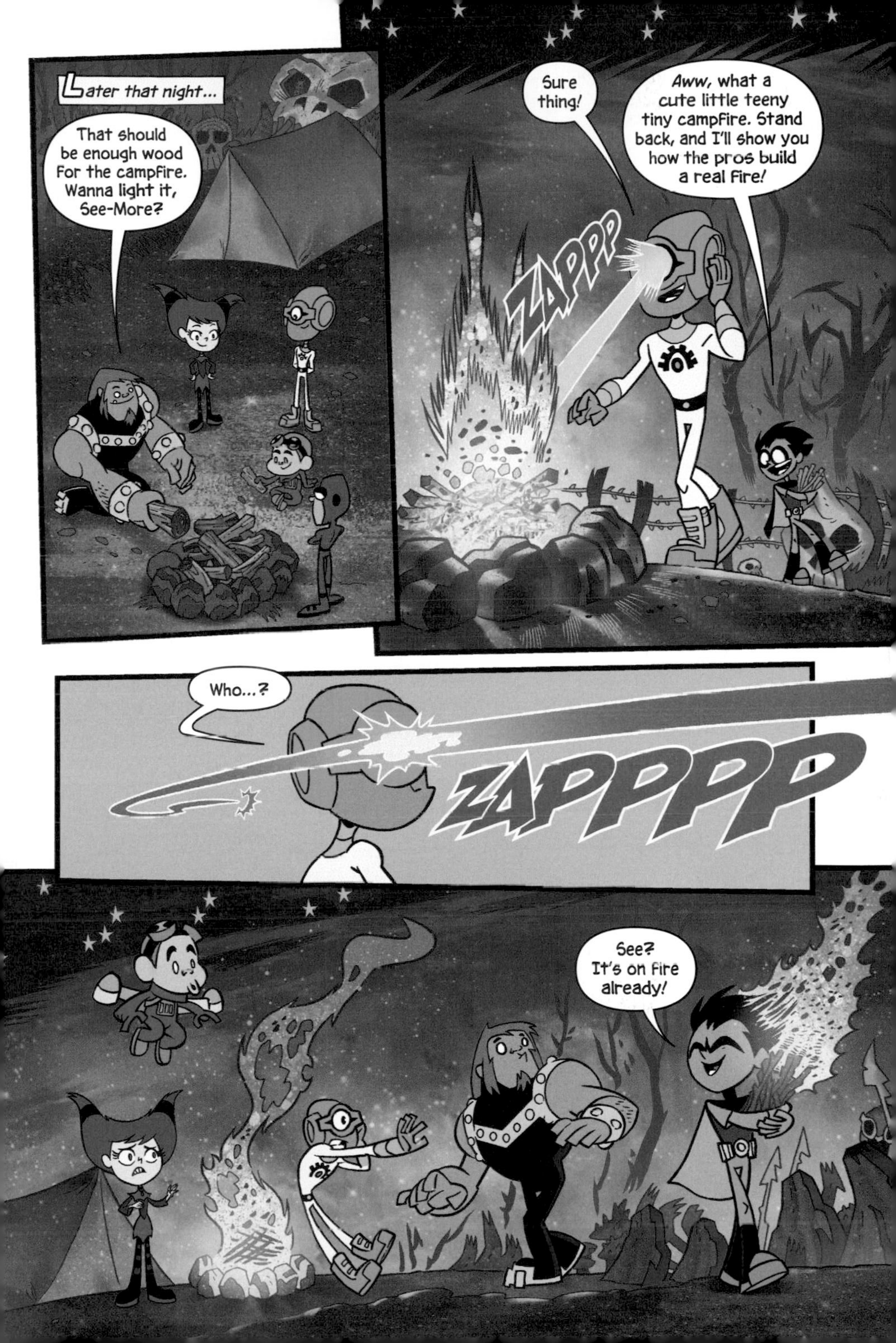
Later that night...
That should be enough wood for the campfire. Wanna light it, See-More?
Sure thing!
Aww, what a cute little teeny tiny campfire. Stand back, and I'll show you how the pros build a real fire!
ZAPPP
Who...?
ZAPPPPP
See? It's on fire already!

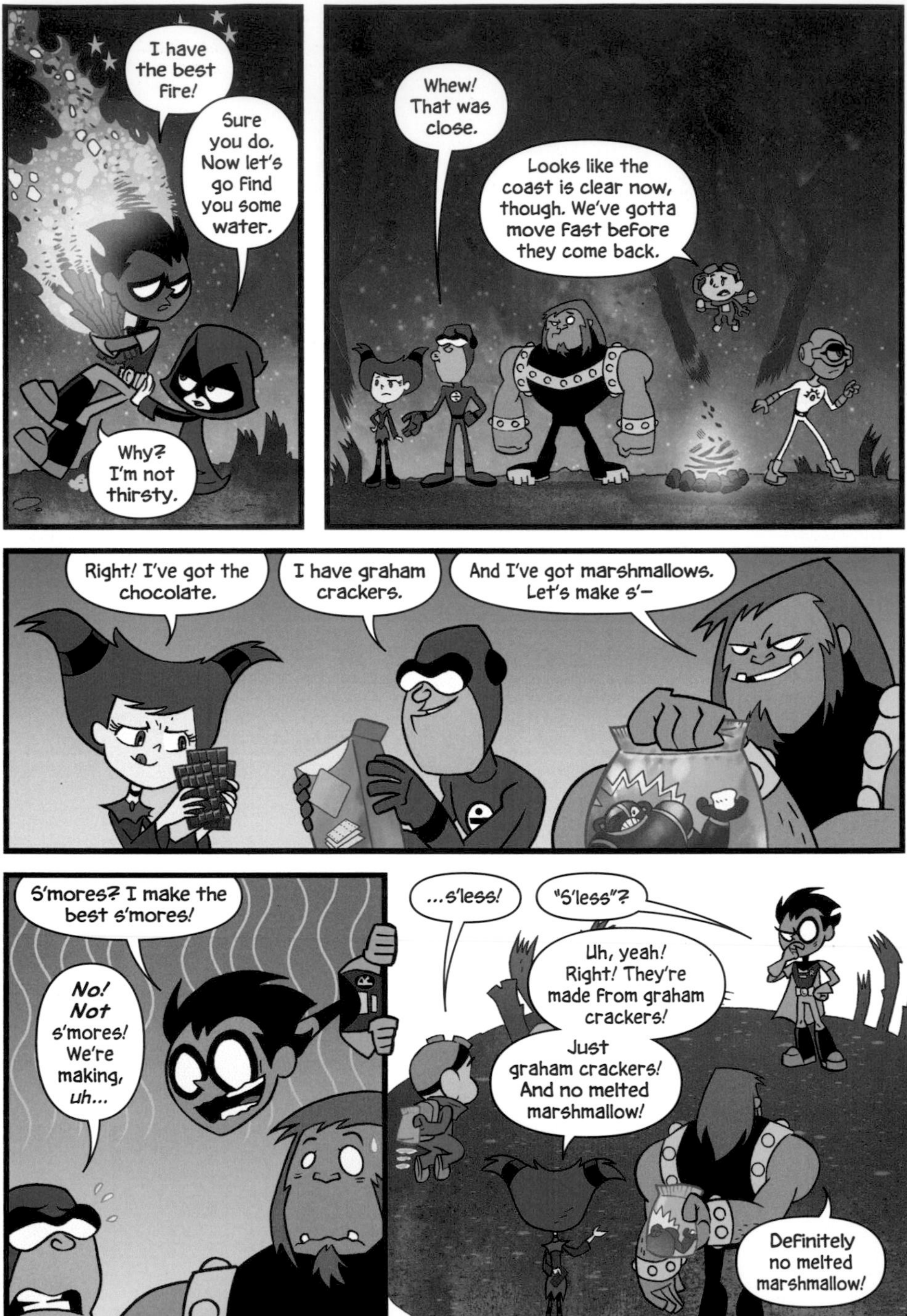
I have the best fire!
Sure you do. Now let's go find you some water.
Why? I'm not thirsty.
Whew! That was close.
Looks like the coast is clear now, though. We've gotta move fast before they come back.
Right! I've got the chocolate.
I have graham crackers.
And I've got marshmallows. Let's make s'—
S'mores? I make the best s'mores!
No! Not s'mores! We're making, uh...
...s'less!
"S'less"?
Uh, yeah! Right! They're made from graham crackers!
Just graham crackers! And no melted marshmallow!
Definitely no melted marshmallow!

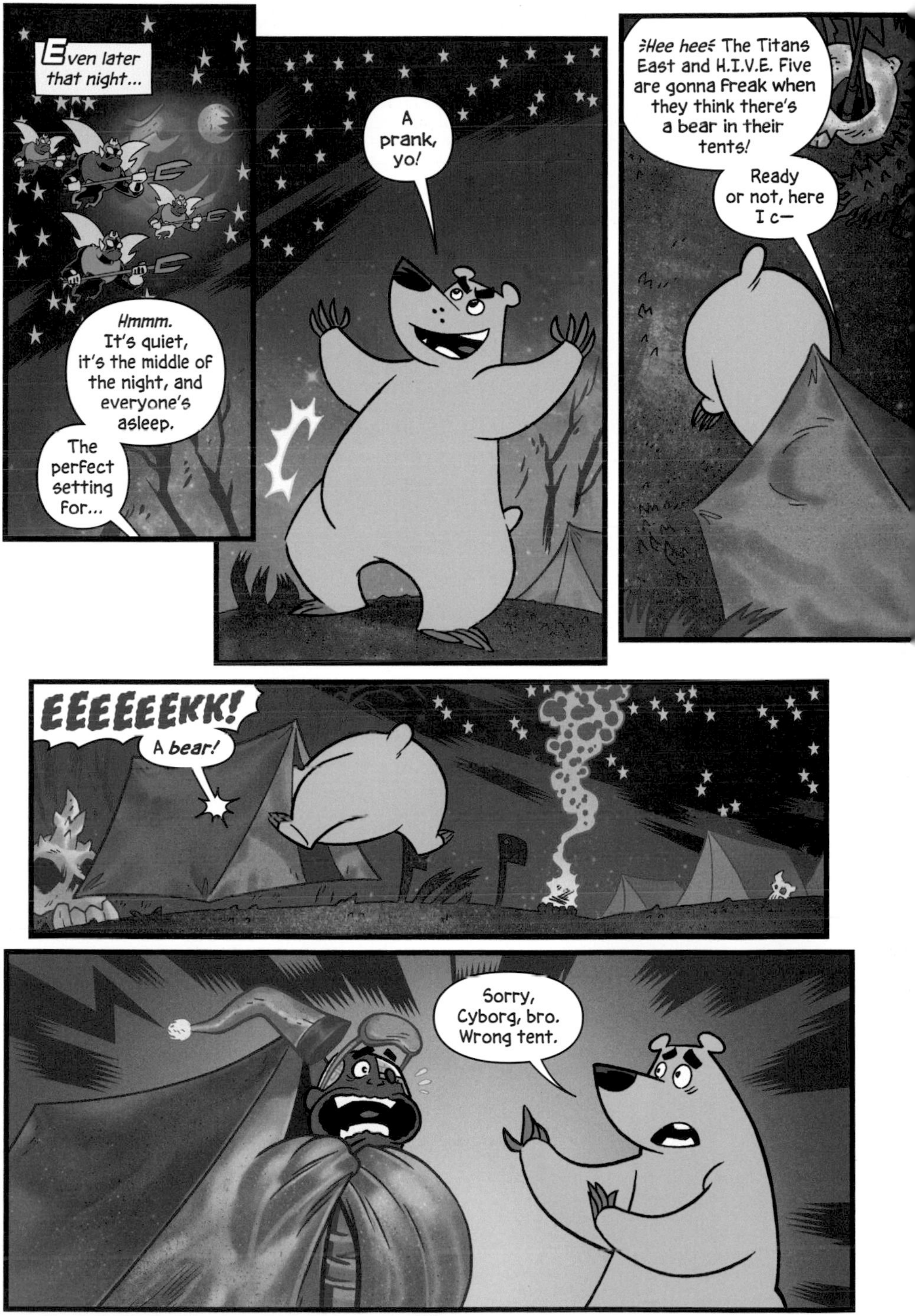
Even later that night...
Hmmm. It's quiet, it's the middle of the night, and everyone's asleep.
The perfect setting for...
A prank, yo!
Hee hee The Titans East and H.I.V.E. Five are gonna freak when they think there's a bear in their tents!
Ready or not, here I c—
EEEEEEKK!
A bear!
Sorry, Cyborg, bro. Wrong tent.

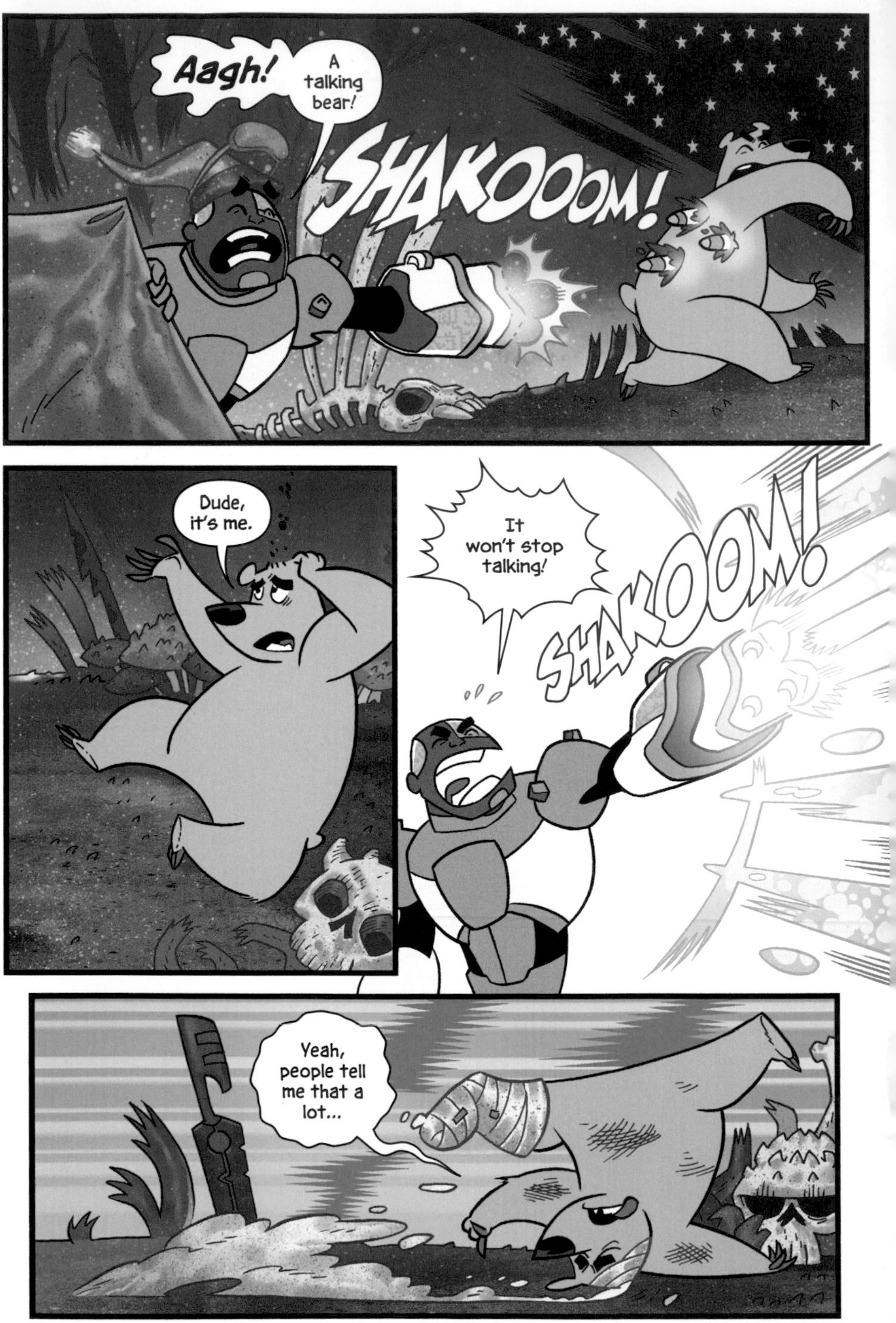
Aagh!
A talking bear!
SHAKOOOM!
Dude, it's me.
It won't stop talking!
SHAKOOOM!
Yeah, people tell me that a lot...

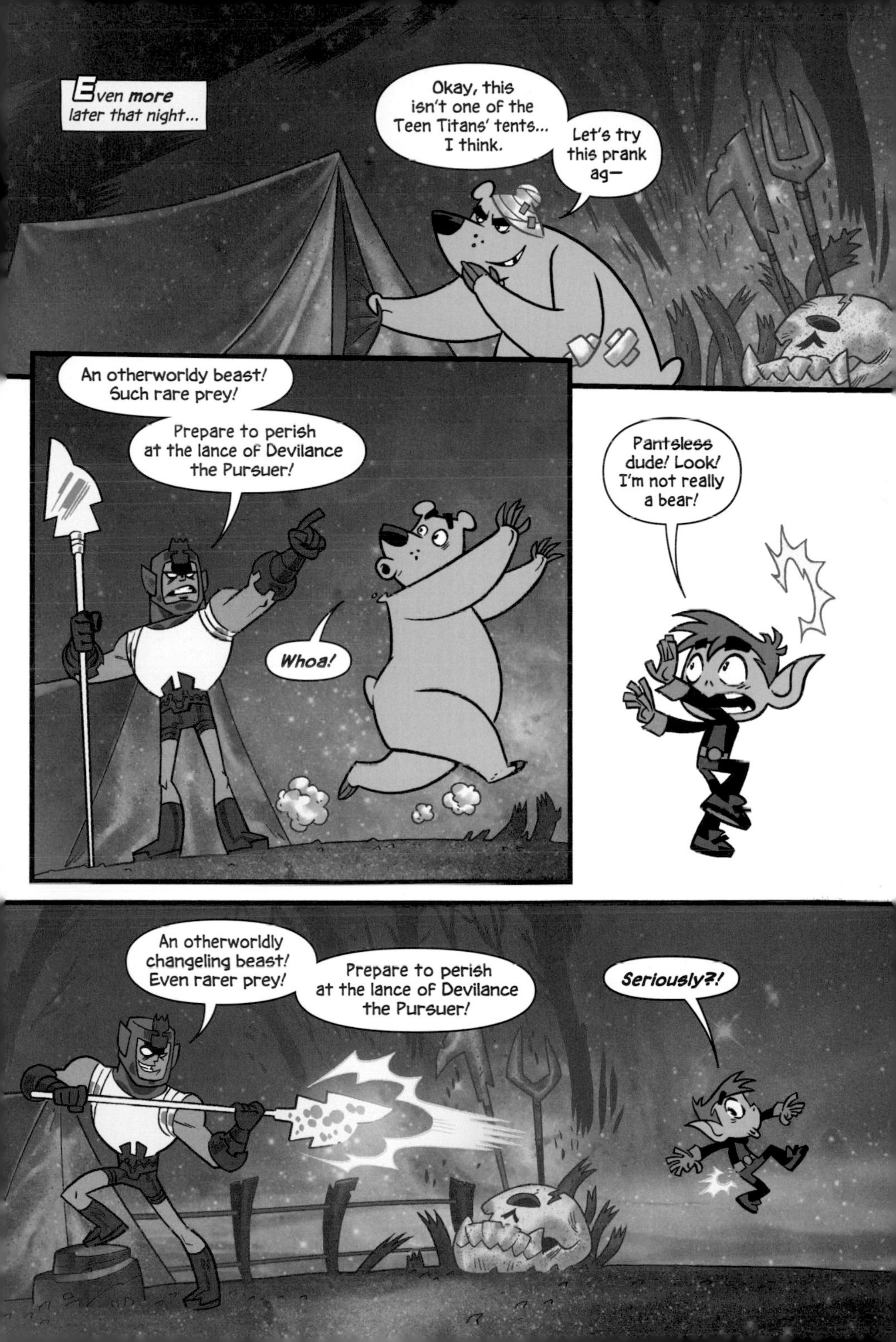
Even *more* later that night...
Okay, this isn't one of the Teen Titans' tents... I think.
Let's try this prank ag—
An otherworldy beast! Such rare prey!
Prepare to perish at the lance of Devilance the Pursuer!
Whoa!
Pantsless dude! Look! I'm not really a bear!
An otherworldly changeling beast! Even rarer prey!
Prepare to perish at the lance of Devilance the Pursuer!
Seriously?!

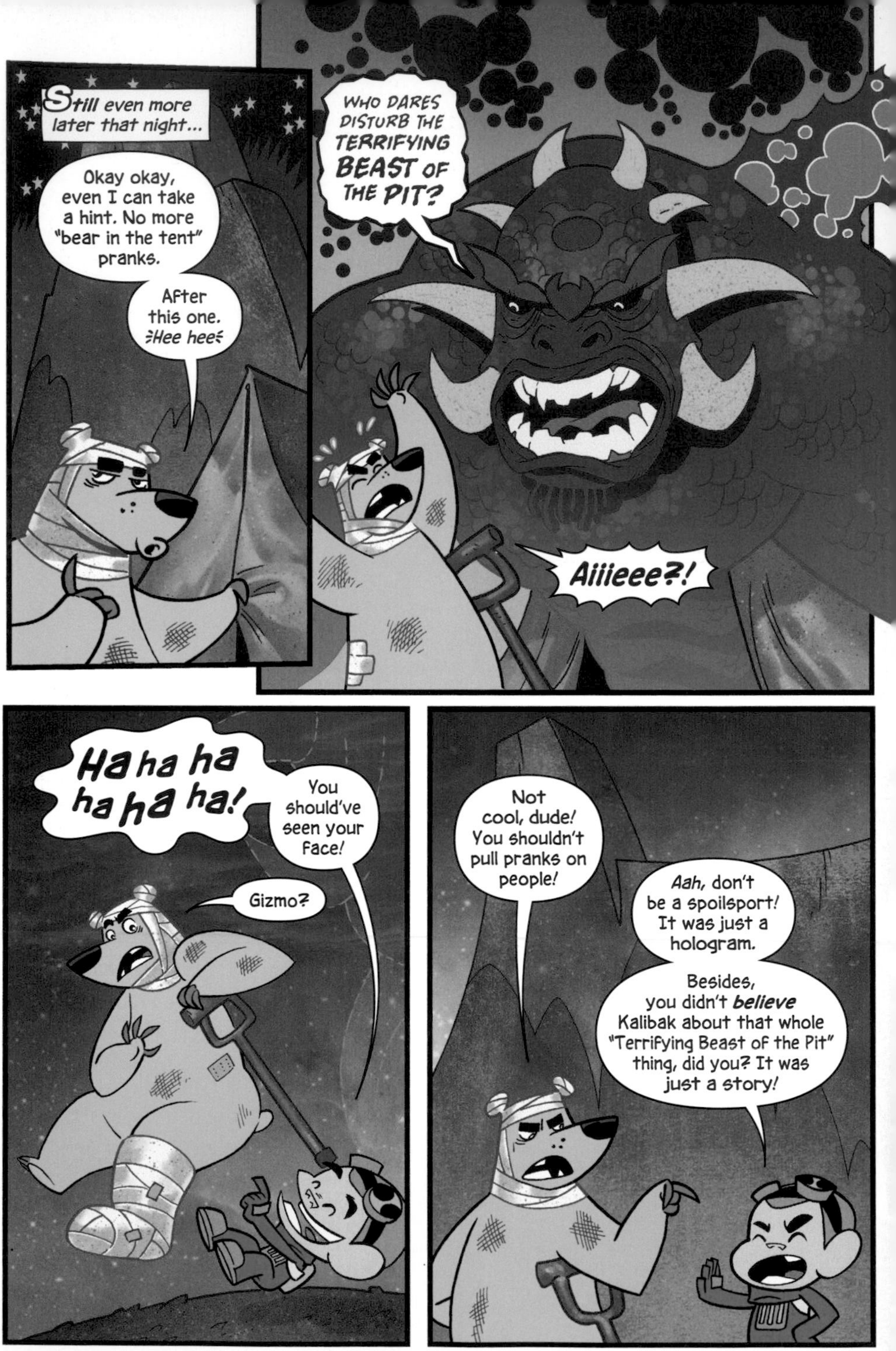
Still even more later that night...
Okay okay, even I can take a hint. No more "bear in the tent" pranks.
After this one. Hee hee
WHO DARES DISTURB THE TERRIFYING BEAST OF THE PIT?
Aiiieee?!
Ha ha ha ha ha ha!
You should've seen your face!
Gizmo?
Not cool, dude! You shouldn't pull pranks on people!
Aah, don't be a spoilsport! It was just a hologram.
Besides, you didn't believe Kalibak about that whole "Terrifying Beast of the Pit" thing, did you? It was just a story!

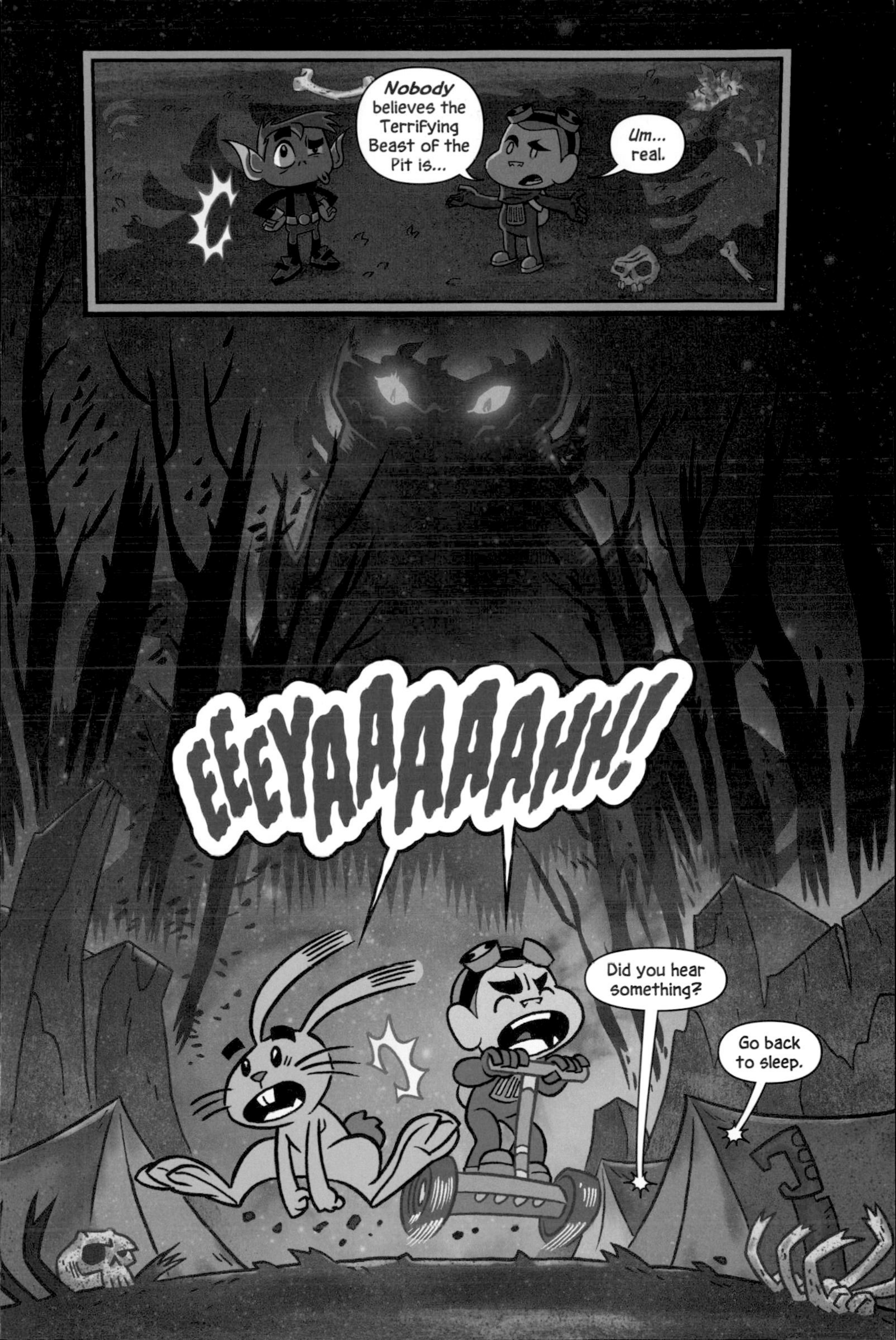

Nobody believes the Terrifying Beast of the Pit is...
Um... real.
EEEYAAAAAHH!!
Did you hear something?
Go back to sleep.

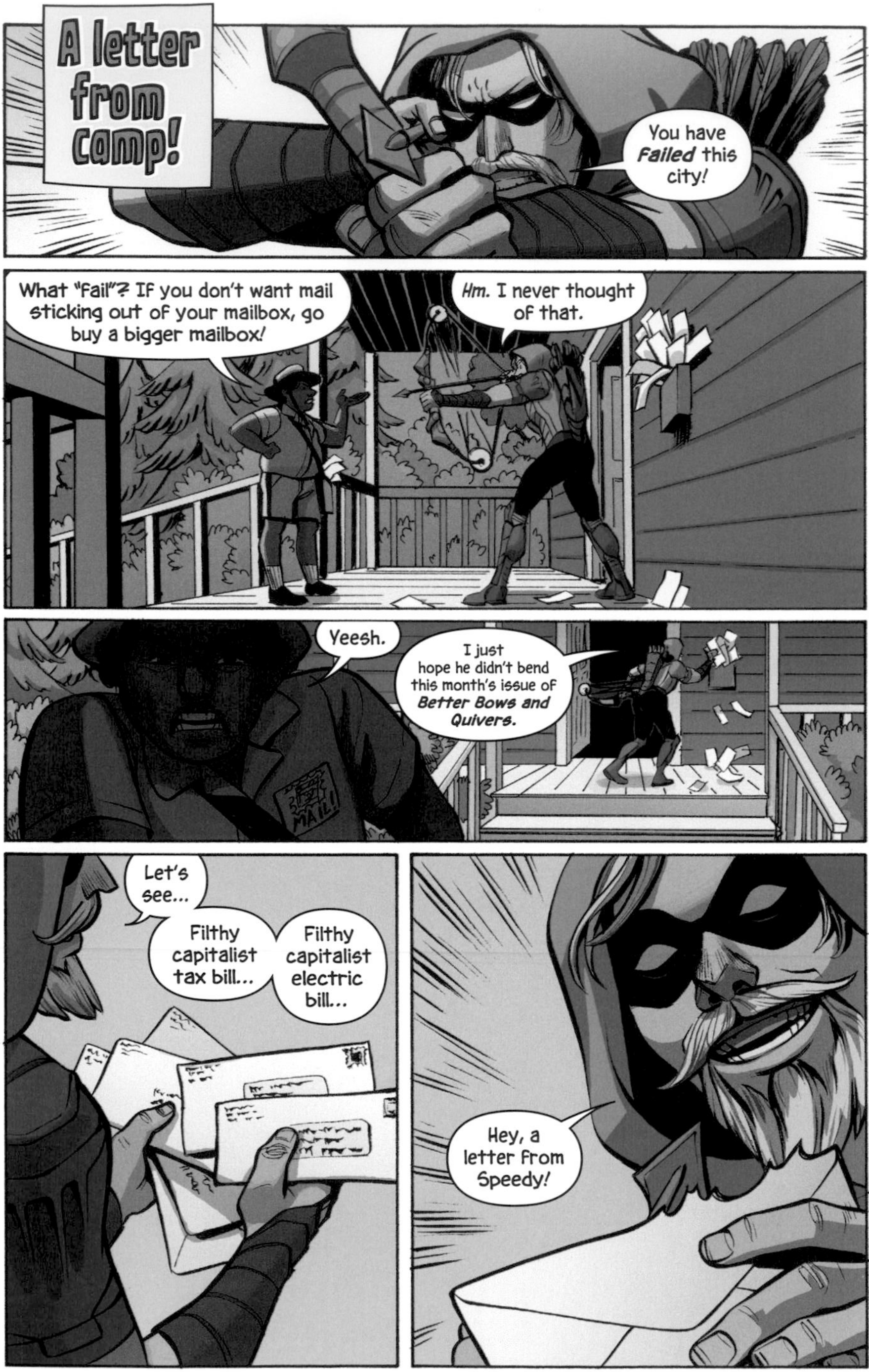
A letter from camp!
You have *Failed* this city!
What "fail"? If you don't want mail sticking out of your mailbox, go buy a bigger mailbox!
Hm. I never thought of that.
Yeesh.
I just hope he didn't bend this month's issue of *Better Bows and Quivers.*
MAIL!
Let's see...
Filthy capitalist tax bill...
Filthy capitalist electric bill...
Hey, a letter from Speedy!

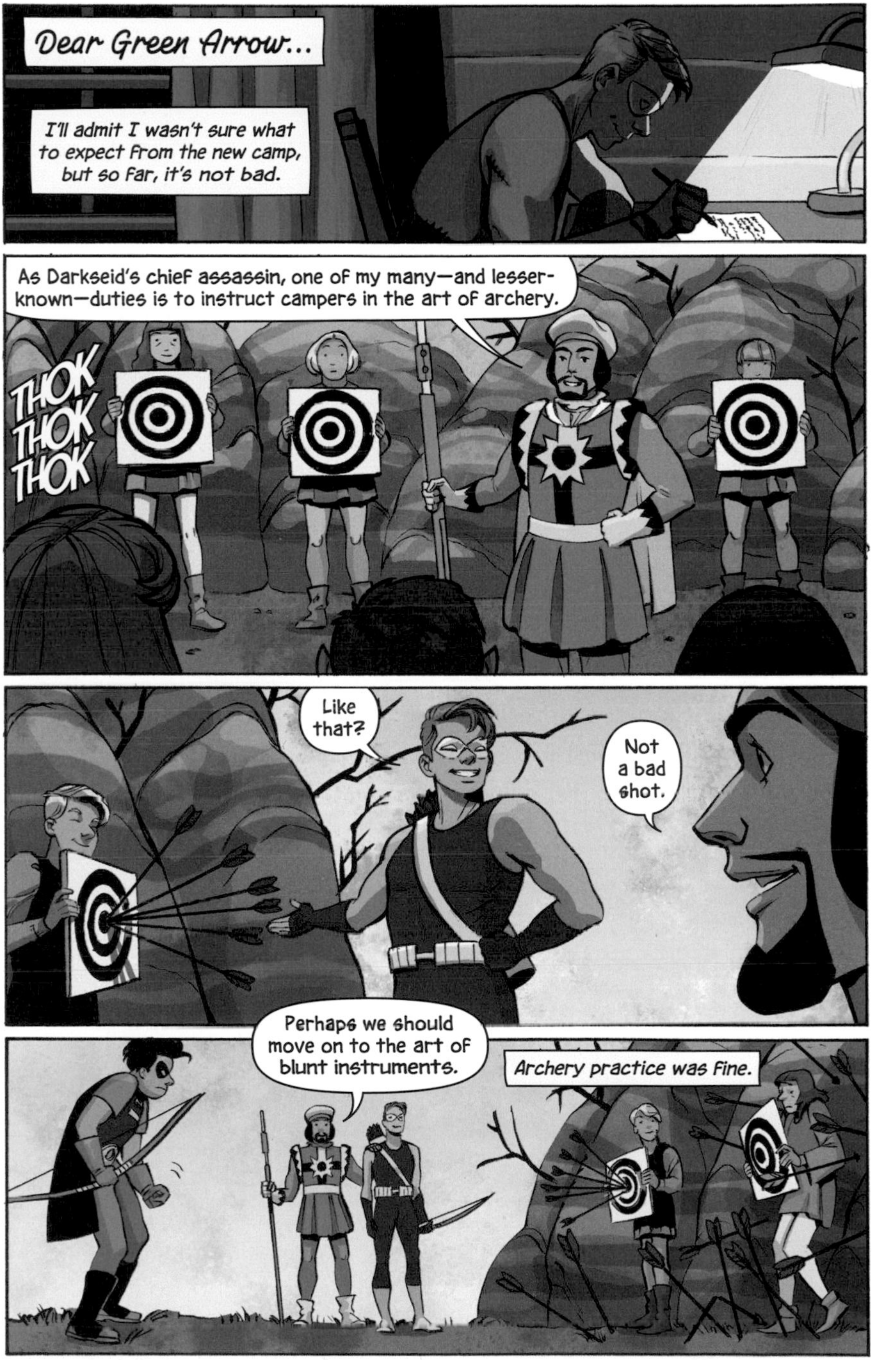

Dear Green Arrow...
I'll admit I wasn't sure what to expect from the new camp, but so far, it's not bad.
As Darkseid's chief assassin, one of my many—and lesser-known—duties is to instruct campers in the art of archery.
THOK THOK THOK
Like that?
Not a bad shot.
Perhaps we should move on to the art of blunt instruments.
Archery practice was fine.

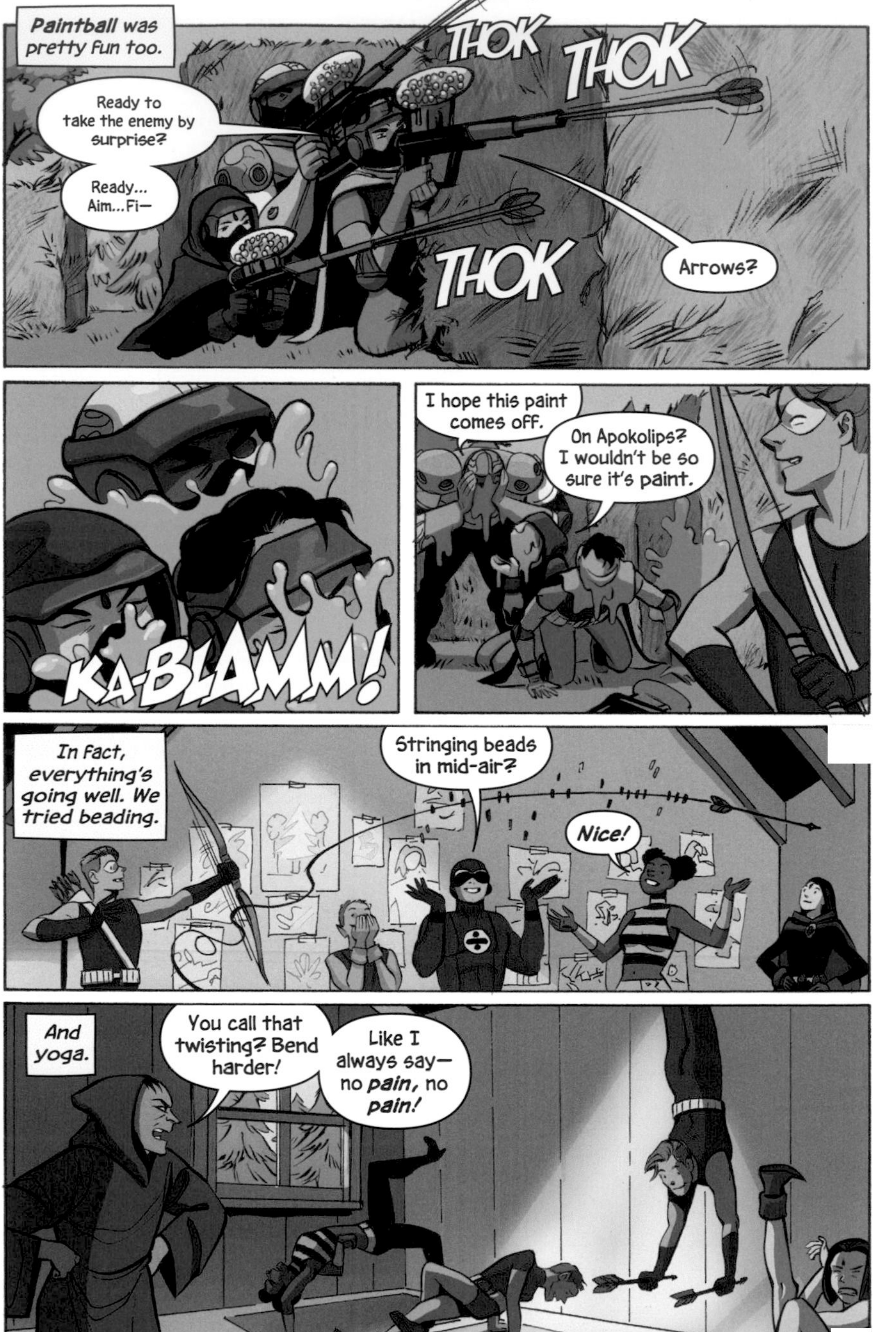
Paintball was pretty fun too.
THOK
THOK
Ready to take the enemy by surprise?
Ready... Aim...Fi—
THOK
Arrows?
KA-BLAMM!
I hope this paint comes off.
On Apokolips? I wouldn't be so sure it's paint.
In fact, everything's going well. We tried beading.
Stringing beads in mid-air?
Nice!
And yoga.
You call that twisting? Bend harder!
Like I always say— no pain, no pain!

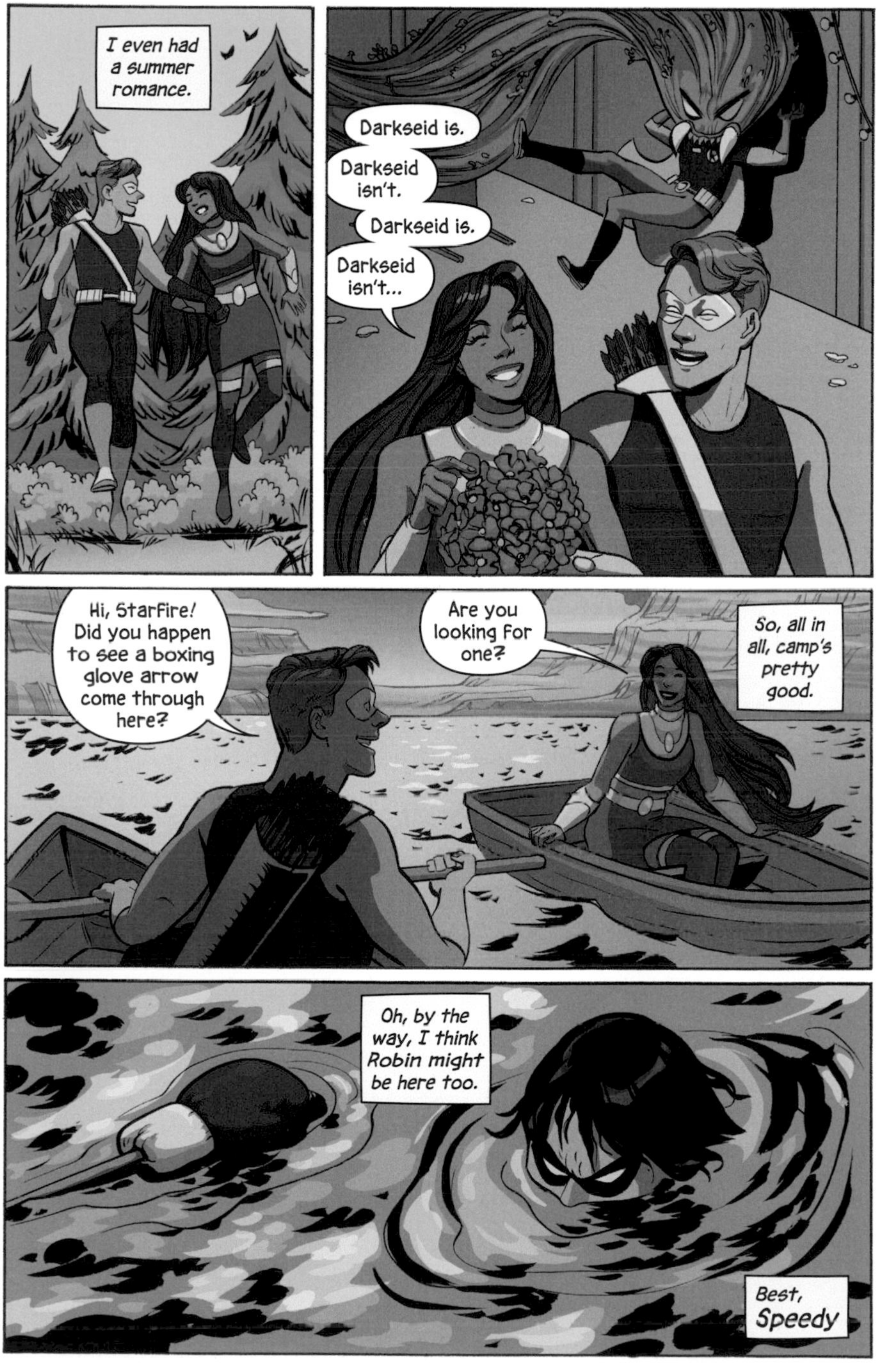
I even had a summer romance.
Darkseid is.
Darkseid isn't.
Darkseid is.
Darkseid isn't...
Hi, Starfire! Did you happen to see a boxing glove arrow come through here?
Are you looking for one?
So, all in all, camp's pretty good.
Oh, by the way, I think Robin might be here too.
Best,
Speedy

Chapter Six

Billy's letter drawn and colored by Erich Owen

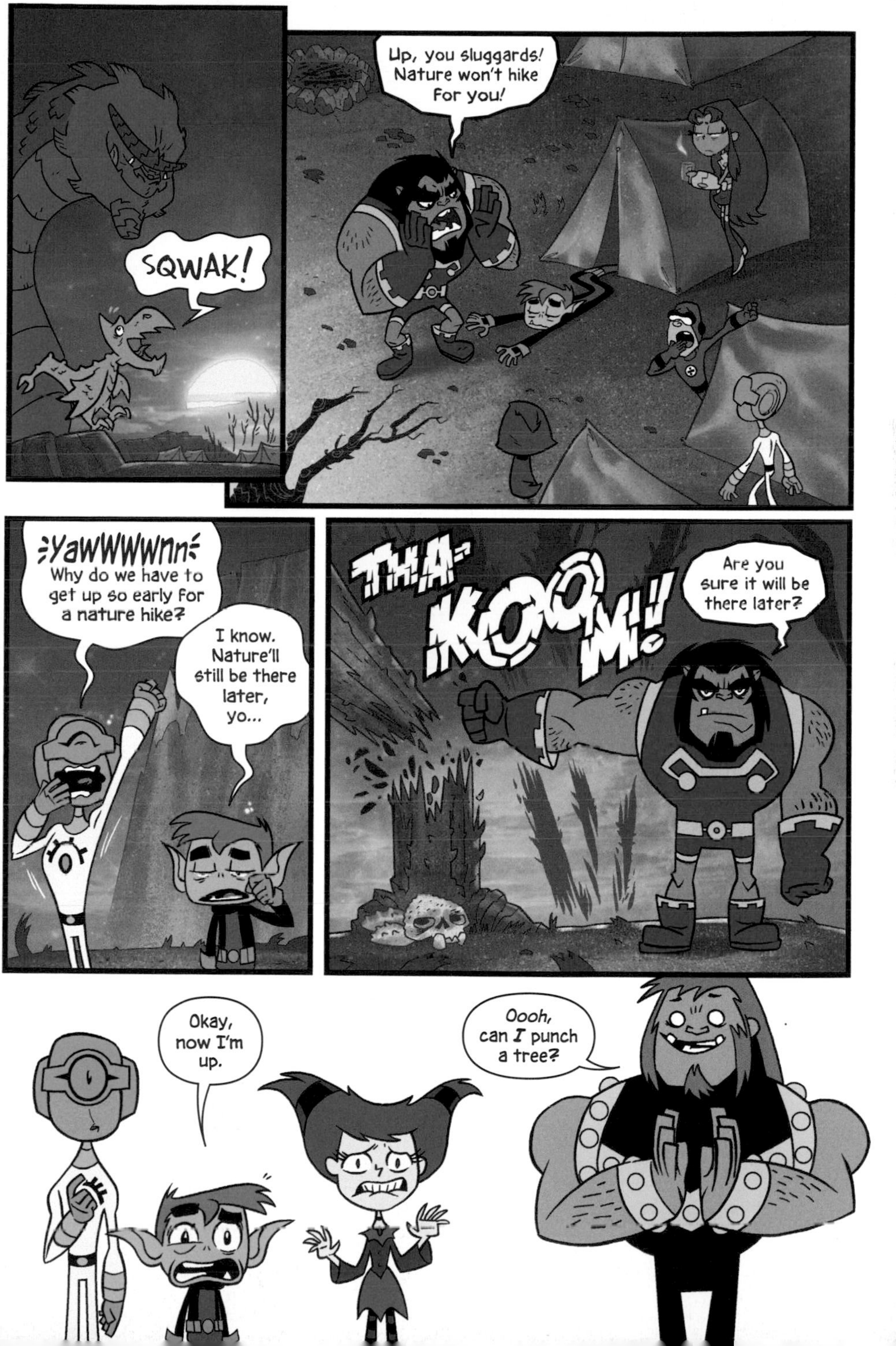
SQWAK!
Up, you sluggards! Nature won't hike for you!
yawWWWnn
Why do we have to get up so early for a nature hike?
I know. Nature'll still be there later, yo...
THA-KOOM!!
Are you sure it will be there later?
Okay, now I'm up.
Oooh, can I punch a tree?

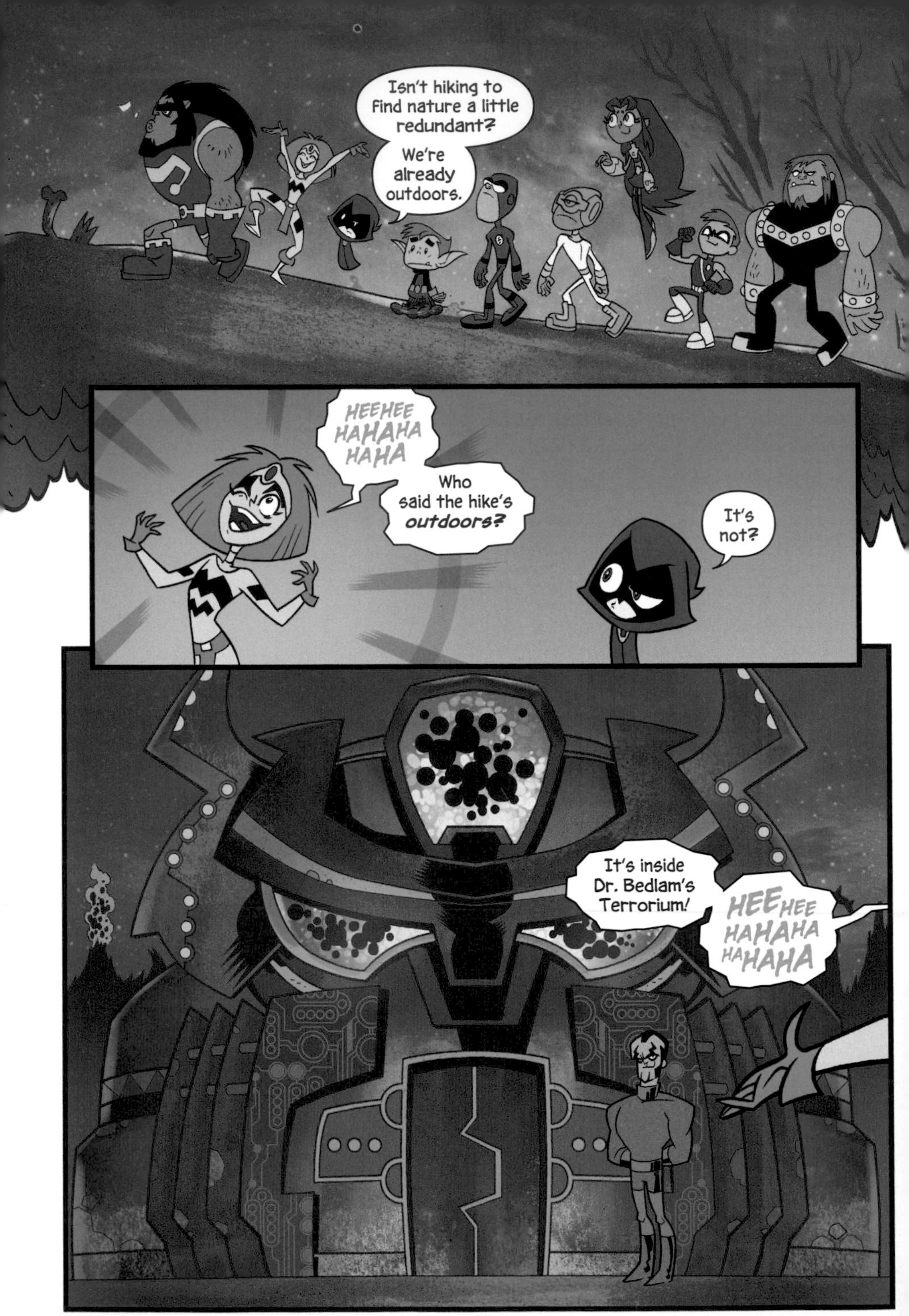
Isn't hiking to find nature a little redundant?
We're already outdoors.
HEEHEE HAHAHA HAHA
Who said the hike's *outdoors?*
It's not?
It's inside Dr. Bedlam's Terrorium!
HEEHEE HAHAHA HAHAHA

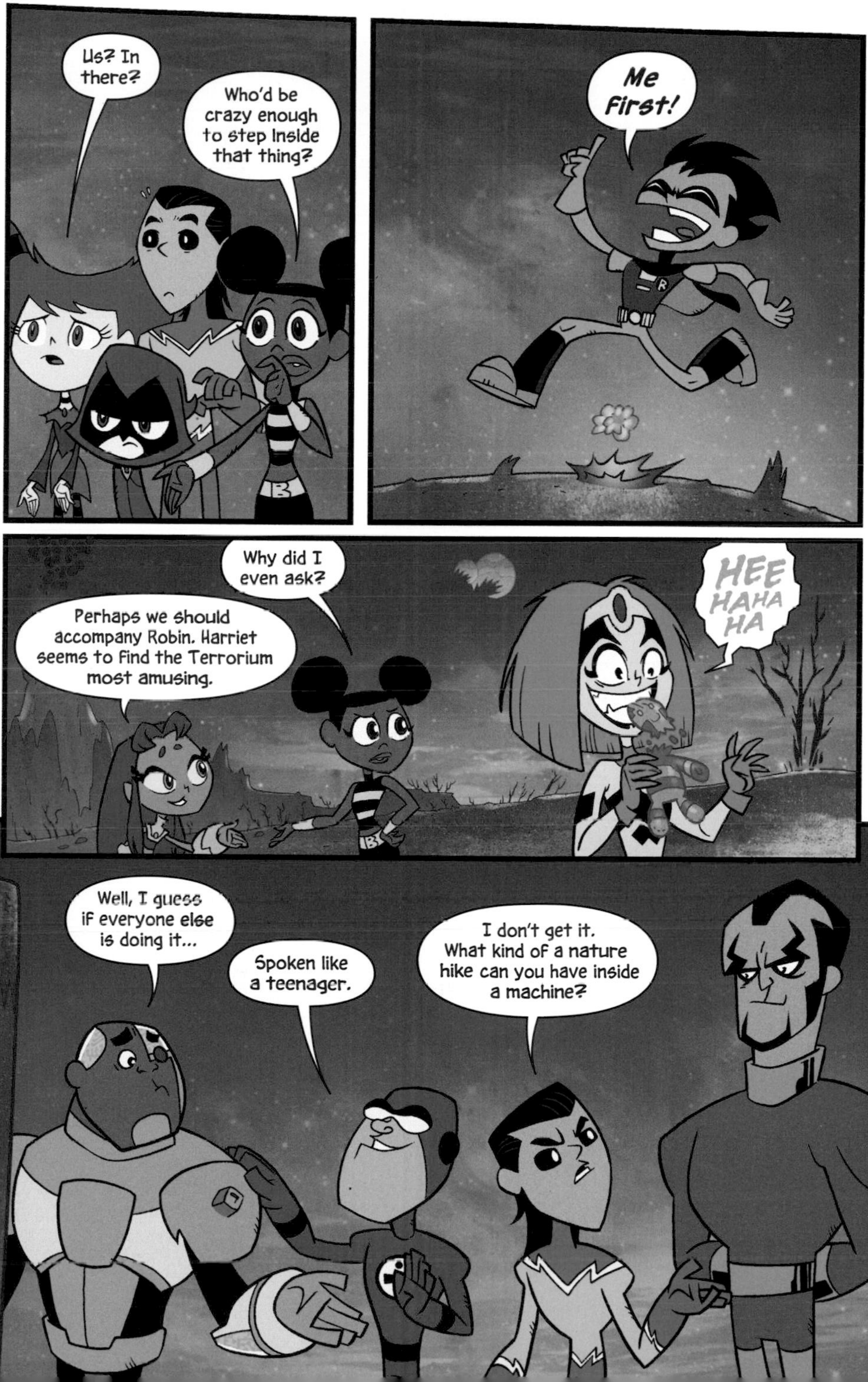
Us? In there?
Who'd be crazy enough to step inside that thing?
Me first!
Why did I even ask?
Perhaps we should accompany Robin. Harriet seems to find the Terrorium most amusing.
HEE HAHA HA
Well, I guess if everyone else is doing it...
Spoken like a teenager.
I don't get it. What kind of a nature hike can you have inside a machine?

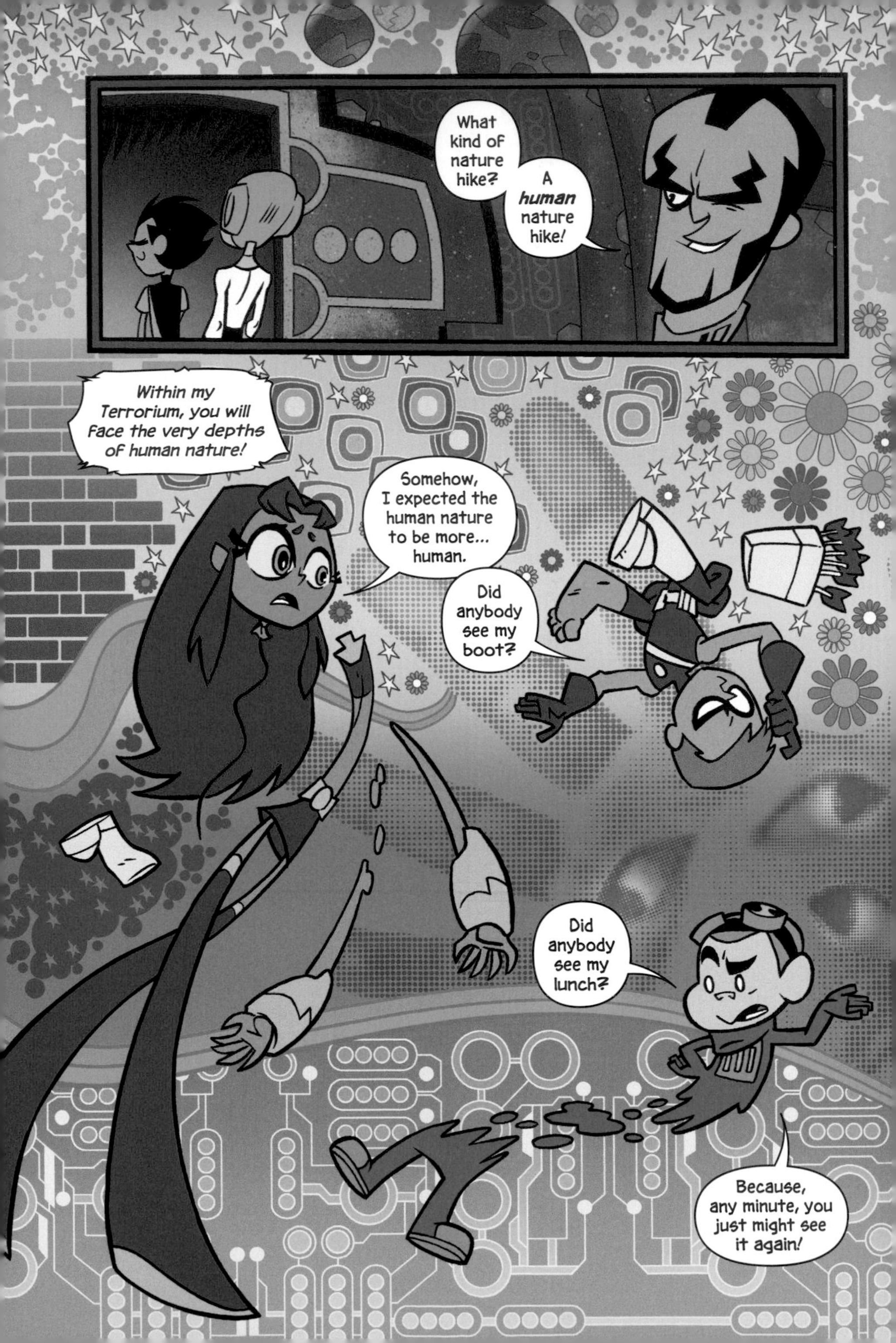
What kind of nature hike?
A *human* nature hike!
Within my Terrorium, you will face the very depths of human nature!
Somehow, I expected the human nature to be more... human.
Did anybody see my boot?
Did anybody see my lunch?
Because, any minute, you just might see it again!

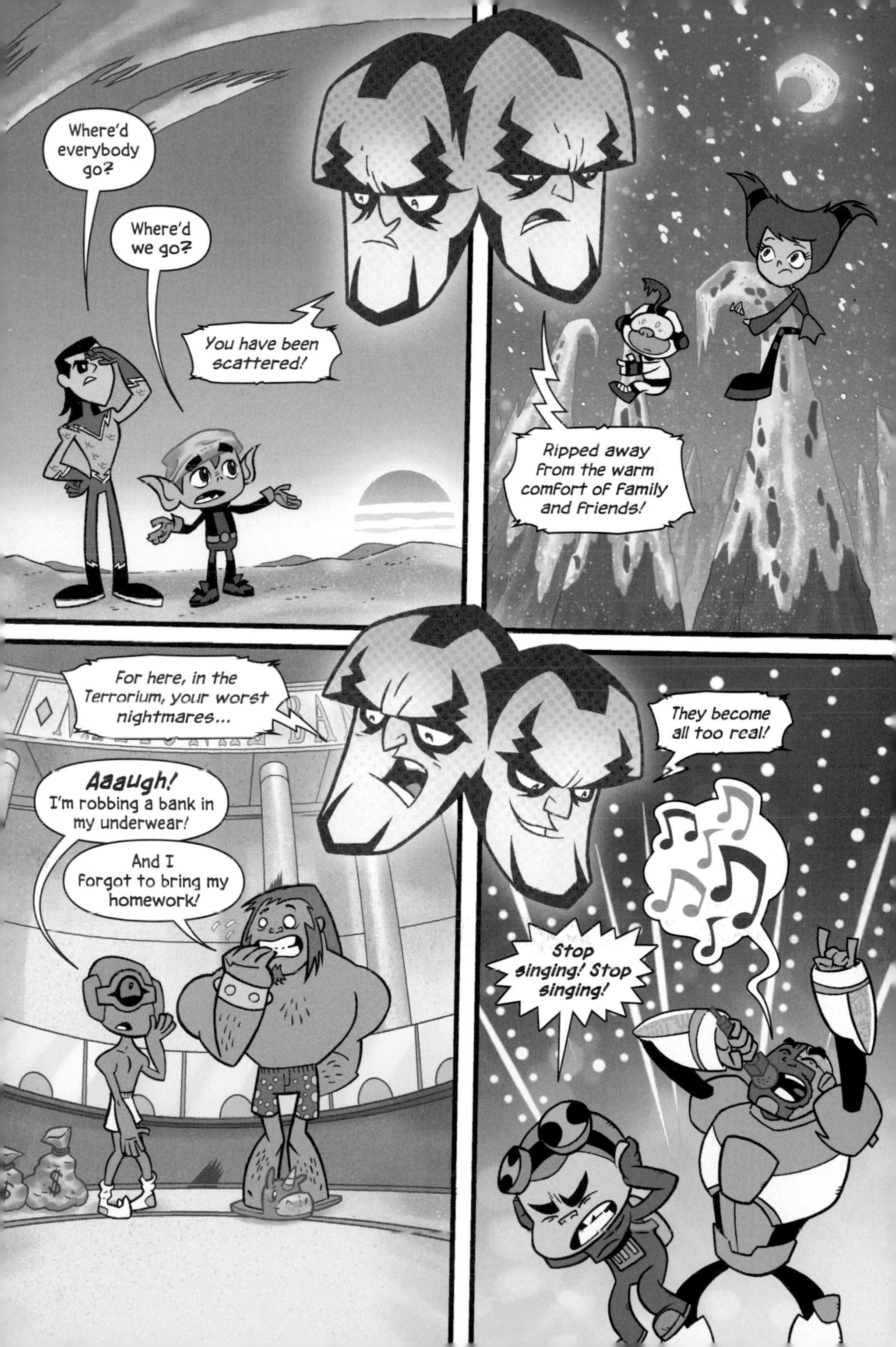
Where'd everybody go?
Where'd we go?
You have been scattered!
Ripped away from the warm comfort of family and friends!
For here, in the Terrorium, your worst nightmares...
Aaaugh! I'm robbing a bank in my underwear!
And I forgot to bring my homework!
They become all too real!
Stop singing! Stop singing!

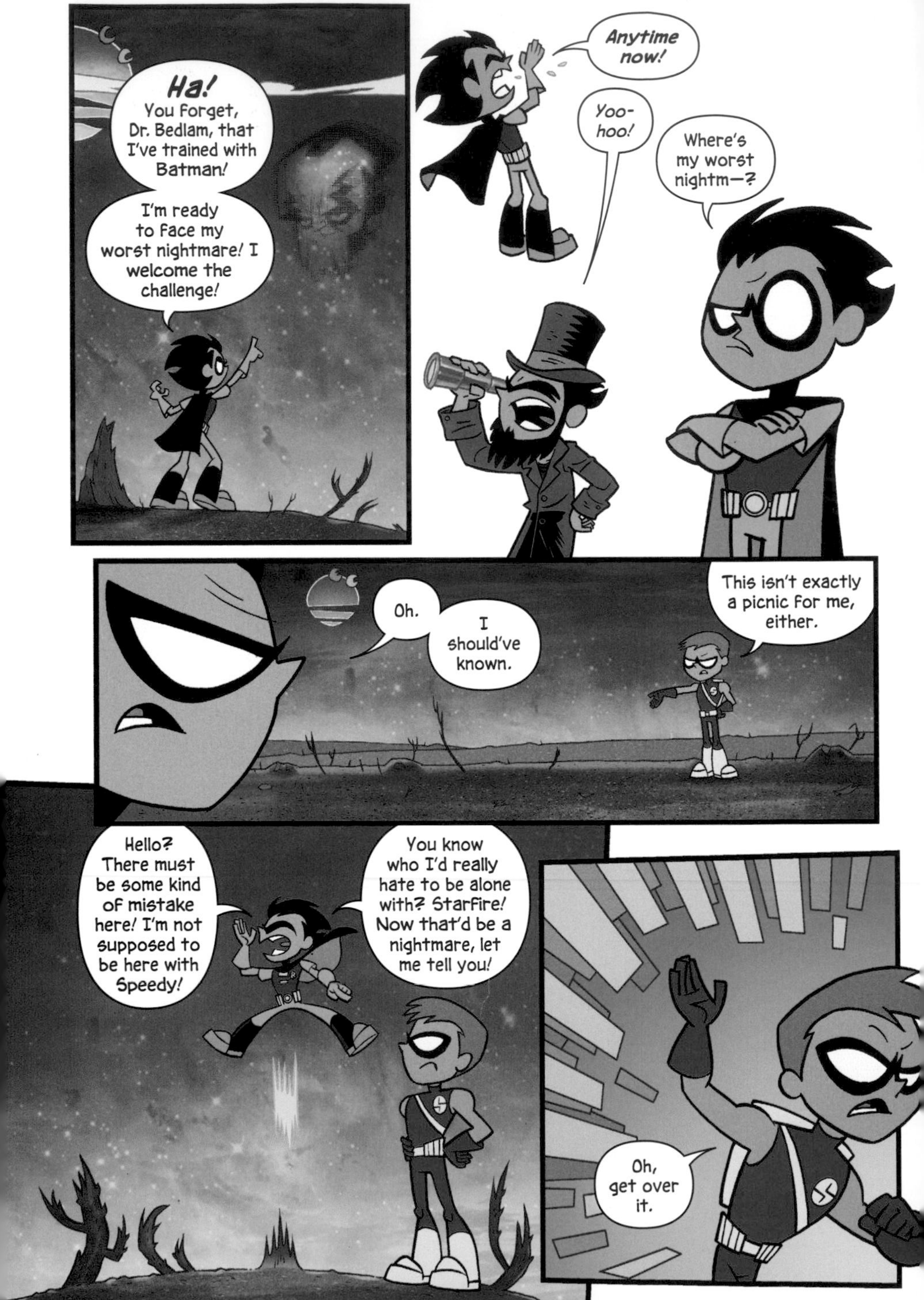
Ha! You forget, Dr. Bedlam, that I've trained with Batman!
I'm ready to face my worst nightmare! I welcome the challenge!
Anytime now!
Yoo-hoo!
Where's my worst nightm—?
Oh.
I should've known.
This isn't exactly a picnic for me, either.
Hello? There must be some kind of mistake here! I'm not supposed to be here with Speedy!
You know who I'd really hate to be alone with? Starfire! Now that'd be a nightmare, let me tell you!
Oh, get over it.

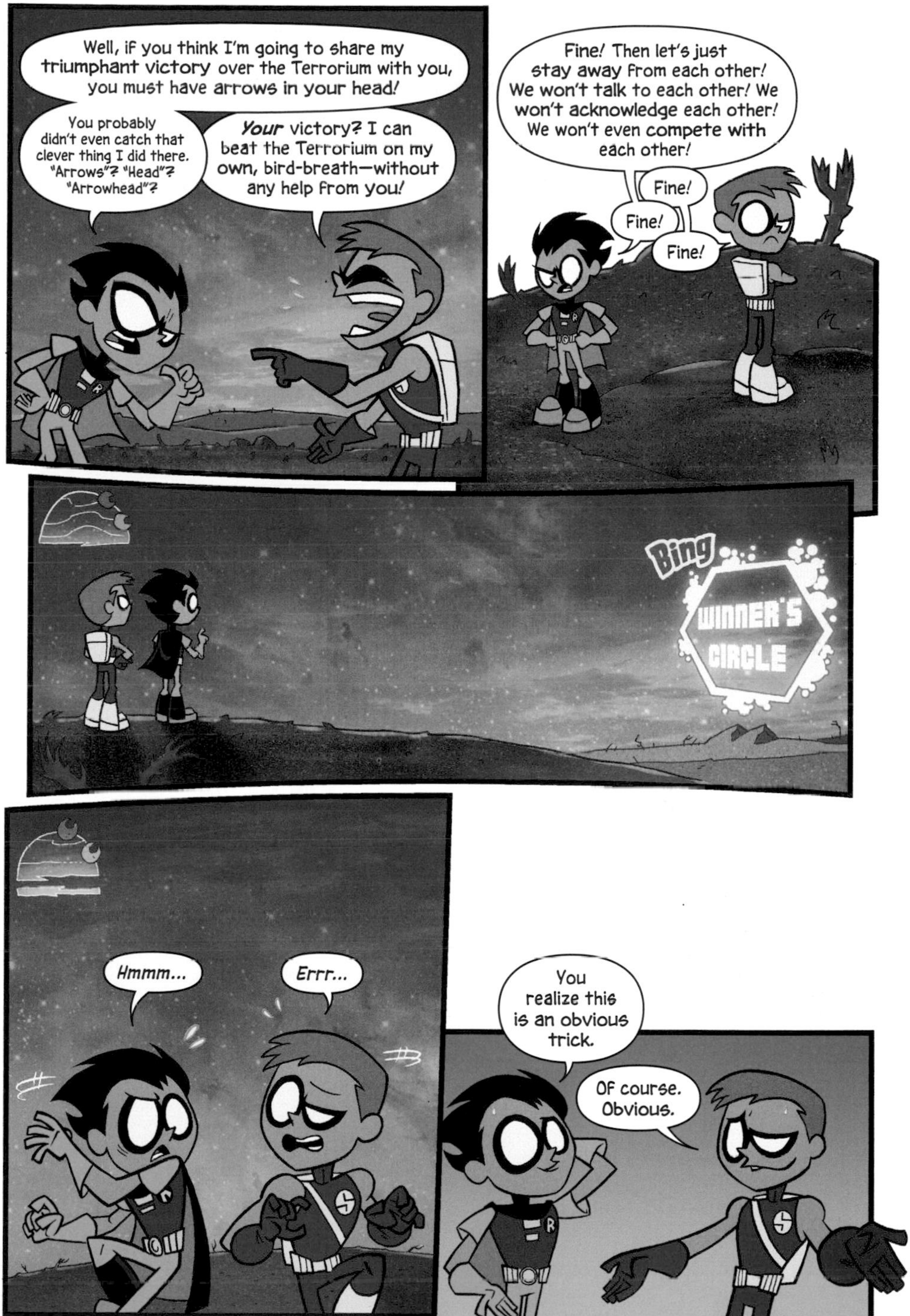
Well, if you think I'm going to share my triumphant victory over the Terrorium with you, you must have arrows in your head!
You probably didn't even catch that clever thing I did there. "Arrows"? "Head"? "Arrowhead"?
Your victory? I can beat the Terrorium on my own, bird-breath—without any help from you!
Fine! Then let's just stay away from each other! We won't talk to each other! We won't acknowledge each other! We won't even compete with each other!
Fine!
Fine!
Fine!
Bing
WINNER'S CIRCLE
Hmmm...
Errr...
You realize this is an obvious trick.
Of course. Obvious.

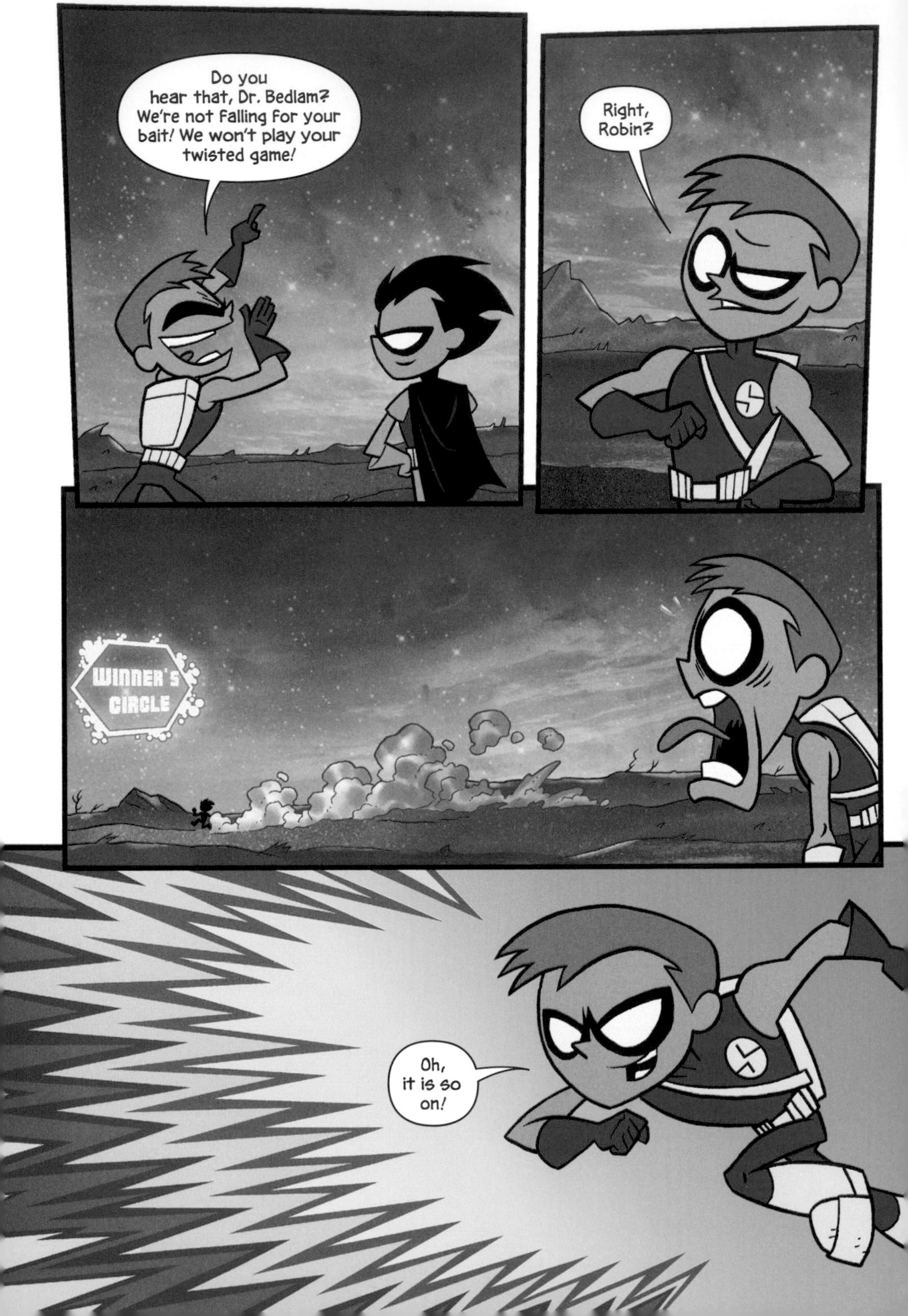

Do you hear that, Dr. Bedlam? We're not falling for your bait! We won't play your twisted game!
Right, Robin?
WINNER'S CIRCLE
Oh, it is so on!

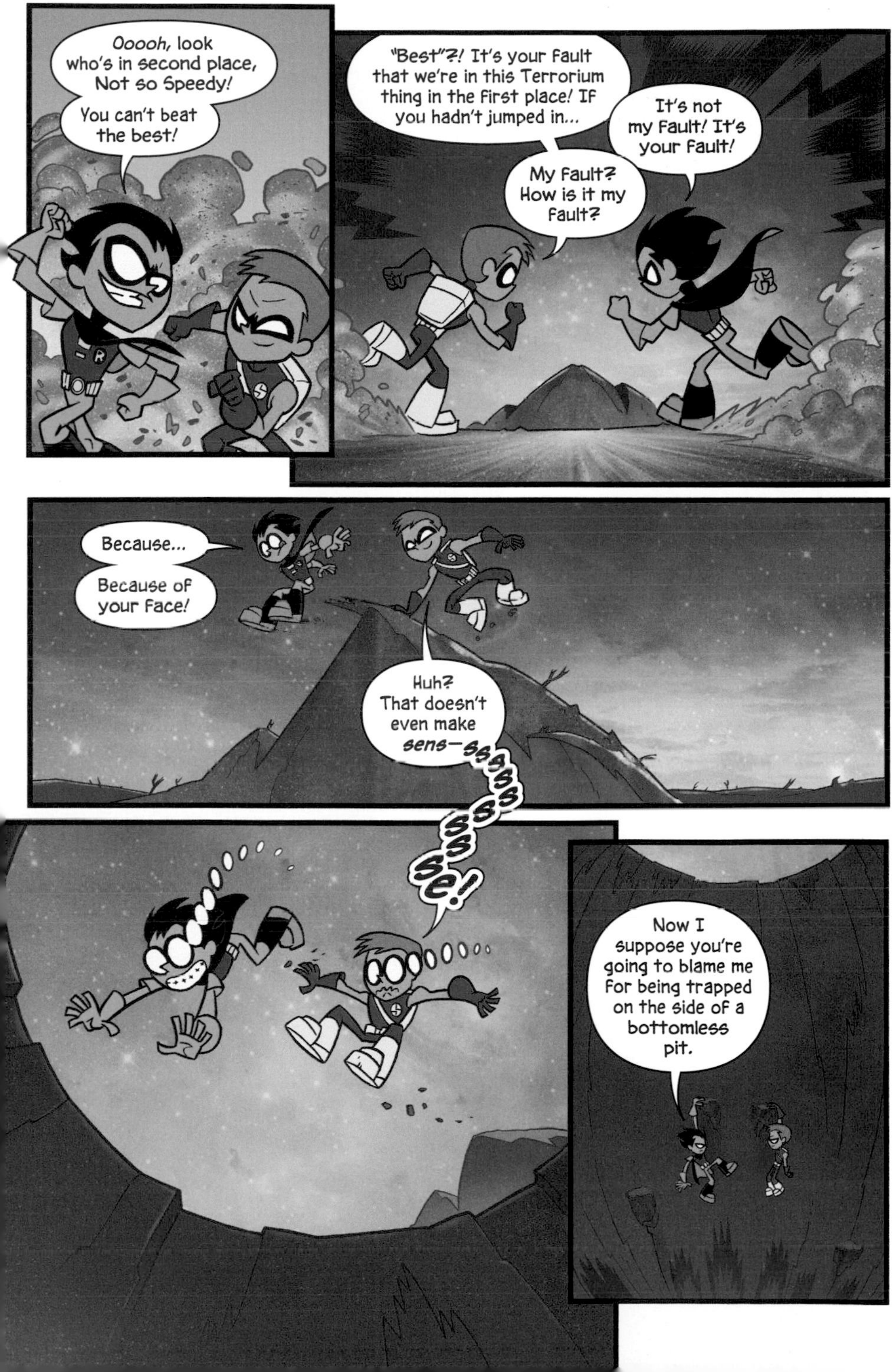

Ooooh, look who's in second place, Not so Speedy!
You can't beat the best!
"Best"?! It's your fault that we're in this Terrorium thing in the first place! If you hadn't jumped in...
It's not my fault! It's your fault!
My fault? How is it my fault?
Because...
Because of your face!
Huh? That doesn't even make *sens—*
SSSSSSSSSSSe!
Now I suppose you're going to blame me for being trapped on the side of a bottomless pit.

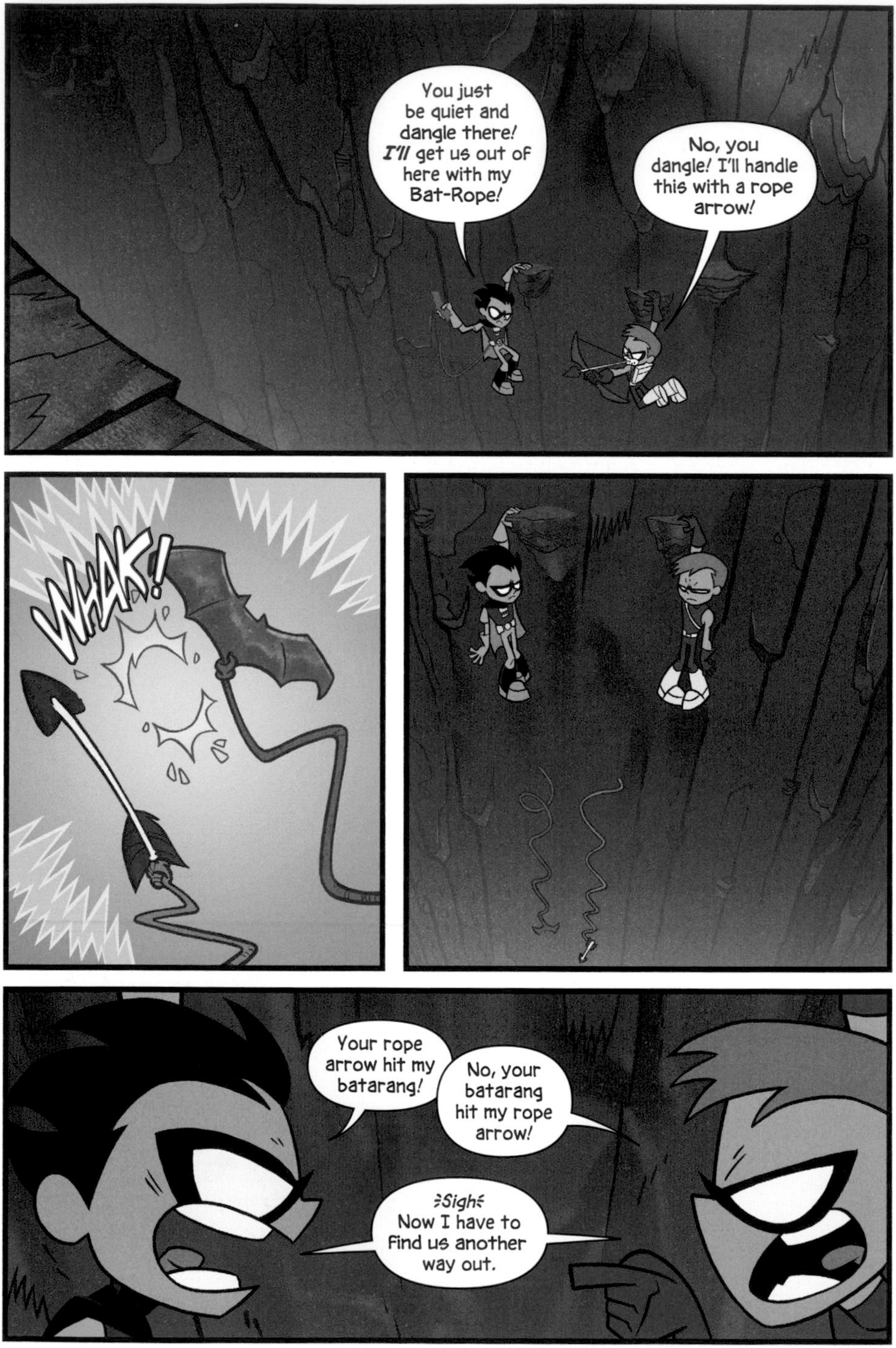
You just be quiet and dangle there! I'll get us out of here with my Bat-Rope!
No, you dangle! I'll handle this with a rope arrow!
WHAK!
Your rope arrow hit my batarang!
No, your batarang hit my rope arrow!
Sigh
Now I have to find us another way out.

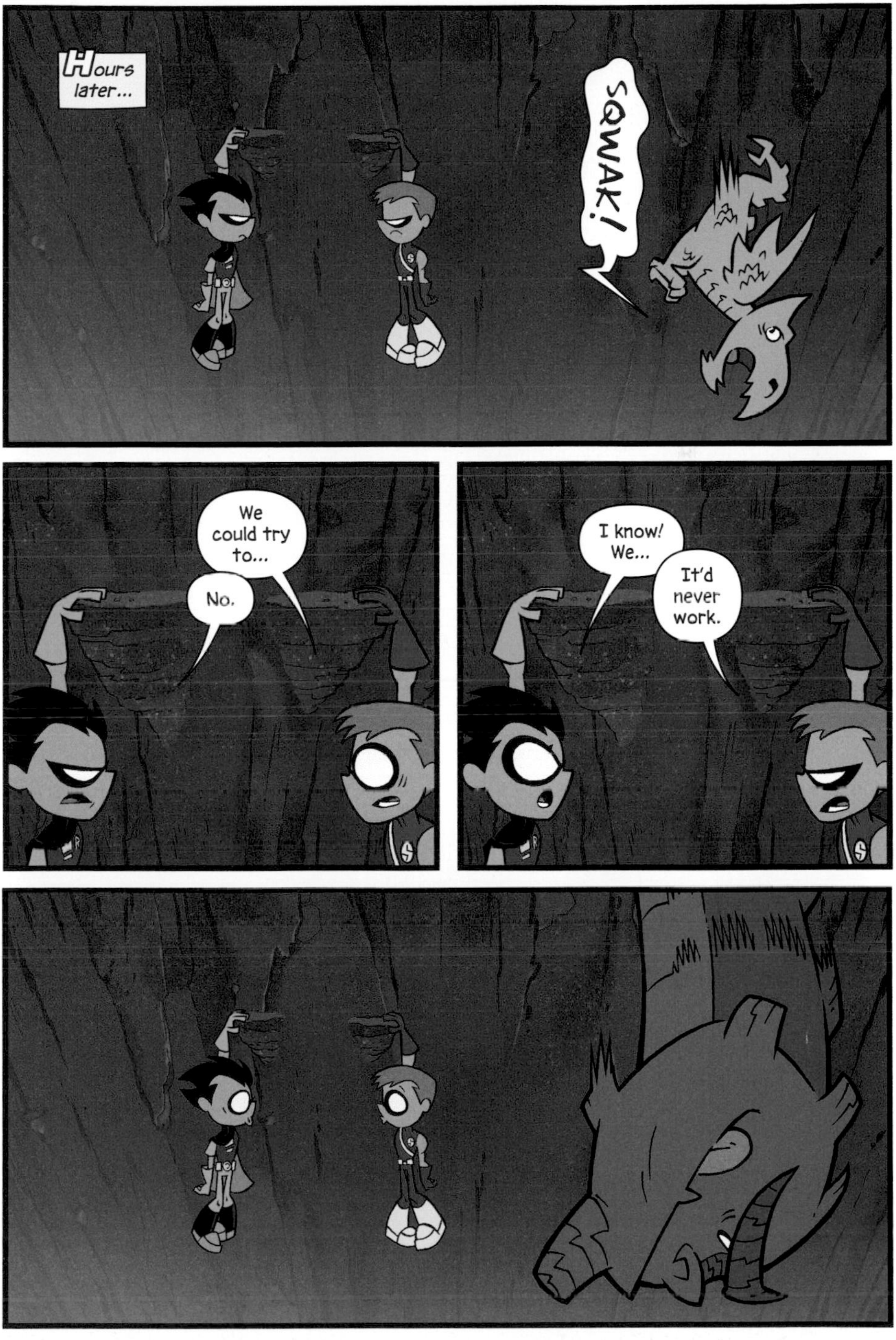
Hours later...
SQWAK!
We could try to...
No.
I know! We...
It'd never work.

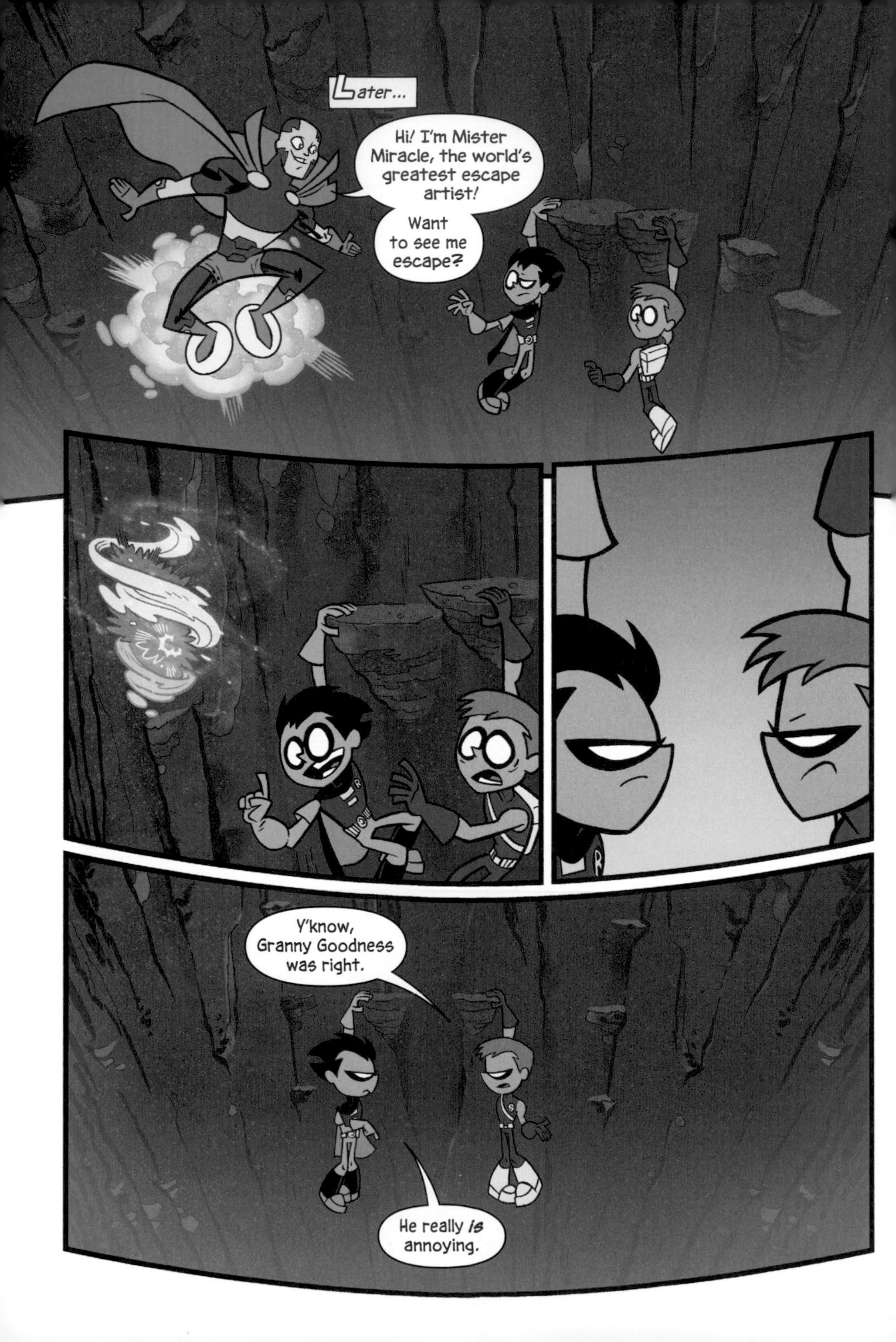
Later...
Hi! I'm Mister Miracle, the world's greatest escape artist!
Want to see me escape?
Y'know, Granny Goodness was right.
He really *is* annoying.

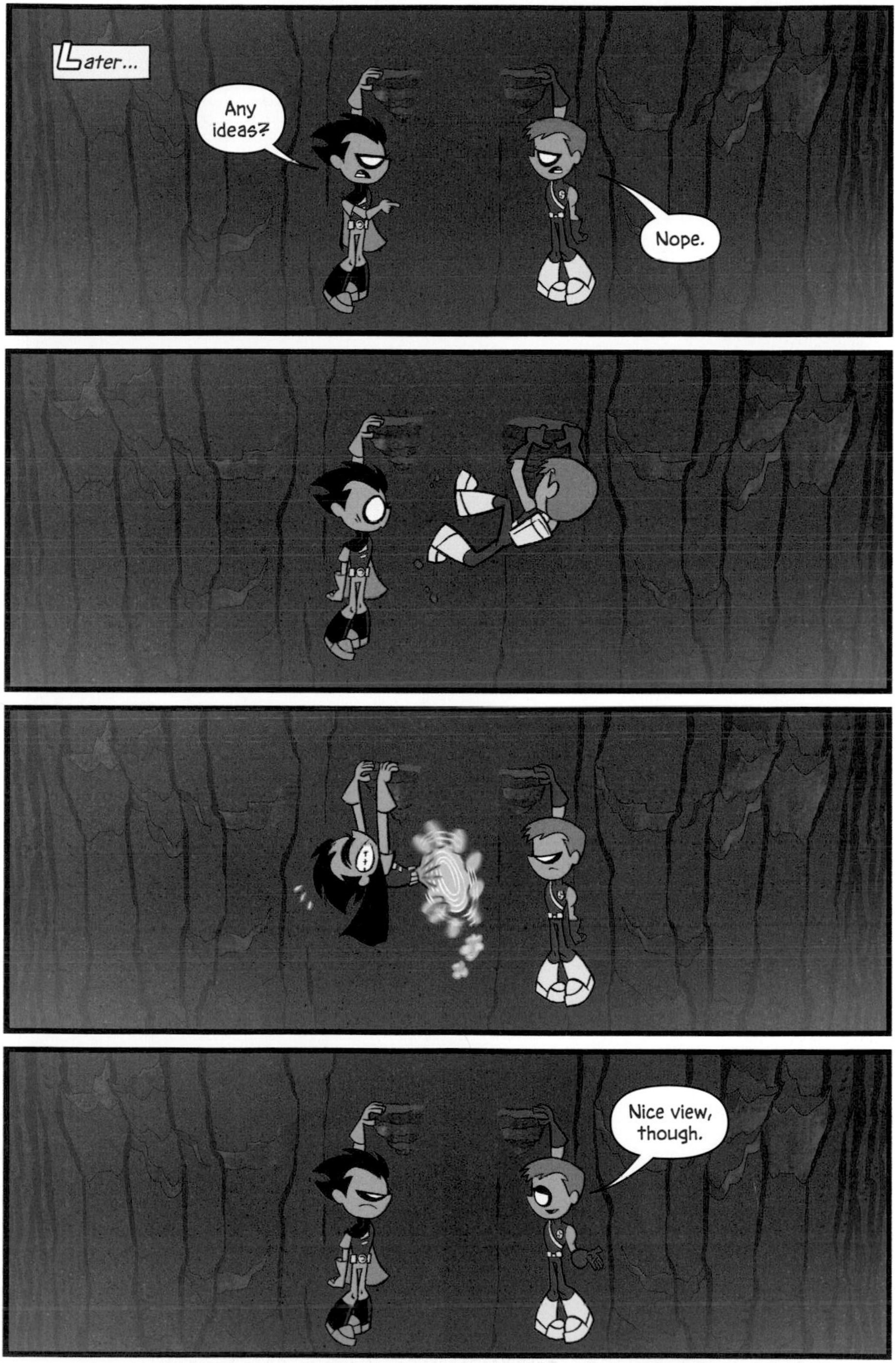
Later...
Any ideas?
Nope.
Nice view, though.

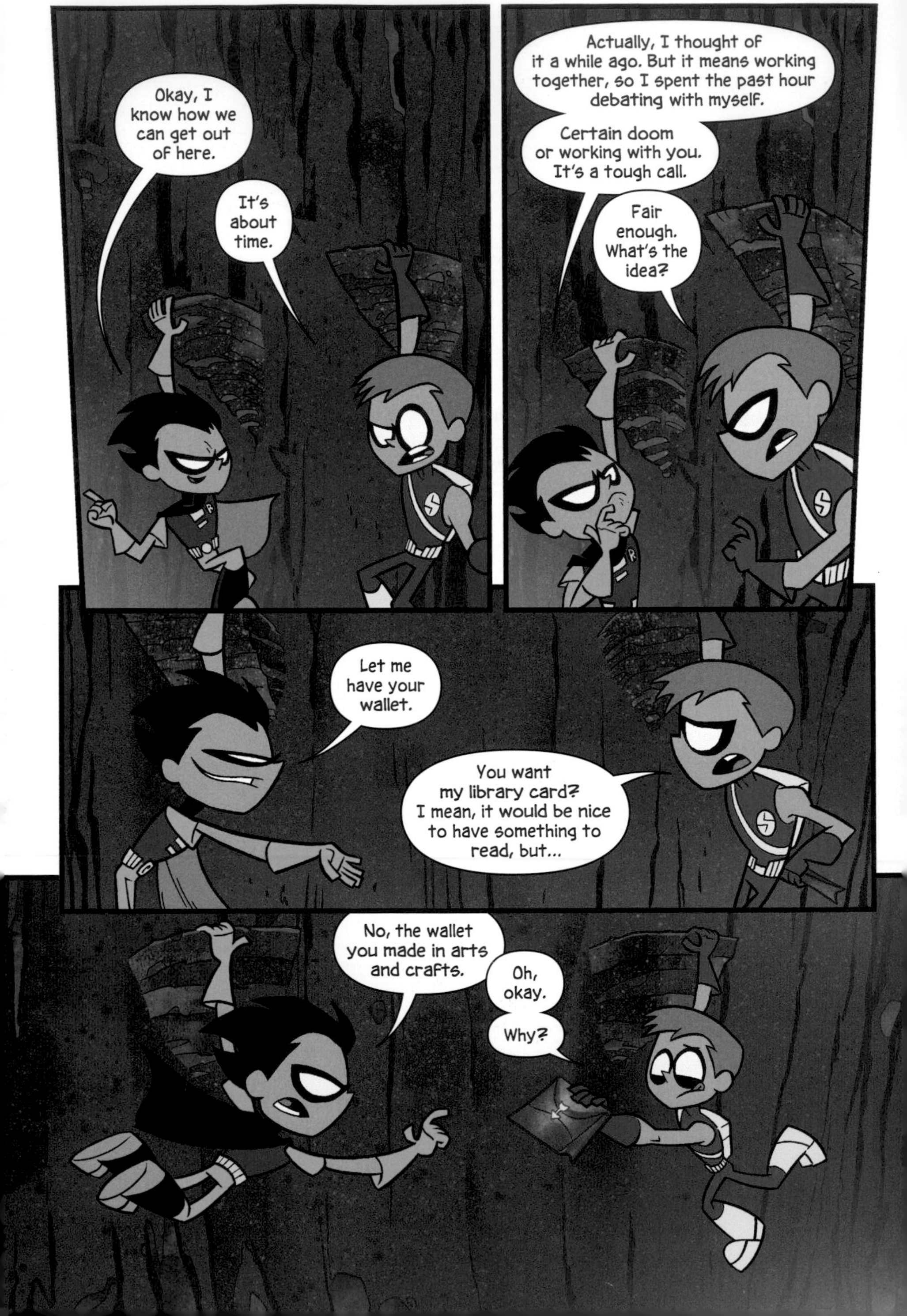
Okay, I know how we can get out of here.
It's about time.
Actually, I thought of it a while ago. But it means working together, so I spent the past hour debating with myself.
Certain doom or working with you. It's a tough call.
Fair enough. What's the idea?
Let me have your wallet.
You want my library card? I mean, it would be nice to have something to read, but...
No, the wallet you made in arts and crafts.
Oh, okay.
Why?

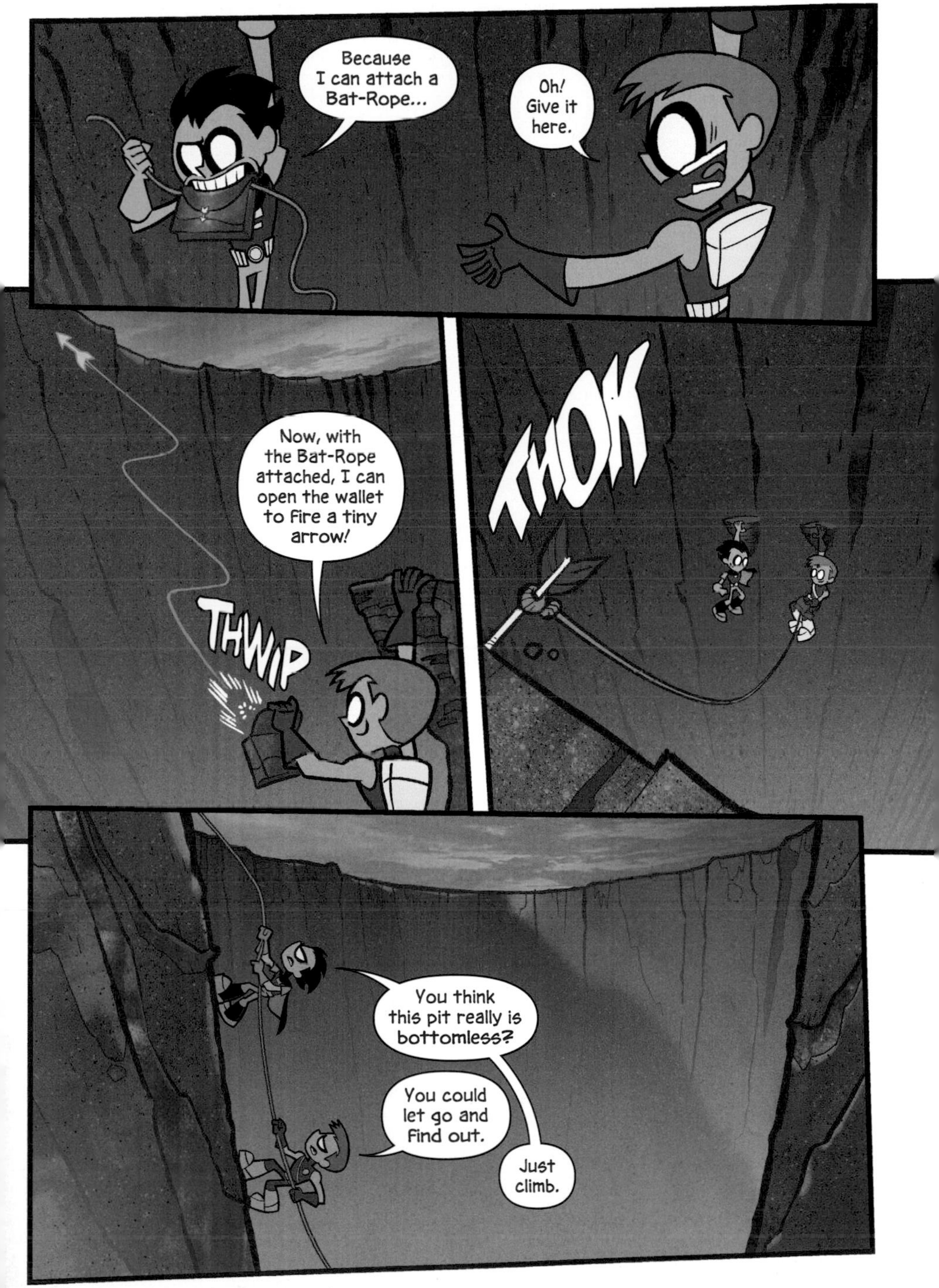
Because I can attach a Bat-Rope...
Oh! Give it here.
Now, with the Bat-Rope attached, I can open the wallet to fire a tiny arrow!
THWIP
THOK
You think this pit really is bottomless?
You could let go and find out.
Just climb.

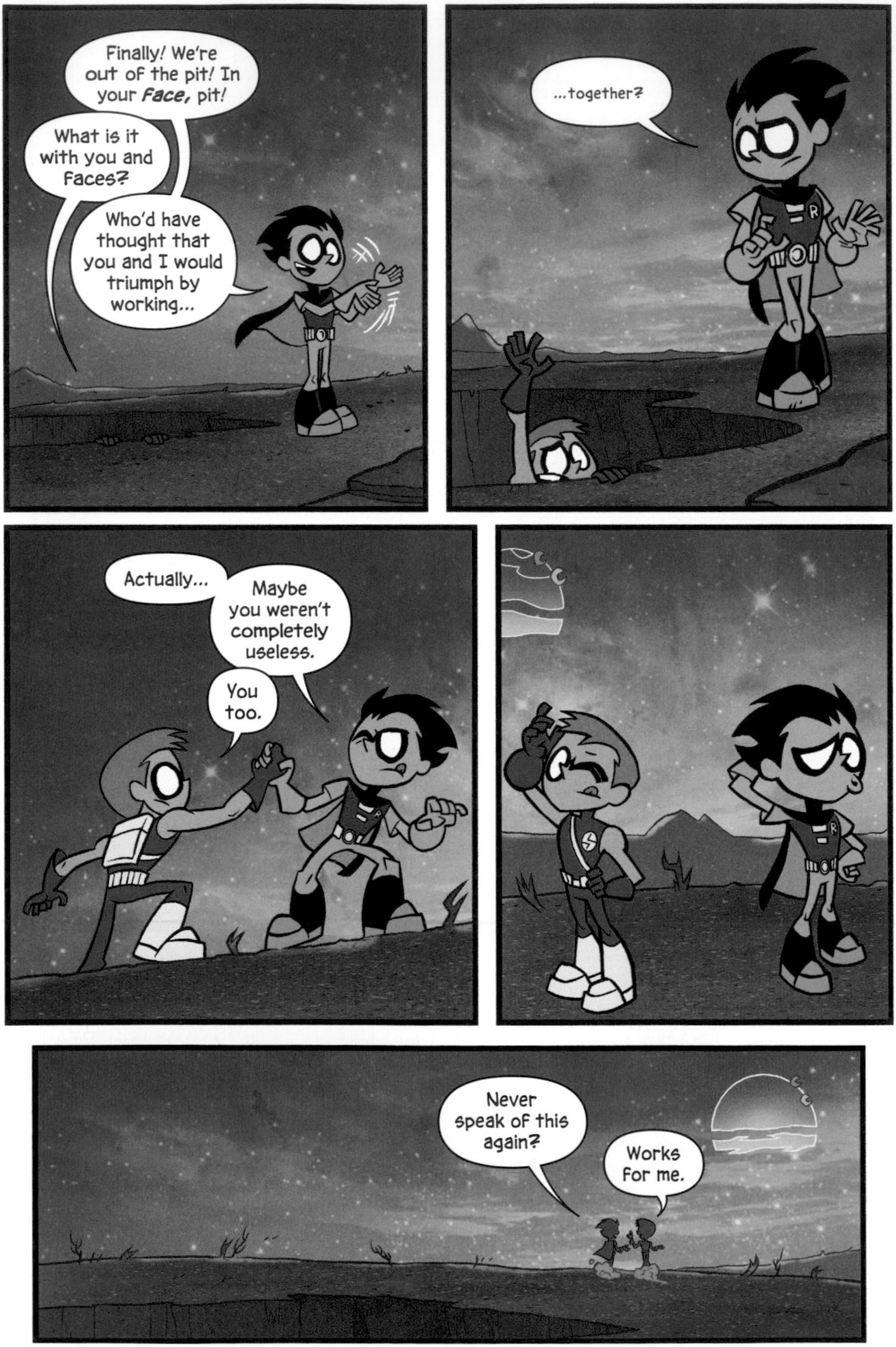
Finally! We're out of the pit! In your *Face,* pit!
What is it with you and Faces?
Who'd have thought that you and I would triumph by working...
...together?
Actually...
Maybe you weren't completely useless.
You too.
Never speak of this again?
Works for me.

A letter from camp!

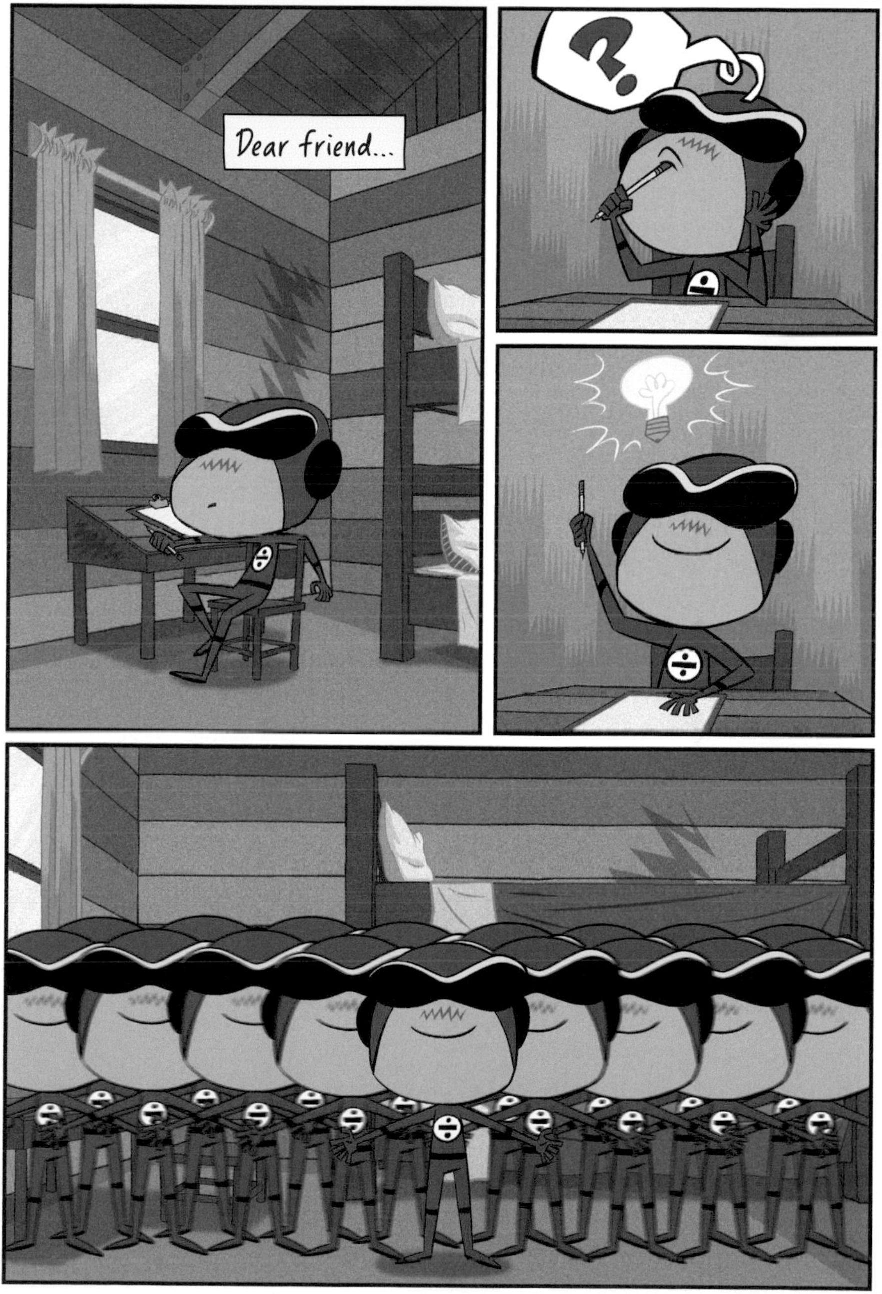

Dear friend...
?

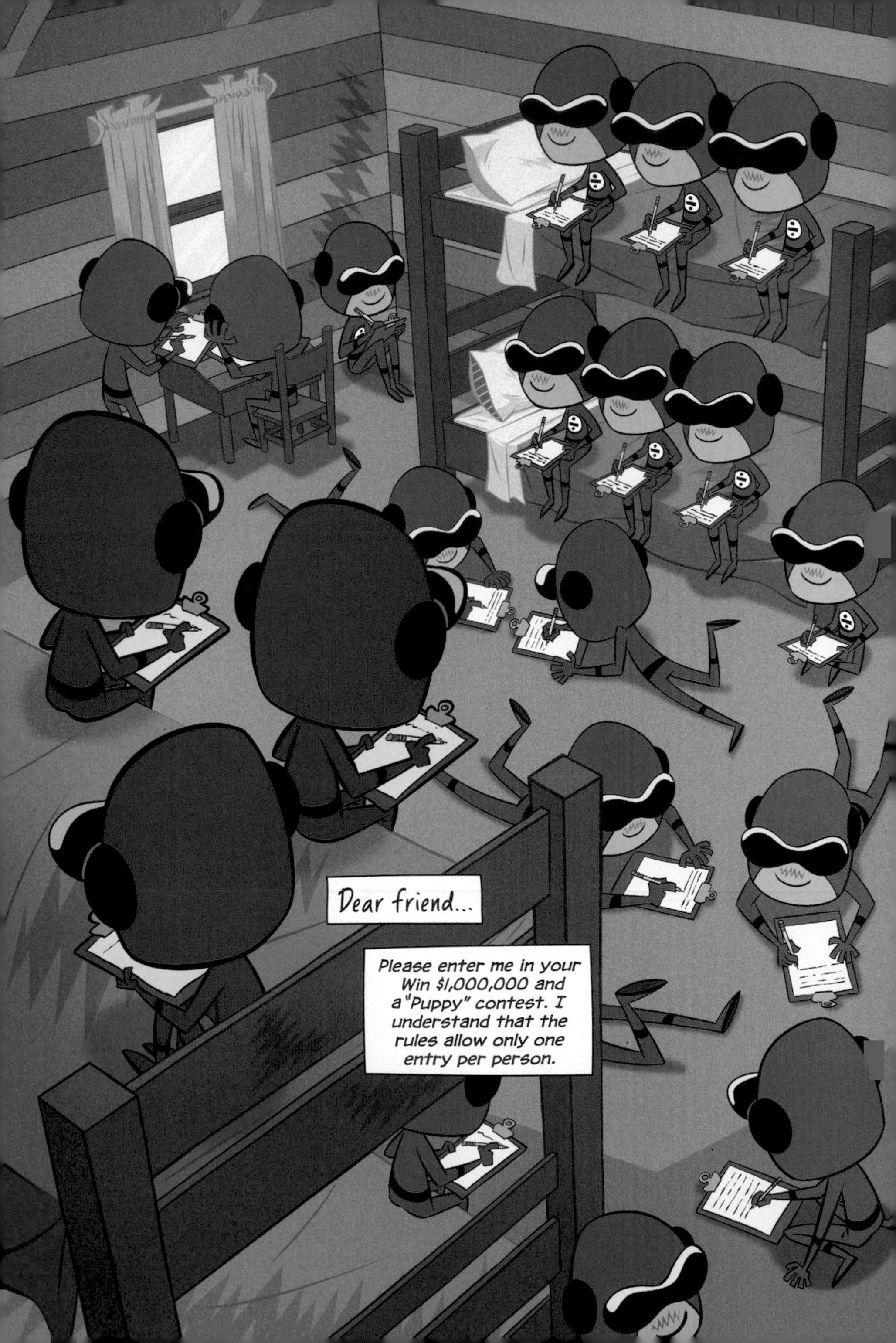
Dear friend...
Please enter me in your Win $1,000,000 and a "Puppy" contest. I understand that the rules allow only one entry per person.

Cyborg's letter drawn
and colored by Jamal Igle
Parademon's letter drawn and
colored by Franco

Chapter Seven

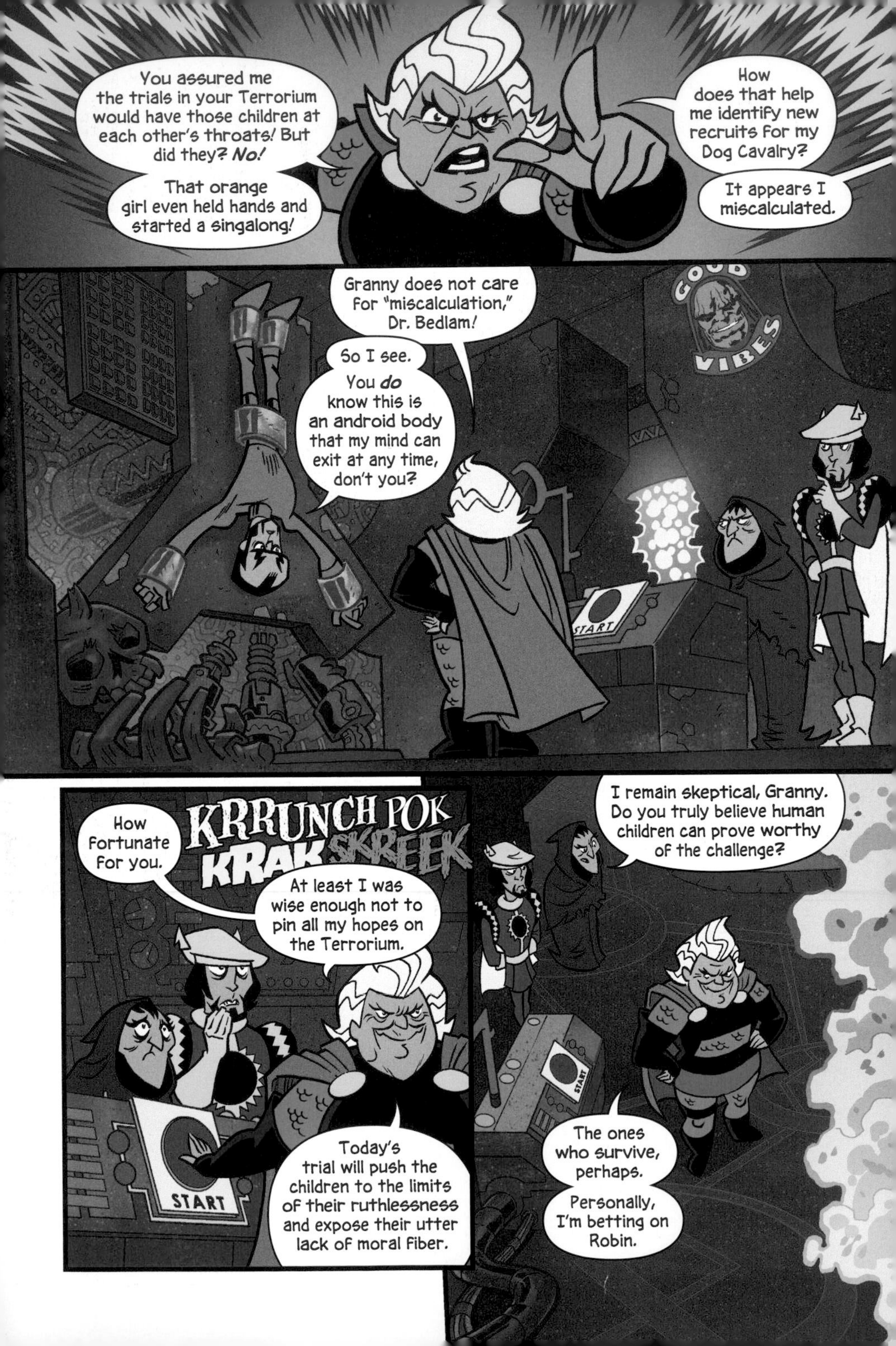
You assured me the trials in your Terrorium would have those children at each other's throats! But did they? *No!*
That orange girl even held hands and started a singalong!
How does that help me identify new recruits for my Dog Cavalry?
It appears I miscalculated.
Granny does not care for "miscalculation," Dr. Bedlam!
So I see.
You *do* know this is an android body that my mind can exit at any time, don't you?
GOOD VIBES
START
KRRUNCH POK
KRAK SKREEK
How fortunate for you.
At least I was wise enough not to pin all my hopes on the Terrorium.
START
Today's trial will push the children to the limits of their ruthlessness and expose their utter lack of moral fiber.
I remain skeptical, Granny. Do you truly believe human children can prove worthy of the challenge?
START
The ones who survive, perhaps.
Personally, I'm betting on Robin.

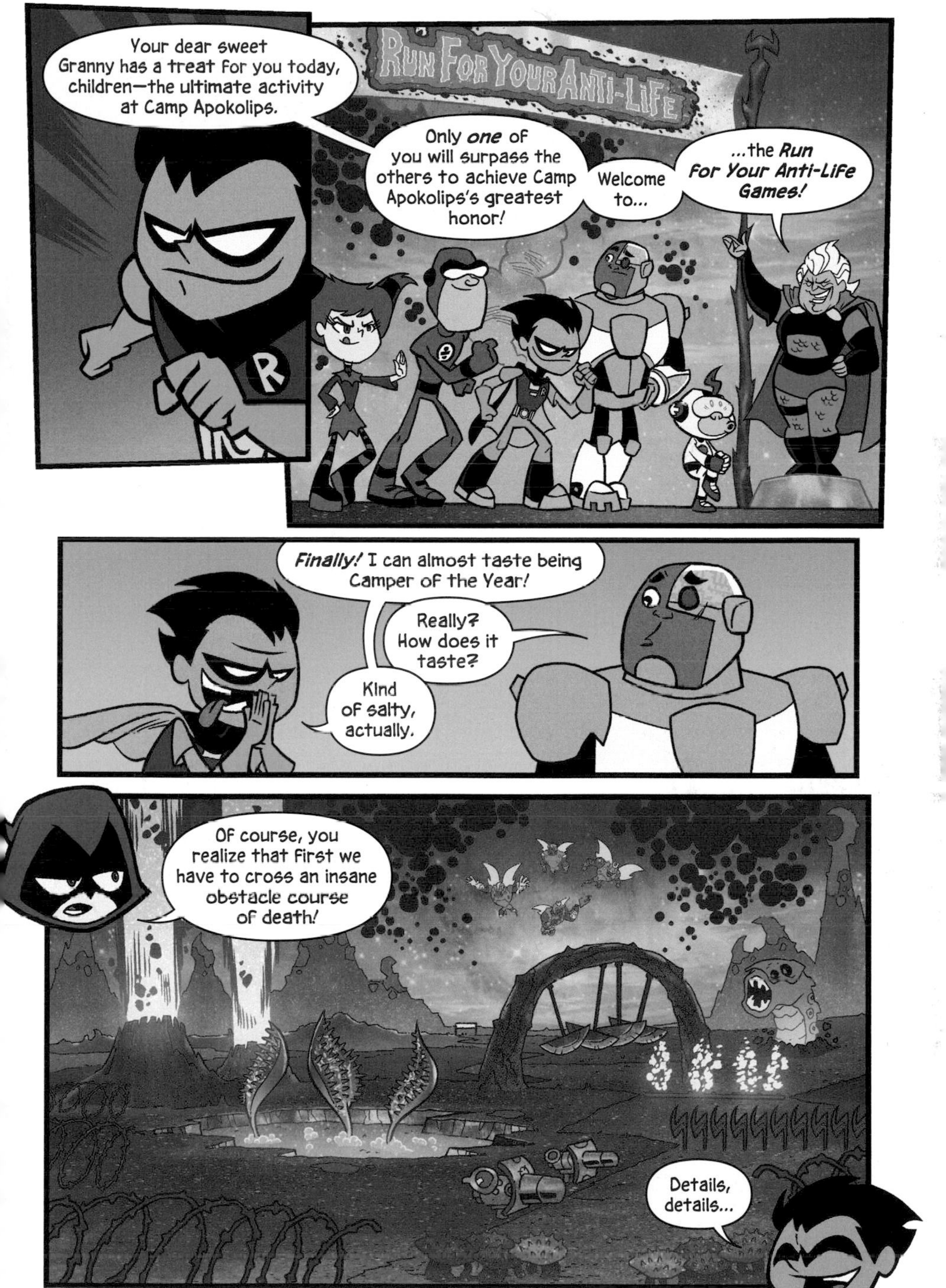

RUN FOR YOUR ANTI-LIFE
Your dear sweet Granny has a treat for you today, children—the ultimate activity at Camp Apokolips.
Only *one* of you will surpass the others to achieve Camp Apokolips's greatest honor!
Welcome to...
...the *Run For Your Anti-Life Games!*
Finally! I can almost taste being Camper of the Year!
Really? How does it taste?
Kind of salty, actually.
Of course, you realize that first we have to cross an insane obstacle course of death!
Details, details...

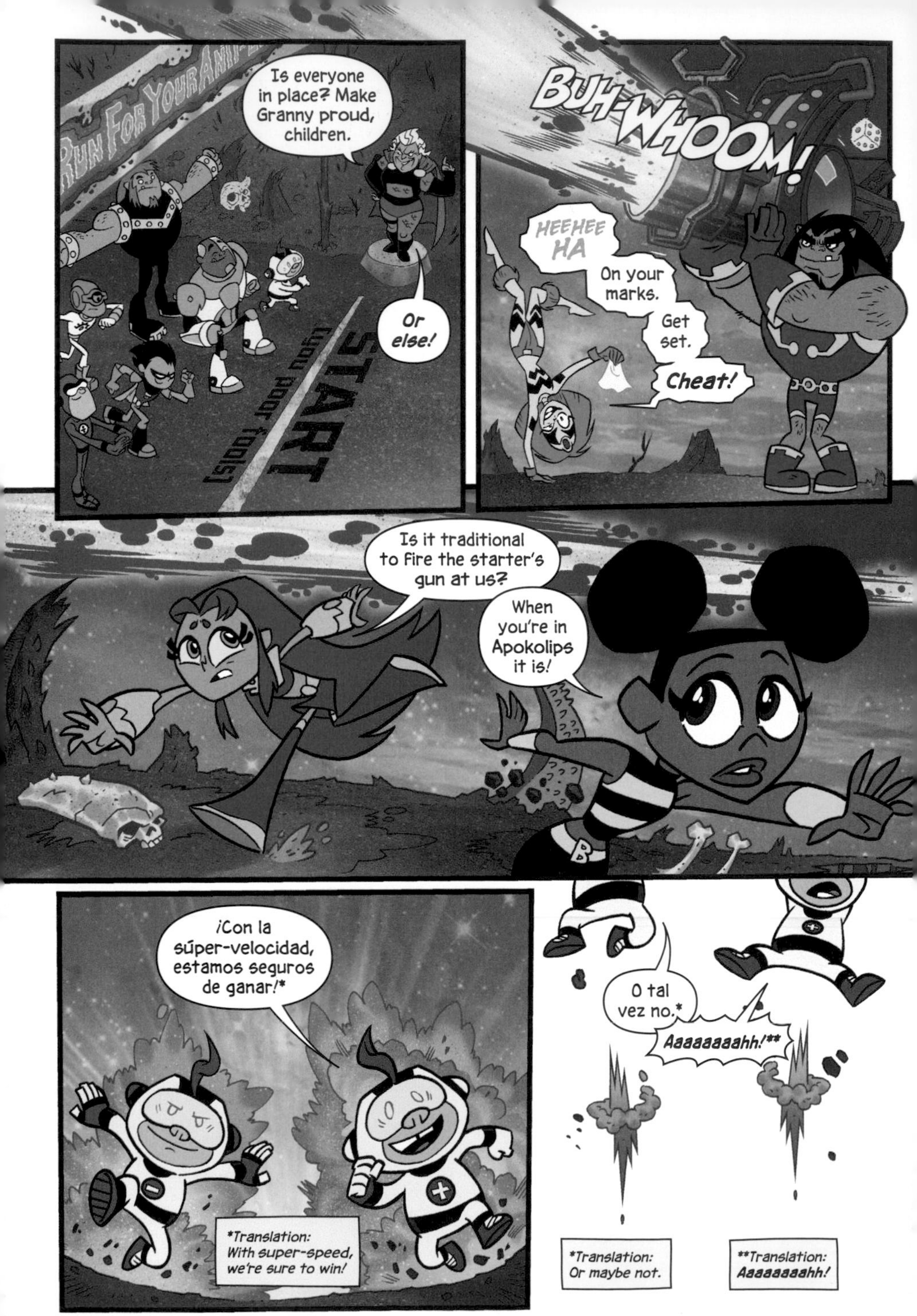
Is everyone in place? Make Granny proud, children.
START (you poor fools)
Or else!
BUH-WHOOM!
HEEHEE HA
On your marks.
Get set.
Cheat!
Is it traditional to fire the starter's gun at us?
When you're in Apokolips it is!
¡Con la súper-velocidad, estamos seguros de ganar!*
*Translation: With super-speed, we're sure to win!
O tal vez no.*
Aaaaaaaahh!**
*Translation: Or maybe not.
**Translation: Aaaaaaaahh!

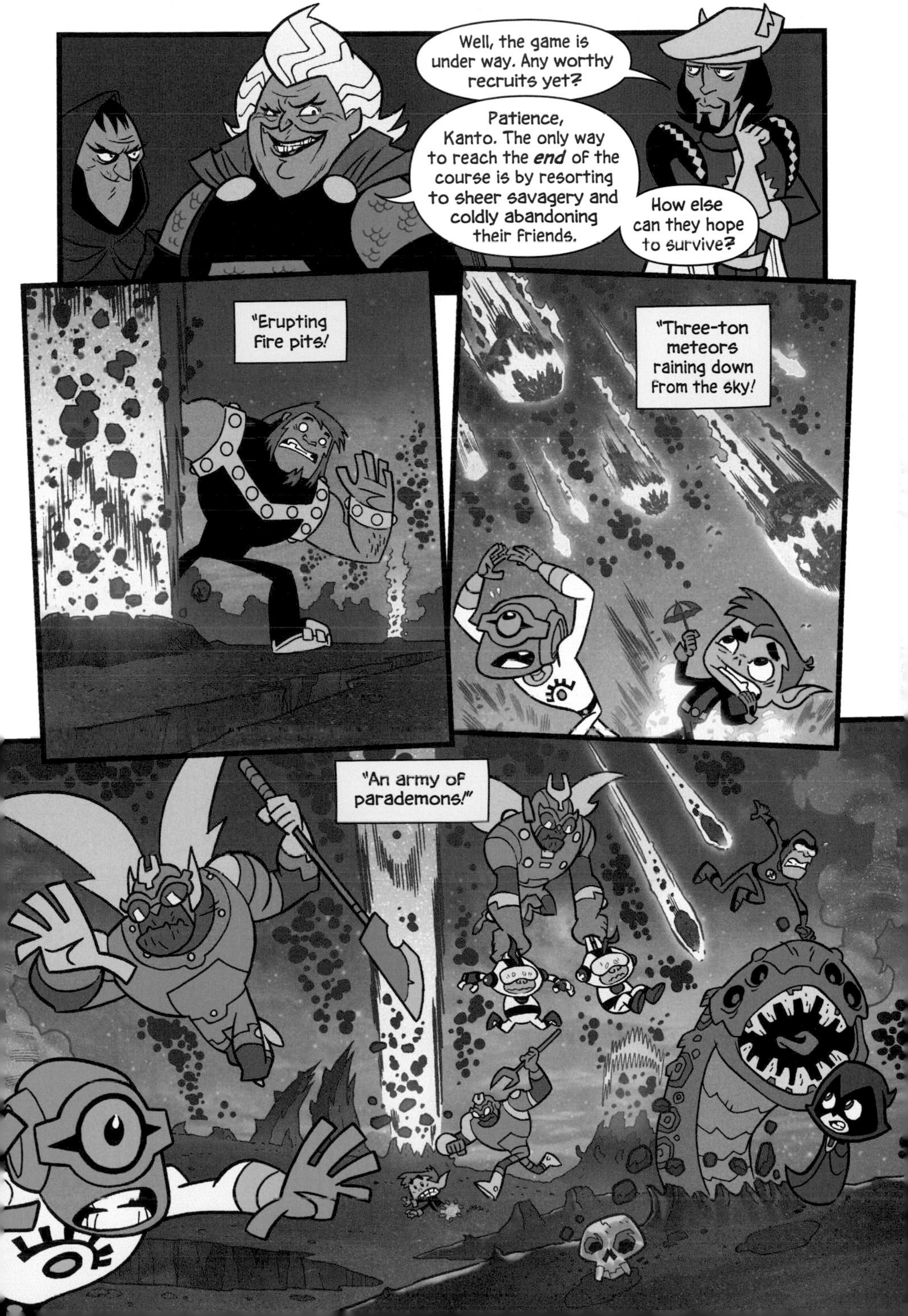
Well, the game is under way. Any worthy recruits yet?
Patience, Kanto. The only way to reach the end of the course is by resorting to sheer savagery and coldly abandoning their friends.
How else can they hope to survive?
"Erupting fire pits!
"Three-ton meteors raining down from the sky!
"An army of parademons!"

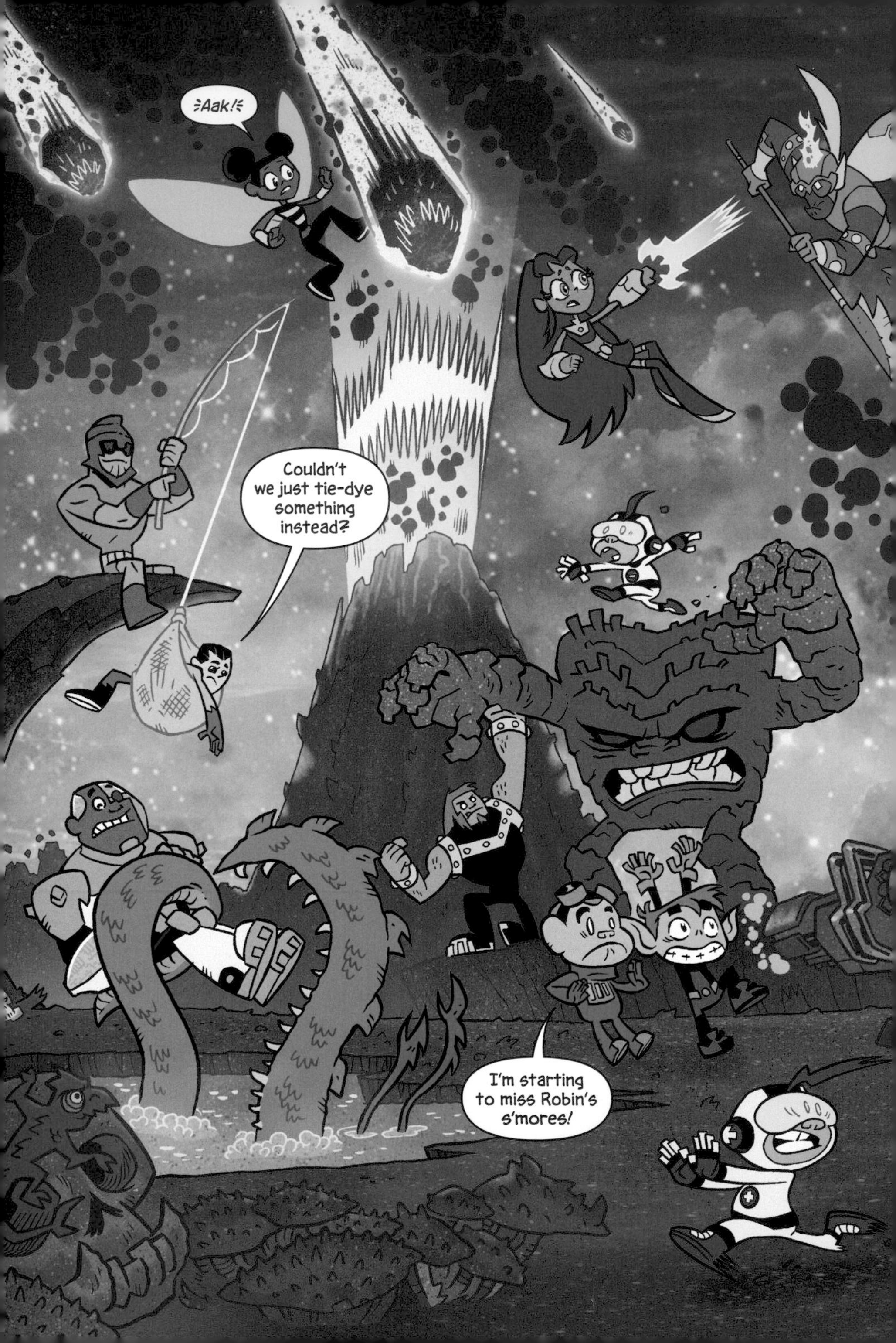
Aak!
Couldn't we just tie-dye something instead?
I'm starting to miss Robin's s'mores!

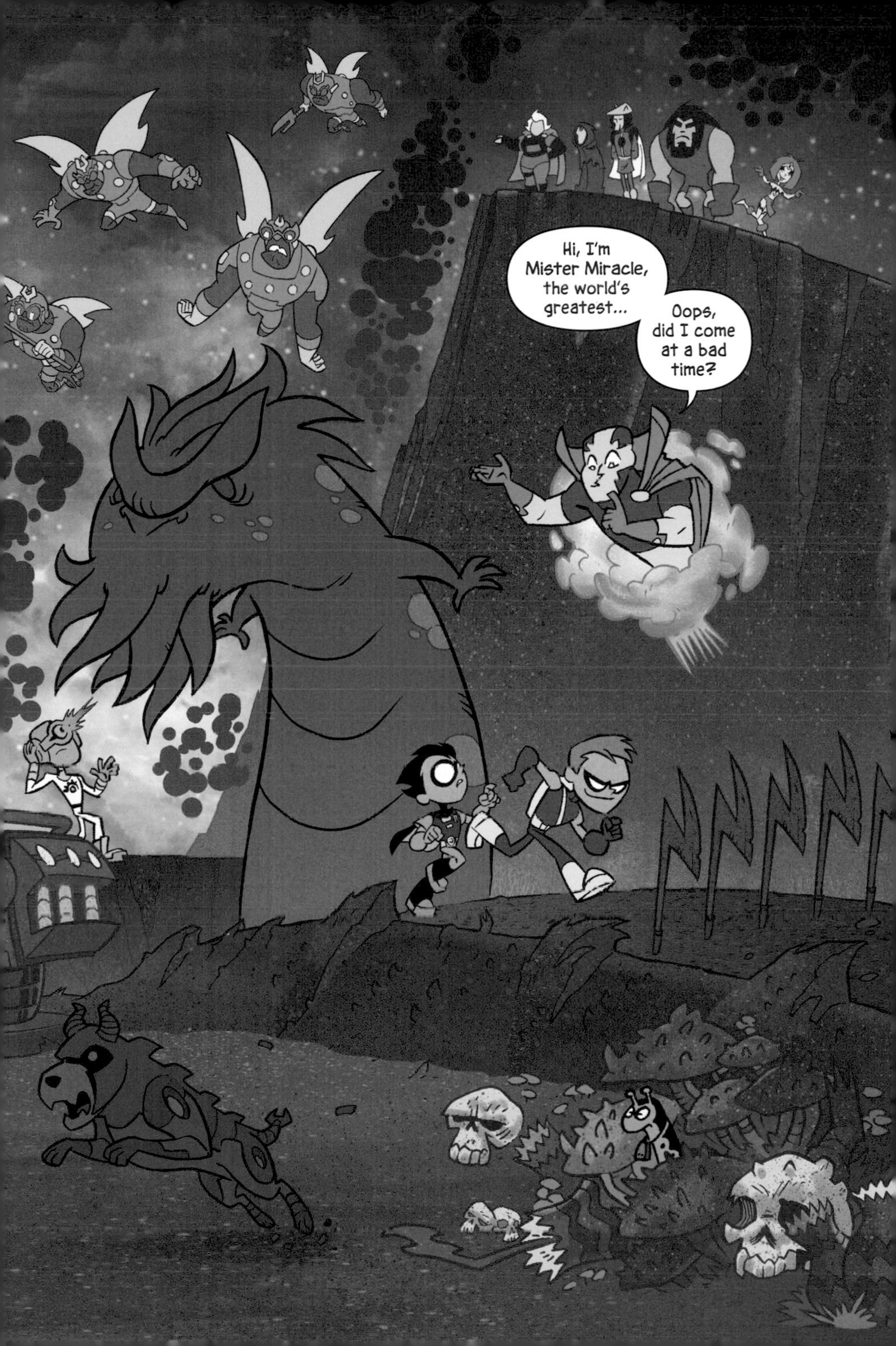

Hi, I'm Mister Miracle, the world's greatest...
Oops, did I come at a bad time?

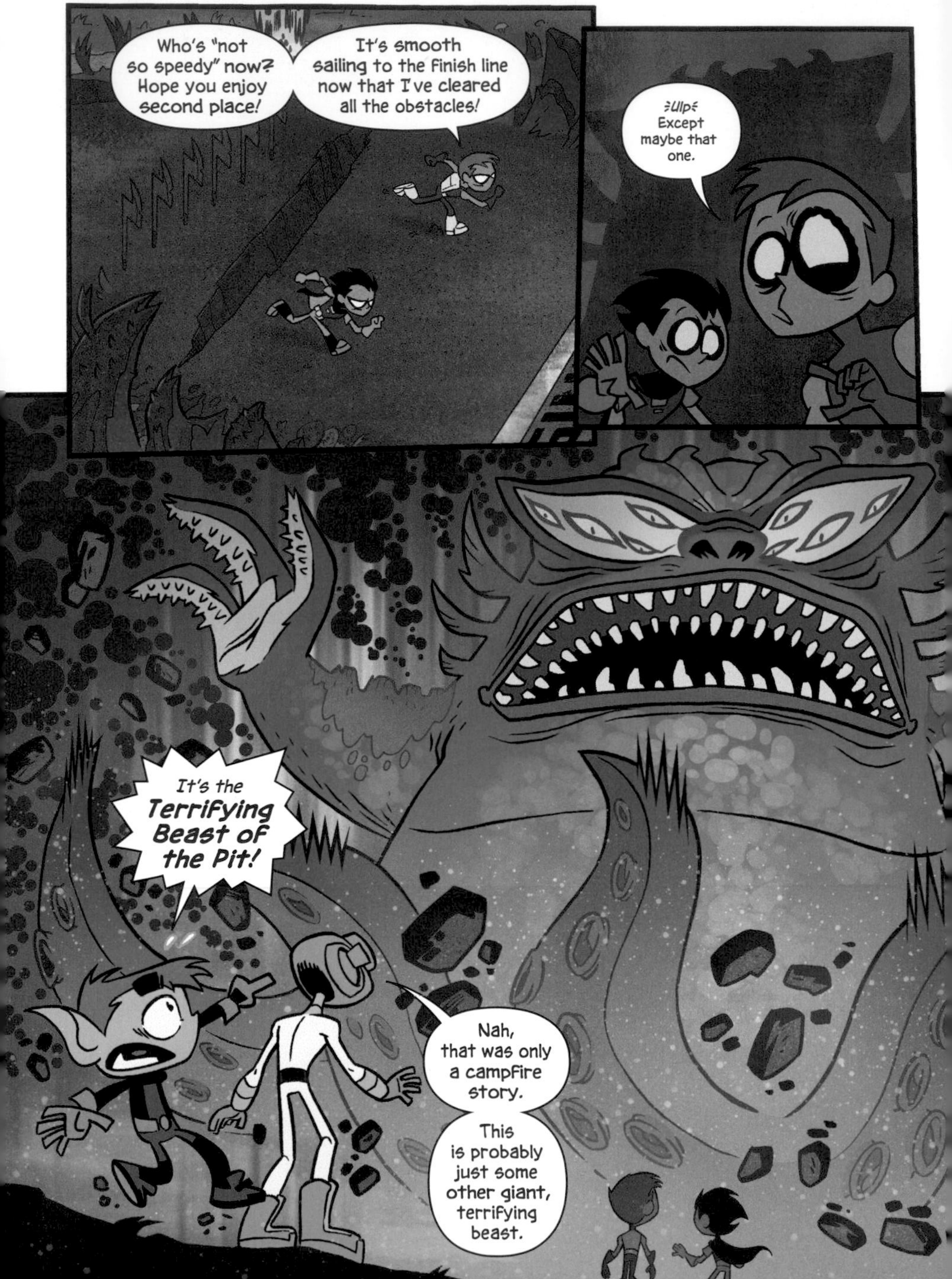

Who's "not so speedy" now? Hope you enjoy second place!
It's smooth sailing to the finish line now that I've cleared all the obstacles!
Ulp
Except maybe that one.
It's the Terrifying Beast of the Pit!
Nah, that was only a campfire story.
This is probably just some other giant, terrifying beast.

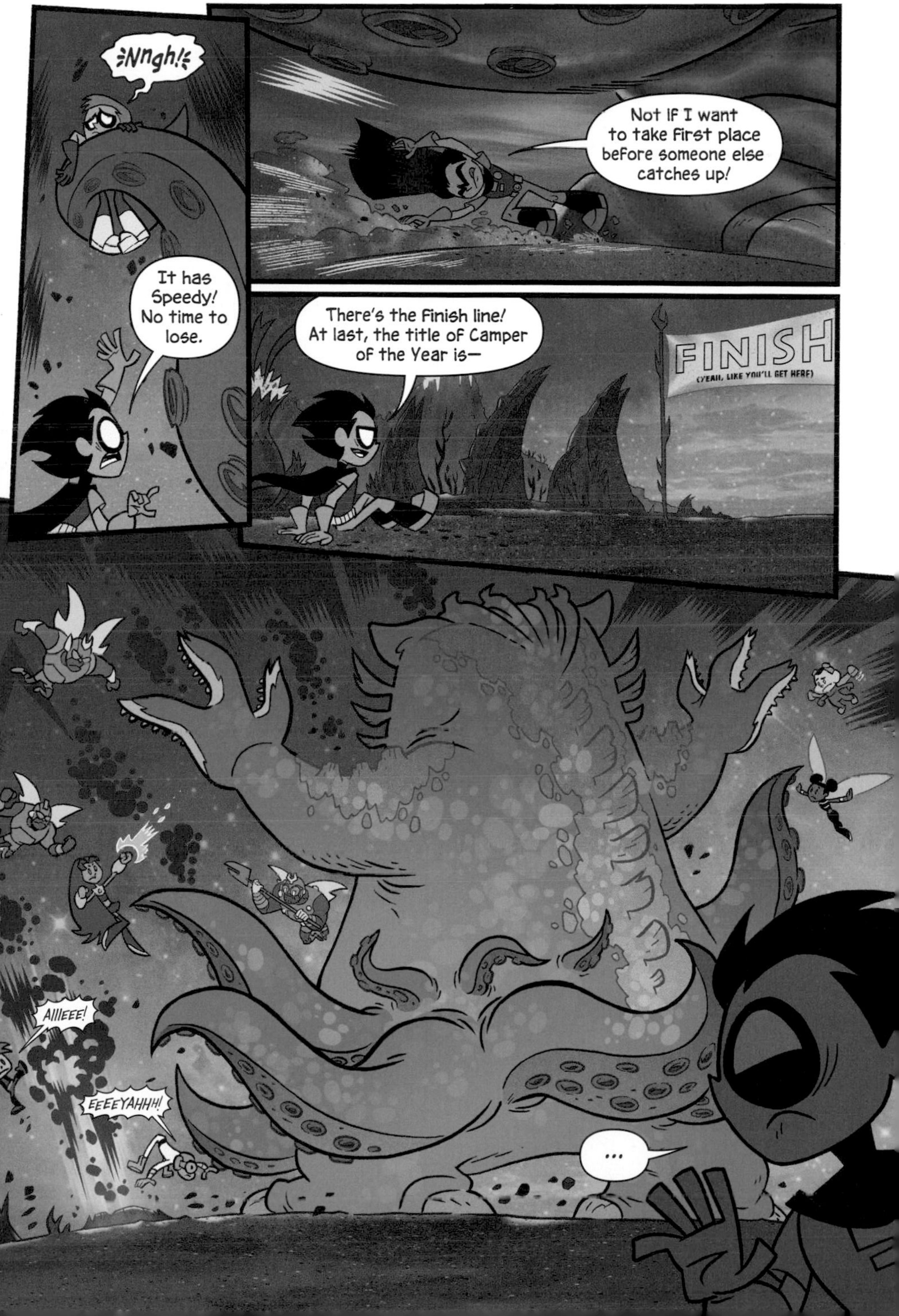
Nngh!
Not if I want to take first place before someone else catches up!
It has Speedy! No time to lose.
There's the finish line! At last, the title of Camper of the Year is—
FINISH
(YEAH, LIKE YOU'LL GET HERE)
AIIIEEE!
EEEEYAHHH!
...

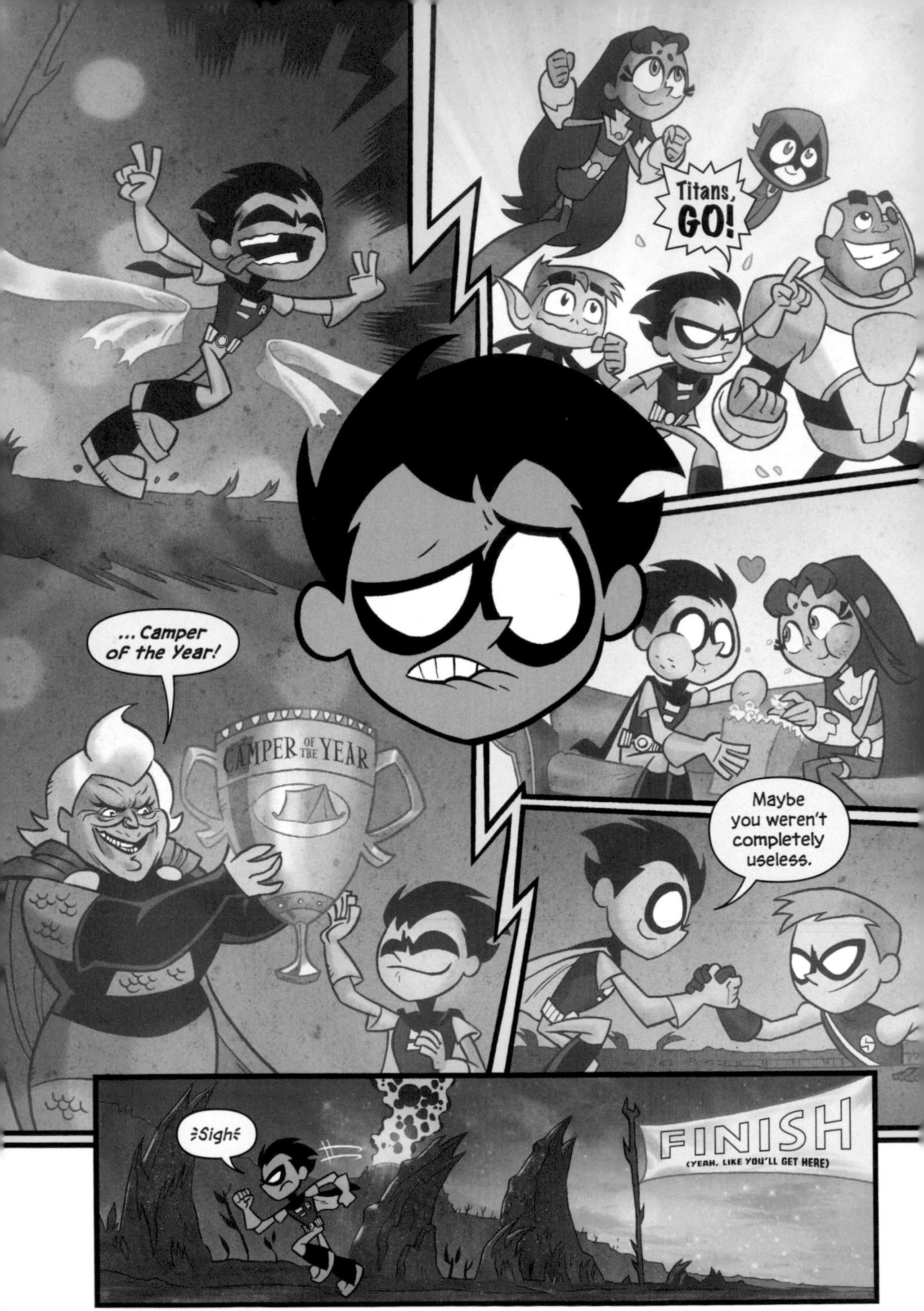
Titans, GO!
...Camper of the Year!
CAMPER OF THE YEAR
Maybe you weren't completely useless.
Sigh
FINISH
(YEAH, LIKE YOU'LL GET HERE)

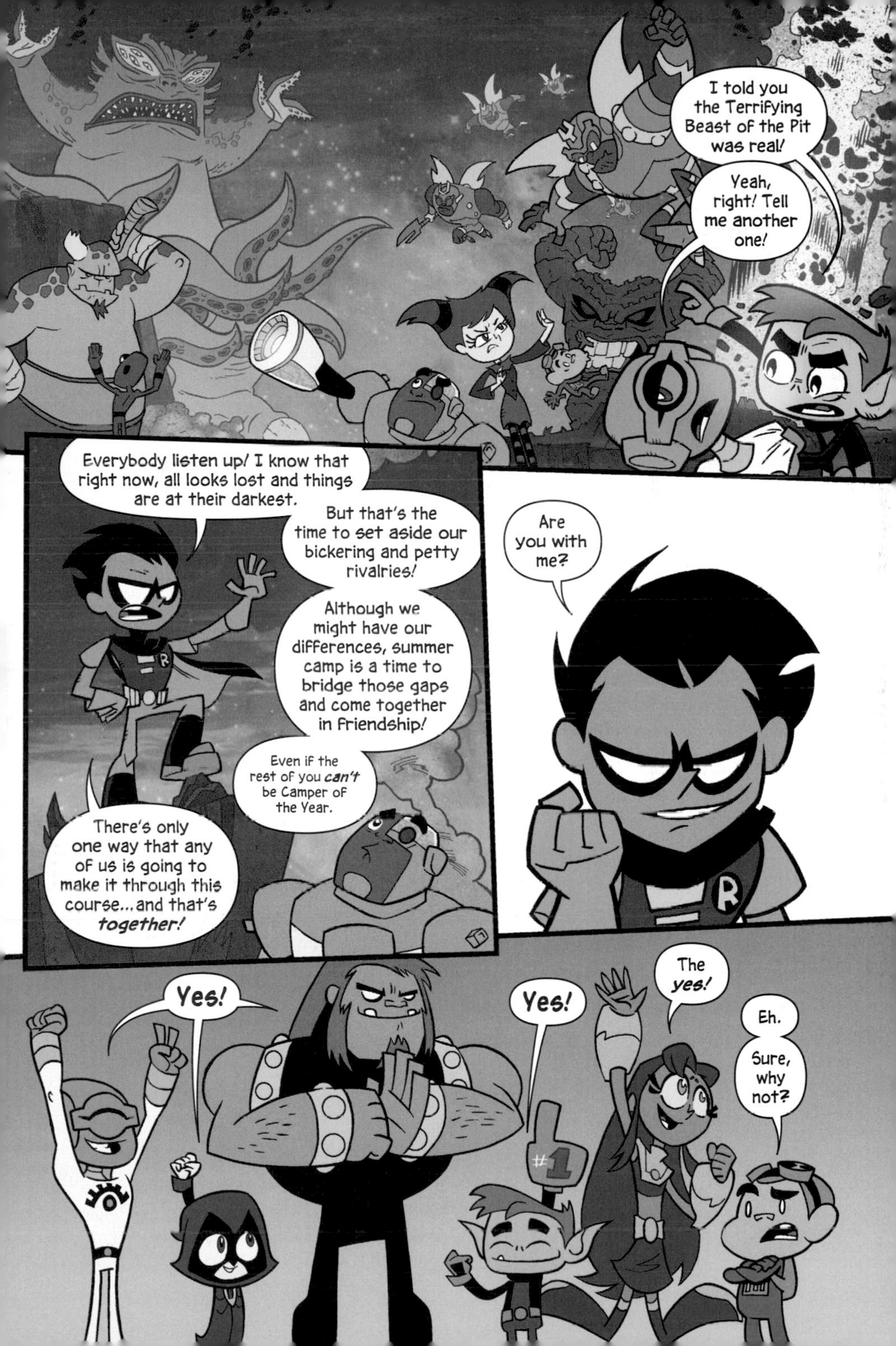
I told you the Terrifying Beast of the Pit was real!
Yeah, right! Tell me another one!
Everybody listen up! I know that right now, all looks lost and things are at their darkest.
But that's the time to set aside our bickering and petty rivalries!
Although we might have our differences, summer camp is a time to bridge those gaps and come together in friendship!
Even if the rest of you *can't* be Camper of the Year.
There's only one way that any of us is going to make it through this course...and that's *together!*
Are you with me?
Yes!
Yes!
The *yes!*
Eh.
Sure, why not?

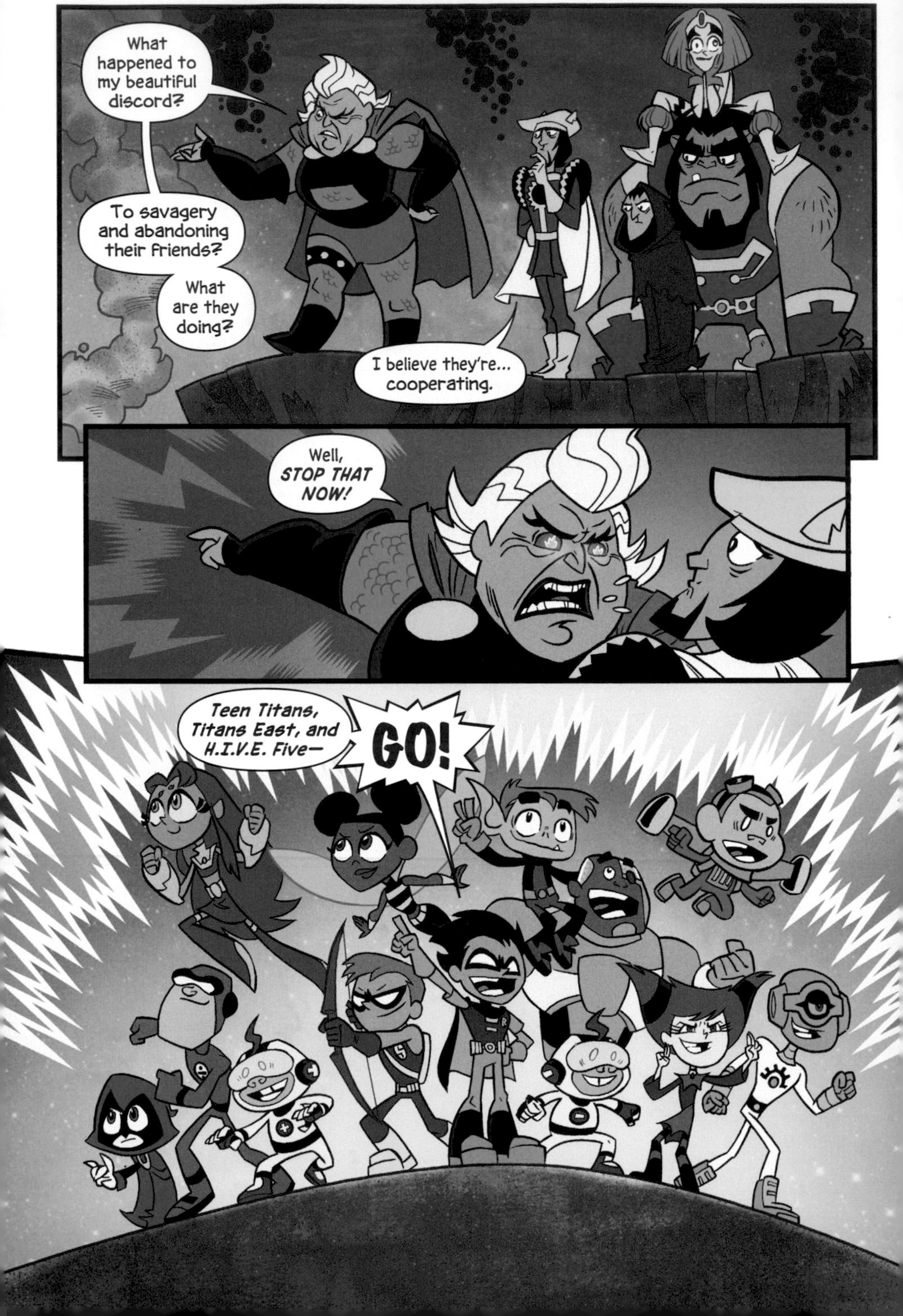
What happened to my beautiful discord?
To savagery and abandoning their friends?
What are they doing?
I believe they're... cooperating.
Well, *STOP THAT NOW!*
Teen Titans, Titans East, and H.I.V.E. Five—
GO!

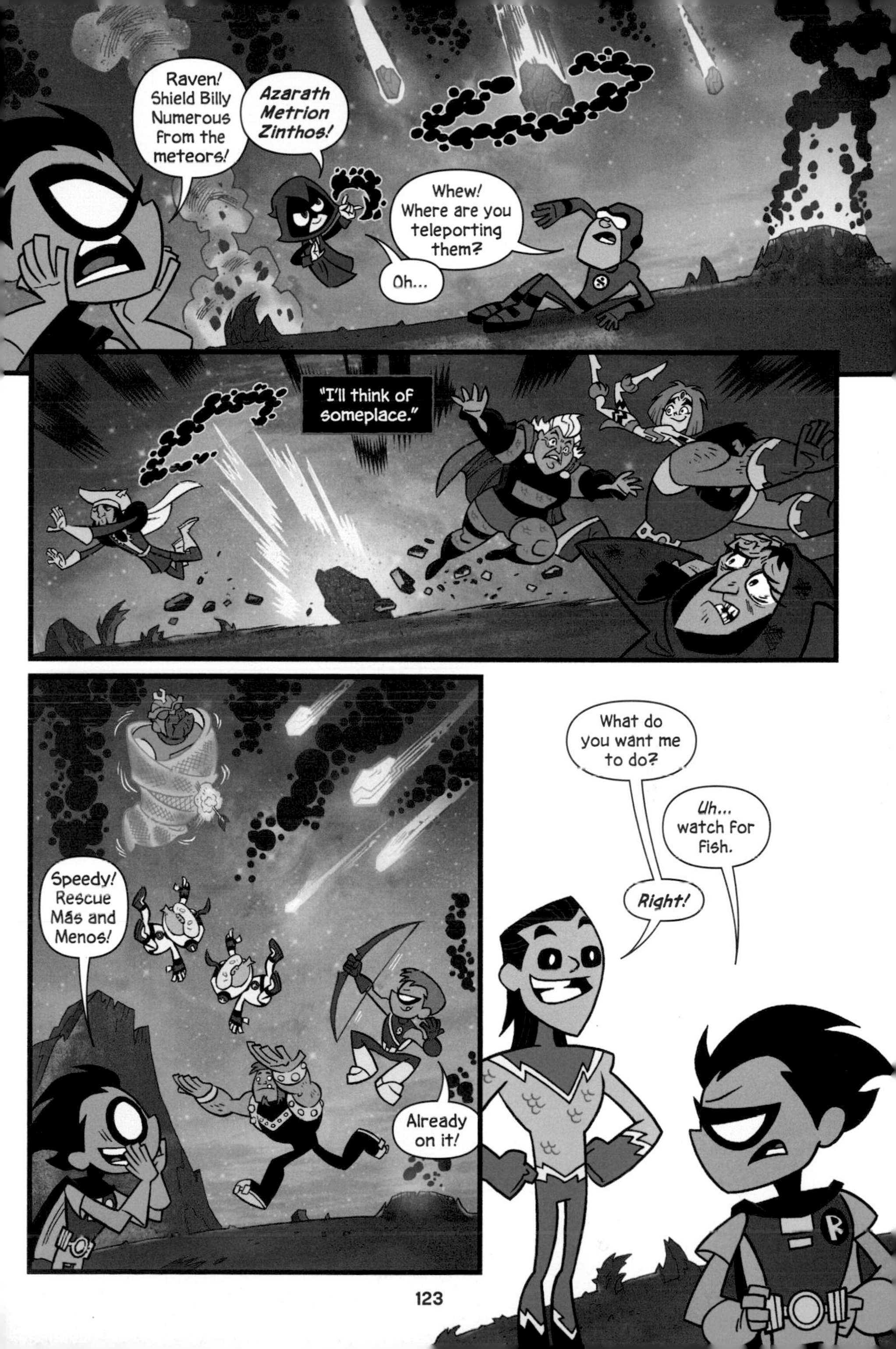
Raven! Shield Billy Numerous from the meteors!
Azarath Metrion Zinthos!
Whew! Where are you teleporting them?
Oh...
"I'll think of someplace."
Speedy! Rescue Más and Menos!
Already on it!
What do you want me to do?
Uh... watch for fish.
Right!

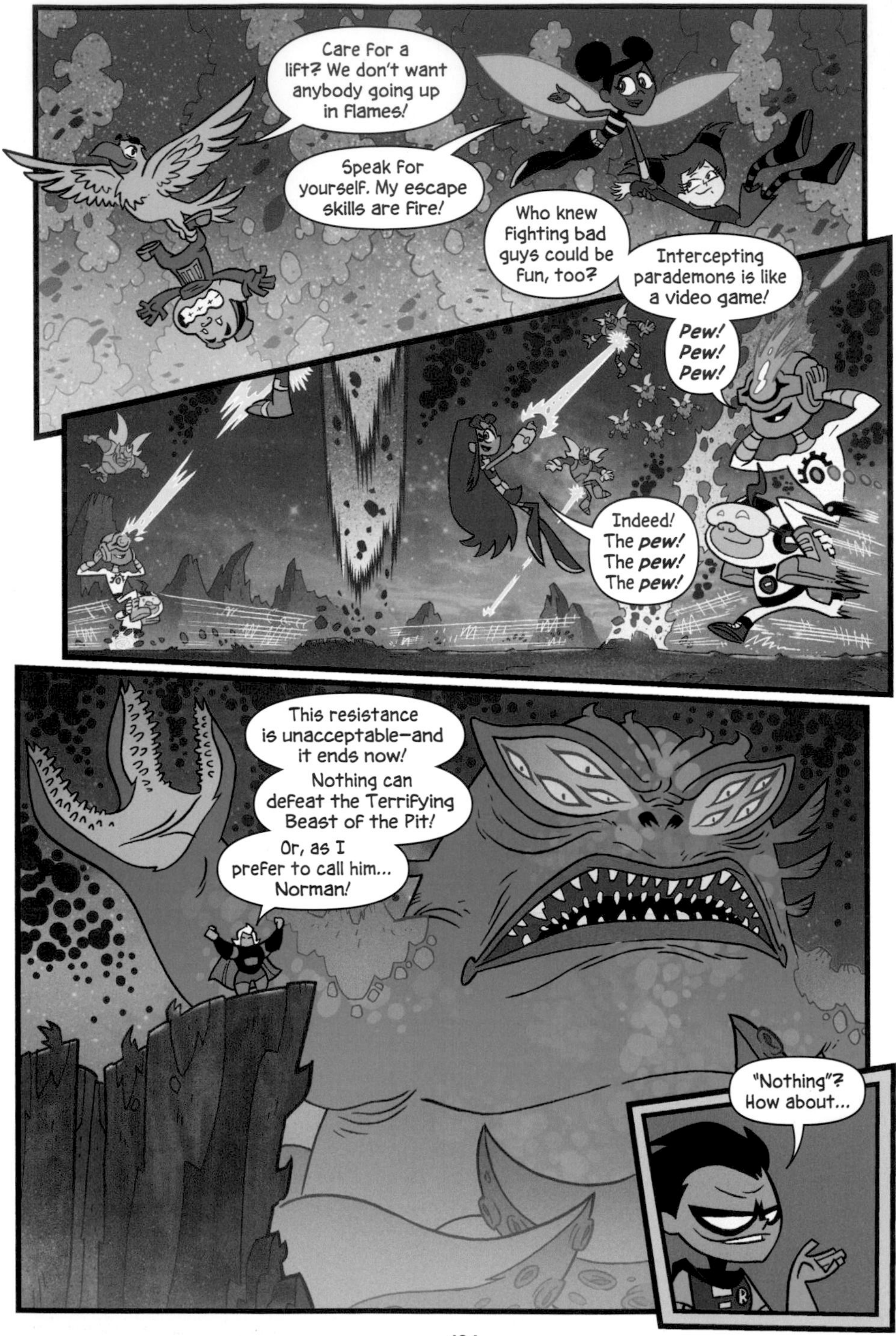
Care for a lift? We don't want anybody going up in flames!
Speak for yourself. My escape skills are fire!
Who knew fighting bad guys could be fun, too?
Intercepting parademons is like a video game!
Pew! Pew! Pew!
Indeed! The pew! The pew! The pew!
This resistance is unacceptable—and it ends now!
Nothing can defeat the Terrifying Beast of the Pit!
Or, as I prefer to call him... Norman!
"Nothing"? How about...

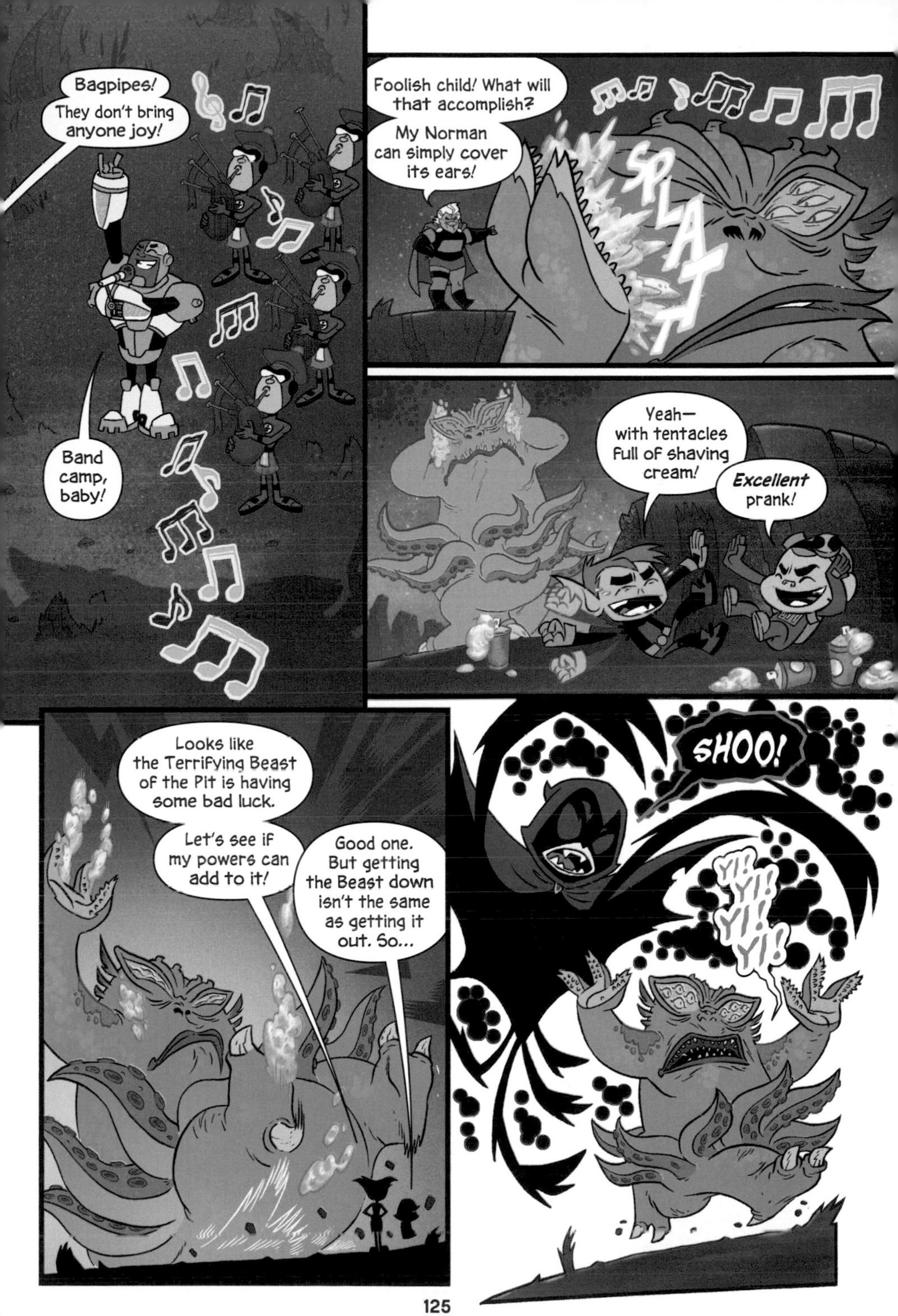

Bagpipes!
They don't bring anyone joy!
Band camp, baby!
Foolish child! What will that accomplish?
My Norman can simply cover its ears!
SPLATT
Yeah— with tentacles full of shaving cream!
Excellent prank!
Looks like the Terrifying Beast of the Pit is having some bad luck.
Let's see if my powers can add to it!
Good one. But getting the Beast down isn't the same as getting it out. So...
SHOO!
YI! YI! YI! YI!

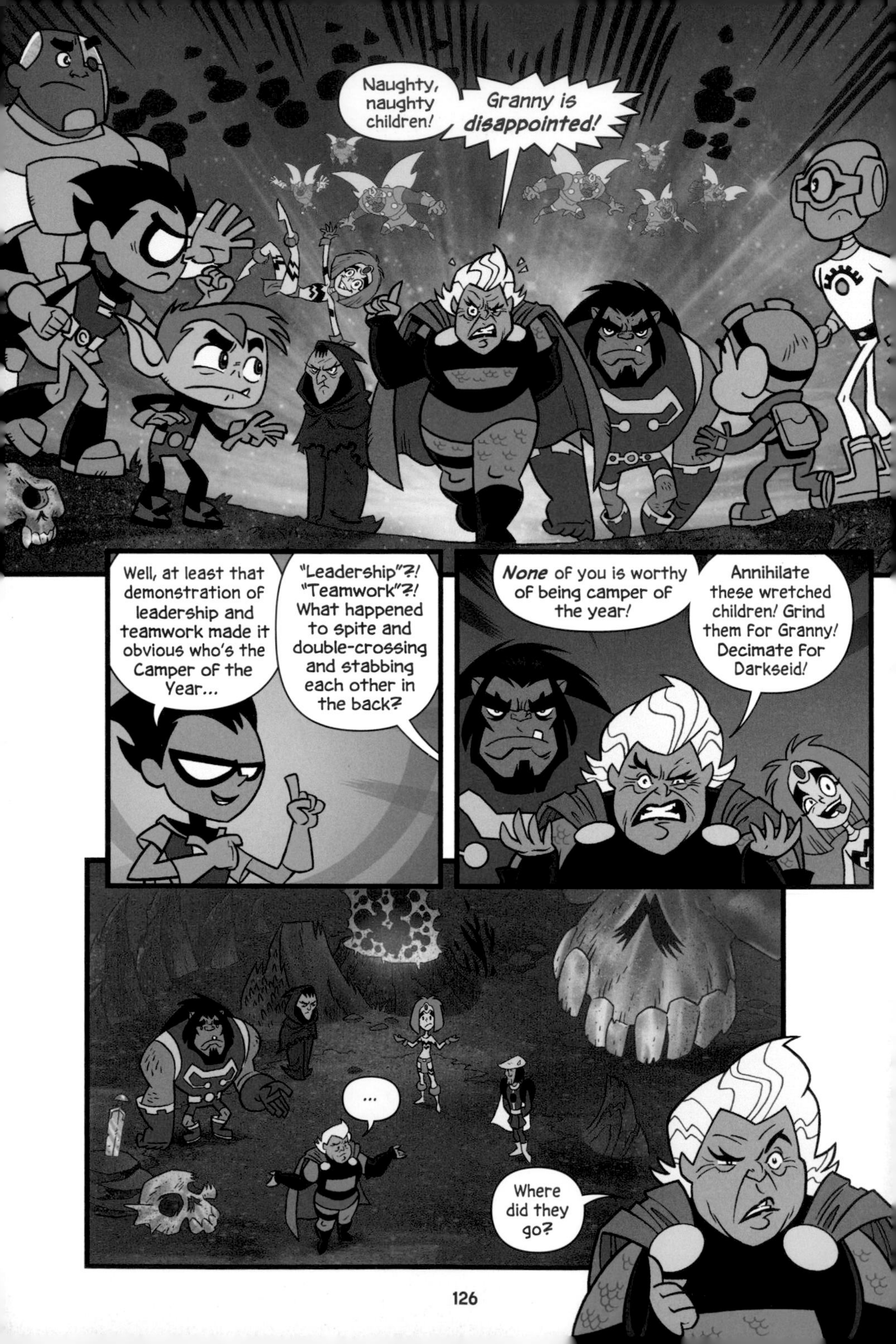

Naughty, naughty children!
Granny is *disappointed!*
Well, at least that demonstration of leadership and teamwork made it obvious who's the Camper of the Year...
"Leadership"?! "Teamwork"?! What happened to spite and double-crossing and stabbing each other in the back?
None of you is worthy of being camper of the year!
Annihilate these wretched children! Grind them for Granny! Decimate for Darkseid!
...
Where did they go?

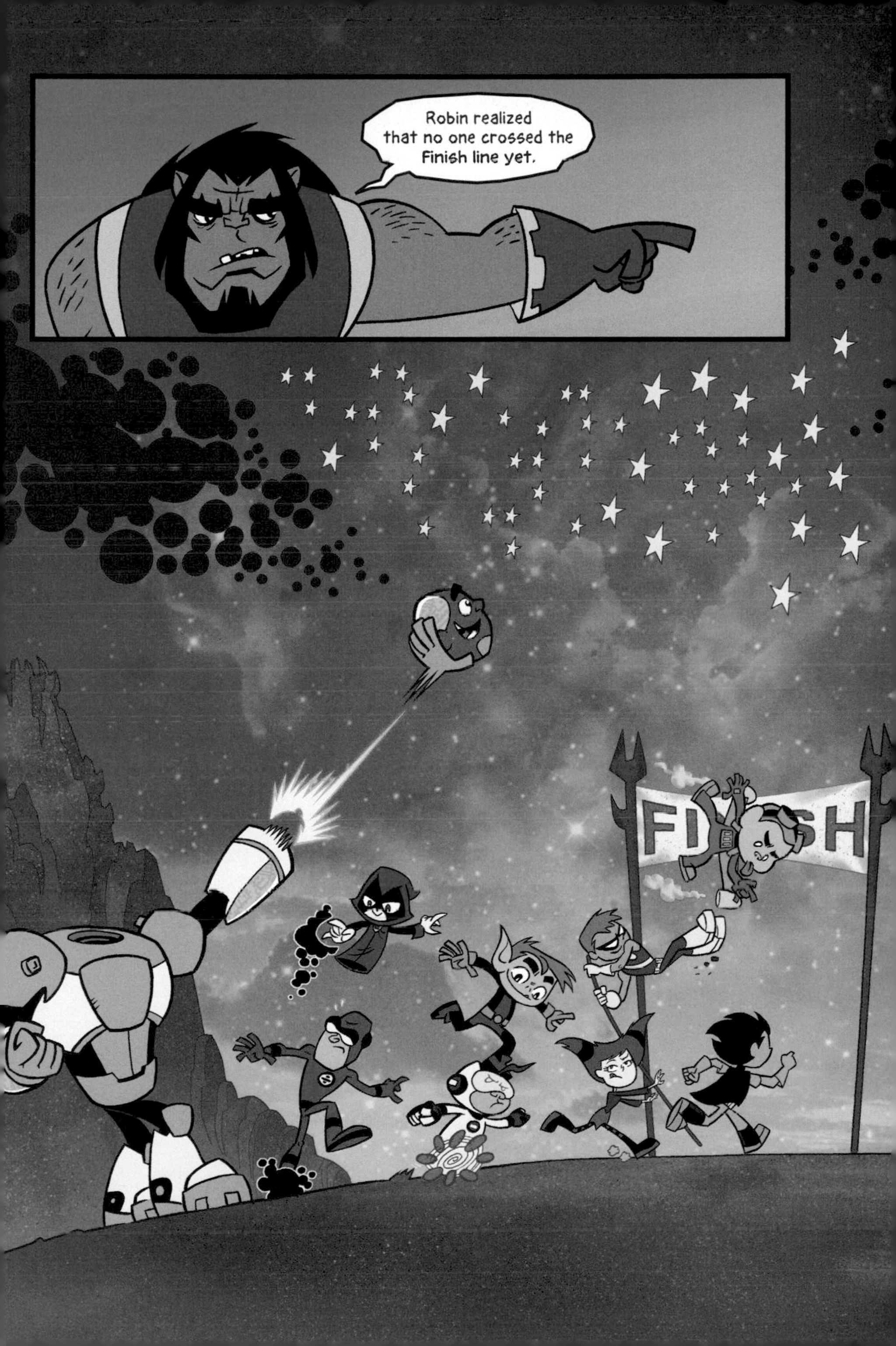
Robin realized
that no one crossed the
Finish line yet.
FI SH

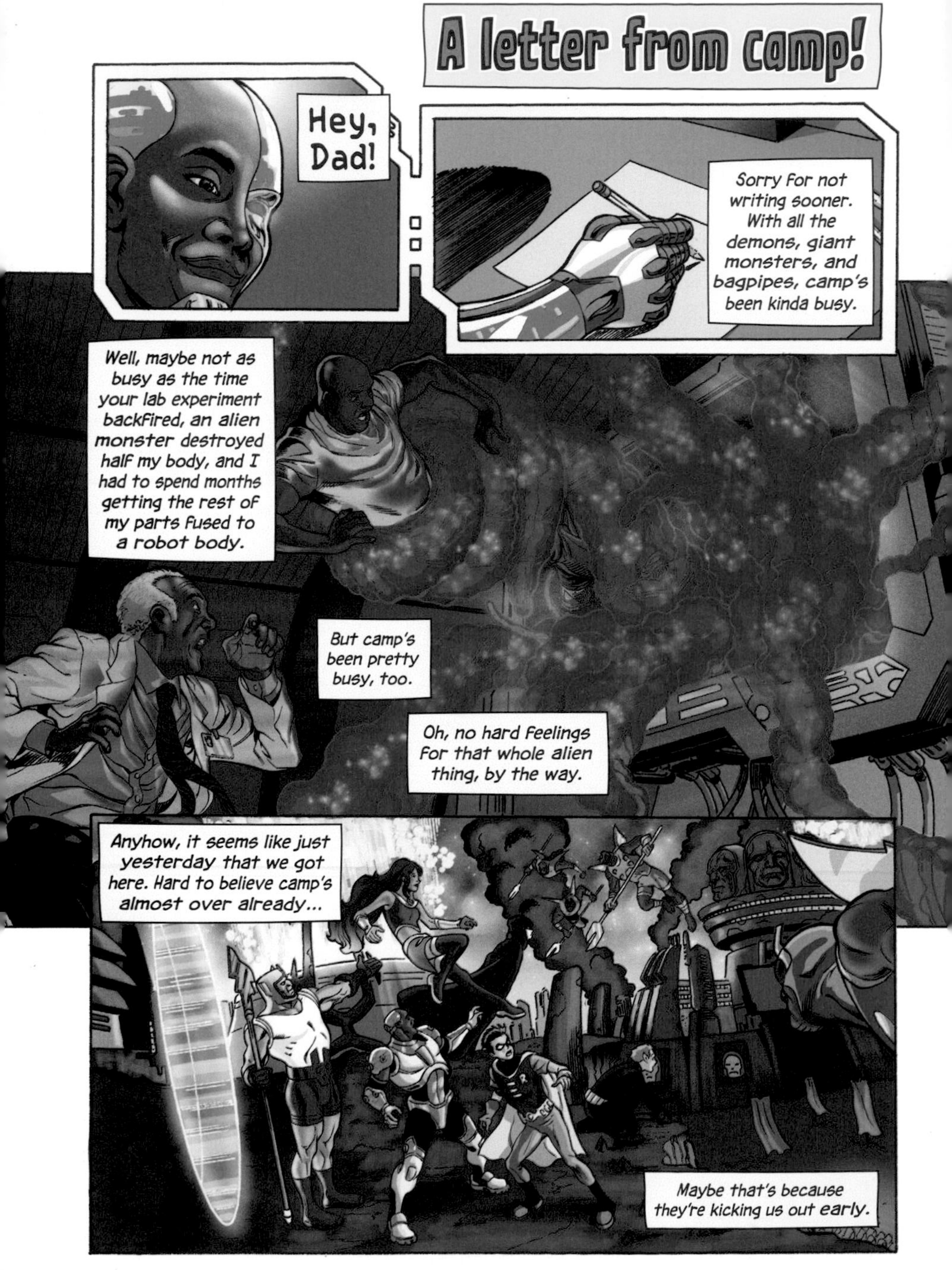
A letter from camp!
Hey, Dad!
Sorry for not writing sooner. With all the demons, giant monsters, and bagpipes, camp's been kinda busy.
Well, maybe not as busy as the time your lab experiment backfired, an alien monster destroyed half my body, and I had to spend months getting the rest of my parts fused to a robot body.
But camp's been pretty busy, too.
Oh, no hard feelings for that whole alien thing, by the way.
Anyhow, it seems like just yesterday that we got here. Hard to believe camp's almost over already...
Maybe that's because they're kicking us out early.

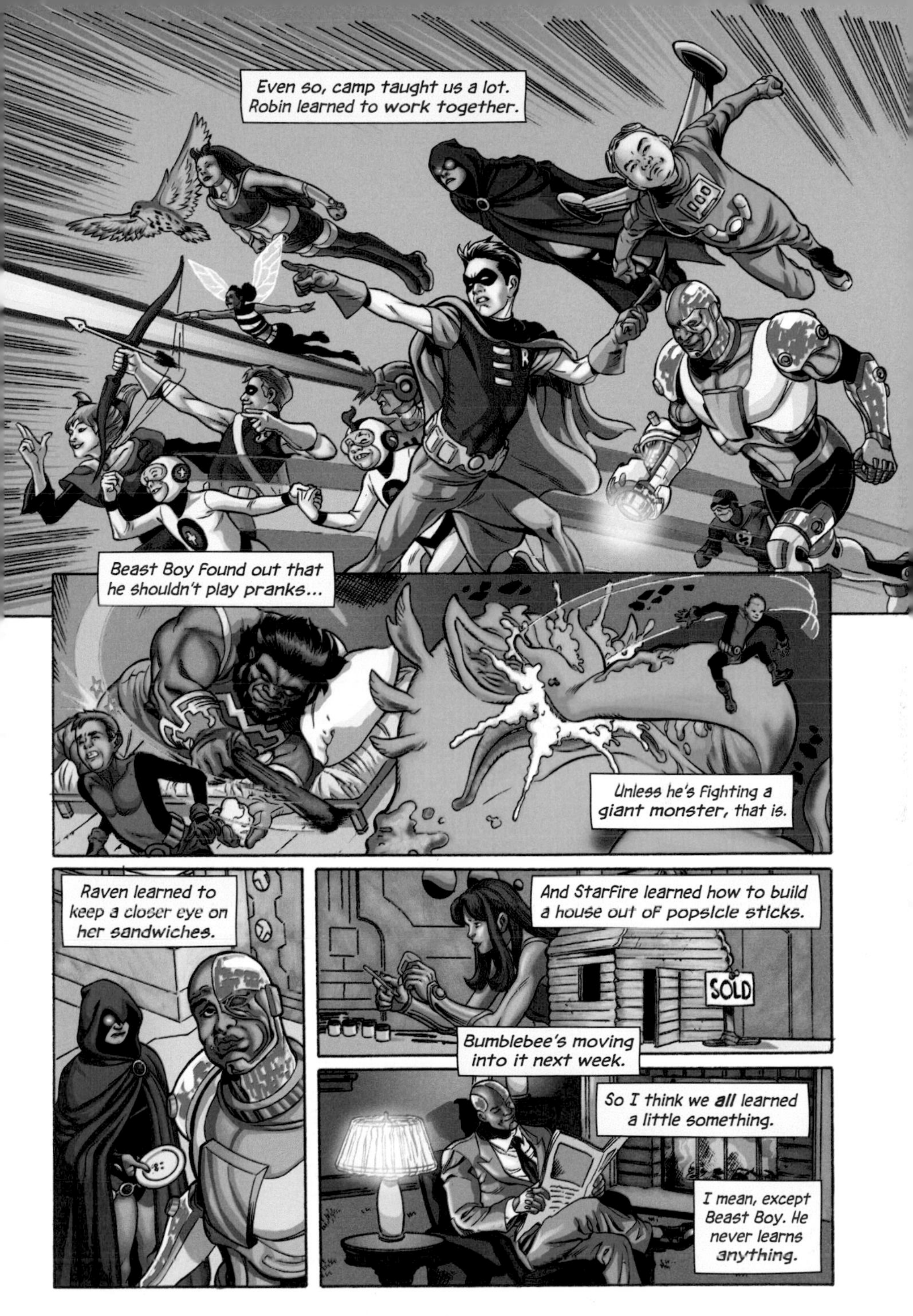
Even so, camp taught us a lot.
Robin learned to work together.
Beast Boy found out that he shouldn't play pranks...
Unless he's fighting a giant monster, that is.
Raven learned to keep a closer eye on her sandwiches.
And Starfire learned how to build a house out of popsicle sticks.
SOLD
Bumblebee's moving into it next week.
So I think we all learned a little something.
I mean, except Beast Boy. He never learns anything.

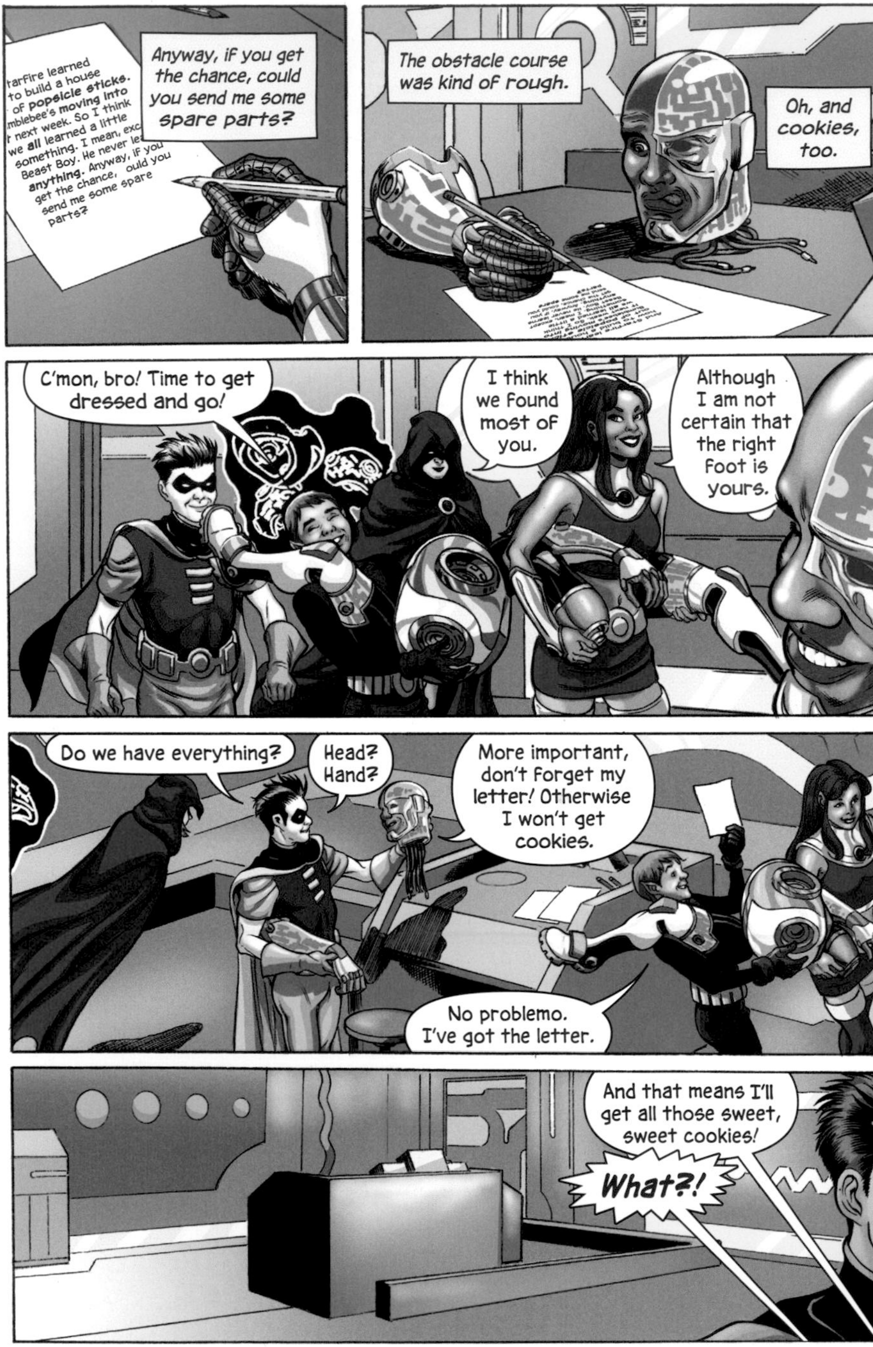

tarFire learned to build a house of popsicle sticks. mblebee's moving into t next week. So I think we all learned a little something. I mean, exc Beast Boy. He never le anything. Anyway, if you get the chance, ould you send me some spare parts?
Anyway, if you get the chance, could you send me some spare parts?
The obstacle course was kind of rough.
Oh, and cookies, too.
C'mon, bro! Time to get dressed and go!
I think we found most of you.
Although I am not certain that the right foot is yours.
Do we have everything?
Head? Hand?
More important, don't forget my letter! Otherwise I won't get cookies.
No problemo. I've got the letter.
And that means I'll get all those sweet, sweet cookies!
What?!

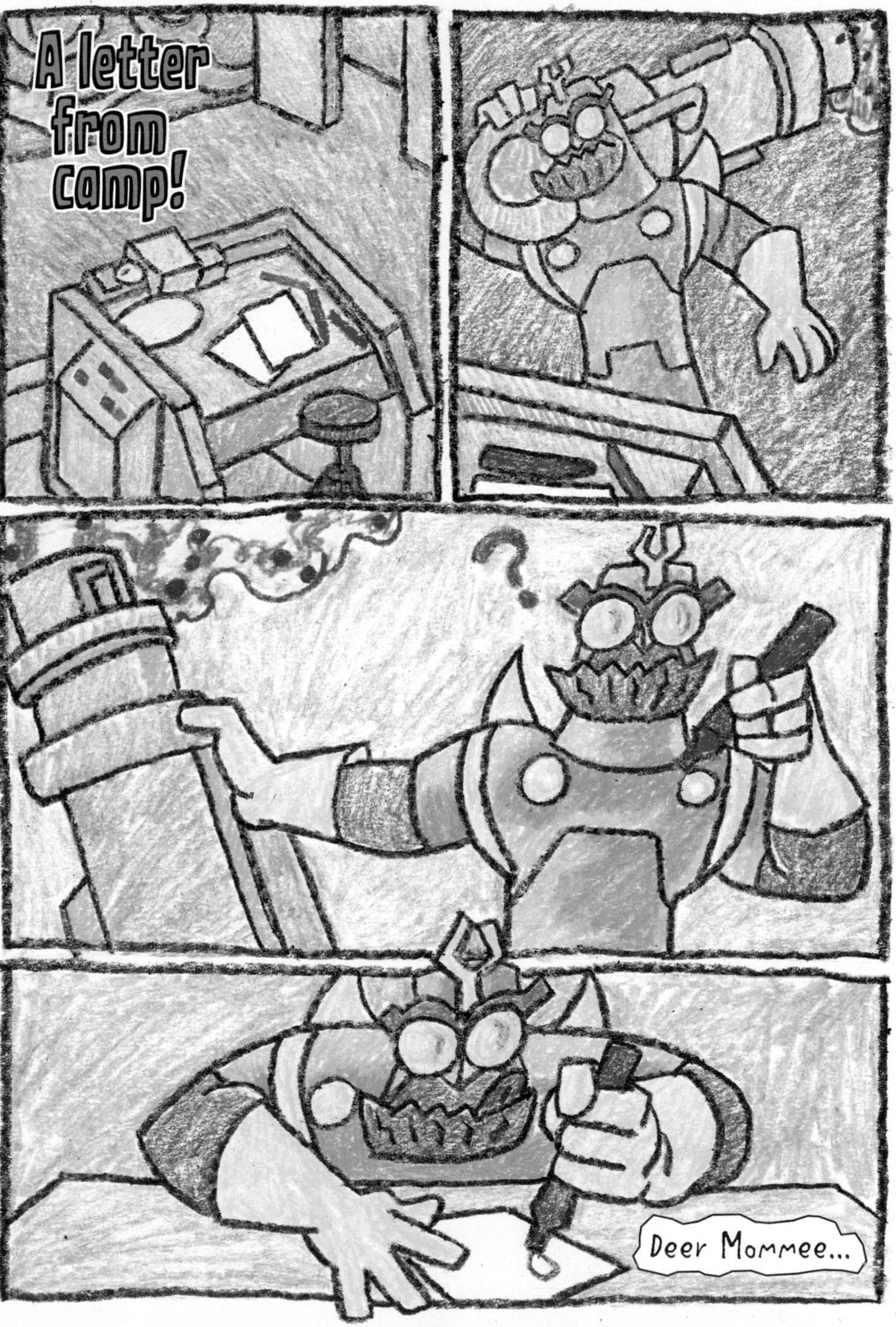
A letter from camp!
Deer Mommee...

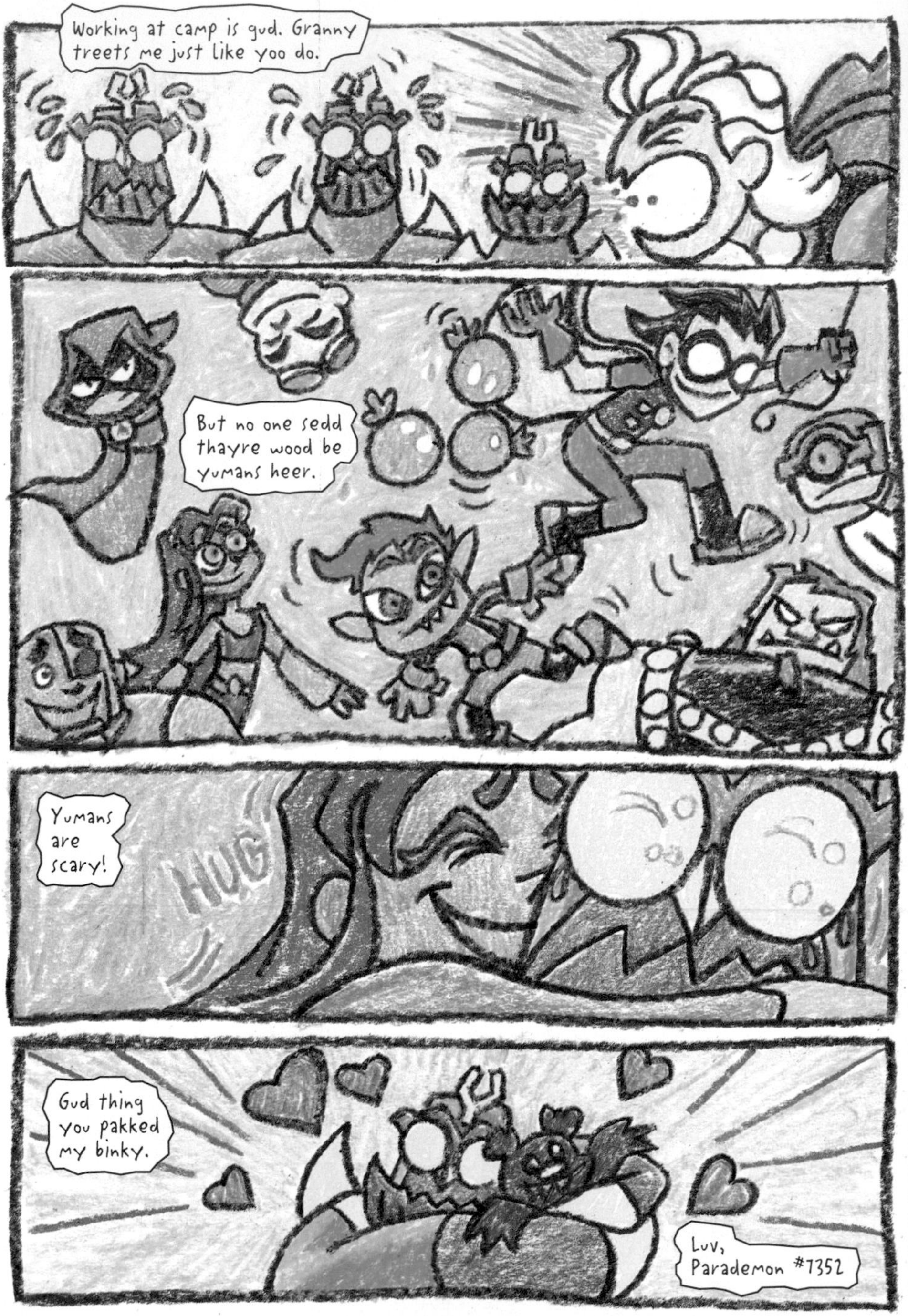
Working at camp is gud. Granny treets me just like yoo do.
But no one sedd thayre wood be yumans heer.
Yumans are scary!
HUG
Gud thing you pakked my binky.
Luv, Parademon #7352

Chapter Eight

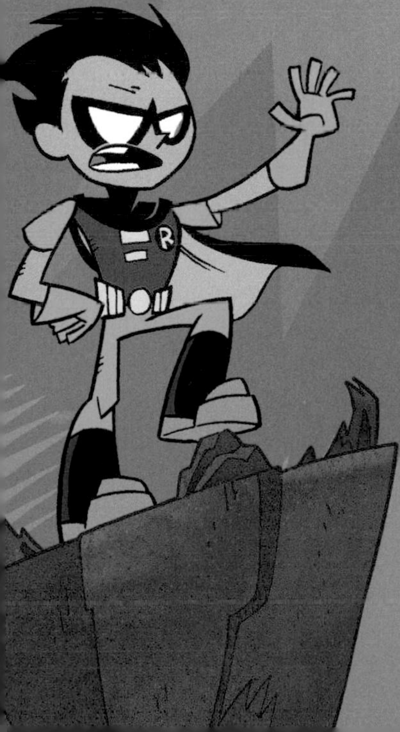

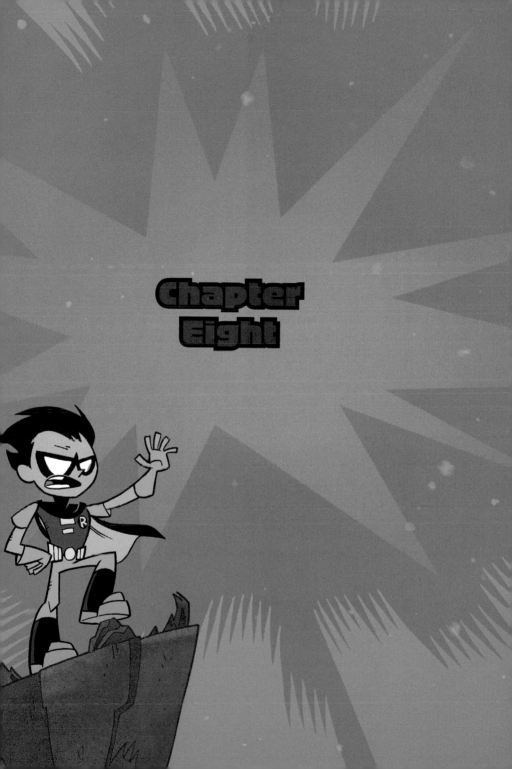

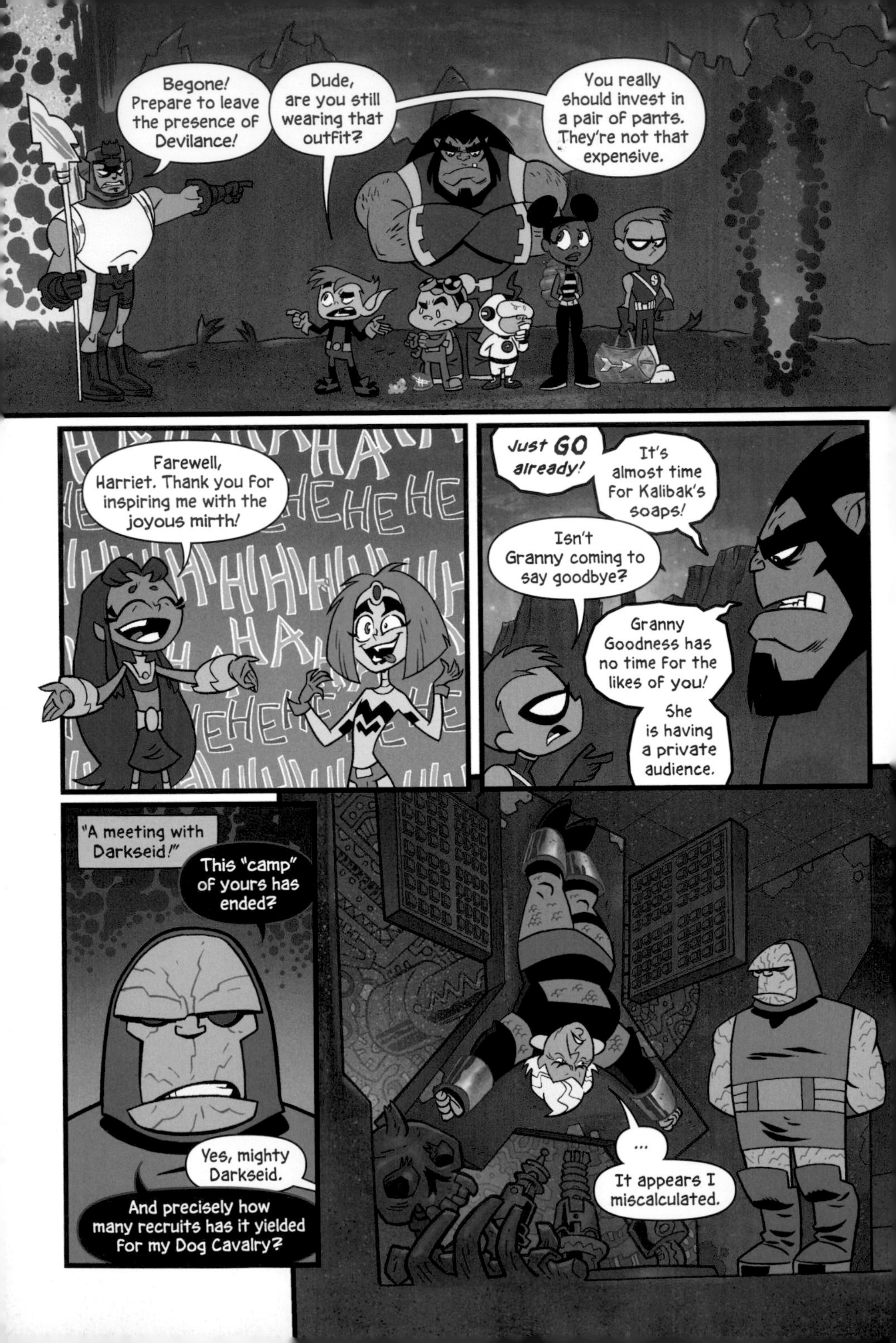
Begone! Prepare to leave the presence of Devilance!
Dude, are you still wearing that outfit?
You really should invest in a pair of pants. They're not that expensive.
HA HA HE HE HE HI HI HA HE HE
Farewell, Harriet. Thank you for inspiring me with the joyous mirth!
Just GO already!
It's almost time for Kalibak's soaps!
Isn't Granny coming to say goodbye?
Granny Goodness has no time for the likes of you!
She is having a private audience.
"A meeting with Darkseid!"
This "camp" of yours has ended?
Yes, mighty Darkseid.
And precisely how many recruits has it yielded for my Dog Cavalry?
...
It appears I miscalculated.

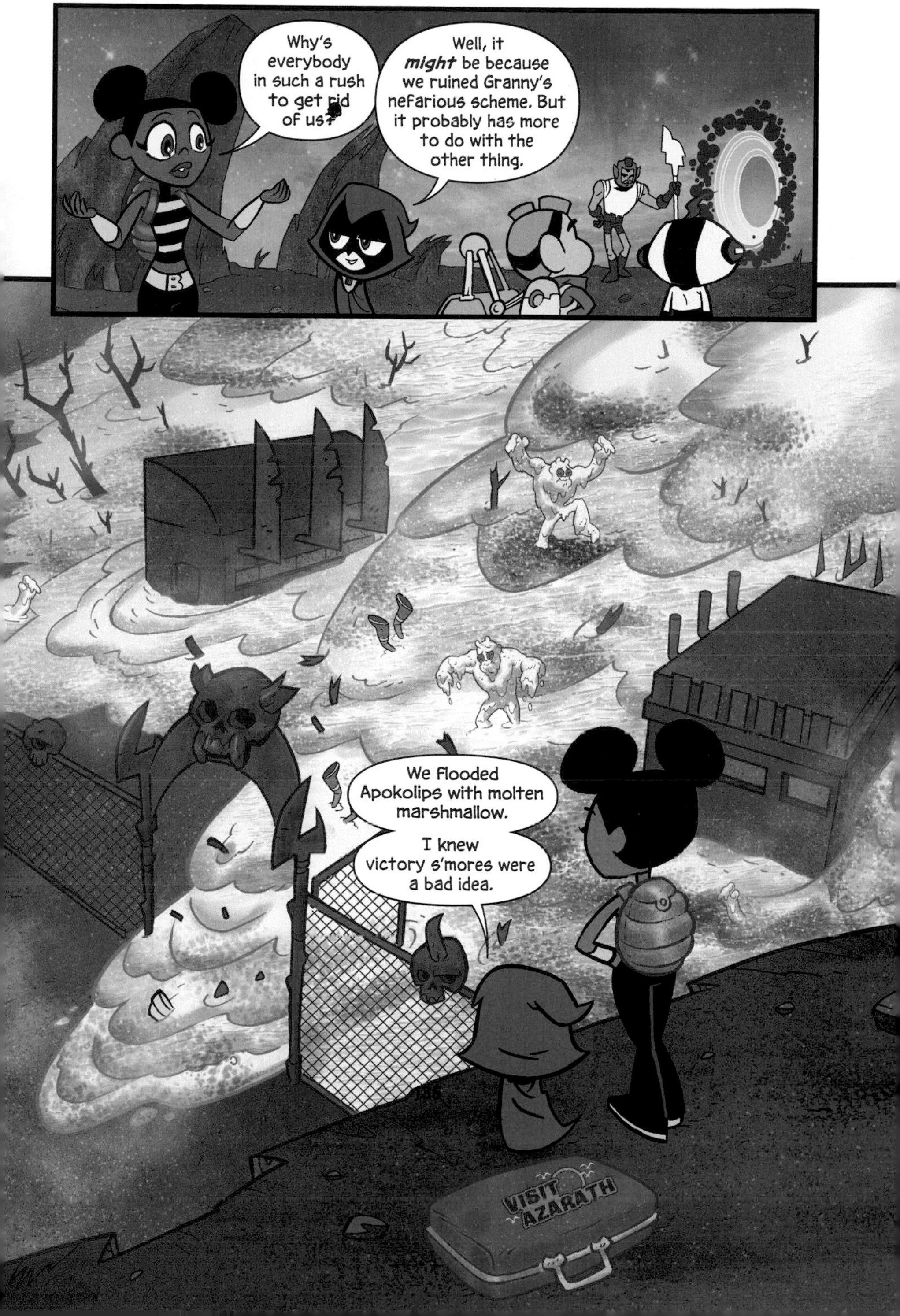
Why's everybody in such a rush to get rid of us?
Well, it *might* be because we ruined Granny's nefarious scheme. But it probably has more to do with the other thing.
We flooded Apokolips with molten marshmallow.
I knew victory s'mores were a bad idea.
VISIT AZARATH

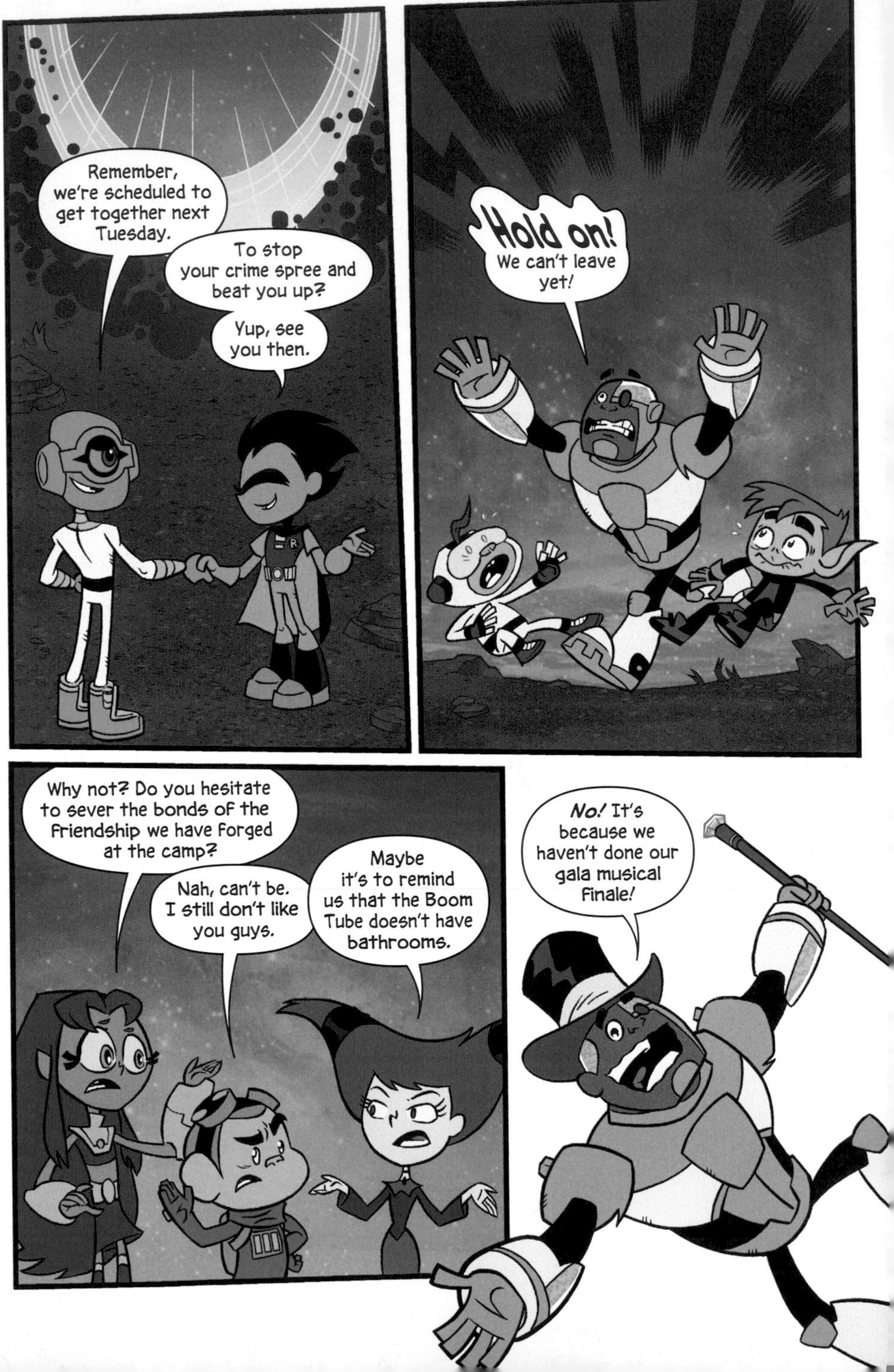
Remember, we're scheduled to get together next Tuesday.
To stop your crime spree and beat you up?
Yup, see you then.
Hold on! We can't leave yet!
Why not? Do you hesitate to sever the bonds of the friendship we have forged at the camp?
Nah, can't be. I still don't like you guys.
Maybe it's to remind us that the Boom Tube doesn't have bathrooms.
No! It's because we haven't done our gala musical finale!

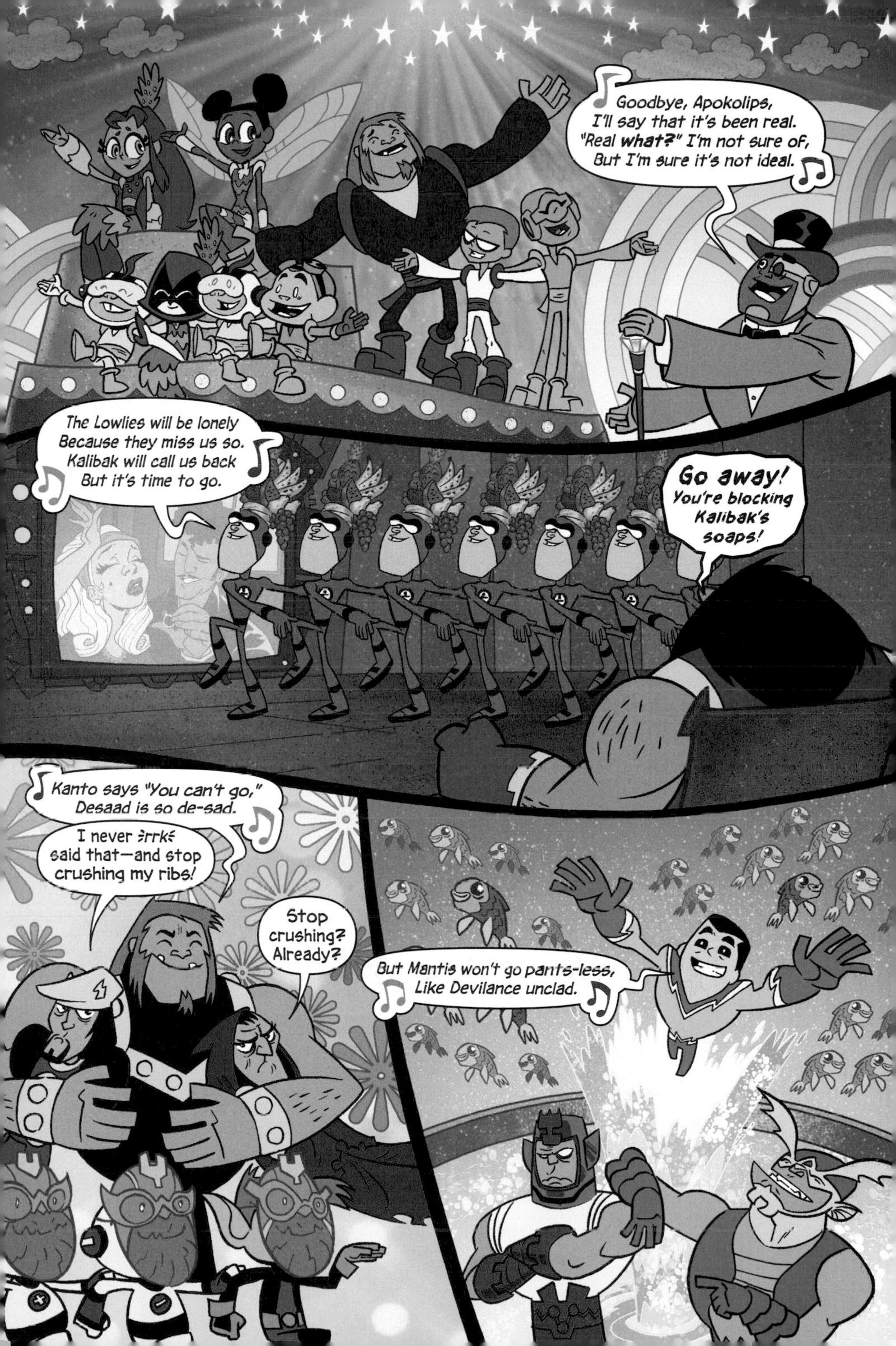
Goodbye, Apokolips, I'll say that it's been real. "Real what?" I'm not sure of, But I'm sure it's not ideal.
The Lowlies will be lonely Because they miss us so. Kalibak will call us back But it's time to go.
Go away! You're blocking Kalibak's soaps!
Kanto says "You can't go," Desaad is so de-sad.
I never ≠rrk≠ said that—and stop crushing my ribs!
Stop crushing? Already?
But Mantis won't go pants-less, Like Devilance unclad.

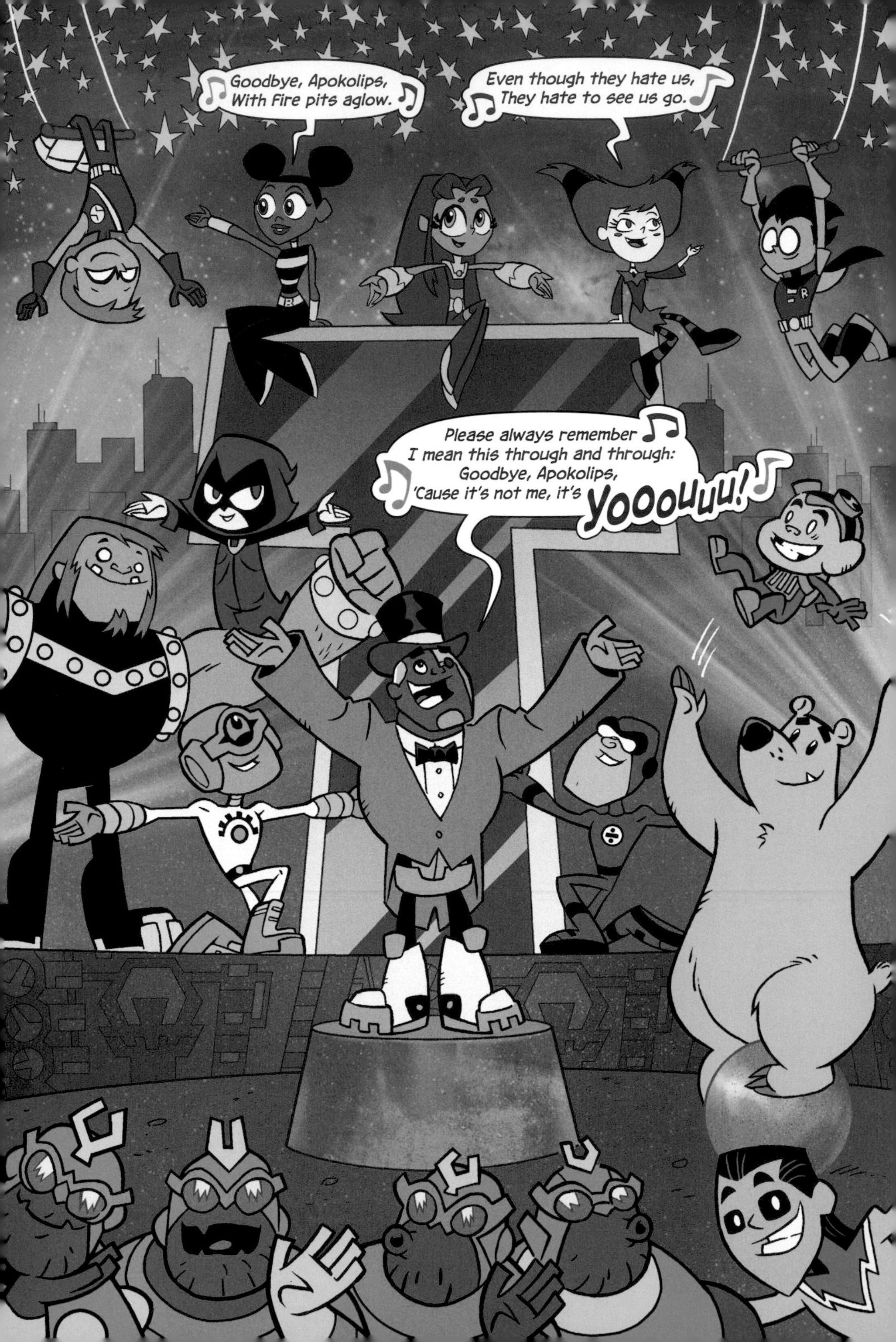

Goodbye, Apokolips, With fire pits aglow.
Even though they hate us, They hate to see us go.
Please always remember I mean this through and through: Goodbye, Apokolips, 'Cause it's not me, it's YOOOUUU!

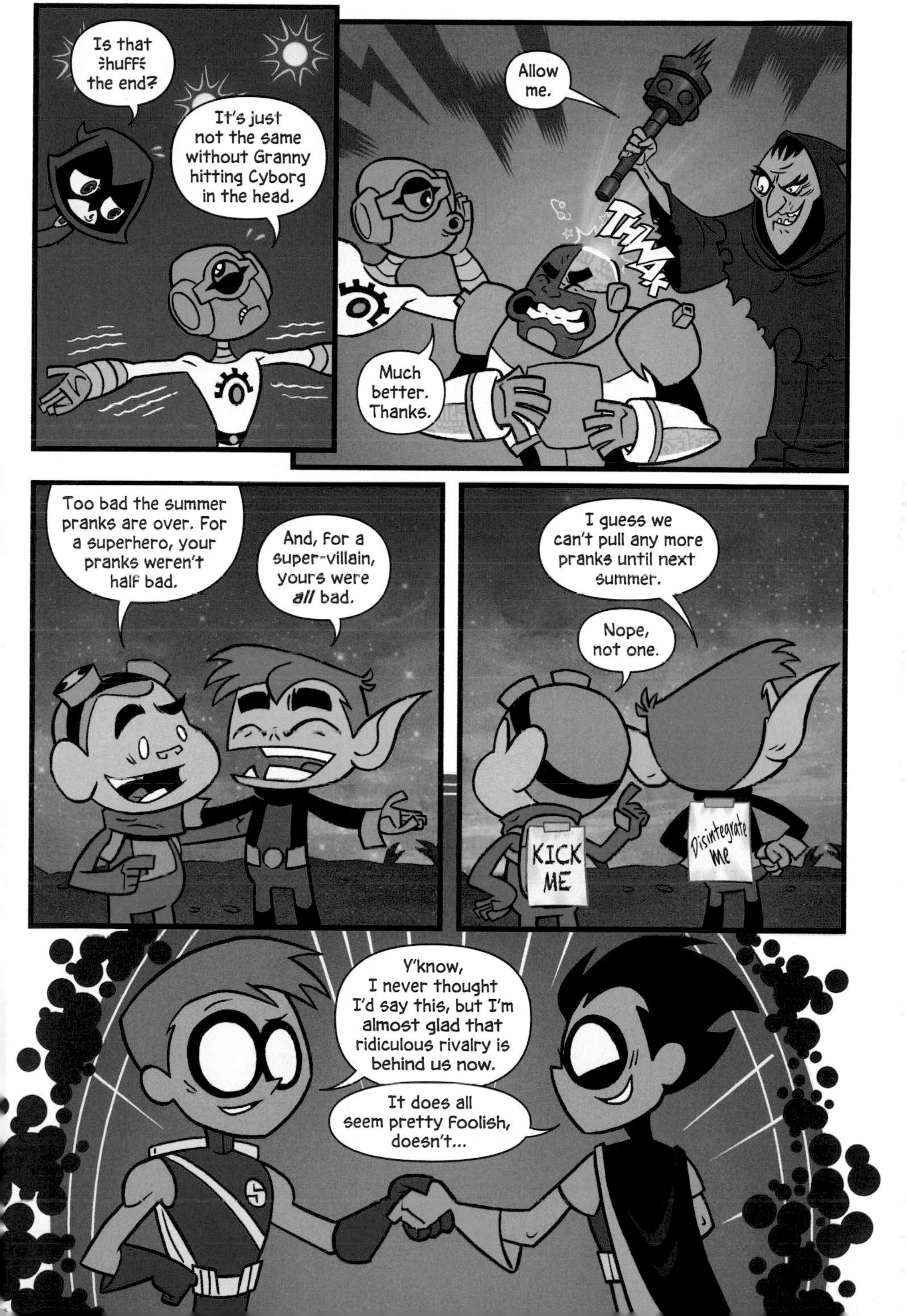

Is that ≠huff≠ the end?
It's just not the same without Granny hitting Cyborg in the head.
Allow me.
THWAK
Much better. Thanks.
Too bad the summer pranks are over. For a superhero, your pranks weren't half bad.
And, for a super-villain, yours were *all* bad.
I guess we can't pull any more pranks until next summer.
Nope, not one.
KICK ME
Disintegrate me
Y'know, I never thought I'd say this, but I'm almost glad that ridiculous rivalry is behind us now.
It does all seem pretty foolish, doesn't...

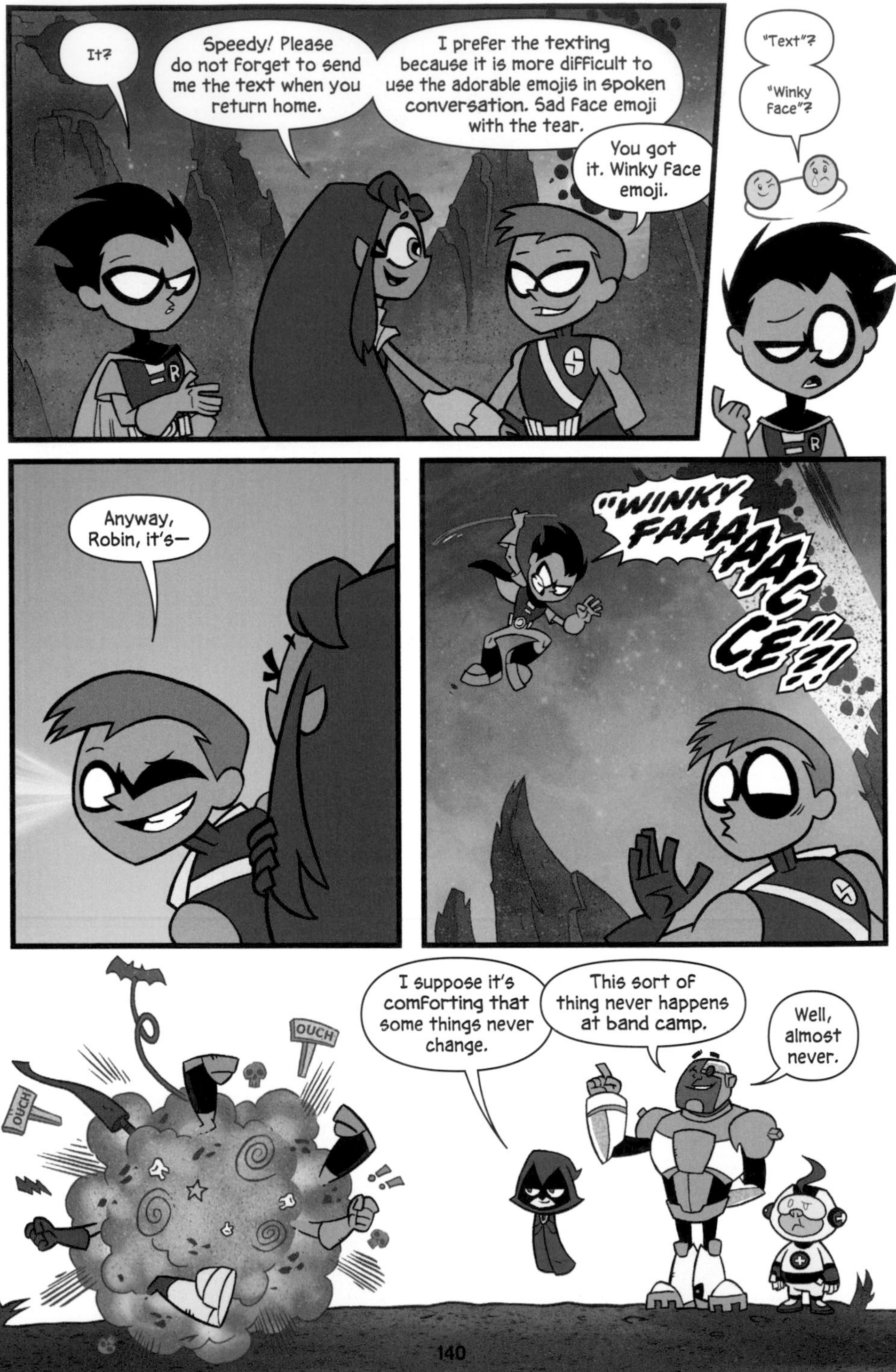
It?
Speedy! Please do not forget to send me the text when you return home.
I prefer the texting because it is more difficult to use the adorable emojis in spoken conversation. Sad face emoji with the tear.
You got it. Winky face emoji.
"Text"?
"Winky Face"?
Anyway, Robin, it's—
"WINKY FAAAAAACE"?!
OUCH
OUCH
I suppose it's comforting that some things never change.
This sort of thing never happens at band camp.
Well, almost never.

Epilogue

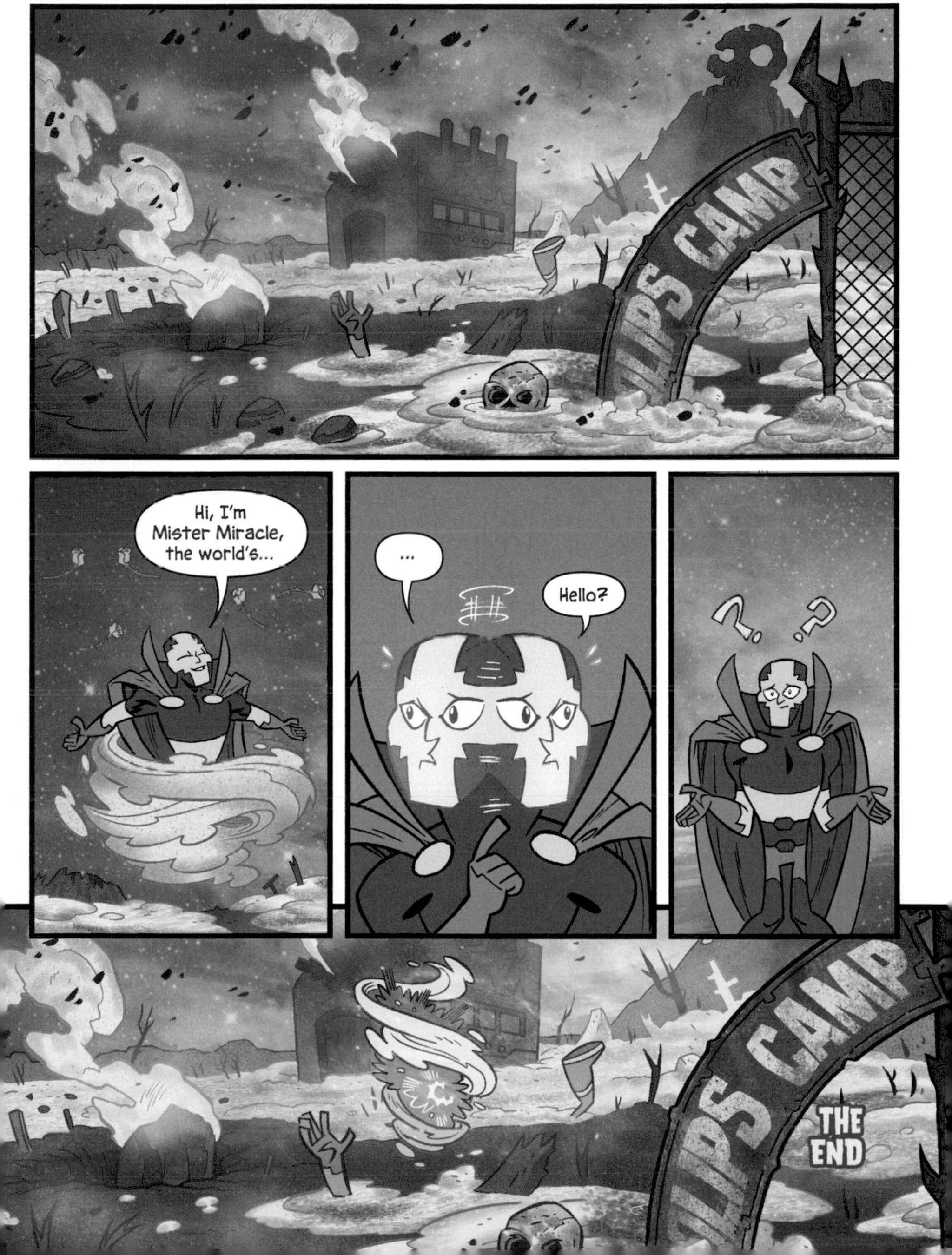
Hi, I'm Mister Miracle, the world's...
...
Hello?
THE END

SHOLLY FISCH is a mild-mannered developmental psychologist who has helped produce dozens of educational TV series, digital games, magazines, and hands-on materials, including *Sesame Street, Cyberchase, The Magic School Bus Rides Again, The Cat in the Hat Knows a Lot About That,* and lots of things you've probably never heard of. He's spent more than 30 years writing everything from *Superman* to *Star Wars* to *Scooby-Doo*. He lives with his lovely wife, Susan, and his brilliantly talented children, Nachum, Chana, and Miriam, who hope he'll get more sleep someday.

MARCELO DiCHIARA, a Brazilian artist, began his career doing illustrations for French publisher Semic. In the United States, he has worked for Image Comics and Marvel Comics on *Iron Man and Power Pack, Marvel Adventures: Super Heroes,* and *Marvel Super Hero Squad*. Since 2014, he has worked for DC Comics as an artist on *Smallville, Bombshells United, DC Super Hero Girls,* and *Teen Titans Go!*

FRANCO RIESCO has worked for DC Comics on *Scooby-Doo Team-Up* and *Teen Titans Go!* Support from his wife and parents has been the key to making his career flourish (but he also wants to thank the one who taught him all about color theory... his dog, Boris!).

AGNES GARBOWSKA has made her name in comics illustrating such titles as the *New York Times* bestselling and award-winning *DC Super Hero Girls* for DC Comics. In addition, her portfolio includes a long run on *My Little Pony* for IDW, *Teen Titans Go!* for DC Comics, *Grumpy Cat* for Dynamite Entertainment, and Sonic Universe "Off Panel" strips for Archie Comics.

SILVANA BRYS is a colorist and graphic designer who has colored *Scooby-Doo, Where Are You?, Teen Titans Go!, Scooby-Doo Team-Up,* and *Looney Tunes* for DC Comics, plus *Tom and Jerry* and many other comics and books. She lives in a small village in Argentina. Her home is also her office and she loves to create there, surrounded by forests and mountains.

DARIO BRIZUELA is an artist who loves drawing kids and superheroes! He's from Buenos Aires, Argentina, and one of his first projects was *Ben 10*. He drew many issues of *Scooby-Doo Team-Up* and is now drawing spaceships and lightsabers. You may soon see his art on really cool toy packaging. He loves his wife Silvina and will be always thankful for her support.

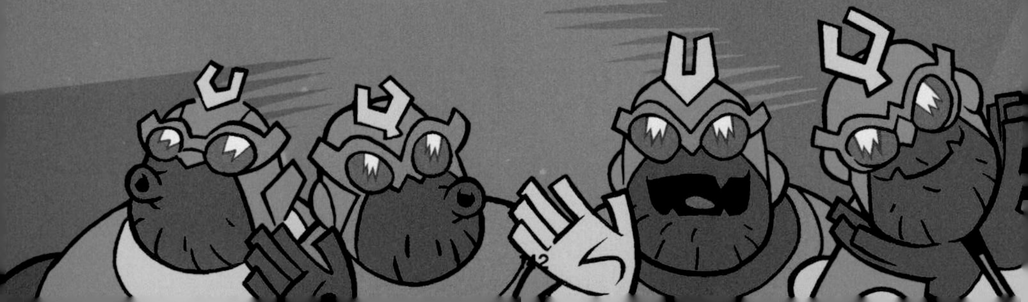

ABIGAIL LARSON is a Hugo Award-winning illustrator who loves all things strange and spooky. She's worked with awesome companies like DC, Universal, Titan, and Syfy in the past, and is very proud to have created a tarot deck, "The Dark Wood Tarot."

EMMA KUBERT is a young and talented artist who has worked for various companies including Image Comics, Dynamite Entertainment, and, of course, DC Comics, where she's contributed to *DC Super Hero Girls: Weird Science* and *Teen Titans Go!* She is currently working with fellow artist Rusty Gladd on their creator-owned project *Inkblot* for Image Comics, which will be published in 2020.

LEILA DEL DUCA is an artist who loves to draw animals, over-the-top emotions, and crazy action scenes. She has worked on many fantasy and science fiction adventure books such as *Shutter*, *Sleepless*, *Afar*, and *Wonder Woman: Tempest Tossed.* Leila has two rats named Troy and Abed and she squeals with delight (and a little fear) when they lick her nose.

MARISSA LOUISE is a colorist who lives in the misty woods of Oregon. She has a background in painting, four cats, and one half-wild dog. She has worked throughout the comics industry on books like *Hex Wives*, *Spell on Wheels*, *Grumble*, and *Semiautomagic*.

ERICH OWEN is a cartoonist living in San Diego. His first graphic novel series, *Mail Order Ninja*, which he co-created and illustrated, was published in 2005. Since then, he's been drawing all kinds of comic book projects! Currently, he draws *Teen Titans Go!* and *DC Super Hero Girls* for DC Comics.

JAMAL IGLE is a comic book industry veteran. His work has been seen in the pages of DC series like Supergirl, Firestorm, and Nightwing. Jamal is also the creator of *Molly Danger* and co-creator of the series *The Wrong Earth.*

FRANCO is the creator, artist, and writer of *Patrick the Wolf Boy* and *Aw Yeah Comics!* He's worked on the Dino-Mike book series and on comics including *Superman Family Adventures*, *Super Powers*, and the *New York Times* bestselling and Eisner Award-winning *Tiny Titans* for DC Comics. His latest works are the original graphic novel *The Ghost, The Owl* by Action Lab Entertainment, and *Superman of Smallville.* Franco is also a high school teacher, a painter who has shown work in galleries around the country, and one of the principle owners of the Aw Yeah Comics retail stores.

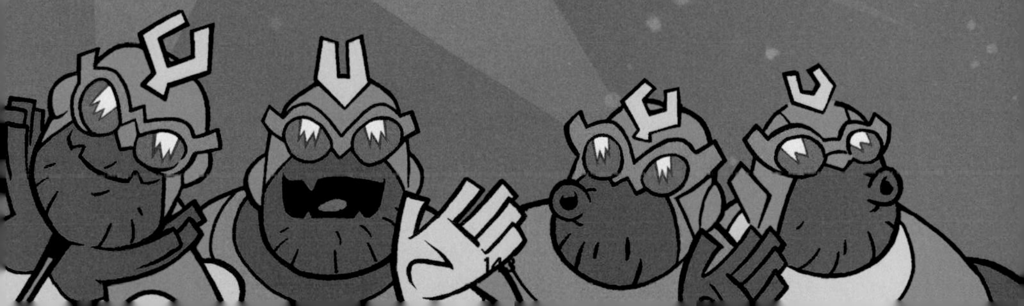

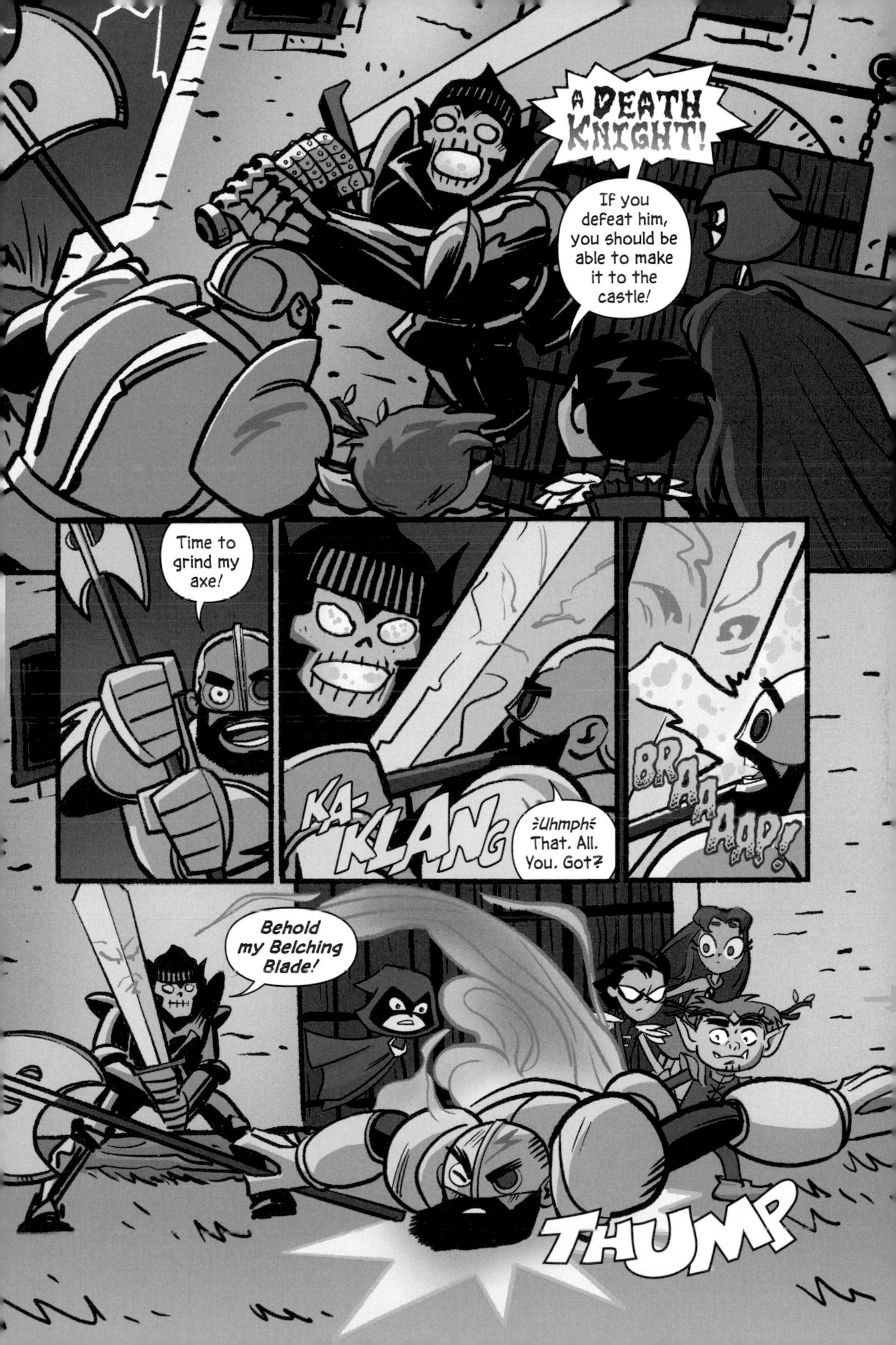
A DEATH KNIGHT!
If you defeat him, you should be able to make it to the castle!
Time to grind my axe!
KA-KLANG
Uhmph That. All. You. Got?
BRAAAAP!
Behold my Belching Blade!
THUMP

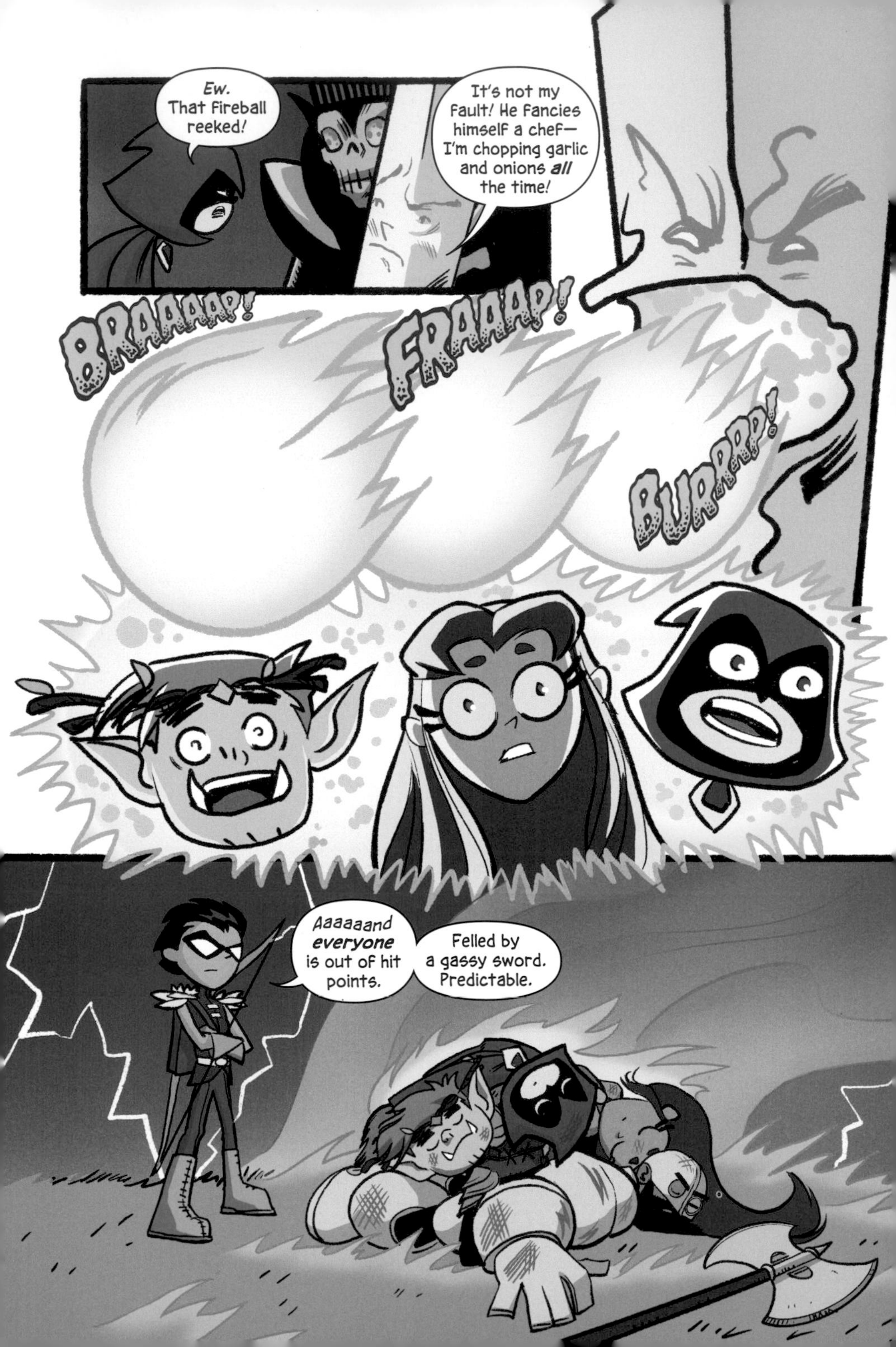

Ew. That fireball reeked!
It's not my fault! He fancies himself a chef— I'm chopping garlic and onions *all* the time!
BRAAAAAP!
FRAAAP!
BURRRP!
Aaaaaand *everyone* is out of hit points.
Felled by a gassy sword. Predictable.

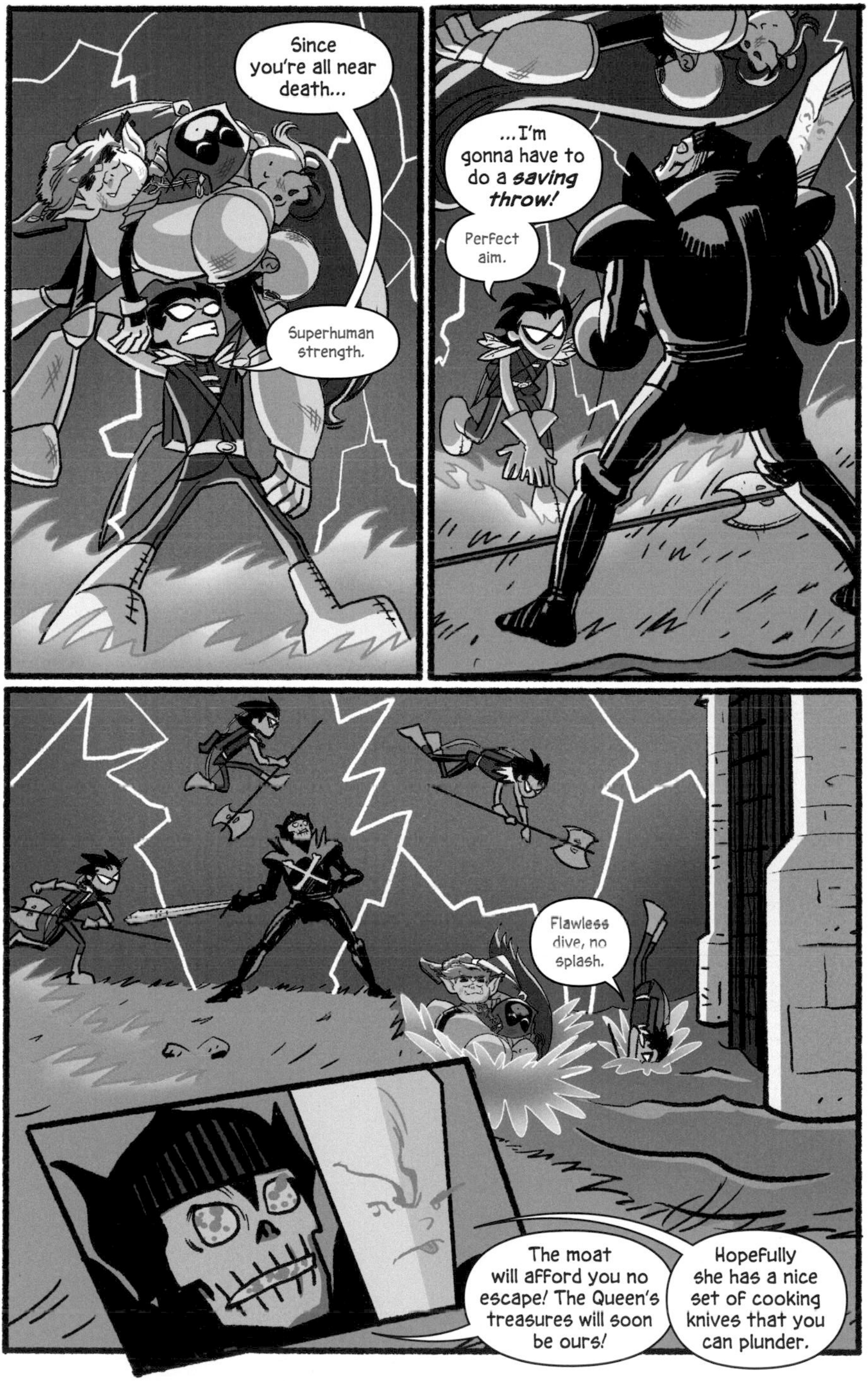
Since you're all near death...
Superhuman strength.
...I'm gonna have to do a *saving throw!*
Perfect aim.
Flawless dive, no splash.
The moat will afford you no escape! The Queen's treasures will soon be ours!
Hopefully she has a nice set of cooking knives that you can plunder.

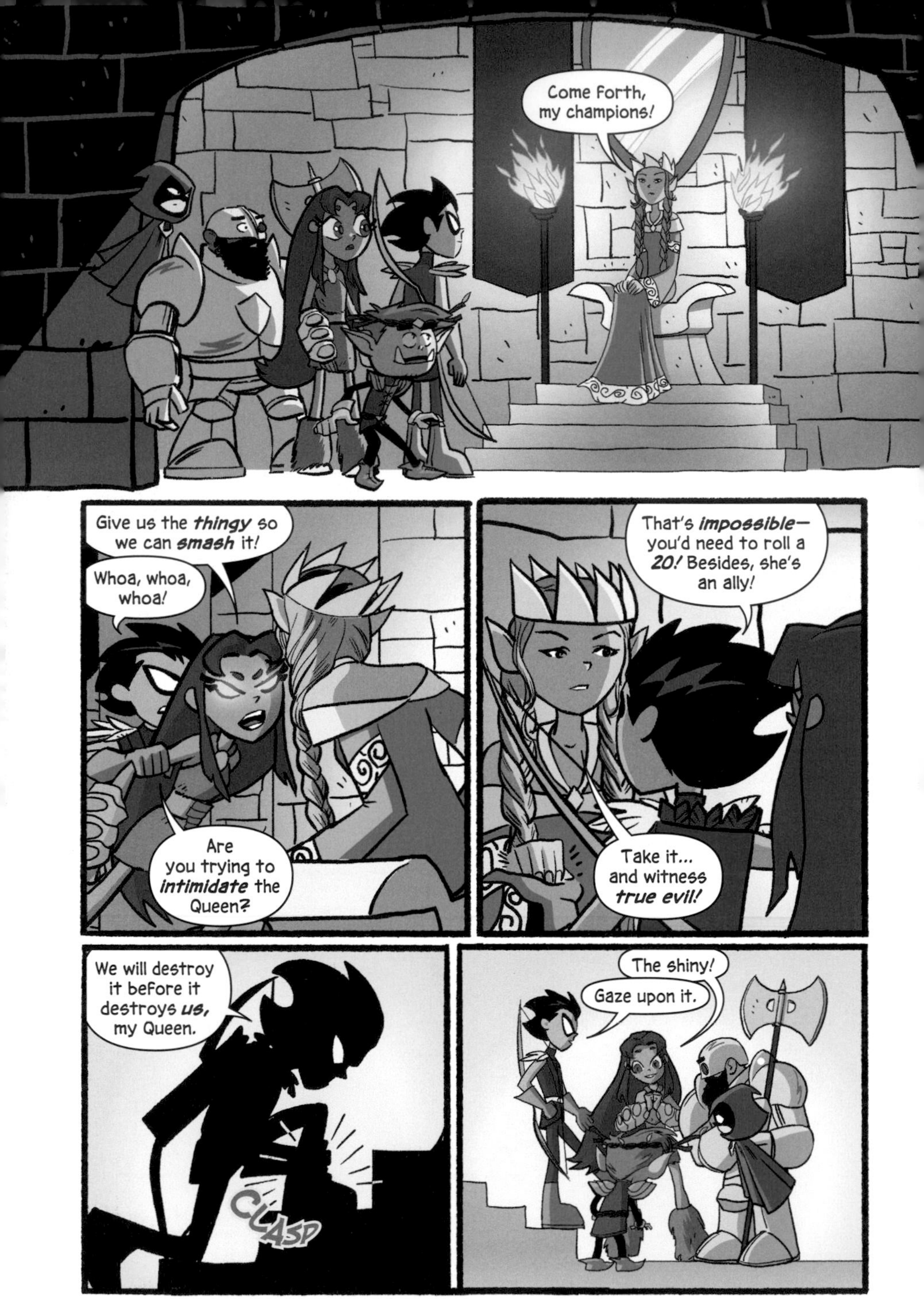
Come forth, my champions!
Give us the thingy so we can smash it!
Whoa, whoa, whoa!
Are you trying to intimidate the Queen?
That's impossible—you'd need to roll a 20! Besides, she's an ally!
Take it... and witness true evil!
We will destroy it before it destroys us, my Queen.
CLASP
The shiny!
Gaze upon it.

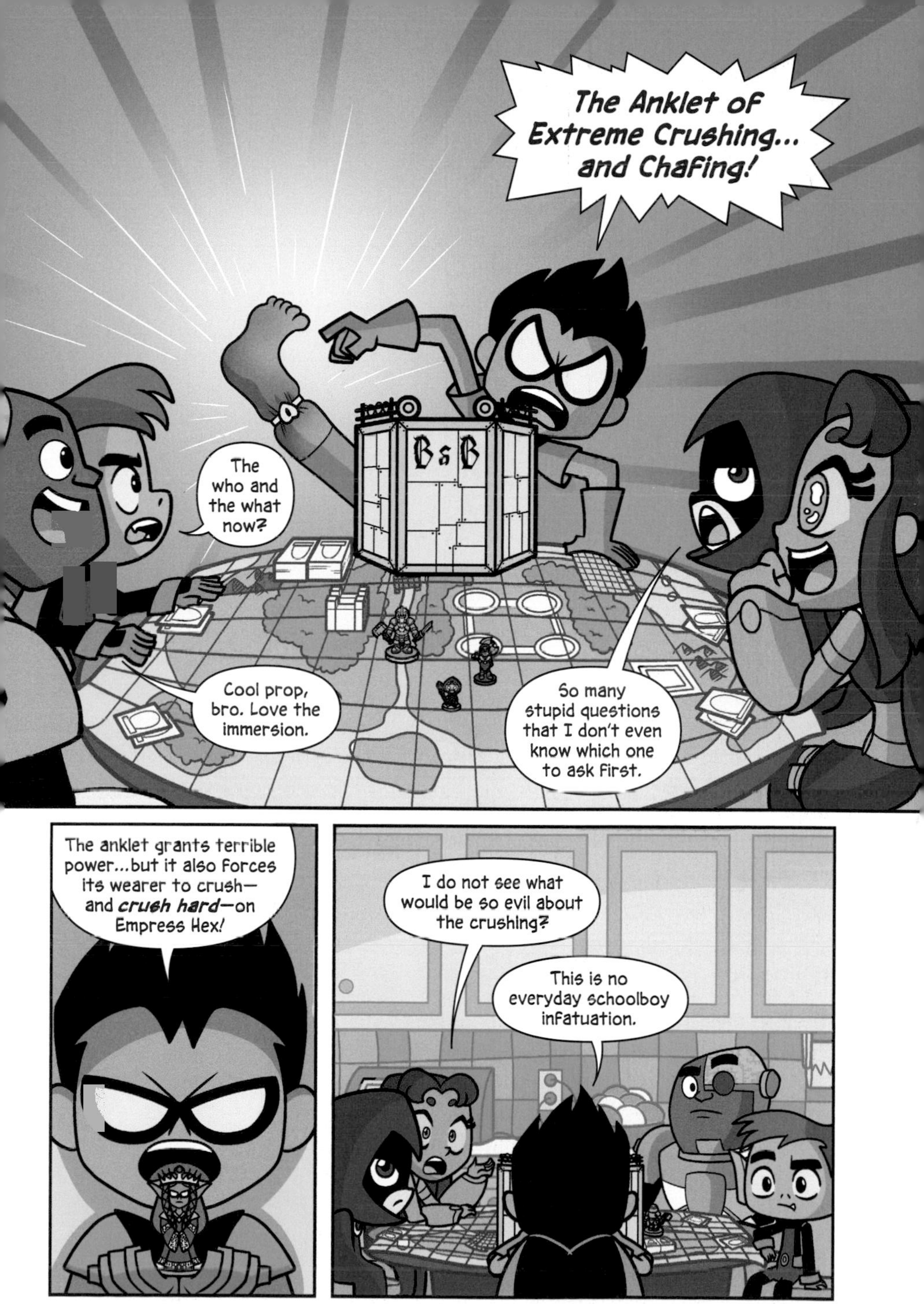
The Anklet of Extreme Crushing... and Chafing!
The who and the what now?
Cool prop, bro. Love the immersion.
So many stupid questions that I don't even know which one to ask first.
The anklet grants terrible power...but it also forces its wearer to crush—and *crush hard*—on Empress Hex!
I do not see what would be so evil about the crushing?
This is no everyday schoolboy infatuation.

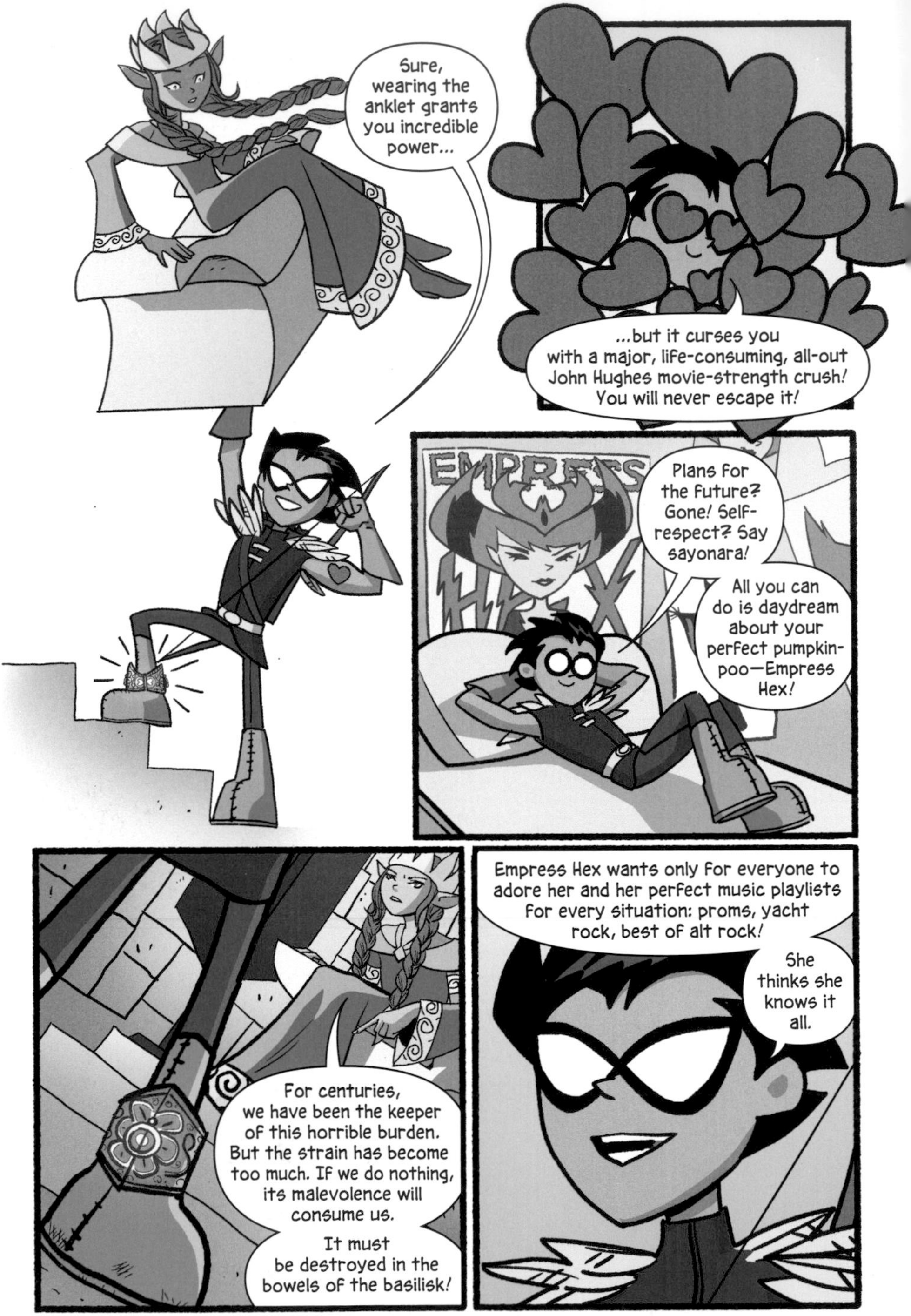
Sure, wearing the anklet grants you incredible power...
...but it curses you with a major, life-consuming, all-out John Hughes movie-strength crush! You will never escape it!
EMPRESS HEX
Plans for the future? Gone! Self-respect? Say sayonara!
All you can do is daydream about your perfect pumpkin-poo—Empress Hex!
For centuries, we have been the keeper of this horrible burden. But the strain has become too much. If we do nothing, its malevolence will consume us.
It must be destroyed in the bowels of the basilisk!
Empress Hex wants only for everyone to adore her and her perfect music playlists for every situation: proms, yacht rock, best of alt rock!
She thinks she knows it all.

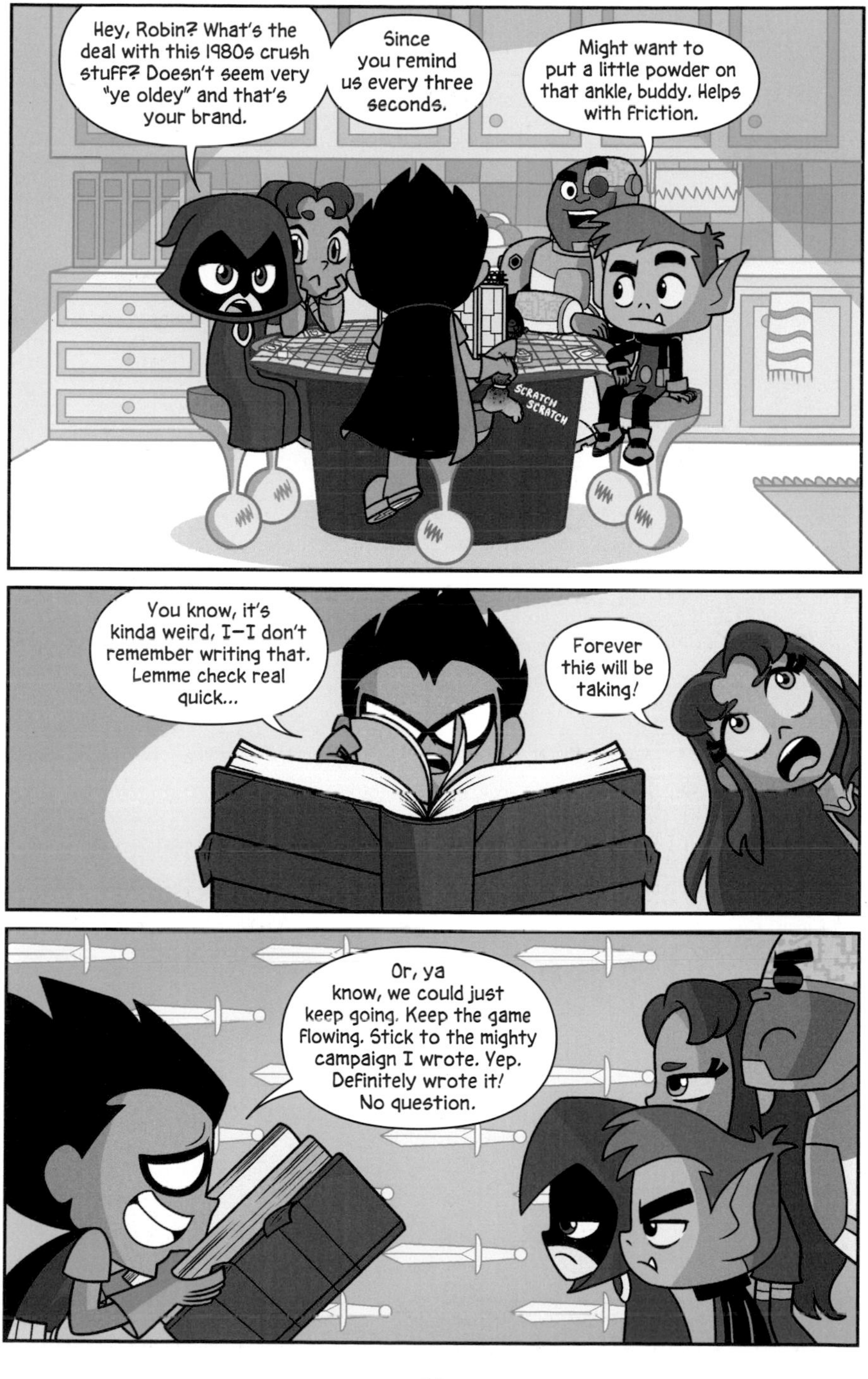
Hey, Robin? What's the deal with this 1980s crush stuff? Doesn't seem very "ye oldey" and that's your brand.
Since you remind us every three seconds.
Might want to put a little powder on that ankle, buddy. Helps with friction.
SCRATCH SCRATCH
You know, it's kinda weird, I—I don't remember writing that. Lemme check real quick...
Forever this will be taking!
Or, ya know, we could just keep going. Keep the game flowing. Stick to the mighty campaign I wrote. Yep. Definitely wrote it! No question.

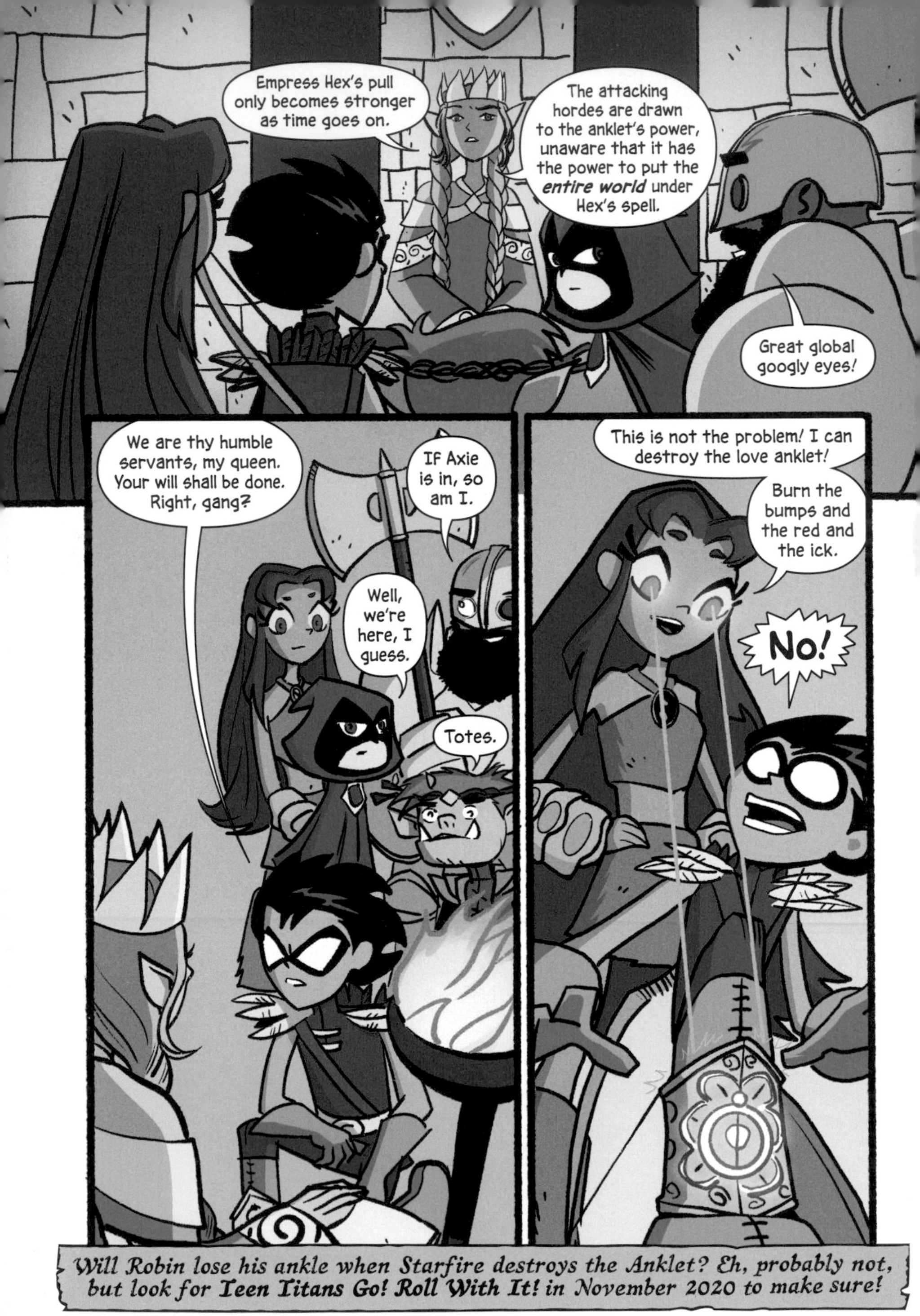
Empress Hex's pull only becomes stronger as time goes on.
The attacking hordes are drawn to the anklet's power, unaware that it has the power to put the *entire world* under Hex's spell.
Great global googly eyes!
We are thy humble servants, my queen. Your will shall be done. Right, gang?
If Axie is in, so am I.
Well, we're here, I guess.
Totes.
This is not the problem! I can destroy the love anklet!
Burn the bumps and the red and the ick.
No!
Will Robin lose his ankle when Starfire destroys the Anklet? Eh, probably not, but look for **Teen Titans Go! Roll With It!** in November 2020 to make sure!